It's a Bomb!

"No question about it . . . thermonuclear . . . the biggest goddamn thing ever. . . . It fits—everything drops into place! That tidal wave in Alaska; the explosion in space, beyond the moon; those phony oceanographic fleets—this is it! A thirty-gigaton bomb!"

And to compound the situation the monstrous device was to be placed on the ocean floor in a volcanic pocket, to trigger a chain reaction far worse than the bomb itself . . . disaster literally beyond human comprehension.

"It would pulverize all of Florida and destroy the coastal regions northward along Georgia and the Carolinas . . . wipe out Miami and many of the Gulf cities . . . could totally inundate the entire state and far beyond . . . destroy the Panama Canal . . . devastate much of Latin America. . . . The tidal wave would be felt around the world. It could kill several hundred million people, perhaps more. To a considerable extent it would affect virtually the entire planet. As bad, possibly much worse than a full-scale nuclear war. . . ."

Another Pinnacle title by Martin Caidin:

ENCOUNTER THREE

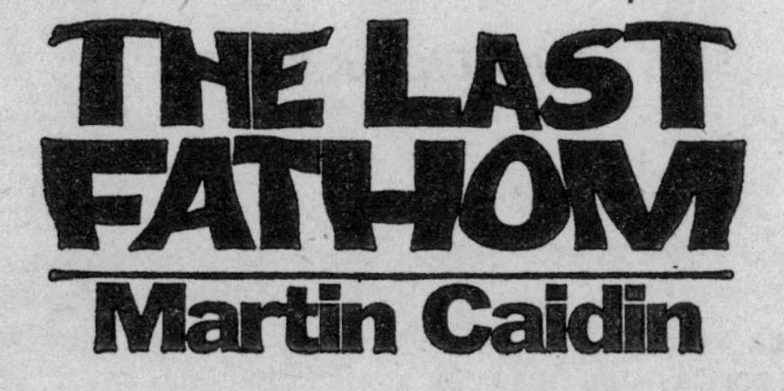

PINNACLE BOOKS • LOS ANGELES

This is a work of fiction. All the characters and events portrayed in this book are fictional, and any resemblance to real people or incidents is purely coincidental.

THE LAST FATHOM

A Pinnacle Books edition, published by special arrangement with Hawthorn Books, Inc., New York.

First printing, November 1974
Second printing, December 1978

ISBN: 0-523-40452-2

Cover art by Randy Weidner

Printed in the United States of America

PINNACLE BOOKS, INC.
2029 Century Park East
Los Angeles, California 90067

This book is for
PAMELA,
who asked that she have one
"for my very own self"

THE LAST FATHOM

1

For three days and nights the gale lashed the North Pacific. Streaming out of the northwest, howling without relief, the winds rushed down from the frozen Arctic. The vast stirring of icy air from the polar regions gave impetus and staying power to the storm. Day and night the wind shrieked, pushing masses of dark clouds swiftly over the foaming sea, building the waters into marching ranks. The great waves paraded endlessly from over one horizon to the other; where their tops surged far above the troughs the wind blasted away the water with such force that it became impossible to separate salt spray from air. Day followed night with a repetitious gray weariness. No sun broke through the thick and leaden clouds. The ghostly phosphorescence of the night yielded sullenly to colorless daylight. And always the wind was there, howling and lashing the waves before its fury.

Four thousand feet beneath the spray-lashed air, silence reigned. In the eternal darkness a cold river drifted downward through the sea, heaving sluggishly along the near-vertical flanks that formed the south walls of the Aleutian Trench. The icy waters moved with a progress measured at less than a mile every hour. A tributary of the river within the ocean slid along a great fault, a huge crevice that had split the steep walls of the trench. The split in the ocean floor widened to an escarpment the floor of which was covered with huge boulders and the debris released by tremors deep within the crust of the planet. Many times in the past the crust had shifted, splitting wider the crevice, weakening the flanks.

Another tremor could bring on disaster, send the spasms of shock racing along the ocean floor northward to the shores of Alaska. A shift in the scabrous surface of the planet so well concealed by the dark waters could cause crustal blocks to seek new footing—crustal blocks made up of entire mountains and the flanks of coastal ranges.

Within the crevice, at the bottom of the huge cliffs of the Aleutian Trench, a knobbed sphere swayed at the end of its cable tether. Invisible in the wet blackness, the sphere hung precisely three hundred feet above the surface of the ocean bottom. Three hundred feet from where intensive study had revealed the beginning of the fault in the terrestrial crust.

It was time.

Within the knobbed sphere a timer closed, tripped an electrical switch, triggered a chain of intricate events. Less than a thousandth of a second later the chain reached the final event. Instantly the knobbed sphere ceased to exist.

Nearly four thousand feet beneath the surface of the wind-lashed seas a small star leaped into existence. Several pounds of plutonium, the casing of the sphere, and everything contained within its knobbed shape vanished. In an instant they were transformed to pure temperature. Four thousand feet beneath the North Pacific a shape with a temperature of forty million degrees came into being.

For that immeasurable moment of time, the bottom of the North Pacific was as hot as the interior of the sun. Everything within reach of that awesome heat converted instantly into gaseous form. Within the space once occupied by the knobbed sphere there existed a pressure of thirty million pounds per square inch.

The pressure rammed outward in all directions, converting water into raging, superheated gas. The original tiny heart of the star punched itself into a ball of blazing energy. A shock wave cracked outward through the cold Pacific.

Within a fraction of a second the shock wave sledgehammered into the weak structure of the crustal fault of the Aleutian Trench.

The massive blow moved a huge section of the vertical wall that made up the base of the trench. Even as a giant sheet of rock began to move, sliding away from the great cliffs, the shock wave bounded through the fault, cracking sharply toward the distant shore. Beneath the still-flaming fireball, many hundreds of feet in diameter, the ocean bottom dished downward. Radial cracks rippled outward like a shattered pane of glass.

The blazing fireball surged for the ocean surface like a thing berserk, pulsating, expanding, and contracting as it ripped upward in a mass of writhing flame and steam. Just beneath the surface, following the shock wave that preceded its passage, the fireball still exerted more than three tons of pressure per square inch. Then, with freedom at hand, it burst away from the depths in the form of a huge pyramidal spray dome. Normally, it would have ascended to perhaps a mile above the ocean surface.

Instantly it appeared the storm struck with great talons of wind. The cauliflower dome of tumbling spray that began to form never took shape. The wind ripped away the shape even as the forces that began the violent events shredded beneath the fury of the Pacific gale. Twenty seconds after its appearance above the ocean surface there was only a great cloud of wind-whipped spray, vanishing swiftly, invisible to any observer who might have been present within the space of a mile.

Far from the original blaze of millions of degrees at the ocean bottom, the forces set into play by that instant of savage energy were just making known their effects. The nuclear explosion, in itself a massive energy release, was as nothing compared to the chain reaction it generated within the sensitive balance of the weak terrestrial crust. This, indeed, was its purpose: to begin a domino-fashion toppling of mountains. . . .

Along the shoreline of the Fairweather Range of the Alaskan coast a huge section of the earth's crust shifted. The sledge-hammer blow ripping through the subsurface strata set off a new chain reaction of events. The crustal uplift within the Fair weather Range sent a tremendous strain coursing through the area. The underlying rocks of the range yielded before that growing strain; long moments later the huge rock masses collapsed, triggering new spasms to wrack the planetary crust.

The blow registered on seismographs around the globe. A sharp and locally devastating earthquake jolted much of the North American continent.

Across the southeast hills and valleys of the Alaskan coastline a nightmare leaped into being. The air shimmered visibly from the shock waves that rippled upward from the suddenly writhing earth. Terrified witnesses stared in openmouthed disbelief as the snow-covered peaks of the mountain range shuddered before their eyes. It appeared as if the great range itself were moving, a spasmodic gasp of a rubbery world. The effect was much the same as if someone had flapped a gigantic carpet to shake loose accumulated debris.

Thunder rolled through the skies as the avalanches began. Clouds of snow and dust and hammered debris boiled into the air, whipping into needle shards as the winds of the gale that had blown for three days and nights snatched at them and flung them away. For nearly one hundred and thirty miles along the coastal lowlands one nightmare after the other exploded into being as the mountains quivered and danced. Huge geysers hissed with crackling roars into the air. Sulfur pools vomited their stench into the wind, which flung away the offending mixtures and sprayed it into the midst of the storm.

Yawning fissures appeared in the ground as a sound of huge tearing and ripping assailed the air; in hundreds of places the earth literally shredded its surface. On the Awekat River, a cluster of homes and trucks vibrated wildly as a huge crack opened at their edge. The people within the buildings barely had time to dash outside when the earth split wider beneath them, swallowing whole the tiny community.

Along the northwestern edge of Litkana Bay, the entire lower third of Capemont Isle heaved itself forty feet above the level of the bay; for a terrifying moment it hung, poised, in the troubled air, and then collapsed into itself. As the waters boiled and foamed upward to engulf the sinking island, the sixty men and women of a fishing hamlet went with them; only three were to survive. A new current pounded angrily through the space where the island had raised from the waters.

The writhing agonies of the earth were not all confined to the alluvial soils of the coastal lowlands or the towering peaks of the three-mile-high Fairweather Range. At sea two fishing boats rode out the gale, bows into the wind, taking quite well the fury of the storm. The men aboard the boats were long accustomed to such weather. But they were unprepared for what happened when the wind-lashed sea beneath them heaved slowly but inexorably, carrying the boats impossibly higher and higher into the air. Nearly a hundred feet above where they had stood into the wind the boats poised along the mound of the great wave that pushed deep within the sea. The break was much sharper than the lifting front of the swell; the boats plunged with heady speed into the dark trough that waited for them.

One boat never again came up. In all, counting those in the bays and harbors as well as the ones on the open seas, thirty-four vessels went down. Frantic, terrified voices burst out of the night as people called out by radio their nightmarish last moments before the final engulfment.

Along the coastline the avalanches grew in violence and number, heaving millions of tons of glacial ice, snow, and rocky debris into the sheltered coves and harbors. Small communities vanished beneath the scouring masses as they roared into the enclosed bodies of water, ripping the bays and harbors into churning maelstroms. Many hamlets that escaped the paths of the thundering slides survived only for moments longer as the waters leaped and foamed fifty or a hundred feet above the normal high-water lines, pounding into splintered kindling the suddenly exposed structures.

But nothing matched the fury that erupted within Litkana Bay. There the world went mad.

Litkana Bay in times of clear weather forms a magnificent amphitheater, backed by the huge mass of the Fairweather Range. It is a natural gem along a forbidding and inhospitable coast; one leaves the cold and leaden sea to enter the bay, passing by the long finger of Solomon Point. At once the relentless foe of the sea is left behind. The seclusion is as close to perfect as a seafaring man may desire. The head of the bay lies eight miles inland, where it branches out east and west in the form of a gigantic cross, the arms of the fjordlike head made up of two massive glacier fronts. The hills rearing up from the protected waters of the bay shine beneath the sun, exposing their lush canopy of evergreens. There is a brilliant contrast between the ice-speckled waters of the bay and the thick carpets of strawberries that abound during their short season. The bay is, among other things, a scene of majestic and protected serenity. And when the weather sours and the massive waves of air descend from farther north, the bay, despite the still-howling winds along the hills, and cold that sinks deep, provides superb protection against the storms that foam the seas.

Along the inland, northern edge of the bay stands Creighton Point, a gently sloping expanse that begins three hundred feet above the sea. Nestling along the lower flanks of the Fairweather Range, the town of Creighton, with a population of some two thousand people, thus is protected against both the fury of the sea and the worst of the storms that howl down from the north.

Perhaps someone aboard a fishing boat in Litkana Bay this night chanced to wonder at the curious rolling thunder that beat sonorously through the mountains, audible even above the howl of the storm. Had he done so—watching one of the last sights of his life—he would have seen a great white cloud appear beyond the turn of the bay. Beyond a sweeping headland the white mist, seen only dimly through the darkness and the rain-sodden skies, would have expanded, looming strangely into view. It would have appeared, through the poor visibility, as a ghost of whiteness, a spreading mirage one would associate normally with snow.

But this was no mirage.

The entire front of the Litkana Glacier heaved with a cry of muffled thunder that shook the world. Beneath the vast river of thick ice a mountain had shifted, breaking free the grip of the ice. In the spasm that racked the forefront of the range, the glacier had shaken loose. And now its millions of tons reared more than three thousand feet over the inland waters of Litkana Bay. For a long and timeless instant massive chunks separated from the high cliffs, falling with what appeared to be slow motion as they tumbled and spun toward the bay.

Then came the ultimate disaster. The whole mass of the glacier forefront fell away from the main river of ice and crashed into the bay.

Millions of tons of ice pounded into the protected waters. What came next was inevitable. The water, seeming to groan from within itself, surrendered to the terrible impact of the collapsing glacier. A wave unlike any other ever known leaped explosively into being.

A single churning wall of water with a billion screaming throats hurled itself over the headland, ripping away trees and soil and boulders. The wave flung itself madly onward, caromed higher and higher.

In the blink of an eye it happened. A huge scraping knife of water obliterated the town of Creighton and its two thousand souls. One moment it was there; the next instant Creighton was a memory vanished within the maw of the thundering, tumbling wave. The wave chewed and gouged and scraped huge timber tracts from the steep slopes.

When stunned scientists would come, many days after,

to examine what had remained in Litkana Bay, they would find a mute evidence to overcome the incredulity that was inevitable. Creighton was gone. Tens of thousands of trees had been scraped from existence. Enormous boulders had been flung about like pebbles. The high-water mark, where the wave scoured everything down to the bare rock, stood two thousand and four hundred feet above the level of the now placid bay.

The lieutenant walked briskly along the hallway. At a door marked with three stars he paused, straightened his posture, and stepped into a large room. A wide desk barred his way. A security officer looked up at him, scanned him from head to foot, acknowledged his recognition.

The lieutenant glanced at the sealed envelope he carried. The security officer rose to his feet. "I'll take it," he said, gesturing at the envelope.

The lieutenant shook his head. "Sorry, sir. Hand delivery is required."

The security officer pursed his lips. He released the flap of the holster at his side, withdrew the weapon, and cocked it to firing position. "Very good," he said amiably. "We will go in now." The lieutenant nodded, and walked ahead of the security officer. The gun in the hand of the officer behind him was of no concern. When it came to dealing directly with the Admiral, such steps were necessary. He entered the Admiral's office, saluted, extended the envelope.

The Admiral cut the seal, withdrew a document, and began to read. Slowly his face creased in a smile.

". . . and at this point monitoring is complete. As of seventy-two hours following the event, no traces of radioactivity were discernible by surface vessels. Further monitoring will be maintained by trawlers for another four days."

2

"Three hundred yards. On course. Maintain depth, maintain speed. We're right in the groove, Con."

Conan Dark shifted his body within the shoulder harness to relieve a pressure point against his skin. His fingers curled around the pistol-grip of the killer submarine's control stick—sensitive, gentle, but firm in their pressure. With the practiced, osmotic motion of the skilled veteran of his business, Dark's eyes flicked across the glowing dials of his instrument console.

He centered his attention on the electronic scope display of the berthing-sonar system. Slightly off center on the display board before him, a circular glowing screen presented to Conan Dark an electronic picture of the killer sub's position in relation to the channel along which they moved. Sonar pulsators imbedded in the channel bottom and positioned to each side of their passage created an aural-electronic passageway along which he guided the powerful Orca. Visually, he needed only to keep the glowing pip that represented the killer sub in dead center of the soft lights showing on the screen. It was as if he could see along a miniaturized, three-dimensional tunnel. The glowing pip on that 3-D screen would respond exactly as he maneuvered the powerful submarine through fingertip pressure.

But that was strictly the visual readout of what was happening. Handling the Orca under these conditions was a bitch, and Conan Dark was acutely aware that a single error on his part could mean a tidal wave of problems. Despite the great mass of the Orca he could feel her respond to the undulating motions of the shallow sea. The sixteen hundred tons of the submarine were in delicate equilibrium with the sea through which they moved with such caution, working their passage along the restricted channel leading to the caverns that housed their base. Conan Dark sensed through the motions of the Orca, registering both in physical movement and the quivering responses of the delicate instruments arrayed before him, that new currents surged through their approach channel, currents that tugged at and tried to worry the killer sub, to compound the problems of their slow movement.

Because Orca—and her crew of two—disliked the need for such torturous progress, the killer sub was built for swift running through the open seas. Her home was the crushing pressure of the great deeps, where her twin screws slashed with all the fury the nuclear turbines could deliver. Orca was a killer that came alive in what Conan Dark thought of as the "black wet," the great ocean depths where you reckoned pressure at tons to the square inch. As it pounded through the great mass of the sea with speeds exceeding a hundred knots, Orca became a bludgeon of tremendous power.

Surrounded by the nerve endings of intricate control systems and panels, Conan Dark looked about him. These were the times, he thought, when he and his close friend and fellow submariner, Larry Owens, truly came to life, with every cell of their bodies and minds performing in harmony with the incredible machine of which they had become a vital part; they were a *gestalt*, a wondrous integration of human senses artificially extended and broadened.

Multicolored lights reflected dully from the faces and hands of the two men. Through the massive structure of Orca they could feel the distant, slow churning of the screws. They could sense the effects of the currents. But that was all of the outside world that reached them directly.

Everything else depended upon the vessel and its systems. Where human vision and senses were concerned, they were sealed off completely from the liquid environment through which they moved. They were attended to and served by electronic systems so complex in their making and so sensitive to external stimuli that they seemed to be compounded more of witchcraft than of science.

The surface of the Atlantic Ocean heaved only forty feet above the dull-black hull of the submarine. Beyond the water it was night, the moon splashing silver off the waves of Bahi a Flemenco, through which ran the below-surface passageway to the base hidden within the underground caverns of Isla de Culebra, twenty-three miles east of Puerto Rico. It was a voyage that Orca made only in darkened waters, concealed from all eyes.

For this was a vessel of which the outside world knew nothing....

Orca was more than a startling advance in submarine technology. The long, flowing shape represented a quantum jump in concept, design, construction, and awesome performance. The sixteen hundred tons of Orca meant a freedom of the ocean depths unparalleled in history. It was a greater leap forward from existing submarines than was the advance from the clumsy, leaking pigboats of World War I to the huge undersea missile platforms that cruised the edge of a third world war.

Yet even the nuclear boats retained the fetters of technological obsolescence and suffered the performance restrictions inherent in dirigiblelike vessels of positive buoyancy. In clumsy fashion they balanced and counterbalanced water and compressed air to maneuver atop and beneath the surface.

Not even their electronic-nuclear wizardry could sever the umbilical cord of yesteryear's thinking. Not even new forms and shapes, radical to the "old hands" of undersea operations, could clear the way to what was truly an undersea renaissance.

It took a small group of daring innovators—prominent among them Conan Dark—to rip away the chains and plunge into the future. It took a decision and a gamble that scaled the sensitivities of military and industrial hierarchies.

The concept was heretic. It was also simple enough.

Get out of the dirigibles and into the true undersea killer.

For decades the submarines had been chained to the principles of positive buoyancy. Like their aerial counterparts, they floated as great swollen lumps within the denser liquid oceans that make of earth a water world. No one had severed the thread that ran all the way back through more than two thousand years of history to Archimedes' discovery of the natural law of buoyancy.

Even with the best the hydrodynamicists and nuclear-drive people could do, the undersea dirigible ran into walls. You could go only so fast and so deep with conventional submarine design. With the inherent limitations of the bulky, thick-hulled dirigible, you were limited in speed and severely restricted in depth. Only the thinnest upper layers of the ocean could be pierced on an operational basis.

To make the quantum jump engineers heeded the experience of those who sailed the air oceans, men who had abandoned the balloons and the dirigibles and put their faith into what had seemed flatly impossible—a machine heavier than air that could fly.

Why not do the same with the submarine? Why not eliminate all the clumsy, chafing restrictions of positive buoyancy? Why not get out of the ocean-going dirigible into the true undersea vessel—a submarine of *negative* buoyancy? A submarine that was heavier than the water it displaced.

But first there were skull-squeezing problems to overcome. One was immediately and painfully obvious. If the vessel lost power and forward momentum, it wouldn't float. It would sink. But the shark was a creature of negative buoyancy, and it had been doing quite well, thank you, for millions of years. Airplanes couldn't float, but they condemned the dirigible to antiquity by utilizing skillfully the fluid medium through which they moved. With aerodynamics a science and powerful engines a reality, men swept with confidence through the air oceans of the planet.

Given the proper technology and, especially, sufficient and sustained propulsive energy, an undersea vessel of unprecedented performance could evolve from new and daring concepts.

It did.

They named her after the slashing killer that was both the most intelligent and the deadliest creature in the sea—the killer whale.

Orca.

Conan Dark was one of the men who had defied tradition and broken from the accepted concepts of submarine technology. His entire life had been linked to the sea and the challenging new world concealed within its depths; this intimacy with the beckoning deeps and a brilliant grasp to the point of genius of new technologies placed him in the forefront of the team responsible for Orca.

Technamics, Inc., a high-powered civilian research outfit specializing in advanced hydrodynamics engineering, hired Conan Dark as their director of research and development to break through the barriers to true performance in the deep hydroworld. But Technamics dealt in brainpower rather than in the production of steel and electronic components. The development of Orca demanded so intensive an effort that a major cross-section of American technology and industry had to be brought into its long period of birth. Conan Dark, representing Technamics, was unquestionably the strong hand at the helm of the project.

Where Conan Dark knew the oceans and showed his brilliance in design theory, Larry Owens was a hardheaded and tough young engineer who dealt with the more immediate realities of materials. As a research engineer with Astro Hydrodynamics, Larry Owens led a project group experimenting with the materials that could replace conventional steels and special alloys to withstand the crushing pressures deep within the ocean. They had achieved spectacular results with fiber-reinforced plastics with a yield strength of 200,000 pounds per square inch—so great that the expression "yield strength" had become meaningless. What raised eyebrows to their highest levels, however, was the work carried out by the AHD team with massive glass structures. The elements developed as experimental materials for deep-submergence proved out with a compressive strength of more than a half million pounds per square inch.

The new materials and the expected progressive advances in nuclear propulsion systems made of Orca a reality. It was not necessary to build an entire submarine with the thick-walled pressure hull common to the operational boats. Despite her projected size—Orca displaced 1,600 tons and measured 120 feet from her smoothly rounded bow to her twin screws—the new undersea killer carried a crew of only two men. They were housed within a massive spherical chamber emplaced amidships of the long and slender vessel, and linked through electronic nerves to the mechanisms of the submarine. Thus the requirement for the controlled environment and life-support systems in a world more alien than the surface of the moon was reduced to the barest minimum.

The thought of only two men to control a vessel of such complexity and performance as Orca defied tradition and boggled the imagination. Yet Orca could be thought of as half computer and half submarine. And if three men could leave the earth in a rocket weighing more than three thousand tons and controlled by ninety-five engines of varying sizes and power, and take that rocket all the way to the moon, why should not two men be capable of integrating their finely honed skills in the submarine-electronics systems built within the massive and intricate hull of Orca?

Conan Dark and Larry Owens were of a new breed of submariners. Theirs was a kinship between mind and artificial senses to a degree never before attempted. They functioned almost as if the sensitivities of Orca were extensions of their own abilities. Without the Orca systems they were blind and helpless within deep hydrospace. Without their capacity of thought, interpretation, decision, and command, Orca remained nothing more than mindless and purposeless complexity.

Together, as a single integrated system—a cybernetic organism of man and artificial sensing and power—they became the deadliest creature within the seas.

The final shape of Orca was based on experience with nuclear-driven attack submarines, the revolutionary concept of negative buoyancy, and new nuclear turbines that delivered nearly 350,000 h.p. under maximum emergency power. The teardrop configuration remained, but with vital modifications to its basic form.

Engineers had long studied the unique methods with which the porpoise—notably the bottle-nosed dolphin—reduced surface friction of its body during high-speed passage through the water. The unique skin of the dolphin markedly reduced the effect of turbulence against it, enabling the dolphin to achieve, from a standing start, a speed of twenty-five knots and greater, within two seconds of thrashing the water. Moreover, the dolphins could sustain their amazing speed. Working with aquarium scientists, Conan Dark resolved that a diaphragm-damping fluid surface could work miracles for any object moving with great speed through a fluid medium. The engineering obstacles under the pressures for which Orca was designed to operate proved insurmountable as a matter of operational efficiency. But heat—heat generated along those specific areas of Orca's hull where turbulence built up to tremendous drag—could greatly affect that turbulence. It could, and it did, reduce by a major factor the forces that restrained and gripped any high-speed submersible.

Because of her great speed and the nature of her performance as dictated by her design principles of negative buoyancy, Orca maneuvered in the deeps along the same principles that governed a high-speed aircraft in flight. Set immediately aft of her center of gravity were stubby hydrofoils, sweeping forward along the trailing edge and rearward from the leading edge, much like the stubby-winged design one expected to find in a supersonic aircraft. The effect of these hydrofoils, along with that of the knife-edged flare that ran the length of the submarine, provided Orca with the "lift" the vessel needed as she maneuvered.

To sustain obedience and purpose from the great machine that was Orca, Conan Dark and Larry Owens needed power and they needed control. And above all else with their mighty, sensitive steed, they needed vision.

There was precious little vision to be found in the great depths that weigh so heavily around the hidden crust of earth. It took a long time for men to realize that the ocean deeps were not as placid or quiescent as in our ignorance we had assumed them to be. Instead, the explorers of the hydroworld crashed into huge waves marching through the deeps, and they encountered a bewildering variety of streams and currents and inversion layers, turbulence severe and unexpected, and other unanticipated forces that created the swirling clouds and mists of hydrospace. There were mysterious deep-scattering layers which in many ways proved analogous to the great cloud formations that brood within the gaseous atmosphere. Men were astonished to find that the clouds of the hydroworld rose and fell; they were possessed of movement, they exhibited height and depth and substance, and they both affected and were affected by their surrounding medium.

Human eyes that stare through water learn quickly that light—everyday, taken-for-granted, normal light—is out of place within the liquid environment. The heaving mass refracts and absorbs light waves and reflects back a weakened, distorted, and unreal picture. Light bogs down in the miasma of the oceans; the water world quickly drains light of its energy, swallowing the most intense beams of light as effortlessly as it absorbs a pebble tossed idly into its maw.

Thus the men who go down deep within the sea alter their vision: they attempt to see by sound. Optics gave way quickly to new sight—sonar, or "sound navigation ranging" But it is not that easy. Sonar vision itself suffers impairment and distortion because temperature and salinity changes in the water bend and twist acoustical signals. Sound beams are swallowed greedily by floating masses and subjected to a host of other forces yet inexplicable and inescapable.

This opacity of the deeps demanded of Orca and its two-man crew a dazzling variety of artificial senses. These ran the gamut from ordinary, restricted human vision along the upper edges of the hydroworld, where natural sunlight, sometimes moonlight, and certainly the brilliant beams of floodlights returned to man a fraction of the sight he experienced in his normal environment. It was possible also to extend this vision through television probes that snuffled ahead of the main craft, but at best this was limited. Within the sea man has long been the beggar and not the chooser. There were other extensions of man's visual capacity made possible through the special systems of Orca. The "liquid radar"—sonar—was of the widest possible use and flexibility. But there was also the ladar, the blue-green modified laser beam of monochromatic light that had brought about a new phase of the renaissance within hydrospace.

Sonar had long existed on the planet, developed eons past by the bat; the ugly little winged creature was adept, where not the faintest ghost of light could penetrate, at guiding itself by projected and reflected bursts of high-pitched sound. But sonar was even more widely used within the ocean depths—an acutely developed sense of the family of whales, from the smallest porpoise on up through the bottle-nosed dolphins, including the orcas and the greatest creatures ever to live on earth, the huge blue whales. Sound, living sound, had been developed within the hydroworld, functioning as sweep radar and employed in swift, high-intensity bursts for communication among the creatures generating the signals.

Orca's sonar functioned much in this same manner. But Dark and Owens were spared the difficulties of trying to interpret the often splotchy pictures of their sonar sweeps. As the sonic beams echoed back to the submarine, they filtered through an elaborate electronic system. A memory computer, working with a speed measured in millionths of a second, translated the sound echoes into clear picturizations on the screens studied by Dark and Owens, and later the data would be distributed to the main oceanographic centers so that they might subsequently be fed into the memory banks of every computer in the far-flung system of all submersible and anti-submarine warfare forces, as well as the shore-based data centers.

There was a world of wonder and mystery always unfolding before Dark and Owens, either through their own senses—with television scanners located about the submarine serving as their visual extensions—or through the artificial senses of the submarine. The different temperature layers, the thermoclines, appeared on the console display screens as layers of greenish fog, wisps that ribboned through the seas and, more often than not, gleamed through the translation of sound into electronic display. At times they ran into unexpected currents or even the strips and eddying movements of swirling rivers, and the men watched in fascination the silvered, glowing bands of light. There were vast schools of fish always to be encountered, and these appeared before them as glittering fogs. More than once they had approached within sonic study of a great movement of whales, studying the sonar-computer system readout as a great teardrop fleet maneuvered past them, stately and undisturbed by the presence of the metal giant scarcely larger than their own bulls.

And deeper, much deeper, into the true depths, a world of luminescent ghosts swimming through a vast space where no star had ever penetrated, the nether world separated always and forever from the "reality" of the nakedly thin surface.

Here, no matter what sea or ocean, no matter what depth or how crushing the brutal pressure of miles of water reaching above, Orca was in her true element.

Now, after her twenty-third trial at sea, a plunge to more than a full day and night, Conan Dark and Larry Owens were bringing her home.

3

Larry Owens switched to close-scan on his berthing display. "Eighty yards, Con," he said. "You can go to visual now."

"Right." Conan Dark punched the mode-selector switch on his control console. The sonar picture vanished and was replaced immediately with a scene of distorted lights. He saw now through the television eyes staring from the submarine's bow. To each side of Orca, rows of glowing lights marked the edges of the underwater approach to Base Savage. Directly ahead of the killer sub, along the sea bottom, blue-white light rippled away from them. Every three seconds the rippling effect repeated itself, the blue-white flashes guiding them directly to the underground caverns.

Owens sighed in anticipation of berthing the Orca and then stretching his legs.

"Christ!" he grunted, "but I'll be glad to get out of this thing for a while. I think I've forgotten what it's like to walk. Two weeks in this mother is enough to make anyone go stir-crazy."

His friend laughed. "Sure, sure," Dark mocked him. "You're hot to trot, huh? It wouldn't be that Betty has anything to do with it, would it?"

Owens returned the laughter as he thought of his wife waiting for him. A vision of her lithe tanned body on crisp white sheets passed before his eyes. "Well," he admitted slowly, "there is a bit of tightness in the belly, I suppose."

Dark glanced into the mirror to his upper right and grinned. Owens' reflection gestured at Dark's control panel.

"Back to your cage, slave," he chided. "I got a woman just aching for me and this is no time to get stuck in the mud."

His voice changed imperceptibly; of a sudden he was again all business. "Fifty yards and we're in the groove," he said. "You can come back on the speed now."

"Roger," Dark said. He reduced the power flow to the screws and with the same motion brought in greater thrust to the fore-and-aft hydrojets. The sound of the jets increased to a subdued whine, caused more by the flow of disturbed water than the smoothly spinning engines. There was a subtle shift in the response of the killer sub as the hydros took on greater control of the vessel's motion.

"Ten yards," Owens called. This close in, his voice was crisp, no-nonsense. Jockeying a mass of sixteen hundred tons into a channel narrow on all sides was no time for banter. Both men saw clearly the darker mass ahead of them, the tunnel entrance to the caverns, framed by a softly glowing ring of light. With small, constant touches to his controls, Dark threaded the needle of the submarine through the glowing eye.

"Okay," Owens said. "We're in. Disengage turbines, please."

Dark moved another control to disengage the twin screws far behind them. They sensed the slight trembling as the screws slowed to a stop. Now Orca moved slowly on the hydrojets alone

"Prepare for grapples," Owen snapped.

"Right," Dark replied. "Leveled and ready for grapples." He held the submarine absolutely level, the forward speed to an even two knots. On the consoles before each man a warning light blinked amber.

"Steady as she goes," Owens cautioned.

Dark did not reply. They waited for the grapples to lock onto the vessel. They could not see what was taking place but they knew every detail of the operation now going on about them. Beneath the rounded hull two semicircular bands moved with the same forward speed as Orca. As the speed matched, steel pistons within the tunnel floor began to rise, extending the semi-circular bands upward toward the slowly moving submarine.

The amber light blinked out. Red flashed steadily at the Orca crewmen.

"Contact any moment," Owens said, more out of habit than a need to pass on the information to Conan Dark. The words had scarcely left his lips when the submarine shuddered; the grappling bands had reached and were now closing slowly for a solid grip on the mass of the vessel. Another light flashed, but Dark had already responded to the trembling quiver of contact. Instantly he shut down the power to the hydrojets to ease the submarine's full weight firmly within the grapples. The vessel rolled slightly, steadied. Now the berthing system moved Orca under station power steadily forward into the cavernous chamber where the project team waited for them. On both control consoles the blinking red lights had vanished. replaced with a steady, assuring green.

Owens breathed an audible sigh of relief. "Whew!" he exclaimed, "I'm glad that's over. This is the only time this tub really has me on my toes." He gestured wearily. "Me for the open sea any time," he added. "I don't go for threading needles, that's for sure."

"Well, you'll just have to keep your pants on a bit longer," Dark laughed at him. "We may as well start shutting down now."

Owens groaned. "Okay, okay, give me a sec," he said. "Have the checklists ready in a moment."

They felt the slight trembling motion of the grapples moving forward along the tunnel rails. It would be several minutes yet before they were in the main chamber and the locks would be closed to start draining the water about the submarine. In the interim they could start the long and detailed shutting down of Orca's power and control systems. It would take them at least fifteen minutes to complete the primary checklist; after that, the project crews could come aboard and continue the job of preparing Orca for an exhaustive study of all her systems.

They were on the last page when they heard the waters sighing away from the flanks of the submarine. Through the massive hull came the sucking sounds of the pumps draining the chamber. They heard the familiar thuds and clanking noises of the catwalk being extended to their entrance hatch. Then a panel scraped; Hans Riedel was plugging in the power communications cable. Immediately afterward his voice crackled in their earspeakers.

"Con? Riedel here."

They could recognize his voice anywhere. Riedel still carried the clipped tones of the former German military officer.

Dark switched to outside communications to respond. "Got you clean, Hans."

"Very good," came the reply. "Starting to release the hatch," Riedel continued. But for a moment the noises ceased. The German engineer would make no further move until he received confirmation from within the submarine. Dark raised his eyebrows to Larry Owens; he received a confirming nod.

"Okay to unbutton, Hans," Dark called. The explosive release switch was closed and the safety wire secured. "Pyrotechnics on safe," he added.

By way of answer air began to hiss from the spherical chamber as Riedel and his berthing crew unsealed the hatch. The thick circle of steel lifted and then swung away. Immediately the wet smell and thudding noises of the underground chamber spilled into the submarine. Dark looked up to see Riedel's grinning face. A hand followed to clasp the one extended by Dark; Riedel shook it vigorously in a steel grip.

"Congratulations, Captain Dark," Riedel said in official tones. "Orca is now fully accepted by the Navy. We have—"

"Later, later," Dark interrupted. "I can wait for the champagne, Hans. Right now all we want to do is climb out of this thing. Okay?"

Riedel scrambled away from the hatch. Moments later a ladder slid through the open hatchway and locked into place. Dark removed his headband, punched the snap release of his shoulder and lap harness, and slid his padded contour seat back along its rails. He groaned as he stretched his muscles to unaccustomed positions, then took a last look around the control chamber he knew so well. Abruptly he swung about to the ladder and climbed out of the submarine.

Atop the catwalk he paused to breathe deeply. He loved the ringing sounds and the smells of the underground cavern. Never had he emerged from a submarine in the heart of Base Savage without feeling the same touch of awe that returned to him now. From the surface of the sea or the sandy hills of Isla de Culebra itself there did not exist so much as a shred of evidence that a huge subterranean chamber had been hollowed out and equipped as an advanced submarine project base. Engineers had discovered a natural fault lying beneath the cornerstone of the slim peninsula that formed the northwestern quadrant of the island. Under a blanket of naval maneuvers in the area they had brought in the equipment to enlarge the naturally formed hollow. Explosive blasts, well concealed by depth charges ripping the seas during the maneuvers, widened and deepened the central chamber and the underground channel. Engineers then built the secret facility for the sea trials of Orca, equipping the base with a major repair and maintenance station, as well as the communications, servicing, administrative, and other logistic requirements necessary to support the project. Other submarines had been accommodated here, but their presence was incidental to the primary mission of developing the deadliest weapon the seas had ever known. Conan Dark knew that this base might never have existed, that Orca itself might yet be imprisoned within some unfulfilled engineering dream were it not for himself and the small project team that had brought the killer-sub program to its present level of great success. He knew this and yet he never failed to acknowledge the fact, at least to himself, that the whole thing seemed always a bit tinged with the sense of unreality.

He looked about him. Overhead, the rough-hewn rock soared in a long sloping roof of dark shadows from which sprouted electrical stalactites placed there by the engineers who had created Base Savage. Brilliant floodlights cast a dazzling blue-white glare throughout the chamber, splashing intense light and stark shadows throughout the structures that reached from the tracked flooring to the light-studded naked rock far overhead.

At the far end of the cavernous chamber, penned within its own steel locks, loomed the rounded flanks of a second Orca. Dark and Owens several months earlier had brought the vessel to Isla de Culebra from the AHD yards in San Diego and, after carrying out the initial sea trails, had turned the killer sub over to Hans Riedel and the Orca project team for progressively more advanced testing.

Dark listened to the sound of water gurgling away beneath him as the pumps sucked the lock free to expose the lower lines and long belly of his submarine. You couldn't get rid of the sound or the touch or the smell of water in the great cavern. Evaporation and condensation were a constant process that kept the walls and metal structures glistening wetly beneath the hot lights. The base throbbed with the hum and clank of machinery. Overhead cranes sang with a muted thunder, and there seemed always to be the shouted conversations of the project crews working with power tools and their specialized equipment. It was all music to the man who stepped quickly along the catwalk to greet the section leaders of Project Orca.

Riedel couldn't wait to get to him. He grasped Dark's hand again and shook it with an enthusiasm that caught his friend by surprise. "I wanted to be first to tell you, Con!" he said, his eyes shining with excitement. "It is official. The news came to us only a few hours ago, and—"

Dark held up a hand to stem the rush of words. "Wait a moment, Hans!" he grinned. "*What's* official?"

"I told you, I told you," Riedel burst out. "The Navy . . . it has accepted Orca! The sea trials are officially over, Con! We've exceeded our specifications for the contract and . . ." He paused to breathe in deeply, his face wreathed in a wide smile. Eight years had reached their fruition.

Dark turned at the sound of Owens' footsteps along the catwalk. "You hear the news, Larry?"

Owens shared their obvious pleasure. He congratulated Dark and went through the hand-pumping enthusiasm of Riedel. "Calls for a party!" Owens shouted. "Tonight, at my place—okay? We've got plenty of time and—"

He broke off and looked beyond Dark and Riedel as a naval officer emerged from the shadows and walked briskly to the submarine, waving in greeting.

"Hey! Steve Marchant, no less," Owens called. "The hot rock from the Pentagon, himself. Must be big doings if we can shake the old four-striper loose from his swivel chair."

Captain Steve Marchant grinned at Owens' banter. Shaking hands with the group, he added his congratulations to Riedel's news. "It's just great, Con," he said. "The brass is delighted with your last run. Nothing like exceeding all the specs to keep the heavies smiling and contented." He gestured at his attache case. "Got your new orders here for Orca. A special team came down with me to rig her out for the ordnance tests. Soon as they're ready you'll be going out again."

Dark whistled slowly. "You people sure don't waste much time," he said. "We haven't got our feet dry and you're hustling us out again. Slave drivers, all of you."

Marchant laughed. "It won't be that quick, Con. Lot of work to do with the boat. Besides, we'll be installing some new equipment. Latest stuff, very hush-hush. Take some time to check it all out."

"Just like that, huh?"

Marchant ignored the barb. "Besides, that's government property you're going to be pushing around from now on, remember?"

"Yeah, that's right." Dark grinned. "Now we can

scratch the paint and don't have to worry about paying for it ourselves." He paused as a thought came to him. He looked directly at Marchant.

"But you didn't come all the way down here just to hold hands, Steve," he said slowly. "How come the special honors?"

Marchant shook his head slightly; the movement was barely noticeable, even to Dark, standing directly before him. It was a clear message to drop the subject. Dark gave no sign of the warning he had received.

"You going to be with us long, Steve?" he asked.

"No, not really. Have to set up things for the ordnance tests, and then I can be on my way." He turned and motioned for a group of men to join them.

"Special team will be working with you from now on," he explained. "They've already met Riedel and the rest of your group here. I want you to meet them."

He introduced each man to Dark and Owens; they had worked with several of the specialists before. Ray Matthia, in fact, was the brain behind many of Orca's advanced electronics systems, and they had worked with him during the design and construction phase of the first submarine. Sam Bronstein was a newcomer to their group; he was a nuclear ordnance specialist assigned by the Atomic Energy Commission to Project Orca. Chuck Harper had been detached from antisubmarine warfare tests; he was straight out of Washington. Dark had heard of Harper before. The man knew about as much of Russian attack submarines as the Soviets themselves. Dark was puzzled with his presence; he pushed aside the questions that he knew Marchant would answer when they were alone. And there was also Derek Fuller, whom Marchant introduced as a submarine ordnance specialist.

It wasn't hard to tell that something was in the wind. Owens showed his awareness of the suddenly accelerated schedule with raised eyebrows; like Dark, he kept his silence and asked no questions. But both he and Dark knew that the advanced ordnance tests for Orca weren't scheduled for another four or five months. Somebody upstairs in Washington was beating the waves for an unexpected acceleration of the program to prove out Orca as a weapons system.

As they walked to the elevator shaft that would take them to the island surface, Dark paused. He watched Bronstein, Harper, Fuller, and a dozen technicians swarming over the submarine.

My God, he thought, they're not even waiting to study the data tapes. The hull's still wet and they're going to be tearing out old gear and putting their new gadgets inside the boat. Steve's got a lot of talking to do.

Dark shrugged and crowded into the elevator. It was a ride of three hundred feet to the surface of the island. He accepted a cigarette from Marchant and sucked deeply of the smoke, swirling it through his mouth and exhaling slowly. After the scientifically controlled air of the submarine the taste was wonderful to his senses.

They stepped from the elevator into a thick concrete building filled with packing crates and construction equipment. Dark glanced at the elevator door closing behind him. There was no sign of an elevator or the shaft; he saw only the rough boards of a crate marked "Machine Tools." One foot away and you couldn't tell that you really weren't staring at a packing crate.

They stopped before a whitewashed concrete wall. Dark heard a slight buzzing sound in the air; in the island security office a naval commander was even then studying their faces over a closed-loop TV system.

"Please go ahead sir." The voice came out of nowhere; the speaker was concealed somewhere within the mass of crates and machinery. The concrete wall slid to one side to expose a narrow passageway. No sooner had they entered the passage when overhead lights went on and the wall closed behind them, trapping them effectively within the confined space. Each man had gone through the process before and evinced no surprise at the severe security measures. One by one they stopped alongside a metal plate imbedded in the wall; each man held up his wrist to the plate, where an electronic scanner studied the molecular arrangement of an identitab about each wrist. A memory computer checked out the identitab, a TV scanner provided visual identification, and a grill of heavy metal slid upward before them.

They stepped outside beneath a sky gleaming with stars. A warm wind whispered from the sea, bearing a taste of salt air. It was clean and refreshing.

"Steve, will you be needing me for debriefing now?" Owens asked of Marchant.

The captain shook his head. "Tomorrow will be time enough," he answered. "Besides"—he grinned—"Betty has promised me a lump on the head if I hold you up even one unnecessary minute."

Owens started down a path leading to the housing area. "It's eleven o'clock now," he called behind him. "Don't forget the party. Drinking time is midnight!"

Conan Dark turned the shower to a hot spray that threatened to blister the skin from his body. After two weeks of being cooped up in the equipment-jammed control room of Orca, the steaming needle blast was sheer delight. He let the water drain down his chest and back, running in hot rivulets across his stomach and down his legs. Finally he could stand it no longer and, with a shout of pain, twisted the shower to off. Several minutes later, shaved and scrubbed, he walked into the living room of his bachelor apartment. Steve Marchant extended a martini that Dark accepted, sprawling comfortably in a deeply cushioned chair.

They sipped slowly, neither man wanting to break the comfortable silence between them. Until, finally . . .

Dark walked across the room to refill his glass. Pouring, his back to Marchant, he broached the unexpected presence of the naval captain at Base Savage.

"All right, Steve," he said. "It's time for fun and games. Why don't you get a load off your chest and tell me that little story that's bottled up in you?"

Marchant waved his empty glass at his host. "It's fun and games, all right," he snorted, "but I think you're going to be in for a number of surprise endings tonight. In fact," he said, pausing while Dark refilled his glass, "I doubt if you're going to get very much sleep before we see daylight."

Dark gestured disdainfully. "And I say up yours, my friend. Orca wasn't built for comfortable sleep and I'm bushed. Besides, I want to crawl back into the boat in the morning. Hans and I have a lot of work to do, and—"

"You won't be working on the boat," Marchant broke in quietly.

Dark stared at his friend. Steve Marchant looked tired; lines creased his leathery face, making the eyes seem hollow and sunken. His shock of thick white hair only accented the contrast. Steve should have been a motion picture star, Dark thought. He even has the air of tragedy to go with his looks.

"Who the hell says so?" he demanded.

Marchant shrugged. "Who else?" he countered.

Dark showed a sudden flare of anger. "For Christ's sake, Steve, then quit beating around the bush and spill it."

Marchant ran his fingers through his hair, sighing heavily. "Sure, sure, Con," he said. "Only it's a bit difficult to find out where to start."

"All right, damn it," Dark shot back at him. "Why not tell me why I won't be working on the boat in the morning with Hans and his crew? That's as good a start as any," he finished impatiently.

The captain looked steadily at him. "Well, among other things, Con," he said slowly, "tomorrow morning you're going to be in a plane on your way to the Pentagon." He held forth his glass in a mocking toast. "With me, of course," he added.

Dark scraped a match into flame and lit up. "Okay, okay, Admiral," he said with a sour tone to his voice. "I'll be good. I won't interrupt your bedtime tale any more. Only tell me your goddamned story and get the hell out of here so I can get some sleep!"

Marchant was delighted with Dark's obvious impatience. The opportunities for needling his old friend had been all too rare. But this wasn't the time to press the advantage.

"Con," he said carefully, "do you remember that, um, that tidal wave along the Alaskan coast about, well, just about three months ago? We lost several dozen ships at sea and in the harbors, if you'll recall. A fair-sized town was wiped out and some rather severe damage raised along the coastline." He paused to review the facts in his mind. "More than four thousand people were killed," he added.

Dark didn't try to temper his impatience. "So? So there was a tidal wave in Alaska, and I'm here in Culebra. Sure, I remember it, Steve. But what of it? What does that have to do with—"

"I said that we lost more than four thousand people," Marchant broke in.

"Well so what!" Dark retorted. "You're talking as if this was something in which I was involved. What's with you, Steve? So they had a tidal wave. So I remember an earthquake in China that killed over eight hundred thousand people, and a fire-bombing in Tokyo that creamed more than a hundred thousand, and a monsoon in India that did in another quarter of a million, and—"

"Hold it!" Marchant said angrily. "Who wound you up, Con? You should know I didn't come here to discuss statistical handbooks with you!"

"I *told* you I was tired, Steve. Wrap it up, will you?"

Marchant's face went blank. He knew Dark was tired; the test runs with Orca could drain the energy from a man's system like water squirting through a fire hose. Yet he wanted to handle this carefully, for the whole thing, even to him, carried the taint of the bizarre. Marchant studied his fingernails, speaking in a deceptively casual tone.

"It would seem, Con, that the tidal wave I'm talking about was not, ah, shall we say, was not natural in its origin."

A long pause followed his words. He lifted his gaze to

match the frankly disbelieving stare of Dark.

Marchant nodded his head. "I know, I know," he said lamely. "In this day and age those things don't happen, or, if they do, we latch on to them right away to see what makes everything tick." He gestured in a reflection of his own impatience, and sighed. He had been going day and night with little sleep and he was almost as tired as Conan. It's just that I'm a bit more accustomed to the routine, he thought with irony, and I don't show the temper as quickly as him.

Dark's harsh reply intruded into his thoughts. "If anyone else had told me that, Steve," he said, "I'd throw his butt out that door and forget the whole thing." Thoughts of sleep were leaving his mind quickly; he should have known that Steve wouldn't come all the way down to Isla de Culebra without one hell of a reason. He tried to read Marchant's thoughts, but the bland poker face stopped him short.

Dark stubbed out his cigarette. "All right, Steve," he said. "Two questions. *What* do you think caused the tidal wave—you can fill me in on the details when you answer—and, second, what has all this to do with me?"

Marchant loosened his necktie and assumed a more comfortable position on the couch. "We don't *know* what caused it, Con," he began. "In fact, there are a great number of people in Washington who are convinced that this is nothing more than a very weak theory, and—"

"Run that by me again," Dark interrupted. "From the way you're acting it's obvious you think it's a lot more than theory. Otherwise you'd never be here."

Marchant smiled. "Let me give you a quick summary," he said. "The pieces will start to fall into place by themselves."

Dark nodded his assent.

"First," Marchant picked up his report again, "have you ever heard of Dr. Franklin Whitelock? Professor Whitelock, of the University of California? He's—"

"Never mind," Dark broke in. "I know Whitelock all

right. Big, strapping guy. Not what you'd picture as a professor. One of the best oceanographic scientists in the world—if not the best—I'd say."

Marchant straightened in his seat. "Of course! I'd forgotten," he chided himself. "Didn't you do your oceanographic studies with Whitelock?"

"*Under* Whitelock would be more accurate." Dark laughed. "I'm a long ways from knowing enough to work *with* him."

"Doesn't matter," Marchant said. "Just so long as you know the caliber of the man I'm talking about," he stressed. "And that's the real point of it, Con. Whitelock has been raising merry hell with the Navy about their official report on the tidal wave. He laced into the Oceanographic Data Center with everything he had; called Dr. Merriweather—he's the head of ODC—a blithering old fool who doesn't know enough to keep his head above water. Well, that's a side issue. What I'm getting at is that Whitelock insists the wave could not be the result of a natural event."

Dark didn't conceal his rising interest. "Go on," he urged.

"The professor is backing himself up with some powerful ammunition," Marchant said. "He even ran a computer check on the possible effects of a crustal-block shift that could bring on a major tidal wave. He insists that what happened—according to all natural law—is impossible." The captain gestured to his attache case. "I brought along a summary of his report; you can read it on the plane tomorrow. Essentially, however, he insists that the wave—actually, there was a dual effect: a seaborne wave effect plus the worst violence caused by the tremors and crustal-block shift along the coastline—defies everything that's known about geology or oceanology. And so forth. The sum and substance of it all—and the professor is very hard-nosed about this—is that there are only two possible answers: First, that we had better revise our understanding of many physical laws—*if* what happened was a natural event. . . ."

"And the second?" Dark asked softly.

A bleak expression appeared on Marchant's face. "And the second," he said carefully, "is that it was *not* natural."

He paused again, not wanting to speak the words. "And the second," he repeated, "is that something—someone—deliberately triggered the whole thing."

For a long moment Dark did not respond to the story offered by Marchant.

"You're trying to tell me that someone—and it's not our team—set off a nuke at the sea bottom to create a crustal shift?" he asked finally.

Marchant sucked deeply on his cigarette and nodded.

Dark placed his martini carefully on the table by his chair. He chewed on his lip and looked up at Marchant. Then he gestured to the cocktail glass. "With stories like that, Steve," he said, "who needs this stuff?"

"I know, I know," Marchant agreed.

"But I don't understand how I fit into all this," Dark protested. "Hell, man, I'm playing nursemaid to a killer sub, not poking around in the sea bottom. So how—assuming that your fantasy tales for tonight are true, that is—do you bring yours truly into this act?"

Marchant climbed to his feet to pace the room. His hands moved in gestures of nervous energy.

"Let me preface what I still have to tell you, Con, with a warning. I've been doing a great deal of mental arithmetic the last few weeks. Trying to see if two and two will add up to four. But they don't." He gestured angrily. "There's a skunk in the woodpile and it keeps coming to the surface no matter how I try to keep things nice and neat. Keep them simple, see?"

"No, I don't see anything of the sort. Not yet anyway," Dark said acidly.

"Hell, call it a hunch, if you will," Marchant went on, ignoring his friend's sarcasm. "The pieces by themselves are enough to make you think. But when you start fitting them together you end up with a man-sized headache."

"Jesus!" Dark swore, "Will you get on with it!"

Marchant stopped in the center of the room and stabbed a finger at Dark. "Six days ago," he said in a voice devoid of emotion, "an ASW force was in the Atlantic on maneuvers. They were working out with some of our attack subs—the new sub killers. As luck would have it, they were moving into an area where we had two oceanographic study vessels, doing bottom soundings." He hesitated. "Con, they picked up two unidentified bogeys. Deep."

"How deep?" Dark asked with impatience.

"Deeper than anything that should have been down there," Marchant blurted. "*Two* bogeys"—he held up two fingers to emphasize his point—"and, no question about this, maintaining at least five to seven knots."

"*How* deep, goddamn it?"

His answer froze Conan Dark in midmotion.

"*Twelve thousand feet,*" Marchant said. "*That's* how deep."

He stared across the room. "Two thousand fathoms," he added unnecessarily.

"You can't be serious," Dark protested. But even as he said the words, he knew that Steve Marchant had never been more serious in his life.

"Serious enough to come down here to take you back to Washington with me," came the reply.

"Yeah," Dark acknowldeged. "I see what you mean. There are three things about which you never joke, aren't there, Steve? The first is your wife, the second is poker, and the third is—"

"Unidentified bogeys at two thousand fathoms," Marchant finished for him.

Dark thought suddenly of Chuck Harper. "Wait a moment," he said slowly as he began associating separate events into a single overall picture, "wait just an everlovin' moment. You said 'unidentified,' didn't you?"

The trace of a smile appeared on Marchant's face. "That's right," he confirmed.

"Then what the devil is Harper doing here?" Dark demanded. "He's our brain boy on the Soviets, and—"

Marchant threw him a salute. "You have just won yourself a cigar, Con."

Dark glanced at the wall clock; it was almost two in the morning. "What time did you say we were leaving for the Pentagon?" he asked.

"I didn't," Marchant countered. "Wheels up at o-eight hundred. We'll have time to breakfast with Larry and his wife before we take off." He started unbuttoning his shirt and gestured to the couch. "I'm sleeping right here," he said wearily. "I'm too bushed even to think of walking out that door."

Ten minutes later he was fast asleep.

Conan Dark slipped beneath the sheets of his bed. He had been exhausted, ready to drop off the moment his head hit the pillow. Now he found his head whirling, the thoughts unsettling.

Two thousand fathoms . . . ! Sure, they could get down there with a bathyscaphe, all right . . . but without mother ships and tenders on the surface? Never. It's got to be something else. And Steve said they had been under way . . . What was it? Yeah; seven knots, maybe. It doesn't add up; it just doesn't add up, damn it. . . .

He fell into a fitful sleep, thinking of the awesome pressure two thousand fathoms squeezed against a conventional hull.

4

Five miles above the earth the silvered machine slid along an enormous sloping wall of cloud mountains and shadowed valleys. Against those massive ramparts of building thunderstorms the swept-wing craft was the merest speck. Down past the tumbled white slopes and gorges the sun splashed blue-green flame against the Atlantic. For the crew and passengers of the jet slicing the heavens between Isla de Culebra and Andrews Air Force Base it was a rare and breathtaking sight.

Steve Marchant stared through the oval window by his seat and saw nothing. The majestic panorama unfolding before him went unnoticed. His mind was active far from the sight displayed to him. He thought of a meeting in the Pentagon and of a tidal wave, inexplicable and terrible, roaring out of the Pacific night and sweeping four thousand human beings to oblivion. His thoughts swirled and eddied uncomfortably; Capt. Stephen S. Marchant, USN, was a man with an orderly mind who went at problems with a cold efficiency and single-mindedness of purpose that invariably produced the results he felt were preordained by such an approach. But now his precious equilibrium in accepting the thorns of his job waned. Keeping the rough and jagged pieces of this jigsaw puzzle in hand long enough to assemble a coherent picture lay beyond his immediate grasp. He felt he was foundering in a shirting kaleidoscope from which he *must* assemble the answers that lay tantalizingly beyond him. For there was a strange sense of dread associated with all that plagued him.

Things were not *right*. That was it more than anything else. Some pieces seemed to fit, but never quite enough. His thoughts refused coherency because of the ill-fitting and . . .

He gritted his teeth in self-anger at his lack of mental precision. A tidal wave that shouldn't be and a shift of the crustal block underlying the Alaskan coastline that at first glance, and on a second look, remained unjustified by all that was known of such matters. . . . And there lay one of the real rubs in the problem. A lack of knowledge could lead to problems created by that very lack; it was too easy to accept the panacea of mystery. Is this what Professor Whitelock had done in his insistence that the tremors and tidal wave could *not* be of natural origin? Or was the good doctor on the right track, while everyone else sought the familiar and comfortable refuge of refusing to challenge the greater weight and opinion of the scientific body that accepted what had happened in Alaska as perfectly ordinary; a bit unusual, perhaps, in the manner of its occurrence, but certainly within what could be expected of the fluid and unstable crust of the planet.

There! Another piece of this blasted puzzle. The body of scientists opposed adamantly to Professor Whitelock's brand of geological heresy had not said that what happened in Alaska *would* be expected, or *should* be expected . . . oh, no. In their own cute little way they were hedging, and they took elaborate precautions, and Steve Marchant knew that their phrase "*could* be expected" was no accident. Pompous they might be in their insistence that the tidal wave and tremors were perfectly natural events; they were also wise in the way of bureaucratic infighting to leave themselves a way out. *Could be* . . . hell, that was tantamount to saying they simply didn't *know*. Not well enough to lay their necks on the chopping block, as was Professor Whitelock. The scientist greatly disturbed Steve Marchant. Despite the coldly polite smiles of his associates, Whitelock simply was not a man to go off half-cocked on theories supported by little more than groping knowledge.

Whitelock, Marchant knew, was as much of a data purist in his own field as Marchant had been throughout his career in the Navy. If the man was certain of something, he didn't muck around the issue; he grabbed it by the tail and he tied it up as best he could.

And that was far from all, Marchant reflected with the displeasure that gnawed constantly at him.

Those mysterious submersibles—he didn't yet dare specify them as true submarines—sonar-tracked at twelve thousand feet; now there was one to give the Intelligence people the headache that binds! The Russians had been probing the deeps almost everywhere around the planet. That line of action surprised no one; their intensive effort had proved far greater than that of the United States and in itself was disquieting, but at the same time it remained within the laws of probable events and actions. What did *not* add up—in fact, it rocked the boat of any good Intelligence team—was that they had been detected at a depth of twelve thousand feet, and that there had been no service or mother craft on the surface within detectable range. That spelled out only one answer: the submersibles—and they *had* to be true submarines, Marchant thought darkly—had range and endurance sufficient to operate through a possible radius of several hundred miles from their servicing vessel. Was that mother ship itself perhaps a huge submarine that lay just beneath the surface when its charges were off probing the deeps? Chalk that one up to likely, but not yet in the probable class. Hell, and don't forget that there had been *two* sonar targets: two subs at that crushing depth. Or, he asked himself, were there really two? Had they detected a single craft disguising or altering its singular position through electronic countermeasures? Had unusual sea conditions, perhaps currents and even several thermoclines, created a false or distorted sonar picture?

More and more disturbed by what was unfolding with frustrating slowness before him, Marchant had already ordered the collection of incidents and Intelligence reports to be combined in a single study project. He had even brought it up as a matter of discussion before the monthly conference of the "Little JCS," the elite technical group that kept their collective eye upon developments concerning the USSR.

Soviet oceanographic efforts had in the recent past gone through an explosive increase in activity. The Russians had been filling the world ocean with many times the ships and manpower in oceanographic studies that had been put to sea by the United States. But even that enormous effort had nearly doubled in the past six months. *And there was absolutely no reason for any such effort to be made.*

Even their fishing fleet activities were causing feelings of disquietude. Here, again, there seemed little enough by itself to raise eyebrows, let alone blood pressure. But there was that same underlying burr of something that didn't fit. New whalers had appeared within the greater bulk of the Soviet fishing fleets operating on every ocean and sea around the planet. *Whalers?* Why whaling ships when the annual whaling catch was going down progressively as the result of stricter controls by the international body on fishing grounds of the world—of which the Soviets were not only willing but even avid supporters! The computer search was still under way, but Steve Marchant would have bet one of his gold stripes that when the run was finished, they would find some of those new whalers where no one even attempted to gun down the great beasts!

Why?

Marchant shifted in his seat, brooding, as he thought of a hundred *whys* that defied answer. Why the completely unexpected—and inexplicable—sudden imposition of severe security restrictions both at Vladivostok and at Murmansk? Why should the major commercial seaport of the Soviets, Murmansk, suddenly he blanked out with a security effort that exceeded anything in the days of even that master at the security game, Joseph Stalin himself? And Vladivostok . . . if the preliminary computer research runs weren't completely off base, then the Russians were starting to concentrate a massive oceanographic fleet effort at the Pacific port. But an increased oceanographic effort that lay obscured by the thick blanket of the intensive new security program? And whoever was running this new show wasn't playing games. CIA had come back with the unnerving reports that at least a dozen suspected—suspected and by no means confirmed—agents or dupes in the Vladivostok area had been stood against a wall and shot.

Was there substance to the drifting and shadowy whispers of a power conflict within the hierarchy of the Soviet government? How the devil do you field *that* one, groaned Marchant, when it drifts out of the miasma of European espionage and counterespionage as a regular course of events?

How did all of this fit into that thorny matter of the crustal-block shift, the tremors and avalanches and the tidal wave? Or did it even fit in at all? There was—hell, yes, there was a lot more to it than just what he had run through his aching head. The tracking ships; of course! One more stinking, ill-fitting piece in the puzzle that defied identification, let alone solution. From where had all those tracking ships, burdened with radar and electronics, appeared so suddenly? And what were they doing across the seas? They were fanning out in the pearl-string patterns to cover everything from the forty-ninth- to sixty-fifth-degree orbital inclinations of the Soviet space shots, as well as the orbital plane along a truer north-south line. But so many of them . . . *twice as many* tracking ships as the Soviets had ever placed around the world, including the times when they'd orbitted their first manned space station and had five Voskhods up at one time.

So how did he reconcile that problem—bad enough in itself—with everything else he was attempting to solve?

The Russians hadn't yet accomplished what they were after. That much Marchant knew. The mysterious activities of the Soviets on and beneath the high seas were suggestive of some long-range goal that would be achieved only at tremendous cost and effort. And the Russians were practical people. They were overly fond of results, and they didn't waste time or energy without damned good reasons for their actions.

Marchant did not *know* what lay behind the obscuring mists of insufficient data. But he knew the Russians well enough to accept the firm conclusion that anything involving mysterious earthquakes and tidal waves, unknown submarines operating at two thousand fathoms, unexplained strict naval security measures, vague reports of upper-hierarchy infighting within the walls of the Kremlin, and those mystifying oceanographic and fishing fleets at sea . . . well, damn them, they were hard after *something*.

Marchant's sixth sense wouldn't leave him alone; it nagged and worried his peace of mind. The more he thought of what that something might be, the more disturbed he became. For there is an old rule in the game of international intrigue and the manipulations of power: never let your opponent set you up. For if he does, especially with the control of massive energy within the hands of both the United States and the Soviets, he can hit you one hell of a blow. *Fast*. Faster than you can react.

You have to keep tabs on the opposition. You smile at Ivan and he smiles back, and you exchange cultural and scientific groups, and you sit at peace tables and mouth much nonsense about treaties, but never for a moment do you trust the son of a bitch so far as to get careless. And if Ivan can set up so effective a smoke screen that he's operating right under your nose, without your knowing what he's up to, it's just as bad as being careless. Because you can't respond, you can't initiate measures on your own, and *he* gets the drop on *you*.

"That has been known to be fatal," Marchant muttered to himself.

Well, he had to make his moves. Number one on the list was the ocean deeps.

The way things were heading, Marchant knew, they were going to have to search not only through every normal channel of political and technical intelligence available to them, but they must get within the ocean proper. Not in those blundering, clumsy and helpless bathyscaphes that bobbed up and down like sodden corks. Or even in the best of the big nuclear subs; not even they could take the squeeze of really far down. They'd crumple like pasteboard and tissue paper. . . . Marchant dwelled briefly on the *Thresher* and shook his thoughts free; he'd lost some very close friends when the ocean depths imploded *Thresher* and claimed her forever. No; they needed something better, *much* better.

Steve Marchant glanced to his side, studying the profile of Conan Dark as he looked through the jet's window at the great clouds sliding beneath them. He's going to go right through the roof when we start pushing him around in his precious Orca, Marchant mused, but there's no helping it. We need that killer sub and we need the one man who can make her perform in the manner that's necessary. There's no time to train anyone else in a test program. It's got to be Con. . . .

Without the knowledge of those involved, Marchant had already selected the members of his specialized team to pursue what had become a matter of critical urgency. It had been a long time since he and Con had worked together; the man who was now the head of Project Orca had once been a wet-nosed boot serving under Marchant's command. They'd put in two years at sea—*under the sea,* Marchant corrected himself—in one of the nuclear attack boats.

And now Conan Dark had, with genius and old-fashioned bulldoggedness, made himself the number one man in the business of deep submergence. Deep submergence, that is, with a freedom of movement that not too long ago had been a wild dream.

Marchant placed his attache case on his lap and released the catch. He withdrew a bound folder, opened it by a tab marked "Personnel," and read the list of names:

Conan Dark; Lawrence P. Owens; Hans Riedel; Raymond B. Matthia; Samuel Bronstein; Charles T. Harper; Derek Fuller; Robert A. Walters . . .

Marchant scribbled in another name—Georgi Rubinov; he would have to borrow Rubinov from NSA. He was their authority on the USSR; what Rubinov didn't know about the intrinsic capabilities of the Soviets wasn't worth bothering with.

There was another name, at the bottom of the list. Jerri Stuart. After her name was the listing: Crowell Institute of Oceanography; associated with University of California.

Jerri Stuart was a beautiful brunette. She had a few other assets, as well. The most obvious was a body that made strong men weep. But Jerri was a brain, a brilliant scientist in oceanography. There were plenty of outstanding oceanographers; Marchant had his pick from several hundred of the best.

Jerri Stuart was special. She had been Professor Franklin Whitelock's assistant for nearly six years; she would be invaluable to Marchant in what lay ahead.

For the first time in hours the captain allowed himself the luxury of a smile. He couldn't help it; he *did* enjoy manipulating people.

Until there had been a star-spangled clash of temperament and a conflict of wills that had since kept them apart, Conan Dark and Jerri Stuart had been lovers. They'd met when the Navy sent Dark to the Crowell Institute in California for a year's intensive studies in oceanographic sciences. There, inevitably, he was thrown in close proximity with Jerri Stuart. And just as inevitably the two had struck sparks with one another.

Steve Marchant wondered what Con would say when he discovered that Jerri Stuart was waiting to meet them at Andrews Air Force Base. Then again—he grinned—she didn't know either that soon she would be seeing Con. It should be quite a meeting. . . .

"Con?"

Dark turned from the window to look at Marchant. The captain held out the folder, his thumb marking the list of names. "Read this," Marchant said.

Dark scanned the introductory heading, raising his eyebrows at the bright-red SECRET stamped at the top of the page. He started down the list of names. Marchant watched him carefully.

He wasn't surprised when Dark's face seemed suddenly to freeze. His finger still poised over Jerri Stuart's name, he turned back to Marchant.

"You son of a bitch, why didn't you tell me?"

Marchant chuckled. "You never asked."

Dark glanced through the window. The silence lasted for several minutes.

"Steve."

"Yeah?"

"Where is she?"

Marchant glanced at his watch. "Just about one hour from now, that's where."

"Jesus Christ! You mean she's waiting for us at Andrews?"

The captain nodded.

"But *why?*" Dark shouted. "Why the hell are you bringing *her* into this?"

The sudden reaction caught Marchant off balance. Carefully, the levity no longer in his voice, he looked steadily at his friend. "Because I need her," he replied. "That's on the level, Con."

Dark glared at him. "You can't tell me there's no one else, Steve. That's just so much crap and you know it."

Marchant shook his head. "Uh uh, Con," he countered. "Professor Whitelock has only one really close assistant, and Jerri is it. She knows just how the old boy thinks. I said I need her in this thing and I mean it. I need an oceanographer a hell of a lot less than I need someone who can keep me in the know about the professor's thoughts. Not only for now," he added with emphasis, "but also for what's coming up."

Dark didn't reply.

Suddenly Steve Marchant was disturbed. He didn't like, he'd never have anticipated, Dark's response in this manner. He'd never dreamed that Con might still be . . . damn it, he should have told him before this.

Marchant shifted uncomfortably in his seat.

"Con, I don't understand," he said softly. "I thought you and Jerri called it quits way back when."

A cheek muscle twitched in Dark's face. "I didn't know it showed," he said angrily. He turned back to the window.

5

The sea brought us together and the sea keeps us apart. And it never let me forget her. As if I could or really wanted to. . . .

Conan Dark stared morosely at the clouds. Glowering masses of gray had replaced the dazzling white pinnacles. The jet plunged into a solid wall of rain, shuddered with the slapping shocks of turbulence, and burst forth into clear air.

No; that's not fair. It's really not true, either, he chided himself, preferring the truth to misplace blame. When we get right down to it, we were simply too strong for each other. She knew what she wanted and so did I. Both of us were determined to have it our own ways. He sighed unhappily. Never fall in love with a brain. That should be the first rule to be observed and never forgotten.

He brought her to mind, seeing her clearly. There was always a struggle to *keep* the image clear. Who was he seeing? Which Jerri? The brilliant young oceanographic scientist, of whom Professor Whitelock spoke with both deep affection and professional admiration? Or the young scientist who was possessed of an incredible memory and a natural affinity for the sea? Jerri Stuart took to the oceans with all the intrinsic understanding and the natural feel that you expected to find in a leather-faced old salt who'd cut his eyeteeth on a wind-snapping two-master. You did *not* expect to find grave intelligence, the cutting edge of a scientific mind, and a motherly instinct for the creatures of the sea in a package of dazzling femininity that stood a diminuitive five foot four, in a girl that could have walked away with any bathing-beauty contest in a state crammed with hopeful pulchritude.

For that was the other Jerri . . . the girl with whom he'd fallen in love. Nothing reserved or calm about it, either. The old-fashioned, head-over-heels kind of love affair. He would have made an utter ass of himself except that Jerri responded in kind. She was open and honest enough not to play games about her feelings. They had loved and made love in a delicious whirl. With the mountains at their back and the Pacific beaches at their feet they had been blessed with the magnificent stage settings of nature that lovers expect to find in fairy tales only.

Dark was a superb swimmer. At the age of two his father had tossed him into the river near their home and commanded him to swim—or else. The simple philosophy worked well; his father's creed was to make the boy swim without letting him realize that at the first sign of difficulty he would be snatched from the water. From that day on, with the lakes of Orlando, Florida as his backyard water playground, and the flat, hard sands of Cocoa Beach only fifty miles away, Dark had been a natural creature in the water.

To his delight, he realized he wasn't quite the swimmer that he discovered Jerri to be. She lacked his powerful drive—Dark had a slew of racing medals to his credit—but she matched him easily in endurance, and compared to her lithe flowing motions he felt like a bull elephant stampeding through a creek when he watched her swim, more seallike than human, apparently effortless as the water flowed before and around her body to yield her passage.

During weekends they drove to her home in Pescadero, where more of the idyl they found so much to their tastes was available to them. Theirs was a love affair of sparkling water and sun-drenched beaches, of sails cracking in the wind and excursions into the nearby mountains.

What they shared in their pleasures and in their passion

they discovered also in their work. Conan Dark had come to Crowell for a year's intensive training and practical experience in the oceanographic sciences; what might have required several years was condensed for him in only one. He had brought with him to the classroom—indoors as well as the sea—his own already extensive knowledge of the oceans; to him the oceanographic studies were simply an extension of what he had done most of his life.

Jerri had already worked several years as a student with Dr. Franklin Whitelock and, after graduation, planned to stay on at Crowell as the Professor's assistant. Dr. Whitelock had found in her an extraordinary combination of dedicated young scientist and human being. The good fortune of their mutual professional activities did no harm in overcoming the expected jaundiced eye that Dr. Whitelock turned to the confident young man who had been sent to him by the Navy. Any suspicions Dr. Whitelock harbored that Conan Dark might well leave in a year's time with his assistant were allayed somewhat by Dark's own knowledge of the ocean depths, the same area in which Dr. Whitelock endeavored to cast the light of some meaningful scientific knowledge. Conan Dark at this time was a veteran submariner, an experienced UDT swimmer, and skilled in deep free dives. But his experiences in bathyscaphe descents down many thousands of feet into the ocean was the clincher that swept aside whatever doubts Dr. Whitelock might have harbored. With Conan Dark available to him for questioning, Dr. Whitelock was somewhat more disposed to encourage his beautiful young assistant to keep Dark within reach, rather than to hope for their parting.

Jerri Stuart and Conan Dark were, of course, oblivious of the machinations conducted by Dr. Whitelock in his own mind. During the heated flush of their relationship, however, it is doubtful they would have heeded the interfering voice of Dr. Whitelock or anyone else. The world was theirs, and in their deepening love there was little room for the intrusions of others.

Lightning ripped the sky. A jagged, curing bolt stabbed his eyes; Conan Dark stared into the flickering afterimage as the storm's darkness again swallowed up the swift aircraft. They hurtled from one line of storms into another, out of fury-lashed clouds into momentary respites of clear air. Dark glanced down to see a shaft of sunlight knifing through the roiling gloom; it speared its way unconcernedly through the violence and gently set its golden wash on the ocean surface far below. Then driving rain obliterated the sight.

The rain . . . a wet blackness in the heavens. He thought back to a time when he and Jerri had stood huddled close together, arms clasped around each other's bodies, laughing at the cold sensation of their wet clothes, watching a summer thunderstorm tearing up the Florida sky. That particular moment and delirious two weeks were a gift from Dr. Whitelock. There was a need for someone from the Crowell Institute in California to visit the University of Florida; Dr. Whitelock managed to arrange matters so that both Jerri Stuart and Conan Dark were assigned to the task; he compounded his manipulation of the Institute's needs by seeing to it that the two young people were not to return for two weeks. That Dark's home was in Orlando, Florida, was a fact not unknown to the Professor, who, it should be noted, denied any role in assuring his favorite assistant and her bright young man an unexpected vacation.

Conan Dark smiled at his memories of Whitelock. The "Bear of the Sea," as his students referred to the gruff old man, could be as soft as putty. He was deeply and genuinely fond of Jerri, who on her part loved the cantankerous old soul; when the situation permitted, Whitelock never hesitated in the granting of whatever favors lay within his authority.

That was quite a trip. Dark sighed. It was like turning back the clock to when he was a kid. But he wasn't any more; he was a man with a beautiful young girl who loved him and who had returned with him to his home. And he'd been given the rare opportunity to take her back in time with him to the places and the sights that the youth he once was had treasured so much. . . .

"Stop it, you idiot!"

He ignored her protest, pressing against her body and tickling her ear with his tongue. He felt her skin react as she twitched. He grinned as he sought a repeat performance. She couldn't resist him, with one hand on the handle of the big frying pan and the other trying to turn over a simmering perch. He moved his body up and down slightly, rubbing his skin against hers, his tongue after her ear again.

She tried to squirm away. "Con, I mean it . . . stop it right now!" He breathed heavily in her ear. "Con, I swear, if you don't, I'll—"

He pressed his weight against her body. "What?" he whispered. "Just what are you going to do, beautiful?"

"If—if you don't keep at least three feet away from me, Con," she said sternly, "I—I'll toss your dinner right into that river!"

"Oh, my God!" he shouted in mock horror, springing away, "anything but *that*, woman!"

He retreated to a canvas chair on the deck and sprawled limply, reaching for a cigarette. She turned to look at him and smiled.

He glanced up and saw the smile. "You're supposed to be cooking my dinner," he chided her with an answering grin. "What are you smiling at, woman?"

Her teeth flashed whitely in the evening shadows. "You," she answered.

He raised his eyebrows. "Why?"

"Well," she began slowly, "at first I was going to say that you looked like a big cat. Something like a cougar, or a bronzed panther."

"Well, no, I—"

"But on second thought," she continued, "the more I look at you and hear that growling from your stomach, the more convinced I am that you're not a big pretty cat. You're just a horrid, lecherous man who wants his dinner and—"

"—will do his damnedest to roll you in the hay afterward," he finished for her.

She turned the perch in the big iron pan, examining it critically. She half turned to glance at him again. "They don't have hay in this houseboat," she said.

He waved his hand airily. "Think nothing of it," he bantered. "What has been forgotten from the farm I more than make up in the arts and techniques of—"

"Dinner's ready," she broke in.

"Hot damn," he said, rubbing his palms together. "It's about time." He flipped his cigarette into the river and brought the dishes to her at the iron stove. "Ummm, but that *do* look marvelous."

They sat together at the low table, the fish he had caught only hours before sizzling on the plates. He took a first bite and closed his eyes, savoring the taste, and then attacked his meal with gusto.

She laughed at him. "I get the feeling that I've been thrown over for a speckled perch," she said.

A forkful hesitated just before his open mouth. "Uh huh," he grunted, gesticulating with the fork. "But only for a little while, you understand. I'm, ah, just building up energy for what comes later."

She stuck out her tongue at him. "Much later, I'm afraid. You're a lousy lover on a full stomach, darling."

Another mouthful disappeared from the plate. "Sure, sure," he countered. "I'll see you when the moon is full. Hay or no hay," he added.

They finished the meal leisurely, helping the fish along with cold beer from the houseboat refrigerator. After Con had swept the remains into the river he arranged two deck chairs together so they could look into the evening skies. Their arms linked, a sense of peace settling about them with the approach of night, they sat quietly, content with the presence of one another.

She loved these moments at the end of the day. Con had equipped the houseboat with a tape player, but to Jerri the music of the St. Johns River was far to be preferred. In the lush growth on each side of the river a thousand voices chirruped and sang in a medley of shrill and bass notes. Against the pale remains of the day, a thin violet light the only evidence of the sun that had eased its way around the distant edge of the world, they watched a long procession of winged creatures that alternately exercised their wings and then glided effortlessly through the air. Beyond the feathered train a star gleamed.

Jerri sighed, her fingers moving slowly along his arm, caressing his skin lightly. All's well with the world, she thought, holding the little-girl wish of wanting to stop time.

But it would end tomorrow. Each of them knew the other had thought suddenly that the morning would bring the last day. Neither had regrets. It was a special kind of miracle when you could live in a world of dreams that seemed real even if only for one week. And it was more than the laughter they had shared, the closeness of their bodies, the growing sense of oneness, the knowledge that they had defied the oppressive sameness of every day by retreating to this timelessness on the river.

They had started their vacation in Florida, grateful for the unbidden meddling of Professor Whitelock, when the idea came to Con that rather than spend their time along the coast, here was a heaven-sent opportunity for a truly rare seclusion for them. His father kept an old, sturdy houseboat at Lamb Stewart's Fish Camp on the St. Johns River, about thirty-five miles from their home in Orlando. Con had spent a good part of his youth on that flat-bottomed pleasure palace; made of planking that would weather another fifty years, she was thirty-two feet from her pointed bow to her squared-off stern.

Excited with the thought of a week along the river, he had told Jerri of his plans. They'd visit his folks for two days, and that would give him a chance to call Stewart at the fish camp and be sure everything aboard the *Old Jackson* was in good shape.

His excitement and his descriptions pleased her; in her own mind she saw in this seclusion the opportunity to know more about the man with whom she had already found so much. Con seemed to . . . well, to bring to life what lay dormant within her.

She was delighted with his family and they—Timothy and Harriet Dark—with her. That they saw nothing odd in a young couple's disappearing for a week was made quite plain to her; apparently Con's mother thought that wholesomeness was a better virtue to be pursued by the family than false modesty.

Only one disappointment met Jerri; she had hoped to meet Con's younger borther, Michael. But he was gone and would be for another year.

Con made a face and said that Michael was an outcast in the family. Startled, she turned to the elder Darks. "Anything that doesn't swim," his father explained, "isn't quite human. At least as far as Con is concerned. And to him, Michael committed the ultimate sin, the unforgivable blasphemy."

"But what did he *do*?" she asked, caught off balance by this unexpected assault on the missing Michael.

"Mike's a fighter pilot, Jerri," Timothy Dark explained, laughing, "and Con's never quite gotten over it, that's all."

"That's *not* all," Con threw back at his father. He turned to Jerri. "It wouldn't be so bad if Mike had joined the Navy," he said, "or even the Marines. The family name could stand that. But, no! The deep and dark truth is that he's a figher jock in the Air Force, of all places," he added with a sour expression. He rolled his eyes toward the ceiling. "The shame of it all," he cried out in mock sorrow. "Four generations of the Darks have gone down to the sea, and my brother—my own brother, mind you!—flaps his way like an old crow around the sky. Besides—"

"Oh, stop it, Conan," his mother said. "Michael is a very good pilot and you know it."

"Sure I do, Mom," he admitted with a grin. "But don't say it so loud. That's my girl over there, and right now I'm the big cheese in this house."

She joined in their laughter. The family joke and the good-natured joshing of their house guest swept aside whatever last fences there might have been with Conan's parents.

On the second night of Jerri's stay in Orlando they all piled into the family station wagon to deliver supplies and fishing gear to the houseboat to which she and Con would return early the next morning for their private vacation. Jerri clapped her hands in delight with her first view of *Old Jackson* and made a quick inspection of what was to be her floating home for the next week. Decades of comfortable use and fishing were stamped indelibly into every inch of the old houseboat; knives and gaffs hung in netting from the walls, the wood was well polished and smooth, and a well-equipped galley with a refrigerator meant succulent meals—if Con kept his promise about tasty morsels from the Florida waters. *Old Jackson* felt comfortable and . . . well, the houseboat even smelled friendly, she thought.

Before sunup the next morning Con roused her from a deep sleep with an unceremonious hard slap on an exposed behind. Dawn was only an hour behind them when Con eased the houseboat away from its landing and swung into the slow river current.

As the lure of the river and the surrounding swamps drew him back to the thrills he had known as a youngster, Jerri discovered in Con a boyishness she had never expected. The no-nonsense demeanor of the intense and hard-working naval officer faded from sight as he guided *Old Jackson* with renewed skill through the byways of the river and the swamps. She had no idea where they were and thought less of it; Con was her world, and the hours of the days and nights revolved about him. Except for basic staples they trusted to the river and the swamp to feed them; for Jerri it was a new sport, an education and culinary raptures all rolled into one. Knowledgeable she might be of the oceans, but the Florida swamps had concealed from her studies the private world that existed within their boundaries. From the waters they pulled bream, speckled perch, black bass, catfish, and others which, while strange to her sight, left nothing to be desired in the way of taste.

He showed her how to watch for and avoid the less friendly denizens of the high-grassed knolls and the river banks, for the swamps teemed with water moccasins, pygmy and the big diamondback rattlers, and other snakes best kept at a safe distance. More than once she mistook the knob-studded back of an alligator to be a harmless floating log; at night, Con frightened her half to death with flashlight forays he made to rope several of the dangerous creatures. He showed surprise at her concern, for he and his younger brother had hunted 'gators since they were kids. Nevertheless she did not conceal her relief when he released the always angry reptiles. Dangerous creatures were common enough to her; she had dealt with everything from moray eels and poisonous jellyfish to sharks and barracuda. It was that very experience that brought on such reluctance to become better acquainted with the huge-jawed Florida alligators.

But most of their week was an excursion into the vivid colors, sounds, smells, and sensations of a semitropical world never before within her reach. Through Con's own excitement and his astonishing detailed knowledge of the swamps they came alive to her. He never tired of explaining or pointing out to her this animal or that feature. He could spot and identify a bird within the high grass by barely more than a rustle of feathers. He would show her a feathery treasure, multihued and dazzling, that whirred overhead or lay hidden in protective growth and shadows: ducks, snipe, quail, dove, wild turkeys, and bald eagles; the graceful beauty of herons; hawks and geese and buzzards; even the gulls drifting in from the coast. On one rare occasion a crusty old pelican far from his usual haunts flapped to the edge of the houseboat and visited them with fearless curiosity, and then, as if to dash their delight at their communion with the wild creature, exhibited only a vast indifference. Such haughtiness deserved respect, they felt, and the big bird was permitted to remain unmolested as long as he desired.

She saw only a few of the animals he described as permanent citizens of the swamps, but once a bobcat hissed from a low branch as they eased by, and several rabbits appeared in furry flashes. One other creature existed in number, and she watched Con at night, gig in hand, stalking the large plump frogs he had selected for the next evening's dinner.

She knew that to Conan Dark the water was a second home; their work together and his past history as a naval officer had told her many things. Their days and nights floating along the river and within the swampy waterways brought out more clearly a side of the tall and powerful young man that she had faintly known existed, but she was to learn, also, that his skills were many—and often a source of surprise to her.

They left the houseboat for several hours one afternoon to attend a snarling, spray-lashed river race of hydroplanes. This was the first time she had been this close to the wicked little speedsters, and Con had to explain to her what was happening. He pointed out the mahogany plywood construction and the reasons for the dope-sealed taut canvas tops. His hands as descriptive as his words and the expressions on his face, he raced through selective choices of motors starting at fifteen and edging up to forty horsepower and then into the more powerful "brutes." When he came to the manner in which a man careened around the buoys, the spray and thunder ripping its own song across the waters chopped up by spinning blades, she looked at him with undisguised astonishment.

She had to shout to be heard over the waspish cries and bedlam as the boats tore by, smashing their way through the tossed surface. "You never told me you used to race these things!" she shouted into his ear.

He gave her a sheepish grin to demean what, she learned later from his proud father, had been regarded as spectacular skill by Con's elders when he was still of school age. Under her prodding and the goad of his own mounting excitement, he explained to her the "guts" of hydroplane racing.

"It's *feel*, Jerri," he said with a sudden light in his eyes. "A guy in one of those things simply must have the feel of everything that's going on, right from start to finish." His finger stabbed the air. "There—see how they come around, the way the boat is just about walking the water in the turn? Okay, every one of those guys is playing that bomb he's riding as if it was about to go off under him. Because," he said grimly, "they *are* bombs and they can go off if you're just a mite careless." He gestured again as three boats leaped from the water and slammed back down again.

"You feel it all," he continued. "The prop is different when you're straight out and driving for all you've got than it is, say, when she comes out of the water. You've got to be ready for that sudden bite when she slams back in again." His hands wove descriptive patterns in the air before him. "You know you're going to get deceleration and that bite and a rapid-fire batch of deceleration and acceleration and you've got to *ride* it, stay right there on top of it, every second, or else, and—hey! Look over there!"

A flash of wet mahogany, a scream of an engine . . . a racer flipped crazily through the air and disappeared in foaming spume. Moments later a helmet bobbed in the water and a hand waved. Dark eased back into his seat and Jerri felt her heart beating again. "He's okay," he said to her unspoken query. "Boat just got away from him." He grinned. "That's a good example of what I mean," he added. "It can happen, without warning. That guy was lucky; no one was right behind him when he flipped."

Moments later the flat-bodied racers ripped by them in an avalanche of snarling cries and sped down the course. He pointed after them. "See how most of the boat is out of the water, Jerri?" She nodded. "Well," he went on, "that prop is really something. The whole design is so set up that with the throttle fire-walled the stern really bottoms in, lets the boat get full steam."

She watched a flat form come out of the water, crash back in, continue screaming along the course. She winced. "Good Lord, Con," she exclaimed, "doesn't that hurt? When he comes down and hits the water, I mean."

"Damn right it hurts," he said. "It boots you right up through your tailbone. When you're moving like that, Hon, even the ripples change. They're not water any more—it's more like you're riding along a metal trough."

His eyes reflected a moment long ago. "I *know,*" he said. "Long time ago—I was about sixteen or seventeen—I almost got creamed out there, right on this same course."

"What happened, Con?"

For a moment he stared at the boats, the lines of his face hard. Suddenly Jerri wanted to reach out and touch him, to run her fingers lightly along his arm. But she stayed the impulse; she knew that Con was as much behind the wheel of the hydroplanes as if he were out there in the water. And he was mixing the two, the immediacy of the moment and what had happened years before.

"I was coming around into a turn," he said, as much to himself as to her, reliving the sensations with suddenly clenched fingers and a quickening of his breathing. "Cut into it real neat, everything balanced out exactly as it should be, and I had the chance to slice it in between some of the other guys. You know, break out and cut for the lead." He shook his head and grinned self-consciously. "The boat was going up and down, just pounding the seat right into my tailbone. Then the acceleration got bad; I mean, it was almost as if I was getting into swells, and they were spaced just far enough apart at my speed to make them really bad. I was surging; the prop was snapping out of the water and chewing its way back in again. It was getting nasty, the jolts were bad—you can *feel* her sluing awkwardly and you know you're getting into trouble—and I felt her starting to porpoise on me."

He glanced at her face. "And when that happens, lovely one," he said with a frank admission of the fright that had gripped him, "you come closest to knowing just how loose your bowels can get."

She met and held his gaze.

His voice was flat. "The wind crossed on me suddenly. I got a wind shift without warning—I don't think I could possibly have foreseen it—at the worst possible moment." He shrugged. "It got under the boat, like a great big goddamned lever, and it lifted, hard and fast and with a lot of power. Next thing I knew a million buzz saws were going off all around me and I was flying through the air. It was the weirdest sensation, Jerri," he said with sudden emphasis, as if trying desperately to convey to her what he had experienced. "It's as if, well, as if it's not really happening to you; it's all happening to someone else and you're a spectator. Well, like seeing yourself—like you're above and a little away from the whole thing—from a distance. A voice in your head tries to warn you desperately that it really *is* you, but it stays unreal because there just isn't a damned thing you can do about it."

He licked his lips, suddenly dry. "And then I felt—for the first time I could actually feel something—I felt my body twisting, sort of spinning around until I was going backward. I could see with really amazing clarity: the spray and the boat smashing itself up—and the water, even the colored flags and the buoys. All of it. Like a brilliant etching. And then I saw what turned my blood cold. Just like *that*"—he snapped his fingers—"it wasn't happening to anyone else. It was me, all right. I was still in the air, coming down, when I saw the whole field behind me. One mass of boats, screaming, bows high, and each one of them looked as if a tornado was following him from the way his prop chewed the water. I knew I would hit just before they reached me, and suddenly they weren't hydros any more. They were real, living things with terrible cutting knives—those props, remember?—and they'd be tearing right into me."

He paused, staring into the water before them. "Somehow I managed to keep my head. I remember telling myself that if I hit the panic button, then my brother was suddenly going to be an only son." He laughed dryly. "So I opened my mouth and took a hell of a deep breath and started letting instinct take over. My folks were watching, it must have been pretty unpleasant for them, and they told me later that I actually twisted in the air and hit the water in a clean dive."

He made that little shrug again, as if to dismiss a label of importance from what he'd been told. "Anyway, all I recall is that the moment I felt my face in the water I was pumping and clawing with everything I had to get *down,* to get as deep as I could. I must have made it, oh, maybe about eight or ten feet down when this tremendous racket exploded all around me. I opened my eyes and nearly passed out . . . there, over my head, I saw a dozen slashing blades just beating hell out of the water and pounding over and by and all around me. One touch of those and I'd have been in pieces."

His breath came out slowly. "But I was completely safe by then. It took only seconds, faster than I realized, before the boats were gone and it was safe to come up again." He grinned at her boyishly. "But you know what I did, Jerri?" He didn't wait for an answer. "I was scared so stupid that I didn't realize I could have come up and swum to the side, near a buoy, where a boat would have picked me up. Instead, all I knew was that I had to get the hell out of the way of those boats before they came around again, and so I stayed under, swimming as hard and as fast as I could.

"Of course, by now everybody thought I had been hit by a prop; Mom nearly passed out, from what I hear. In the meantime"—he laughed—"old stupid me was thrashing along like a walrus, my lungs about to burst, and I came up about a hundred feet or so from where everyone had seen me hit the water.

"It was a stupid thing to have done, I suppose, but all I could think of was to get away before those props were on to me again." He fished for a cigarette. "Anyway, that's what happened. Right out there." He gestured, feeling uneasy at the blurted admission of his fear.

Later that night, snuggled comfortably within his arms, she found herself thinking about Con's frank and revealing words. She found it difficult to reconcile this powerful, intelligent and confident male animal with someone so frightened he would panic—as Con indeed had admitted doing. It was difficult to understand this not simply because she had come to love and to know well this man, but because she knew also of his background before and after he joined the Navy. Con was a man among men.

He was unbelievably adept beneath the surface, the kind of diver even the fish would accept as one of their own. It wasn't simply a skill he had developed in mechanical fashion; Con was gloriously in his element when the ocean surface closed over him and he eased into the pressure always waiting beneath the thin mantle of the air. He had told her, long before, of weeks spent in the Bahamas and off Puerto Rico, in the clear waters of the Caribbean; as a youth he and three friends had pooled their money to rent a forty-footer and sailed away for three months of joyous freedom known to few youths or adults. Then on the horizon of that youth appeared storm clouds never before encountered by Con. Screaming troops poured across a geographical line on some forsaken, distant peninsula that everyone would come to recognize as Korea, and with the onset of the war Con, then nineteen years old, enlisted in the Navy.

With his powerful, lithe body and superb skills underwater the Navy regarded Con as a natural for a combat swimmer—one of the elite that formed the Underwater Demolition Teams. Con knew how to swim, all right—he would take second place to no man in this regard—but he did *not* know the diverse and extraordinary skills and demands of the UDT swimmer. What he had developed as a natural talent the Navy whipped into blue-steel hardness and greatly expanded underwater horizons. He went through four months of basic UDT school and plunged into six weeks of underwater-swimmer training. He learned to function within the darkness of the nighttime sea in neoprene foam-rubber suits; he became adept with the paraphernalia of his trade—gloves, masks, fins, knives, guns, and other equipment; he gained perspective and equilibrium in the no-gravity blankness of dark waters through the use of compass, watch, and depth gauge. He accepted as second nature explosives and diving rigs, he did hydrographic reconnaissance, lived with SCUBA and new rebreather equipment as extensions of his animal body. And then something happened: he left the UDT team. It seemed no loss to the Navy as Con went into the submarine service and exhibited the engineering genius and the promise that led eventually to the killer-sub program—Orca.

She discovered, in his arms that night, that the man she loved was no stranger to fear. She learned, also, what many women never understand, and men, neither: that all truly brave men know fear, and that what separates them from the others is their command of that fear. There are degrees of control just as there are degrees of effort necessary to achieve and sustain that control. Con dismissed the incident with the hydroplane as the kind of panic that any man might have displayed under the same circumstances. He considered it controlled panic; he hadn't foundered helplessly but had taken the steps necessary to save his life. It was good, old-fashioned fright. That same afternoon he was back in a boat and racing again, and he was so damned mad at having been tossed he frightened half the other racers and stormed to a crowd-cheering victory.

But the UDT team . . . that was different. Con had fought, and won, a violent battle of his own emotions. He gave her only the sketchiest of details; she sensed his misgivings and did not irritate old wounds.

As part of his UDT training, he explained, the men received three weeks of airborne training. Every UDT man had to be a qualified parachutist, jumping both from planes and helicopters, over land and into the water. They made static-line jumps, with long webbing straps opening their chutes automatically. Except for their final leap into the ocean. Burdened with bulky and clumsy equipment, they tumbled away from the jump plane, fell freely for three to five seconds, and then hauled on their D-rings to open their life-saving canopies.

"My chute didn't open."

His matter-of-fact statement in the twilight gloom sent ice water through her veins.

It took him only a moment to realize that death waited but seconds away. He carried no reserve pack; there wasn't room with all the equipment strapped to and hanging from his body. Fighting down the fear bubbling into his throat, he clawed desperately at the ripcord housing.

"I was tumbling," he said, almost in a whisper. "I remember the horizon rolling around at some insane angle and the waves getting larger and larger. All this time I was tearing off fingernails trying to get that stinking chute out off its pack. What was so crazy was that I wasn't even scared. Just cold, through and through. Cold and everything clear to me, and I knew it was too late. There wouldn't be enough time. I quit." He looked up at the stars. "I just plain quit, and I didn't even know the canopy was streaming out, trying to deploy. It never really opened; not fully, anyway. It slowed me down some. Then I hit the water and"—his shrug was eloquent—"I woke up a couple of days later in the hospital. It was a miracle. I broke a leg and got scraped up a lot, but that was all."

She kissed him lightly, wanting him to go on. He drew deeply on a cigarette, tossing the butt over the side. It hissed when it struck the water, then the night sounds of the swamp again filled the air.

"I didn't really become frightened until a couple of weeks after I came out of the hospital," he said. "Suddenly I was faced with reality—going back to the team. I just about fell apart. The reaction took that long to set in. My

God, I shook like a leaf and the sweat poured from me. I was scared out of my wits. I never wanted to step into an airplane again as long as I lived.

"But I did," he said with a heavy sigh. "I put on all my gear and they set me up for a static jump, but I wasn't having any of that. I was white as a ghost, and they didn't want me to jump, but I raised all kinds of hell and insisted I was going out in free fall.

"I almost didn't make it," he said in a whisper she could barely discern. "When I got to the door and looked out I felt a knife being twisted in my guts. I threw up. Didn't even know it was happening until I was sick all over myself. The boys figured I'd had it then. But I told the pilot to go around once again and I wouldn't budge from that door."

He was silent for several minutes.

"I jumped," he said finally. "I jumped, and I did it alone, because I had to. I simply, absolutely *had* to get out of that thing, and on my own. The minute I fell away from the plane I knew I had it whipped. I delayed the pull; let myself fall. I wanted the belly sensation, the wind, that insane horizon, and when I had it all, and knew I was in control, I pulled.

"But I never went back. I quit UDT that same day. I was still afraid to jump. Afraid? I was scared silly into the middle of next week. Oh, I knew I *could* jump. I'd proven that to myself, and the others didn't count. But as God is my witness I knew I'd never go out of a plane again unless it was so critical that life literally depended upon it. I *could,* but I wouldn't. They understood, of course. Hell, they never expected me to go back up again. When I did, they figured I was okay, and anything I decided from that moment on was all right with them."

He grinned self-consciously. "So there it was. I certainly wasn't going back up any more. I did a lot of thinking and all of a sudden, it seemed, everything became crystal clear." He nodded toward the water. "Down; down there was home to me. It was as though I had known it all the time but never took the trouble to recognize the fact. I wanted to go deep, *really* deep. Maybe it was a psychological compulsion. I don't know and I really don't care. I went to submarines like a lost soul. . . ."

Later, after a long silence, he closed the issue with her. "I grew up then, Jerri," he said carefully. "Not when I jumped that last time, to prove something to myself. Later. When I made my decision not to go back.

"Every man's got both eagle and chicken in him. Few men dare to admit that to themselves. But I figure I'm ahead of the game. I learned it a long time ago and I don't mind living with it."

She loved him wildly that night.

She had always loved him well, her body released to accept his powerful surging motions. Their last night on the houseboat carried them beyond an unexpected threshold. A mood had settled over them, a calm in which easily and without conscious effort they were free to enjoy the presence of one another.

Shortly after sunset there began a windless downpour. The rain fell straight down from the leaden skies, building up to a steady serpentine hiss in the air. From the banks of the river and the water itself mist formed in the conflict of heat and drenching humidity. Soon they were in a world separated from reality by the hissing rain and the mists that swirled across the river and spilled silently across the deck of their houseboat.

He came to her and his desire was clear. He wanted none of their long and tender togetherness before they were joined. Not now; not this moment. She saw this and although she did not entirely understand, unhesitatingly she gave herself in a willing acceptance of her lover. Soon the intensity of his passion swept aside her conscious thoughts and she returned his fierce thrusting. He took her in silence, not a sound, not a word from him; when his shuddering release racked their bodies he kissed her roughly with frightening strength, forgetful of everything save the instant.

Later, she saw the surprise in his eyes when he noticed the trickle of blood from her lip. Surprise, but not regret. Something deep within Con had taken place; she did not search it out, for she was grateful. A man comes to his woman in such a manner only when he has accepted within his own mind and free of all reservation, that she, and no other, now fills his life.

Neither found it necessary to speak of marriage; each accepted the inevitability of joining with no more thought than of the morrow's breath.

They looked at the rain. . . .

Now the rain blotted out the wing extending away from the window through which Con stared. He was startled to note the spoilers extended upward from the metal surface. He tried to see through the torrents beyond the Plexiglas; the airplane was in a steady jolting descent toward the ground. He glanced at his watch and could hardly believe that they were due any moment to land at Andrews Air Force Base.

His thoughts returned with a rush to Jerri, for *she* was down there, waiting. He frowned; he was going to see her and that was that.

Two years. . . . She had been crying when he'd last held her in his arms. He'd wanted her then and there to go with him to his life. But it meant a jagged tear in her own promising and challenging career. She wanted to wait, and they both knew it might be for a period of time much longer than they'd planned. Dr. Whitelock tried not to interfere, but Jerri realized only too well his dependence on her. He had been ill and she had taken up the burden of detail in his work; she could not leave him then.

Stupidly, Con had resolved the problem in his own mind and come to a decision. He threw away reality and climbed onto an ego pedestal of his own making, with results that were inevitable. And finally he stormed off, his smarting pride overwhelming a heart beginning to crack on all sides.

The clouds shredded away from the wings and the

outlines of the airfield heaved into view. The minutes fled from him.

Quite suddenly he knew it would be all right. He was so struck with the thought that burst into his mind, he laughed aloud.

Steve Marchant studied his unexpected emergence from the long and moody period of self-reflection. "Care to include me in your joke, Con?" The question came out cautiously.

Dark smiled at him. "Joke's on me, Steve," he replied. "I don't think there's any real sweat with Jerri."

"Oh? Mind telling me what this is all about?"

"Maybe it's impossible to do that, Steve," Dark said. "I was just thinking of something I told Jerri a long time ago."

"What's that?" his friend prodded.

"Just that every man has some eagle and some chicken in him. And it's about time I smoothed out my ruffled feathers. I'll tell her that, Steve. I think she'll understand."

They settled gently to earth.

6

"We haven't much time before the conference, so I'll fill you in now on the people involved." As the helicopter blatted its way over the capital from Andrews Air Force Base to the Pentagon, Steve Marchant glanced at his watch and frowned. He'd hoped for at least several hours of briefing with Conan Dark and Jerri Stuart before they attended the monthly session of the Little JCS panel.

He glanced at his companions—no sparks there yet, he thought gratefully—and opening his attache case, he held out a printed roster. "There's the scorecard of the Little JCS," he said. "Go down the list of names. If you recognize anyone, you're that much more ahead of the game."

They both looked at him with surprise. "Hey, here at the top of the list," Dark said, tapping the paper. "Reads like some guy named Stephen S. Marchant, Captain, USN, et cetera, is chairman of this group of bigdomes. You never told me that, Steve."

"It's not important at this moment, Con," Marchant said brusquely. He was impatient and he didn't try to conceal it. "Please read the list," he urged them again.

Dark held up his hand. "Peace," he said, grinning at Marchant's evident champing at the bit. Dark had yet to accept Marchant's somber mood about their sudden flight or the forthcoming meeting. His attention suffered, understandably, from the pressure of Jerri's warm body against his own in the helicopter as it swayed in turbulence.

Their first meeting after the long separation had been

quiet. It had also been beholden with promise. When he emerged from the plane, Jerri stepped up to him and brushed her lips quickly against his; she murmured something about night being time enough to catch up with each other. He had stared openmouthed at the stunning girl before him; Jerri's striking beauty after all this time still threw him off balance. Then he grinned and they ran arm in arm through the rain to the waiting helicopter.

He glanced now at the lines on Marchant's brow and turned his attention back to the paper, which Jerri scanned with him. Moments later he whistled softly. The list of names represented a scientific-military powerhouse of government; he had had no idea of the strength that made up the Little Joint Chiefs of Staff. He returned the paper to Marchant.

"Recognize any of them?" the captain asked.

"Hell, I recognize all of them," Dark replied, "but that doesn't mean I'm on speaking terms with that kind of crowd."

Marchant nodded. "Okay, I'll run through the list. If you have any questions, hold them for later. I want to get this over with and go on to other matters."

He lit a cigarette and began describing the people they would soon meet.

Marchant looked up as the helicopter lurched to a stop and the cabin door slid back. "This is it, kids," he snapped. "Let's go."

He set a brisk pace through the labyrinthine corridors of the Pentagon. Minutes after they entered the military command bastion Conan and Jerri were hopelessly lost. Marchant turned one corner after the other and led them along unmarked stairways and gloomy halls branching off from main corridors. As they worked their way to their destination the captain continued a running commentary of the Little JCS.

"There will be some people at the conference," he explained, "whose names don't appear on the roster you saw.

In addition to the 'standards' who represent a group or an agency, we try to keep fresh blood and changing attitudes at each monthly session. We call these people our rotating group of experts and they come from anywhere; they're from—In here," he broke into his narrative to indicate a sharp turn into a tubular corridor; their steps echoed hollowly, ringing along the passageway. Dark felt as if he were an actor in some sinister movie committed to appear before a tribunal of security-mad generals and scientists.

Marchant turned to a door marked "Janitor's Closet" and motioned them inside. Dark exchanged a hurried glance with Jerri and rolled his eyes; Marchant ignored the silent comment and closed the door behind them. A light flashed on, they heard a relay buzz, and a steel door slid before them, closing again as they entered a small room. Three burly Navy security guards greeted them with blank faces. Marchant offered his identification and while Con and Jerri did the same, continued talking as if the guards weren't even present.

"All in all," he went on, "we've proven out our theory that these meetings expose us to Soviet developments and trends we could never get in any other manner. We've found that we can detect greater meaning—and follow through—on certain developments that otherwise would have slipped through our fingers."

He gave them a sharp glance. "I want to caution you about one thing, however," he said. "We make it a rule to waive the niceties and the social order you usually find in such groups. At this round table," he grinned, "name-calling is perfectly acceptable. You'd be surprised what this can do to these types who are always functioning within rather severe limitations in their professional life."

Jerri Stuart felt her head spinning. "But what—I mean how can *I* help with this group? I don't know anything about the"—she shook her head in confusion—"what I'm trying to say, Steve, is that I'm no authority on the Soviet Union, or—"

"You'd be surprised," Marchant broke in. He made no attempt at levity.

She started to reply, but Marchant turned to the security guard holding out their identification papers. "Please go ahead, sir," the man said quietly, depressing a hidden button. Another door slid aside for them.

"Okay," Marchant said, "this is home base." He led them into the conference room.

". . . simply no reason for the growth as we have it tabulated." Comdr. Robert Decker glanced at the papers spread out on the table before him. "In summary, their data retrieval and dissemination system cannot absorb the results of so many oceanographic research units. There is a definite correlation between the two, as you all know. Umm, another point that bears on this. Even without their satellite and planetary probes they would quite literally be inundated with raw data. I think that's important." Decker tapped the table to emphasize the point. "They have tripled their research-satellite launchings in the last eight months and, I'm sure you're aware, they have been having phenomenal success with their systems. They are making up for lost time in their lunar effort. Their failure rate has dropped from eighty percent to less than twenty percent. All this, plus the new manned flights with their Pyotrovisk spacecraft, has swamped them."

Decker toyed with a pencil. "The conclusion would appear to be inescapable. Not even their crash program to produce cybernetics data-handling systems could bear up under this load. The *full* system—the avenues and tributaries that permit the data to be utilized properly—does not yet exist.

"So, we have once again the enigma wrapped up in a riddle, so to speak," Decker said. He pursed his lips and continued. "We have an oceanographic fleet that by every rule of logic—ours and theirs—should not be. But," he held out both hands in a gesture of frustration, "it's there. We'd like to know *why*."

Willis Houseman motioned to Decker. "I can tell you what those ships are *not,*" said the CIA man.

Heads turned in his direction. "We've been dogging this stuff ever since you people sent us your memo on it," Houseman continued. "You can usually get some live-wire information by going far enough down the line; somewhere along the way the best cover-up job shows through. I can give you the details later if you want them, but the gist of it is that these are not oceanographic vessels. They're a sham."

"But how can you tell that?" demanded Helen Constance-Smith. Mrs. Constance-Smith, who was today representing both the Bureau of Standards and the National Science Council, was always suspicious of alleged scientific flimflammery.

"There are different ways, ma'am," Houseman replied. "We managed to get some very clear close-up photographs of some of these ships after they'd returned from a few months at sea. The cable winches had never been used; it's obvious they weren't using normal equipment for lowering and raising instruments. There were other signs, of course, but that's only one point among many." He leaned back in his seat. "You're welcome to examine what we have gathered," he said politely, "but I am telling you that at least a certain portion of that fleet is simply a fake."

Decker picked up the train of thought. "Nothing seems out of the ordinary at first—or even second—glance," he said. "It's the assembly of different things that jogged our attention. For example, the Soviet fishing and oceanographic fleets maintain a rather standard ratio of men and women as crew and scientific staff. It lies in the sixty-forty- and forty-sixty-percent bracket; there are extremes, of course, but you end up with an average of evenly mixed crews."

He rested his elbows on the table and leaned forward. "So we consider it significant that on those vessels we have listed for surveillance *we have yet to see a single female crew member or scientist.* That is not only significant, it's so unusual—so great a departure from the norm—that it becomes vital data.

"Now, we begin to put all these bits and pieces in the hopper and we find out something even more puzzling: we can't get any solution other than that the Russians are going to an enormous effort to disguise something. Here, I'll give you one more example."

He turned to face the visitors. "Miss Stuart?"

Jerri was startled. She sat up quickly.

"This is Miss Jerri Stuart," Decker said to the assembly. "You will understand her position better when I explain that she has been Dr. Whitelock's assistant—and an extremely capable one, I should add—for some years. Now, Miss Stuart, you coordinate much of your oceanographic studies with an opposite number, an institute in the Soviet Union, don't you?"

"Why, yes, I do," Jerri replied.

"What group is that, please?"

"Well, Commander, there are many oceanographic and hydrographic centers we deal with." She thought for a moment. "But I don't believe there is any doubt as to the central authority; the center of research, I mean. That would be the Institute of Oceanology; their main headquarters is in Moscow proper."

"Do they specialize in a specific geographic or hydrographic area, Miss Stuart?"

She shook her head. "No; that's why I singled them out. Their area is all-inclusive. They consider themselves not only a direct research organization, but also a clearing house, oh, a central coordinator, you could say, for the other organization. Their publication—it's a monthly issue—is considered the gospel word. The leading academicians and scientists write for their publication, by the way. It's considered an honor to have your material printed by this institute."

"How many other oceanographic institutions are there?"

Jerri searched her memory. "All in all, Commander, about one hundred and ten. But that includes even the smaller research centers. All of them, however, fall under the jurisdiction of some sixteen ministries and agencies, and—"

"Excuse me for interrupting, Miss Stuart," Commander Decker broke in. "How many major organizations —comparable to your own Crowell Institute—would you estimate?"

"Oh; I see. At least five."

"Thank you, Miss Stuart. Now, let me keep one thing clear. You receive the major Soviet periodicals and reports in the oceanographic sciences?"

"That's correct," she said. "Crowell acts as a clearing house for many of our centers, and we prepare a condensation of all their publications as a regular service."

"You've heard the details of the tremendous increase in the oceanographic forces of the Soviets, Miss Stuart?"

She smiled. "Yes, sir."

He kept his face blank. "Why are you smiling, Miss Stuart?"

"Because I believe I see what you're getting at, Commander."

"And that would be?"

"There's nothing in what we receive—either in volume or representative of new research efforts—that reflects any significant growth in equipment or manpower. Nothing at all," she stressed, "and that is odd."

It was Decker's turn to smile. "One more piece to the puzzle," he said to the group.

Marchant picked up the ball; Dark had already heard much of the argument and it didn't seem any less complex when he listened for a second time as Marchant addressed the attentive group. The captain went through a series of reports, the problems they presented, and the difficulties in achieving the solutions the Navy felt were imperative. He spent some time on the fact that a number of surveys and reports had clearly overt significance, while others were seemingly innocuous. He discussed the huge new whaling ships appearing on the high seas and the unusual number of smaller vessels that accompanied them; he detailed the dual incongruity of whalers showing up and remaining in areas where the Navy had confirmed whaling operations had not been carried out for months.

Damn it, Steve's right, Dark thought. The more he keeps stirring up his pot of incongruities, the worse the stew begins to smell. And there's still more to come. He shook his head slowly. But I still don't figure out what I have to do with all this; I've got more than I can handle with Orca.

Marchant read to the conference group the report of two unknown vessels being sonar-tracked at a depth of twelve thousand feet. When he finished, Dr. Fred Kuiper turned his attention from Marchant to Dark.

"Mr. Dark, I would appreciate your answering some questions for me," he said. "Your opinions are as valuable to us as what you may construe to be hard fact. Whenever I deal with anything that lies more than two miles beneath the ocean surface, I find myself disposed to look suspiciously on what is reported to be 'fact.' Opinion—the expert opinion of hard experience, sir—is often more to be coveted. Thus, you may see that you are at the present in a position of demand."

The group joined in laughter at his disarming salutation. It was Dr. Kuiper's way—and he was good at it, Dark noted with a responsive smile—of easing whatever tensions Dark may have held before he was dragged into the bullring of interrogation.

"I'll do my best, Dr. Kuiper," he replied.

"I'm sure you will," said the scientist. The representative of the National Academy of Sciences and the National Science Foundation pushed away the notes on the table before him. Without further preamble he began firing questions.

"Mr. Dark—straight out, sir—do you believe this reported sonar contact?"

"That's like asking me if I believe in God, Dr. Kuiper," he replied.

His answer caught the redoubtable scientist off balance. He looked at Dark, a puzzled frown on his face. "Would you explain that, sir?"

"No offense meant, Dr. Kuiper," Dark said. "I've read the report and it leaves out too much to satisfy me. In effect, you might say I'm being asked to believe—beyond any doubt at all—the presence of two submersibles, holding formation position, moving under their own way where the pressure exceeds five thousands pounds per square inch. Then I must throw into this conditional situation the fact that no mother ship was seen for several hundred miles from the sonar pickup." He smiled. "That doesn't mean it wasn't there; just that we didn't see it. Or it could mean a submersible tender was used. Or even," he said with a touch of sarcasm, "that what was picked up with the sonar had long-range capabilities and was operating nonstop from a land site."

He shifted in his chair, leaning forward, caught up with the opportunity to shred some of the things that had so effectively dented his credulity and kept him off balance.

"I should add, Dr. Kuiper, although I'm certain you're well aware of it, that we have made some rather drastic errors of identification before." Dark waited for the reply.

It came quickly. "You'll find no contest of *that* with me, young man," the scientist affirmed. "That problem with the one-thirty rpm fish, or whatever the thing is, had the Navy Department and half a dozen agencies in an uproar for months."

Sanford Nelson showed a look of complete disbelief on his face. "A *what,* Dr. Kuiper? Did I hear you say a one-thirty rpm *fish*?"

"You did," Dr. Kuiper said with an impatient note in his voice. "Exactly that. We have tracked—oh, several hundred times now—some form of animal life in the sea that produces a sound that is exactly, and I mean *exactly,* the sound that is also produced by a deeply submerged propeller turning at one hundred and thirty revolutions per minute."

"But that's ridiculous!" exclaimed the NASA representative.

"Yes, yes," Dr. Kuiper said dryly, "but no more so than for you to assume I would waste my time and that of these people here with fables. Shall I—despite your reticence to accept what we consider to be incontestable sonar tracking—continue?"

Nelson's face showed a rising flush. "Of—of course, Dr. Kuiper."

But the scientist had already turned away from Nelson and was looking at Conan Dark. "What is your evaluation, sir, of the sonar pickup itself?"

Dark shook his head slowly. "I don't like to act the role of the disbeliever," he said, "but I'm not left with very much choice. The report shows that the tracking was carried out by an ASW team—a hunter-killer group—on maneuvers; they were involved in tests when suddenly they began to get this deep reflection. Right there's a problem, Dr. Kuiper."

"Why?" The question snapped out without hesitation.

"Wrong equipment," Dark said. "It can pick up sound sources from great distances—depth in this case is the point—but its accuracy is questionable because it wasn't designed for that task. Then there are other points that tear some gaps in the report."

"Go on," Dr. Kuiper urged him.

"Well, no one had a reading on the sea conditions at that time, sir," Dark explained. "As I understand it, there was a sea running and a wind strong enough to produce whitecaps. Unless the sonar system is intended to take out those problems, you get aural absorption from the bubble concentration—the aeration—just beneath the surface. Then you have wake problems; surface disturbances from the ships as well as the submarines that were participating in the maneuvers."

He warmed to the moment, at long last feeling alive by contributing instead of having his ears beaten in for several hours.

"What were the temperature conditions existing in the area—" Dark shrugged in an emphasis of his point. "No one knows, but there could have been a whole series of thermoclines involved that affected the sound. Oh, yes; the echo response. In other words, it was accidental, and this sound was picked up as a source transmitter rather than an echo response. In other words, it was accidental, and this only adds uncertainty to the accuracy of the equipment involved. There are many other problems, of course, that simply stamp a question mark on this. What was the DSL at the time, and—"

"DSL? You've got a whole new language there, Mr. Dark," broke in Otto Warwick, the president of the National Industrial Association. "You'd better help me out."

"Sorry." Dark grinned at him. "Deep scattering layer; it's made up of, well, of a great variety of life forms in the sea. One example is the colonial hydrozoan jellyfish. We find them in enormous concentrations, spread out in the form of huge layers. Each one of these creatures has a gas-filled flotation bubble, and when they're all together they play havoc with your sonar beams. They give echoes so strong that some scientists have sonar-recorded a bottom of twelve hundred feet below them, for example, when it was actually more than thirteen thousand. And we have no way of knowing the DSL conditions in the area where the echoes we're discussing were picked up. There's more: bottom effect, reverberations, divergence, refraction . . . you have a problem on your hands with sound that could have bent, split, been distorted and a half dozen other things before it was picked up. Without specialized equipment for the sonar tracking, Dr. Kuiper, and real-time readout data breakdown, well"—again Dark shook his head—"I just cannot buy this report as *fact*."

The scientist turned to Marchant. "Captain, any comment? Your young submariner appears to have demolished our precious sonar tracking, wouldn't you say?"

Marchant grimaced. "We have thought of these effects," he said, not particularly pleased. "In fact, I personally discussed them with Mr. Dark at some length." He sighed.

"But I wanted you to have his own opinion and just as you heard it."

Marchant studied Dr. Kuiper with great care. "I want to make something quite clear"—he glanced about the room—"to all of you. By itself the sonar report leaves too many gaps to justify a major effort to track it down. It was a happenstance thing and it suffers from all the problems you just heard Mr. Dark mention, who I daresay, is better acquainted with deep-ocean operations than any man alive.

"But we are not considering this sonar report as an incident unto itself. That is very important. It's this report and the exploding size of the oceanographic fleet and the whalers and the lack of data-processing systems, and a couple more, *but*"—he was coldly serious—"above all it ties in with the report of Dr. Franklin Whitelock. You have all read his opinion?"

They nodded.

Jerri Stuart nudged Dark. "Look around the room," she whispered, "at their faces."

He saw what she had already noticed. Several of those present in the room were taking no pains to conceal their smiles at the mention of Dr. Whitelock's report. Dark leaned over to Jerri. "Look at Whitelock; he's already fit to be tied," he said quietly so that only she could hear his voice. "They're all but laughing out loud at the old boy."

Jerri nodded, her lips tight. "Con, he's liable to lose his temper completely," she warned. "I know him! He never wanted to come here in the first place, and—"

"Shh, he's starting."

Jerri slipped her hand into Dark's. She was much more upset than she indicated. Professor Whitelock was at the breaking point; he had little enough patience to begin with and that was almost gone. He was a purist in science; he pursued knowledge for its own sake and he really didn't give much of a damn whether a conference room chose to believe in him or to deny the validity of his report. But the Crowell Institute of Oceanography to a large degree subsisted on Navy contracts, and it was with this bludgeon that Marchant had persuaded him to appear at all.

In cold terms that one expected an angry professor to use with a class of unruly miscreants, Dr. Whitelock reviewed in detail the characteristics and the effects of the earth shocks and resultant tidal waves and avalanches. He did not hedge, not anywhere; he stepped aside from the safety of the overwhelming body of scientific opinion and stated that "there exists nothing in the field, historically or relevant to contemporary findings, that could possibly permit a natural origin of these phenomena. The seismographic studies themselves defy the norm. All things being equal there is nothing that may be found—in terms of atmosphere, the condition of the geologic area involved, the state of the sea—*nothing* is acceptable to the objective viewpoint. The conditions as I have described them to you are not found—they are unknown—in nature."

They could hear the drumming of Dr. Kuiper's fingers on the table in the silence that followed. It lay heavy and stifling in the room. And because none of those present were of the knowledge or the experience openly to contest Dr. Whitelock—none, that is, save Dr. Kuiper—they yielded the moment to the government scientist.

Dark whispered to Marchant. "The old boy's had it, Steve. Kuiper doesn't buy his story, and he's just thinking of some way to cut him down. There's going to be some chips flying any moment."

"I know, I know," Marchant mumbled. "Here it comes now. I wish I'd stayed in the fleet."

Dr. Kuiper did his best to impale Dr. Whitelock with an icy stare he had affected over the years. It failed to dismay the oceanographic scientist; if anything, it honed the man's temper that much closer to the snapping point.

"My good Dr. Whitelock," Kuiper began in a syrupy voice. "Are you expecting *me* to believe"—he waved his arm to take in the room—"and these people as well, that there is absolutely *nothing* that could have caused this, ah, disturbance?"

"I don't give a drat what you believe," Whitelock snapped. "You're a scientist, Dr. Kuiper, but at this moment it is difficult to reconcile your background with your attitude."

The syrup became heavier. "Ahh, I shall ignore that, Dr. Whitelock, for I know you have had a long and tiring trip."

Marchant groaned. Dark glanced at Jerri; her face was pale.

"Then," Dr. Kuiper went on, "in effect, you are saying that the disturbance—the seismic shock, the tsunamic effect, and the rest—*is of an artificial origin*?"

Exclamations and sudden conversation filled the room like a swarm of excited bees.

"Gentlemen! Gentlemen . . . please!" Decker banged the gavel against the table. Peace and order came slowly.

Kuiper looked at Whitelock with a blank face; he was openly baiting the Crowell scientist. Finally Whitelock stirred. As he replaced papers in his briefcase, he glanced around the room. His answer came with deceiving calm.

"Why, yes." He smiled. "I am saying precisely that, Dr. Kuiper."

"Are you saying that this was deliberate, Dr. Whitelock?" Kuiper's voice had lost the syrup; it was harsh and biting.

Whitelock never changed the expression on his face. "I congratulate you, sir," he said to Kuiper. "You have finally concluded what has been openly obvious."

"That's ridiculous and you know it!" Kuiper shouted.

"By my calculations, gentlemen"—Dr. Whitelock addressed the entire group—"it is approximately two to three hundred kilotons ridiculous, at a ridiculous height above the ocean floor of, also approximately, two to five hundred feet."

They looked at him in open astonishment.

"But there's been no trace of radioactivity!" Kuiper insisted, slamming his fist against the table.

Whitelock rose to his feet. "No, Dr. Kuiper," he said coldly. "That statement is inaccurate. Placed in its proper context, it is that no search was made for radioactivity until"—he glowered at Marchant—"several weeks after the incident. However, this is no longer any concern of mine. Good day, one and all."

He stalked out without a backward glance.

The noise in the room swelled again to a roar.

Dark turned to stare at Marchant.

"A *bomb*?"

"You're saying that the Russians set off a nuke just to create that whole mess?" Dark's voice was openly incredulous.

Marchant lit a cigarette and flipped the match onto the floor. He looked back at Con and Jerri.

"Welcome to Cloud Nine," he said wearily. "And I might add," he said after a pause, "I'm afraid this is only Act One."

7

He sprawled loosely across the bed with his arms and legs outstretched. A warmth diffused his body. In the room's dim glow the perspiration glistened on his heaving chest and he gave a long, shuddering sigh of complete relaxation. He didn't think or try to think; the moment was everything to him.

Jerri lay curled on her side like a cat arched comfortably, warm against his skin. Her hair spread across his chest silken and fragrant. He breathed deeply, a male animal afterglow of overwhelming release. He felt a finger tracing a slow line along his chest and then down the flat of his stomach. The finger curled, teased, then stopped.

"Mmmm, now, that's interesting," she murmured.

"Huh?"

"That's what I appreciate." She sighed. "A typical, young intelligent male for a lover who goes 'huh? Very romantic."

"Knock it off, pussycat," he growled. "What's so interesting?"

"Mmmmm."

"Stop purring or I might decide to rape you. You sound better when you're moaning happily."

Her hand brushed him lightly. "Braggart," she said. "All talk and promises." She laughed easily.

"You just wait . . ."

"Oh, my," she said with exaggerated sweetness. "I'll have to, won't I?"

"My God, woman, we just—"

"Shhh, don't waste your strength, darling," she cooed. "You're going to need it."

He changed the subject. "*What* was so interesting?" He felt her finger moving again, tracing a sensuous path along his skin.

"Your navel," she said.

"What about it?"

"Well, I just learned what it's really for."

"I admit defeat. Tell me."

"It's to connect everything, I guess."

He groaned.

"Really, it *is* to connect everything together. There are certain types of people, sweet, who are held together in a very special fashion." Her finger stabbed into his stomach. "And you, lover boy, are one of them."

He lifted his head to look at her. "All right, beautiful," he went on. "What kind of certain people?"

"Distinctive," she murmured.

"How?"

"Well, for one thing . . . um, really, it's the main thing, though. It's just that you're such a bastard," she purred.

He stared at her.

"You can talk, lover," she teased. "Even bastards have the right to self-expression."

"Yeah," he said. He dropped his head back to the pillow. "Well, I suppose we had to come right up to it sooner or later. This is all too high in the clouds to last without bumping into something."

Her finger began to move again; he twitched.

"How the hell can we talk seriously when you're doing that?" he demanded.

"Who's serious?"

"Well, bastard is hardly a term of endearment."

"Oh, my, not at all," she said, biting him sharply and bringing a sudden yelp of pain. "Not when you're a real, true-blue bastard like you, Con."

"Am I really?"

"You *are* serious," she teased. "That stern tone of voice! It must be terribly important."

"It is, Jerri. It's about us."

"Who?"

"Us, damn it. You, me; *us.*"

"I don't know that person, Con." He detected a sudden, almost inperceptible hardening in her voice.

He hesitated. Christ, how do you pick up a conversation like this after two years? And . . . and here we are in bed with one another, and it's like it was only yesterday since . . .

Abruptly his temper came. "Then what the hell are we doing here?" His voice was harsh.

Her hand slid in a warming circle around his stomach. "We're making love, Con," she said slowly. "That's what we're doing here." She paused. "We're making love. Like two prime young animals. Like we did many times a long time ago." Her head moved gently to rest on his stomach.

"Well, that's what I mean. I want to talk to you about us, and—"

She broke in quickly. "I told you, Con," she said, her voice clear and smooth now. "I don't know that person. I did once. But that was two years ago. I once knew—"

"Now, wait a—"

"No, Con; you wait. It—there isn't much I want to say to you. First, you're wondering how, after two years, I could just walk in here and climb into bed and make love with you. It *has* been something for you to consider, hasn't it?"

"Well, I—"

"Mmmm, and it's got my handsome young animal all upset." Her voice dripped honeyed sarcasm.

He kept his tongue. She waited just long enough to be sure of his silence.

"You're a handsome young animal; really. And I've known for a long time that you can—well; I don't want to build up your ego too much, darling. Let's just say that we're very good in bed together." Her voice had changed again; she spoke with a self-assurance he had never known in Jerri before. A feeling that he wasn't really running this show began to creep into his mind."

"Shall I go on?"

He mumbled something she couldn't make out.

She shrugged. "What you say really doesn't matter, anyway," she said. "You are also a brilliant young man. Oh, yes; I hear many wonderful things about you. Dedicated, tremendous drive, great future—all the goody words."

She stretched her arms and paused. The seconds went by slowly while she waited to continue.

"You are also pigheaded, conceited, self-centered, and, I might add, a dyed-in-the-wool bastard."

"Damn it, Jerri, I—"

"No, darling." She turned to press a finger against his lips. "Don't talk, not yet. I want you to know that I don't mind your being a bastard. Really I don't, Con. It's just that I wish I had known it a long time ago."

She rested on her elbows and stared into his eyes. "You know where you did me wrong, Con? Two years ago? Not because we couldn't see eye to eye, darling. Couples have that problem all the time. What you did was worse. You tried to force me into your terms, your world, your life, your everything." She spoke faster now, what had been bottled up coming out with increasing intensity.

"You never asked me to share it with you, my sweet. Did you ever realize that, Con? Not once. There wasn't any asking. There was never a hope for sharing. Mmmm; that hurt, when I finally cleared away the cobwebs and could think straight. You laid it out, cold, efficient, put together by some special slide rule for your boy-girl relationships. And it was take it or leave it." She sighed. "It must be nice to be a romantic hero, and—"

"Now, just a goddamned minute, Jerri!" His face was black with anger and she knew he was about to explode.

She smiled at him. Her voice came to him low, unhurried, and she slipped it nice and neat through his ribs.

"Are you going to lose your temper again?"

She stopped him as if he had been pole-axed. The last time, two years ago . . . oh God, he swore to himself, she's right. It's exactly what I did the last time. Me and my temper and my big mouth, and. . . .

Her voice came through his thoughts. "No recriminations, Con. This isn't the weepies." Her voice went just a trifle flat, cold. "But this time you're going to listen to me or you can walk out again, if that's the habit you've gotten into. Just put on your pants and place one leg before the other and repeat that tricky little step and before you know it, why, you'll be gone again, won't you? It's easy, Con. You know what it's like—after all, you've done it before."

Now she was twisting the knife she had placed so neatly between his ribs.

He glared at her, fighting a battle with his temper. "Do you want me to apologize, Jerri? Is that it? Is that what you want? For me to tell you I was wrong and—"

Her finger rested gently on his lips. "Shhh. No, Con"—her voice was soft again—"I don't want that. I don't need you to tell me or to apologize to say anything at all about it. I know you were wrong; you know it." Her bare shoulders shrugged. "So that doesn't matter. What matters if that you've kept me waiting two years to tell you what I thought, and felt, because you were so damned busy, Con, trying to fill up the whole world with yourself."

Her voice trailed away. She bit her lip, and tossed her head to remove her hair from before her face.

"I—I don't want this, Con. But I want you to know what went wrong. I told you that you never asked me to share anything with you. You demanded that—" She stopped in mid sentence. "Yes; that's it. Do you know what you demanded from me, Con? Not of myself. You already had that, even if you didn't know it. Oh, how I loved you," she whispered. Her voice gained strength again. "You demanded that I walk out on a wonderful old man, that I simply leave Dr. Whitelock, who . . . who was like a father to me. More than that, of course; my work, the things I was doing, the people who counted on me, and . . ."

Again that sudden shake of her head. She looked directly into his eyes. "None of that is important now. But I will tell you what happened. To me. You were the only man I ever loved and you tore something into little pieces inside me." She stared into the distance. "After a while I . . . I tried, in different ways, I mean, to . . . to forget you. I . . . I went to bed with other men. Did you know you were my first, Con? Did you?"

"Please, Jerri." His hand stroked her cheek; she ignored the feel of his skin and shook the hand away.

"No; I want it out. I went to bed with, well with more men than I counted. It didn't do much good. I thought it would take me years to cleanse myself because of what I was doing. And then"—she took a deep breath—"I caught myself. There was still time. There was still time to stop, to come back to the Jerri Stuart I once knew. I did that; I came back. The shock of it all, of what I was doing—maybe I was trying in a childish way to punish you by sleeping with other men; I don't know—cleared the fog out of my brain. It's quite a thing to come back into focus."

She felt for his hand, brought it cupped in her own to the side of her cheek. She looked at him and smiled.

"I beat you, Con."

He stared at her.

"I beat you when I realized I was still in love with you."

She let her words sink in.

"It was that simple. I was still in love with you—I was in love with a hard-nosed bastard and that's all there was to it. And that's what set me free, darling. I wasn't running any more; I was facing up to me.

"You remember, don't you, Con, what that's like? You told me yourself and—"

"Yeah." His voice was husky, choked. "Yeah, I remember. I was going to talk with you about that. We're all part eagle and part chicken." He closed his eyes, shut them tightly. "I remember."

She rubbed her cheek against his hand. "Well, that was it. Once I accepted the fact that I was still in love with you, Con—*then I was free of you.* Running away from the fact was what tore me up; you can't really, run away from yourself. So I stopped and took a look and—just like that, *zing!* It all became very simple. I was in love with you, and you loved me, but you loved yourself and what you were doing far too much to make compromises."

She reached to the night table and picked up a cigarette, lighting it quickly. She took a long drag, then placed it gently between his lips.

"I knew you were in love with a machine, that—whatever it is you call that killer thing that's taken up your whole life. And it's stupid for a girl to fight a machine. So I quit fighting, and I stayed in love with you, and it didn't matter much any more."

"But when you saw me—I mean, at the airport," he protested. "Steve told me you didn't know that I was—"

"Steve was right; I didn't," she agreed. "But I had plenty of time and I went into base operations and in a conversation with some people there—the dispatcher, I think—I said I was waiting for Steve Marchant, and he checked the lists, and there was your name. It nearly floored me."

She took back the cigarette, drew deeply again, and returned it to his lips.

"So I had those two hours to think about you, darling. And me, of course. And I found out I wasn't nervous and I was actually glad, very much so, in fact, that I would be seeing you. And . . . and tonight.

"You know what?" she said suddenly. "I'm glad we're in bed with each other, Con."

He smiled.

She wiped it off.

"You didn't take me to bed, sweetheart," she said softly. She looked at him. "You have quite an expression on your face, you know that? No, you didn't take me to bed. I went to bed with you. By myself; *my* decision." She placed her hand tenderly along his neck. "And I can leave any time I want to, my darling. I'm free. No strings. Not even of the heart; see?"

"You said, you loved me," he said, his voice grating. "Did you mean that, Jerri?"

She nodded.

"But then—"

"You weren't listening, love," she said, smiling. "I told you I loved you. I still do. I love you—but you don't own me.

"You did once. Really and truly, you owned me heart and soul because I gave it all to you. But you gave it back, Con, and you don't own me any more. And what I have learned, more important than anything else, is that I can love you and still be free of you."

She stubbed out the cigarette and sat straight up in bed. He looked at her body, that beautiful face, her breasts proud before him, and he didn't know what the hell to say or to do.

"End of speech, Con."

He raised up on one elbow.

"What about you—you and me, now, Jerri?"

She snapped her fingers. "Just like that, Con? Just like that it's 'you and me'; what about 'us'?"

He swung his legs to the floor and looked blankly at the wall.

"Yeah."

"I hope to enjoy us, Con," she said after a pause. "What we had was very beautiful and I long for it. But I don't know if it's still there."

He turned slowly to her. "Do we find out?"

"Why? Why, Con? Do you want me so badly now that we're together and we're making love and you know you don't own me any more?"

His eyes locked with hers.

"I was wrong, Jerri."

"It's nice to know," she said, not trying to hide the sarcasm. "When did you find out—thirty minutes ago?"

"What the hell do you want me to do, then! I admitted I was wrong and—"

"It doesn't matter who's right and wrong, Con. I can't live yesterday over. Neither can you."

"We can try, Jerri. We can try or—or we can give it a fresh start."

"Do you really want to?"

"Yes."

"I don't know if I believe you, Con."

"I'll make you believe me, damn it."

"You can try."

"Yes," he said. "And I will—that, and more."

He pulled her down onto the bed with him, held her close.

Suddenly he felt as if he were holding someone else. A different, almost a new woman in his arms. Somewhere deep inside him there came a great silent shout for joy.

You didn't often get a second chance. . . .

"Jerri?"

"Hmmm."

"Remember that last night on the river? Remember how it was? The rain, and . . ."

She nodded, her hair brushing along his cheek.

They went back. . . .

8

The theater filled with darkness. As their eyes adjusted slowly to the gloom, the briefing officer standing behind a podium control panel resolved into a shadowy silhouette. The shadow moved slightly and they heard a click; moments later a voice spoke to them. They were startled; the voice materialized from thin air, close to them.

"I am Colonel Albert Starnes," the voice began, "briefing officer for the Space Systems Command, Air Force. You will notice that my voice seems to originate from directly before you. Each of you, no matter where seated in this theater, will experience this same effect of directional aural control. If you will please move your right hand to the front of your right armrest, you will notice a button. At any time during the briefing you find it necessary to clarify a point you may press this button. As soon as a light appears, please feel free to speak. You may do so in a normal conversational tone; sonic-beam pickups will relay your voice to me directly."

Dark shook his head, almost dazed by it all. He glanced to his left at Jerri and then glowered at Marchant. He didn't hide his annoyance as he settled back in his seat. He was tiring very quickly of marathon walks through the Pentagon's endless corridors. And while yesterday's session with the Little JCS had been illuminating, very interesting, and even downright startling, it didn't help him one damn bit with getting Orca back into the sea for her ordnance tests. Leaving a job in the middle always rankled Dark; he was a perfectionist engineer and . . . damn it, and now this secret mucking-about in the Pentagon again and an Air Force briefing, for Christ's sake! A muffled sound drew his attention; he turned to see Jerri stifling a laugh.

"Oh, your face! If you could only see y——"

The screen came to life with a shattering demand for attention. It was impossible to ignore the pulsating distortions of the pattern stabbing TOP SECRET into their eyes. They blinked their eyes rapidly, caught off balance by the withering optical blast. It was an extraordinarily effective means of assuring their attention while stamping into their minds the retinal warning of Top Secret.

Moments later Conan Dark sat bolt upright in his seat, his annoyances swept from his mind. The screen faded into darkness, the retinal afterimage of its shock opening diminishing quickly. And then his stomach almost went out from under him.

His eyes riveted to the vertiginous sight of the earth's horizon oscillating wildly, intense light gleaming like a knife blade along its curving edge. The eye-wrenching sight came jerkily to a halt as orange-red glows spattered the picture and vanished as quickly as they appeared. Then the scene was still, the horizon sensible but curved, as if seen from an immense height; Dark stared at several brilliant pinpoints of light against a backdrop of darkest velvet.

"You are looking at the terrestrial horizon from an altitude of one hundred and twenty-seven nautical miles." The words floated from the thin air about them; Dark glanced at the barely perceptible face of Colonel Starnes behind his briefing console.

The picture screen froze; not only motion but the

camera itself had been stopped.

"The footage you are studying is from the Samos Mark Four reconnaissance satellite," explained the ghostly voice. "For the moment I have halted the sequence to better acquaint you with the unique vantage from which the subject matter will be studied."

Steve still hasn't said a word about what we'd be seeing today, Dark thought, but he sure set up one hell of a beginning. . . .

"The motion picture sequences," the voice continued, "are taken with a motion rate of six frames to the second. Interspersed throughout this reconnaissance study will be still pictures taken with advanced long-range photographic equipment; their purpose, as will be evident to you, is to obtain extreme clarity and definition of the subject matter. As for the picture on the screen at the moment, the bright pinpoints of light are certain celestial bodies which the Samos Mark Four employs for navigational-coordinates verfication for evaluation of the target subjects.

"Now we will switch from the stellar acquisition system to the infrared. The IR mode employed for the next scenes is extreme range. The visual angle you will see is twenty degrees from the vertical; the scene is night at approximately two A.M. local time—local time in this instance being the South Atlantic Ocean."

The screen blacked out, came to life again. It was incredible. It appeared to be . . . a sharp X-ray or negative film was the closest simile Dark could imagine. Patches flowed along the view; he knew enough of infrared to recognize clouds picked up by the IR sensors.

Then, along the far left of the screen, nine long objects slowly came into view. Jerri leaned close to him—she never thought of the interrogation button mentioned before by Colonel Starnes—to ask about the strange objects. It *was* confusing to see things in their reverse of black and white on the IR film. Before Dark could reply, he realized their briefing officer had heard the question. His voice came out of the air.

"You are looking ahead of the path of flight, Miss Stuart." The unexpected direct answer from someone at the opposite end of the theater startled her; the explanation also swept aside other thoughts.

"There are nine targets in question and these will gain definition as the slant range decreases and automatic focusing equipment provides greater clarification."

Starnes's voice faded out as the viewing angle brought them closer and closer to the scene below. Then they were looking almost straight down and the picture brightened.

"A digital computer analysis considering all factors such as light, distance, and movement," Starnes continued, "enables us to obtain an infrared picture definition considerably improved over the original film. The scene just observed will now be repeated with the computer-definition film."

The scene unrolled slowly before their eyes, sharper in detail. Now the nine long objects were discerned with greater clarity.

"But what—" Jerri interrupted herself and pressed the button. The picture before them stopped its motion and a light glowed. "Yes, Miss Stuart?" came the immediate response from Starnes.

"Excuse me, Colonel, but *what* are we watching? You mentioned the South Atlantic, so I assume they are ships of some sort."

"That is correct, Miss Stuart. In a moment we will switch from motion to still photography. The clarity of the scene will be enhanced further; please bear with me until that moment."

Jerri nodded; a moment later the signal light before her—the "speak" light, she thought—winked out.

The picture changed to bring a startled exclamation from Dark.

"Those are *subs!*"

Marchant remained silent; he had seen the film before

and did not wish to break into Dark's interrogation. Starnes was an expert at this.

"I'll be damned," Dark said with rising excitement, jabbing an elbow painfully against Jerri's arm. "Subs, for Christ's sake. But . . . what the devil are so many subs . . . ?" He stabbed the button at the end of his armrest.

Colonel Starnes had anticipated the reaction. "You are observing an oceanographic expedition of the Soviet Union," he said.

His words brought startled exclamations both from Con and Jerri. They knew perfectly well that the Russians, or the United States, for that matter, had never placed an oceanographic expedition at sea with so many submarines.

"I don't believe it," Jerri announced.

"Please follow the arrow," came the voice of Colonel Starnes as a thin white arrow appeared on the screen. "Note these two vessels"—the arrow moved back and forth between the two largest objects—"at the center of the picture. You can see they are considerably larger than the other seven craft. The smaller vessels in sight are submarines of the Soviet Navy, carrying out a secret rendezvous—the time is two A.M., remember—with the two large vessels. Ostensibly these two large ships constitute an oceanographic expedition. However, the vessel at the right"—the arrow shifted again—"classifies as a modern whaler; it is possible to just make out the stern ramp equipment."

For the first time Steve Marchant broke in. "For the record, kids, they weren't hunting whales."

They glanced quickly at his form slouched low in his seat.

"We were able to carry out Samos passes during both day and night for a period of ten days," Colonel Starnes went on.

"During three night passes the rendezvous was again detected; twice with four submarines, and once more with the full seven that you see before you now."

The picture changed to a daylight scene; the sudden

brightness hurt their eyes. As Colonel Starnes kept up his running commentary, they were startled with a spectacular full-color close-up view of the two surface vessels. These had been taken with still-picture equipment whose powerful lenses enabled them to make out details of the ships. The lead vessel displayed extensive equipment and gear which Jerri identified as standard for the latest class of Russian oceanographic vessels. It was the second ship—the whaler—that baffled her, and she said so. Colonel Starnes verified her doubts when he stated that while much of the equipment of the whaler was easily identifiable, successive photographic passes showed that not all that equipment could be accounted for in terms of a whaling expedition. "You will notice, also," he went on, "that during a period of some eight days there is no evidence—deck condition, placement, and so forth—that this equipment has been used."

Dark stabbed the button beneath his right hand; the light went on at once.

"Colonel, did you ever pick up those subs during daylight hours?"

"No."

Dark rubbed his chin. Night rendezvous for combat-training missions was one thing. But with *seven* subs? Uh uh; there was more to it than that. Marchant was one of the best men in the world when it came to combat-sub operations, and he had been strangely silent about that part of the puzzle that grew ever more baffling.

"Do you have any ID on the types?" he asked.

"Positive identification was obtained, Mr. Dark. All seven submarines tracked are nuclear-drive. From what could be determined with the limitations of the infrared system, we do not believe them to be of missile-carrying configuration. They fall within the attack and general-purpose categories."

"Any theories on why they should show up several times within the time span you told us, Colonel Starnes?"

"Negative, sir. It is one of the reasons Captain Marchant and his staff have been using up aspirins at an alarming rate."

Dark smiled at the personal reference. The more he learned of the frustrating pursuit carried out by Marchant and his staff, the better he could understand the harried look on the face of his old friend.

Marchant pressed his signal button and waited for the light. "Al, you can kill the rest of the Samos material," he said to the briefing officer. "They saw the part I wanted them to have now; we can give them the rest at a later time. Are your people ready with the Bottle pictures?"

The screen went dark as Colonel Starnes acknowledged Marchant's request. "Be right there, Steve," came the reply. He spoke into a separate microphone to order the new films.

What had Steve said? Dark turned to Marchant. "Didn't I hear you say 'Bottle pictures'? *Bottle?*"

Marchant nodded, a trace of a smile on his face. "You heard me loud and clear, Con," he said. "Orca isn't the only trick we've got up our sleeve. The Bottles, now, are— Let it go for a moment," he interrupted himself, "I'll pick it up again as soon as we see this next sequence." Then, to Colonel Starnes. "Any time, Al."

Blue-green light splashed across the screen. The sequence pictures they watched were sometimes clear, more often blurred and even shaky. But they were unmistakable and a shock to Dark when the sequence halted on a single frame.

He let out a breath long held. "I'll be a son of a bitch," he said slowly.

"That is exactly how I felt when I first saw this," Marchant joined in. "Sort of grabs you by the short hairs and hangs on, doesn't it?"

Dark whistled. "Christ, how big is that thing?"

"Hang on to your seat," Marchant said dryly. "The best estimates—and that's leaning to the conservative side—agree on twelve thousand tons."

"Twelve thous—!"

He turned back to study the screen. He had never seen a submarine before that displaced anything like twelve thousand tons. The huge shape before them had the classic lines of the nuclear-drive class, but with a ring throughout the structure of utility. As good as the picture was, he wished it were clearer, that he could see more of the thing.

"Christ, and I thought *Triton* ran away with the heavyweight honors," he said.

"Will somebody please fill me in?" Jerri exclaimed. "I know that's a submarine and from what you're saying, it's big—"

"Big? That isn't *big,* Jerri," Dark replied. "The goddamn thing is just about impossible. It's several times bigger than the Poseidon class." He shook his head slowly in wonder.

Jerri looked at Marchant. "Then it's"—she gestured at the screen—"a Russian submarine?"

Marchant nodded. "Uh huh. And just like Con said, we used to think that *Triton*—she's our biggest, with twin reactors and about eight thousand tons—was really it. But that thing cops the honors coming and going." He reached into his pocket for a cigarette. "And we don't know if they have any more where that came from."

"You're leaving a lot of empty spaces in all this, Steve," Dark told him.

A flaring match lit up Marchant's face. He blew it out and returned to the shadows.

"We got that picture by a stroke of good fortune," the captain explained. "It was taken off the coast of South America, by the way. From what we have been able to tell—we'd just about sell our souls for a couple of really clear frames—it's a special utility boat. There's no evidence of tubes fore or aft and there isn't any reason to employ something that big as a missile platform. So we've pretty well knocked out any guesses that would lead to some sort of weapons system."

His cigarette weaved a glowing pattern as he gesticulated. "We went the whole route—radar picket, supply, oceanographic, hydrographic, any and all kinds of research. We drew a blank every time. Different things just didn't fit together. We even played with the idea that someone in their Navy had gone ape and sold their big boys a bill of goods. It was ridiculous, but we played with it for a while, and, like the rest of it . . ." He shrugged.

"Then we started to get smart," he continued. "This is where little pieces of information mean everything. After all, it only takes a small key to open a very big door, and—"

"Hold on," Dark broke in. "You mean that sonar report? That pickup at two thousand fathoms? You're connecting the two of them and *now* it fits?"

"That's the general idea," Marchant said to confirm Dark's conclusions. "Finally, we got the fit we were looking for. Oh, I know the areas were different and all that, but so were the times—in fact, the sonar report and the time this picture was taken were several weeks apart."

Something nagged at Dark's mind. "Hey, wait up there, Steve. If you had this picture and you knew about that monster"—he jerked his thumb at the screen—"then why the fat-and-dumb routine yesterday, at that meeting? Why didn't you let on there? And, for that matter," he said angrily, "why the hell did you need *me* to be a patsy!"

Marchant dismissed Dark's anger with a wave of the hand. "Back off, Con. You know better than that." He straightened in his seat and looked at Dark. "In this game you don't always play all the cards on the first deal. I told you we were trying to get something to fit and what we finally came up with seems to be the answer. But we can't swear to it, we're not positive, and even though we don't think so, we *could* be wrong." He jabbed his cigarette into his ash tray. "So we wanted you to come out with what you thought of that sonar report as it was given to you in detail, and we didn't want you second-guessing before Kuiper could ask you all his questions. *Now* you can reevaluate, if you like. Maybe you will, maybe you won't."

Dark sat back in his seat, immersed in thought. Finally he pointed again to the screen. "Any details?"

Marchant didn't answer for a moment. "Not really," he said cautiously. "Just some hints and leads. We've had the interpretation people tearing out their hair with that picture. Called in some of our best engineers."

He pressed his armrest button. "Al?"

"Go ahead, Steve."

"Put the arrow along the lower hull, will you please?"

The arrow moved along the screen and pointed to a dull line. In the blurred scene it was almost impossible to make out any detail.

"What do you make of that?" Marchant asked.

Dark looked at the screen. He raced through his memory, running through details of design, variations in hulls and . . . "Never saw anything like that before," he said, shaking his head. "But I could make an educated guess."

"Go ahead."

"First, I'll change that; I'll do more than guess." He nodded emphatically. "Only thing it could be . . . um; hell, yes, it's *got* to be," he said, thinking aloud.

Marchant and Jerri waited.

The sound of Dark's fist smacking hard into his palm was startling in the quiet that had filled the theater.

"Those are bay doors," he said finally.

Marchant didn't reply; Jerri was trying hard to keep up with words and phrases unfamiliar to her. But she sensed that an interruption on her part to ask questions would only distract the two men; she could wait. There was plenty of time to have it all spelled out later.

"Don't quit now," Marchant urged. Jerri noticed the dour expression had left his face.

"Sure, that's it all right," Dark said with mounting excitement. "They're doors to a pressure bay, and I bet if we could see more of that thing—the underside, I mean—we'd find another set. You know what I mean, Steve? A hull that big—why, it wouldn't be any trouble at all . . . they could build in the systems without any sweat. With nuclear drive in her belly and no ballistic canisters or tubes, there'd be more than enough room to handle two small boats!"

Again he pounded his fist into his palm. He had come to grips with something tangible, he was in his element now. "There's that damned missing piece of yours, Steve—that's their mother ship for those deep submersibles!"

Jerri waited for their rapid-fire exchange to subside; for nearly twenty minutes Dark and Marchant discussed the details of what they had seen—not only the mighty submarine but the Samos pictures as well. There was still the enigma of the seven submarines rendezvousing at night with two mother ships, one of which was obviously a cover of some kind. But what Dark had just seen, placed in a fresh perspective by the man who had made more deep dives and spent more time in the true deeps than anyone else in the country, kindled a new series of possibilities. At least there had been achieved some narrowing of the field.

Finally both men fell silent with their thoughts and the swirling tide of extrapolation opened to them. Jerri took the opportunity to ask the question that had bothered her ever since she first saw the full screen-sized view of the mystery submarine. She was not unfamiliar with underwater photography; she was, in fact, one of the more successful scentists in the field, enjoying as she did the facilities of Crowell Institute and the full backing of Dr. Whitelock in her field studies—the deep waters off the California coast.

Steve Marchant said the picture was taken—where was it?—oh, yes, off the coast of South America. But that meant . . . well, it meant that someone, somehow, *beneath* the surface, had to get close enough to that *thing* to get that picture! And that was impossible. . . .

"Steve? The picture; that submarine. How on earth did you ever manage to get it?"

Her query penetrated Dark's preoccupation. He pushed himself to an upright position. "By God, I must be slipping," he said. "How could I have missed *that?* Jerri's right." He thought of the possibilities. "We must have one hell of a wild-assed boat captain to have gone in that close to—" Abruptly he shook his head, angry with himself. "But that's impossible . . . no way to *take* the damn picture even if . . . and—oh, hell, Steve, spill it, will you?"

"Yeah; the pictures. I almost forgot," he said. A wide grin appeared on his face. "Score one for our side, kids."

He pressed the armrest button. "Sorry we took so long to hassle, Al," he said to Colonel Starnes.

"No sweat," came the reply.

"Are you ready with those scenes of the Bottles?"

"Ready and waiting. Want them now?"

"Right. Roll 'em, please."

Two porpoises in a huge tank swam lazily just beneath the surface. Below them, sluggish and unconcerned with the mammals that moved overhead, drifted a shark. He was a big white, a killer, every bit of twenty or twenty-five feet long.

They watched the scene for five minutes and nothing changed. Dark fidgeted in his seat, trying to figure out what Marchant was trying to prove. The minutes dragged by, without a word from Colonel Starnes or from Marchant. Finally even Jerri began to shift uncomfortably in her seat.

Dark gestured at the screen. "That's very pretty," he announced to no one in particular. "And it's very boring and I might imagine that you're playing games with us, Steve except that we wouldn't be in *this* place just to look at that aquarium waltz you've got."

Marchant was noncommittal. "Look at the screen," he said. "It's all there, right in front of you."

Dark looked at Jerri and slumped back in his seat "Well, it is time for fun and games," he muttered. "Here we go again."

Beside him Jerri was staring hard at the screen. Slowly she came to her feet. She pointed at the screen and turned to Marchant. "Why—why, that's impossible!" she exclaimed.

"Oh? Why do you say that, Jerri?" he asked.

Dark interrupted before she could reply. "Oh, oh," he warned. "I know that sweet innocence tone in his voice from way back. You bastard," he said in mock anger to Marchant, "you're pulling a fast one on us, aren't you?"

The grin spread across Marchant's face. "Don't ask me," he retorted. "Look at *her*." He nodded to Jerri. "She's fit to bust. Why—"

"Oh, shut up, Steve," she said. "Your film, that—that thing"—she jabbed her finger in the direction of the screen—"why, it's just a big fake."

Dark stared at her puzzled. "A fake, Jerri?"

"Con, look at the screen!" Jerri's voice was impatient, reproving. "The porpoises. *Look* at them." Before he could reply, she rushed on. "We've been looking at that same scene for, oh, maybe fifteen minutes now. Con, *they've* never broken the surface to breathe."

He kept his attention on the screen. "I'll be damned," he said softly. "I never noticed it."

"Not only that," Jerri added, "but the shark . . . it's a fake, too, just like the porpoises. Have you noticed, Con? There's no movement . . . the gills, the mouth. They haven't moved at all. And those porpoises . . . look at them again. They always keep the same distance between them. See? And the one on the outside, closest to the wall of the tank, see him? He's always the exact same distance from the tank wall, and the one with him maintains his exact distance. Why"—she was almost spluttering for having been deceived for so long—"it's all a big fake. They're not *real,* Con!"

They sat in silence as the engineering development film showed them the scientific miracle of what Steve Marchant called the "Bottles." Colonel Starnes' voice maintained a running commentary of explanation throughout, and Dark realized now why there had been a note of triumph in Marchant's voice when he had said, "Score one for our side."

The Bottles came in two classes—porpoises and sharks. In the purist sense they were animal cyborgs—cybernetic organism adaptations of real-life creatures of the sea. The porpoises, dark-bodied and amazingly fluid and lifelike, had an outer skin covering of flexible plastisteel. Beneath the outer skin went an ingenious framework, rigid for the most part, but capable of movement in the fins and of limited vertical movement of the flukes. In the heart of each porpoise—Dark found it difficult to think of them by the project code name of Bottles—was installed a powerful nuclear reactor adapted from the reactor developed for permanent installations on the moon. During open-sea cruising, for purposes of speed, the Bottles used a small hydrojet; a panel slid open by the "mouth" and aft of the artificial animal to permit the hydrojet to function. Close to their objectives the hydrojets were shut down and the animal cyborgs moved in to extreme close quarters through their artificial flukes and fins. The shark models had a limited movement capability of the main fins and the powerful tail. Both models—porpoises and sharks—also had flotation bladders to compensate for the basic body rigidity and extreme weight.

Each Bottle had a radius of action from its mother sub, or surface vehicle, of approximately one hundred miles, with a staying time in its target area of one hour. The Bottles were capable of remote control by radio signal if they were sufficiently near the surface for a slender whip antenna to be effective. Otherwise they functioned through their computer systems, an intricate electronic maze of gyroscopes, computers, sensors, and other devices adapted from nuclear-submarine as well as spacecraft systems.

The "eye" of each Bottle was an advanced optical-electronic system that gave stereoptic effect, so vitally needed for under-water reconnaissance. Motion pictures were obtained through the eyes of the Bottles, and the lenses of the still-picture cameras were mounted in the dorsal fins. Depending upon geographical location, sea conditions, and other factors, either the sharks or the porpoises would be sent out on a mission, and at times it was desirable to send both.

Not even the Bottles could overcome the dangers inherent in approaching a submarine or a fleet unit that maintained a thorough electronic-aural scan of the immediately adjacent waters. It was still too much to expect of the system, at least at this stage of the Bottles' development, that they could adopt the random directional movement of live creatures. Once a Bottle picked up its target on its sonar and the computer digested the factors of time and distance and programmed into its memory banks, it kept the Bottle moving unerringly toward its objective.

The few pictures they had seen of the great Soviet submarine—apparently the mother ship to deep-living submersibles—was all that could be salvaged of the rare opportunity to get the photographs. Intelligence had passed the word that "something big" would be moving southward from the Soviet Union and would follow a course to bring it along the coastline of South America. There had been just enough time to crisscross the anticipated course of the known target with long-range planes equipped for submarine surveillance. A P3V with its MAD—the Magnetic Anomaly Detector—got a reading on a "whopper" beneath the surface, and the Navy rushed the one boat it had in the area, with several Bottles aboard, ahead of the Russians' course.

The boat deployed three porpoises along the anticipated course line of the unknown target bearing south at high speed. From what they knew and could extrapolate, the Russians picked up the sounds of the incoming Bottles. Maybe one of the hydrojets failed to shut down properly and alerted the Soviet specialists that something just didn't sound right. Of course, that alone raised a point. What was a research submarine, or what appeared to be a research submarine, doing with extremely advanced military detection systems? And, for that matter, what happened next —in the opinion of the American specialists—was enough to make a man think very hard.

The American sub—which remained passive and undetected by the Soviet systems—later retrieved only one

Bottle. The sounds captured on its tape could have been made only by a swarm of high-speed homing torpedoes fired by the Russian craft—high-speed torps with solid-propellant rockets instead of screws, so that you could release them in a swarm, each torp equipped with a rudimentary sonar-detection-homing setup. They could home in to their targets and detonate within any preset range instead of requiring a direct hit. The Bottles were so designed that when their guidance, power, or homing systems were damaged and incapable of a minimum performance, an intense incendiary charge tore the mechanisms into a shapeless blob and committed the artificial animal to the depths.

"And these pictures," Marchant said, "were worth it all."

Dark mulled over the film and the detailed explanations. "Yeah, it was worth it," he agreed. "And I'm certain the same question that occurs to me now has also popped up in your devious little mind."

"Which is?"

"Easy enough," Dark said. "What the hell are the Russians so trigger-happy about that they'll release torps in the South Atlantic at what could only be an unidentified bogey on their screens?"

"You're right," Marchant agreed. "That thought has also occurred to us. I'd say it leaves room for sober thinking, wouldn't you?"

Steve and Jerri drove him to Andrews Air Force Base. After three days of briefings, meetings, and new orders for the Orca ordnance tests he was taking with him back to Isla de Culebra, Conan Dark felt as if a knot had been twisted within his brain. Somehow he had the feeling he should have been clicking his heels about a whole new world opening up—that second chance with Jerri. Despite their making love with the same uninhibited responses they'd known before, he was also aware that Jerri was very much fully in control of what she was doing, and that—well, damn it, he *knew* she was really one step beyond his reach. He had visitor's rights instead of a place to hang his cap permanently, and if he wanted the latter, she had made it very clear he had his work cut out for him.

He would return alone to Base Savage and to his Orca project team. There would be two or three days of fitting himself into the ordnance systems and making preliminary checks, and then he and Larry Owens would take Orca out to sea and the ordnance test area to see just how sharp and powerful her bite could be.

"I'm flying with Jerri to the West Coast first thing tomorrow morning," Marchant explained as he turned onto the airbase road. "In about a week or so Jerri will become part of your group at Culebra." Dark's eyes widened at that one; a quick squeeze by Jerri's hand told him that she knew of the move. "A cargo plane has already flown a good part of Jerri's files to the base," Marchant went on, "and we've arranged for both teletype and other channels for her to keep tabs on what our Red friends are doing in the oceanographic and fishing world."

He glanced at her. "The oceanographic data center is providing you a direct link to their memory computers, Jerri," he added. "It's just about set up now through the military comsat system, and—"

"The what?"

"Forgot—you've got a new language on your hands. The communications satellites—comsats—will carry our communications loads. No tapping of the line, so to speak, and it's round the clock. As I've told you before, Jerri, you've got to be our bloodhound. You'll be able to keep tabs on what the Russians are doing at sea, anywhere and any place. If you need to make telephone calls or send out wires or letters, we've got it all arranged so that everything will seem to originate from your offices at Crowell

Institute. Because you're well known to all the parties in question and this is normal routine as far as your last several years are concerned, you aren't going to raise any eyebrows. It all fits quite neatly."

He pulled into the parking lot by base operations; Dark recognized the jet that had flown them to Washington. Marchant parked but did not move to leave the car. He still had something to tell them.

Jerri sat silently for a moment. "Do you think there's a chance that, well . . . what I mean, Steve, is what about the fact that I'll suddenly be missing from Crowell, while all this activity is coming from me? What if someone—they—check on this?"

"A very good point, Jerri," he said, smiling. "When we get back to Crowell, you'll see your stand-in. From a distance your own mother couldn't tell you apart."

She waved her hand weakly to dismiss the subject. "Please forget that I even bothered to ask," she said. She looked at Marchant in wonder. "Have you people forgotten *anything?"*

"Sure they have," Dark said.

Marchant cocked his right eyebrow. "I'm fascinated, Con. Tell me where we slipped."

He thought of the Little JCS conference and laughed at the memory. He shifted in his seat and looked at Marchant.

"The last view—it was a rather hurried one, if I recall—I had of one Professor Whitelock," Dark said, "was from the rear, and he was departing in both undisguised anger and a great determination never to have a thing to do with the likes of Kuiper, Marchant, or anyone else of that crowd. How are you going to steal away his right arm and mess up his office routine by sending Jerri down to Culebra?"

Marchant pushed open his door and started from the car. "We'll get your bag on the airplane, Con," he said. His face remained blank.

Dark shrugged and helped Jerri from the car. Ten

minutes later they were within the privacy of the jet.

"Okay, Poppa," Dark said. "Tell us how you're going to tame the ferocious Dr. Whitelock—who never wants to see your face again." He grinned at Jerri; she found it anything but funny. This problem was something that had not occurred to her.

"I have some goodies for our Dr. Whitelock," Marchant said.

"Oh, for Christ's sake, Steve," Dark said impatiently, "you've got canary feathers smeared all over your face. Spill it, will you?"

"Like I said—I have some goodies for the professor." He unlocked his attache case and held out two glossy photographs for them to study. They looked at a mixture of light and wavering shadows; the pictures had been taken in deep water. Deep enough for a complete absence of natural light—these were either floods or, more likely, Dark thought, a float pattern of flash bombs to provide light for the camera.

The picture to their left showed the major part of a great shallow depression in the sea bottom. Much of the inward-sloping surface was bare and . . . Dark looked carefully; it was unnaturally smooth, artificial in nature. He studied the second photograph. It lacked the clarity or distinction of the first picture, but clearly it indicated the same type of depression.

Dark looked up at Marchant. He gestured to the photographs. "They won't win any picture contests."

The captain pursed his lips. "No-o-o," he said slowly, "that they won't. But they're guaranteed to hold your attention—and to utterly captivate Dr. Whitelock, I would say."

Jerri frowned. "But what are they, Steve?"

"The scene to your left—this one—was taken in 1956 at a depth of two thousand feet, in the vicinity of Eniwetok Island in the Pacific," Marchant explained. "We were carrying out a series of advanced bomb tests. And one of those tests was a small device—oh, twenty or thirty kilotons—detonated at a depth of two thousand feet. That would make it, ummm, just about three hundred feet off the bottom."

He tapped the photograph lightly. "What you see—the photography could be better, of course—is the fused glassy surface of the depression punched by the fireball into the ocean bottom."

Dark's eyes were widening as Marchant went on.

"And this second picture . . . ?" Jerri started.

"When did you get that?" Dark snapped at him.

"Oh, about four o'clock this morning," Marchant said with a bland expression on his face. "I was dragged out of bed and rushed to the Pentagon just to look at it. I should add that it was well worth the trip."

He slid the pictures into his case. "That second photograph—did you notice the same general pattern of the fused surface, despite the cracking along the slopes?—was taken at a depth of four thousand feet."

"Where, damn it?"

"Exactly where the caclulations of Professor Whitelock indicated we would find the evidence of his, ah, theories. Due south of the Alaskan coastline and—well, you've heard that story before?"

He stood up to leave, his face grim.

"You see, he's been right all the time. Someone triggered that seismic effect; the whole thing. You could say they murdered four thousand people.

"And you don't need a crystal ball to guess that it's probably going to happen again."

9

Thick clouds tumbled thirty thousand feet above the hidden surface of the planet. Higher still in the night vault a winged form swept through a miles-wide pattern over a specific area beneath those clouds. Moonlight rippled from the metal wings; the pale spray washed the nocturnal mists below into an other-world of silvered valleys and ranges. Within the machine six men listened intently through radio headsets to an electronic ritual rushing through its final moments; far below the speeding airplane a skilled crew within a domed concrete bastion completed the last chords of their technical orchestration.

Beyond the sloping concrete walls a light rain fell from the dark clouds. No human figure or animal shape stirred the night. A cylindrical giant girding for a fire convulsion was the only life as the final seconds slipped away.

"Tri . . .

"Dva . . .

"Odin . . ."

Fire exploded into being—a cataract of flame hellish from the instant of birth. The giant heaved slowly, snapping the thick links of the gravity chain binding it to earth.

The cataract became a screaming pillar lengthening swiftly, whipping and lashing all within its reach.

The sound, then. Ponderous; rolling waves of deepest thunder shaking the ground, rattling even the thick concrete dome.

Higher.

Sunburst; ripping away from earth, kindling golden conflagration through the waiting cloud bellies, reflecting back to terrify the night creatures for miles around. The sun tearing outward through the night-blanketed world.

A billion dinosaurs screaming in the golden darkness. Night again; pulsations heaving earthward from on high, dying away in the endless chambers of echoes.

Then but a whisper. Banks of glowing instruments and dials to register what is happening.

But not for six men forty thousand feet above the smoking launch stand. The pilot listened to the voices; from past moments he knew what to expect. The yoke in his hand eased to the left and his foot exerted slight pressure to bring the machine about smoothly. Six men peered through windows at the cloud valleys and mountains. The machine banked steeper; they saw almost straight down.

The world below them began to burn.

Silver flame.

There was nothing else like it. The conflagration appeared first as only a needle of silvery light. Swiftly, then, it raced outward in all directions to tear away clouds and the night.

A flicker of savage flame; their first view of the giant rejecting a planet. Still it was below the upper levels of the clouds, the fire gashing the swirling mists all about. Silently to its watchers, unreal, it sundered all within reach.

The silver flame-knife pierced the upper cloud ramparts, acceleration exploding it higher and faster, with a silver-blue-green-orange pulsation trailing the fire source. High above them, almost crossing the face of the moon, bending over more and more to the horizontal, the flame subsided, visually pale, an enormous plasma spreading in near-vacuum.

Flame withered; died. They watched a silver shape slide away from the plasmic teardrop.

A tiny spark as new flame gushed, ripped the discarded cylinder, tumbling it madly like a giant's toy discarded at the top of the world.

The new flame pulsed, flickered, rushed beyond the sight of men.

". . . and the latest space shot of the Russians still remains more mystery than fact. Tass announced a giant new step in Soviet mastery of the cosmos is now under way, but we're not sure just what that step may be. Yesterday morning the Russians sent a huge payload into orbit about the earth. American scientists estimate it weighed more than sixty tons and that it was placed in parking orbit. That's a necessary step for a shot to the moon or beyond. The big surprise came only several hours ago, when our tracking stations discovered a second launching. It's confirmed now that the latest shot is one of the new Pyotrovisk spaceships, which can carry up to six men. The Pyotrovisk has made a rendezvous with the giant rocket already in orbit. Several cosmonauts are now outside their own ship, connecting a booster stage to that mystery payload. No one knows for certain what's going on, but correspondents in Moscow report the Russian capital is filled with rumors about the first atomic drive for space and that this is its test flight. However, there's no confirmation of this report.

"Meanwhile, Dr. Frederick Kuiper of the National Academy of Sciences said in Wahington today that . . ."

"There goes that goddamned bell again."

The news editor swore softly and walked to the teletype, which was announcing a special wire service bulletin. He punched the cutoff button for the bell and tore the sheet from the clattering machine, scanning the paper quickly.

"Mike! We got less than ten minutes before the next newscast." He handed the paper to his copywriter. "Put this together in time for the regular news. Bulletin-shmulletin; crap. One more failure don't mean that much any more."

The copy writer nodded, returned to his desk. He laid the bulletin out before him and began to read:

DATELINE: ENGLAND

JODRELL BANK OBSERVATORY

FIRST LEAD BULLETIN, STORY AS FOLLOWS, SCIENTISTS HERE AT THE WORLD'S LARGEST RADIO TELESCOPE HAVE BEEN TRACKING THE LATEST RUSSIAN SPACE SHOT. FROM ALL INDICATIONS IT APPEARS THE RUSSIANS HAVE CHALKED UP ANOTHER FAILURE IN THEIR LUNAR PROGRAM. THE GIANT PAYLOAD FIRED TWO DAYS AGO FROM ITS PARKING ORBIT TOWARD THE MOON IS DEFINITELY GOING TO MISS IT'S TARGET. BRITISH SCIENTISTS HERE AT JODRELL BANK SAY THAT THE RUSSIAN SPACESHIP, WHICH IS STILL UNNAMED BY MOSCOW, WILL MISS THE MOON BY MORE THAN EIGHT THOUSAND MILES. THEY BELIEVE IT IS TOO LATE TO FIRE ROCKETS THAT MIGHT BRING THE HUGE SPACECRAFT BACK ON A COURSE TO THE MOON. THE RUSSIAN SHIP WILL FALL PAST THE MOON AND GO INTO ORBIT AROUND THE SUN. 2ND PARA. BRITISH SCIENTISTS DISCOUNT THE RUMORS FROM MOSCOW THAT THE RUSSIANS ARE TESTING THE WORLD'S FIRST ATOMIC SPACE DRIVE. THEY POINT

OUT THAT THE FLIGHT PATH OF THE RUSSIAN SHIP THAT WILL SOON FALL PAST THE MOON IS NOT THE MOST EFFICIENT FOR THAT KIND OF TEST. ONCE IT LEAVES THE VICINITY OF THE EARTH IT BECOMES INCREASINGLY DIFFICULT TO OBTAIN INFORMATION BY RADIO OF HOW A NUCLEAR ENGINE WOULD BE WORKING. IT IS THEIR OPINION THAT THE RUSSIANS WERE ATTEMPTING TO LAND A LARGE SPACESHIP ON THE MOON'S SURFACE THAT WOULD START THEIR PROGRAM FOR A PERMANENT LUNAR BASE. HOWEVER, THERE'S STILL NO WORD FROM THE RUSSIAN GOVERNMENT AS TO EXACTLY WHAT THEY ARE DOING WITH THE BIGGEST PAYLOAD EVER FIRED INTO INTERPLANETARY SPACE. END BULLETIN.

DATELINE: ENGLAND

JODRELL BANK OBSERVATORY

THIRD LEAD BULLETIN FOLLOWS. THE MYSTERY RUSSIAN SPACESHIP LAUNCHED SEVERAL DAYS AGO FROM PARKING ORBIT AROUND THE EARTH HAS PASSED THE MOON. BRITISH SCIENTISTS HERE AT THE WORLD'S LARGEST RADIO TELESCOPE, WHICH HAS BEEN TRACKING THE GIANT SPACECRAFT, ANNOUNCED THAT THE MISS DISTANCE WAS 8,150 MILES. CODED TELEMENTRY SIGNALS ARE STILL BEING TRANSMITTED FROM THE SPACECRAFT TO RUSSIAN RECEIVING STATIONS ON EARTH. SCIENTISTS HERE REMAIN CONVINCED THE RUMORS OF AN ATOMIC SPACE ENGINE HAVE NO BASIS IN FACT, AND THE RUSSIAN SHOT MUST BE LISTED AS

ANOTHER FAILURE IN THEIR LUNAR PROGRAM. END BULLETIN.

". . . interrupt this program to bring you a special news bulletin. Scientists of the deep-space tracking network for our Apollo moon program report a tremendous mystery explosion in space. First reports indicate that the space blast took place about fifty thousand miles beyond the moon. Scientists at two observatories report photographic plates completely burned out by the intensity of light from the blast, which they describe as 'incredible.' Other reports from the space agency in Washington confirm that the space explosion was more than a hundred times as bright as the sun. There's no question but that the mystery space blast is somehow connected with the Russian ship that missed the moon yesterday by more than eight thousand miles. James Holworthy of our space agency insists that . . ."

DATELINE: MOSCOW

URGENT BULLETIN URGENT BULLETIN

THE SOVIET NEWS AGENCY, TASS, HAS ANNOUNCED THAT THE MYSTERY EXPLOSION THAT TOOK PLACE FIFTY THOUSAND MILES BEYOND THE MOON WAS A FAILURE OF THE FIRST ATOMIC DRIVE ENGINE FOR SPACE FLIGHT. END BULLETIN. NOTE TO EDITORS: EXPECT FOLLOW-UP FEATURE FROM CARLISLE, MOSCOW, RE SOVIET NUCLEAR PROGRAM. END NOTE.

"Commander Decker? Your call to Captain Marchant is ready, sir."

Decker punched his extension line and jerked the telephone to his ear. "Steve? Decker here. Listen, I've been trying to get you for the last couple of hours. You heard the announcement from the Russians? Yeah; I know, I know. Steve, *listen.*

"They're lying through their teeth. That was no nuclear reactor. What? Hell, yes; we *know*. All right, I can give you the details later. The figures? Sure, but they're only a rough guestimate at this point.

"Okay. But I think you'd better sit down before you hear what the boys from AEC have to say. . . ."

DATELINE: MOSCOW

URGENT BULLETIN URGENT BULLETIN

THE SOVIET GOVERNMENT STATES THAT DESPITE FEARS TO THE CONTRARY, THERE EXISTS NO DANGER TO THE MOON OR TO EARTH FROM RADIATION RELEASED BY THE EXPLOSION OF THEIR ATOMIC SPACE DRIVE. "STRICT SAFETY MEASURES WERE OBSERVED THROUGHOUT THE FLIGHT OF THE COSMOS NUCLEAR ENGINE," A MEMBER OF THE ACADEMY OF SCIENCES SAID. HE CLAIMED THAT THE FLIGHT WAS "CARRIED OUT IN SUCH A MANNER AS TO GUARANTEE A MINIMUM RELEASE OF RADIATION IN THE EVENT OF A FAILURE OF THE MECHANISM. THE VALUE OF THESE PRECAUTIONS AND THE SOVIET GOVERNMENT'S GREAT CONCERN FOR THE WELFARE OF ALL PEOPLES WAS AMPLY DEMONSTRATED." THE SCIENTISTS SAID THE NUCLEAR ENGINE WAS NOT TURNED ON UNTIL THE ROCKET WAS NEARLY 300,000 MILES FROM THE EARTH. WHATEVER RADIATION WAS RELEASED IN THE TREMENDOUS EXPLOSION, ADDED THE SCIENTIST, "COULD NEVER REACH THE SURFACE OF THE EARTH

BECAUSE OF THE INTENSE MAGNETOSPHERE AND THE RADIATION BELTS SURROUNDING THIS PLANET." HE POINTED OUT THAT THE "INTENSELY RADIOACTIVE DEBRIS OF THE DESTROYED ROCKET IS NOW HARMLESSLY IN SOLAR ORBIT." ANY RADIATION FIELD NEAR THE MOON, HE SAID, "WOULD BE SWEPT TO THE OUTER REACHES OF THE SOLAR SYSTEM BY THE EFFECT OF THE SOLAR WIND STREAMING OUTWARD FROM THE SUN." END BULLETIN.

Admiral Vadim Doroshinskaya, hands clasped behind his back, stared through the window. Far to his left he could just make out the higher buildings of Archangel where it lay at the edge of the White Sea. From the highest level of the new headquarters building of the Soviet Navy he could see the waters of the sea itself. Archangel was nearly twenty miles distant; the admiral's headquarters were effectively isolated. The nearest road entrance to the naval headquarters complex was eight miles away, and a series of intricate and lethal security measures assured that its isolation would remain enforced.

Without turning from the window, Admiral Doroshinskaya spoke to the men assembled in his office suite. The day was good; much had been accomplished.

"Oleinik, there is no question?"

Dmitri Oleinik was a nuclear scientist, a specialist in thermo-nuclear reactions. Reticent by nature, normally slow to answer, this time he did not hesitate.

"None, Comrade Admiral," he said.

"The yield, Oleinik?"

The scientist permitted himself the luxury of a rare smile. He glanced at his assistant. Nikita Fyodorov was a brilliant weapons specialist, as important to him as his right arm. Fyodorov gestured with the slim briefcase chained to his left wrist and nodded.

"Approximately"—he hesitated only a moment—"one gigaton, Comrade Admiral."

Doroshinskaya turned slowly. His eyebrows went up.

"Really, Oleinik? You are *that* certain?"

The beaming faces of Oleinik and Fyodorov answered for them. The admiral returned to his desk and took his seat slowly. His face showed a sudden intense concentration.

"A billion tons," he breathed. For several moments he remained lost in thought.

He looked up suddenly and studied the eyes of the scientist. "You know the dimensions?"

Oleinik nodded.

"There will be no problem? Be absolutely certain of your answer!"

"There is no problem, Comrade Admiral. Of that we are certain." Oleinik smiled again. "Indeed, we expect a five-fold increase in the thermal factor. Everything has worked out precisely as we anticipated." Again he nodded. "We are *very* certain, Comrade Admiral."

A powerful hand crashed against the desk. "Good! I am pleased, gentlemen, I assure you," Admiral Doroshinskaya boomed with sudden open enthusiasm. "It appears we may commence with the remaining steps. Now, comrades, if you will take your seats"—he gestured to the conference table—"we will review all the latest reports, yes?"

One by one they detailed the progress with Operation Giant. One by one the admiral's aide checked off the names:

Dmitri Oleinik; *nuclear scientist*
Nikita Fyodorov; *weapons specialist*
Yuri Ryzhak; *expedition commander*
Grigor Y. Malinovskii; *oceanographic scientist*
Ivan Kuinzhi; *American Intelligence*

Sergei Smirnov; *naval Intelligence*
Gherman Trofimuk; *internal security*

The admiral listened to everything, took nothing for granted. He knew they would be here for many hours. Their success or failure depended entirely on how things would go with Operation Giant.

Tomorrow there would be the political meeting.

Admiral Doroshinskaya was leaving nothing to chance. He must be as certain of the readiness to strike politically as was his staff with Operation Giant.

He listened to the breakdown of logistics support for the expedition. Yuri Ryzhak was as imaginative as a block of granite, thought the admiral. But then—he smiled to himself—he is also as durable and reliable as that same granite. And I need not imagination; I must have reliability. . . .

10

Red panel lights glowed softly in the darkened cockpit. The two pilots, straining forward to look through the Plexiglas sheets fronting the helicopter, ignored their instruments. Five hundred feet below them a miracle of life spread as far as the eye could see. Through the darkness phantom light gleamed and flashed in a pattern of coruscating unreality.

"My God,"—the copilot breathed in awe—"it looks like the whole Milky Way fell into the ocean."

The pilot nodded; there was really little to say about the fantastic sight. He had never before seen an ocean glittering in every direction to the horizon. The radiance in the water was coming from billions of ghosts, tumbled and frothed by wind and waves into a phosphorescence of liquid jewels. Within the sea the mysterious swarming of the protozoa *Noctiluca* was painting its glowing miracle. The process of luminescence took place at different times of the year, with different creatures throughout the planet, but none so overwhelming as was this moment.

The two men in their machine five hundred feet above the ocean were not here, however, to observe the phenomenon of *Noctiluca.* Military helicopters have other purposes and needs and their missions are coldly realistic; this was no different. The machine had departed Isla de Culebra twenty minutes before Conan Dark and Larry Owens slipped the killer submarine Orca through the subsurface tunnel shaft that linked the underground caverns of Base Savage to the open sea. It had been standard practice from the beginning of the sea trials that the waters leading to and from the underground caverns were to be swept from the air to assure that no surface craft had strayed into the area. Sonar detection systems attended to the security of submerged visitors and radar maintained a round-the-clock vigil of the skies. Surface craft presented their own problems best solved through the clumsy but particularly efficient helicopter.

The big Sikorsky accomplished yet another purpose for the Orca crew. As they eased their way through the shallow waters immediately adjacent to the hidden base, Owens released a long whip antenna that trailed behind and well above the slowly moving submarine. This was their final opportunity before seeking the greater depths to test their electromagnetic communications equipment.

Orca reached the edge of the shallows to the north of Isla de Culebra, moving across beds of sand that sloped with a gentle downgrade to a sudden precipitous drop. The sand lowered until the fathometer showed the bottom three hundred feet below the surface. Then there appeared the sudden plunge of another three hundred feet and a bottom composed essentially of mud. It was at this point, moving to the north, that Orca approached the high ramparts of the great Puerto Rico Trench. From the mud flats six hundred feet beneath the waves the ocean floor dipped in a terrifying plunge that sent the bottom from its mere six hundred to more than twenty thousand feet. And deeper still, to twenty-four and twenty-six thousand feet. And into a hellish gouge in the scarred face of the earth more than thirty thousand feet down.

As quickly as Conan Dark could take her sleek shape safely through the shallows to where the ocean bottom fell away freely beneath them, Orca would be in her true element. They had in the past plumbed those depths, taken the powerful killer sub down and down and still farther down until the deeps clawed at Orca with a pressure of more than six and a half tons per square inch.

There was a last call yet to be made by the helicopter pilots, a ceremonial *bon voyage* of friendly sarcasm from the men who drifted like animated seed pods through the naked air. And who took no pains to disguise their own fears of venturing into a world of alien, overwhelming, suffocating pressure. Behind the bandied words lay the deep respect such men hold for one another.

The helicopter maintained its station to the right and behind the submarine, the pilots still gripped with the dazzling sight below them. To the delight of Dark and Owens, the two men drifting through the night air had described in great detail the glowing ocean and, in particular, the glittering swath created by Orca's own passage through the shallow waters. It stretched for miles behind the invisible submarine to blend finally into the coruscation of the night ocean itself. The copilot tapped his companion on his arm and pointed to the ocean surface below. The pilot nodded; then, unthinking of his words, brought momentary alarm to the Orca crewmen.

"Bandit One from Foxtrot."

"Bandit here," Dark replied. "You clowns *still* up there? I thought you peapods didn't like the water. G'wan, beat it before you get your feet—"

"You got company."

Instantly Dark's hand shot to power control, poised to ram the maximum energy of the twin nuclear turbines to the screws, to send Orca plunging into the depths over which she now poised. The action was reflex, instinctive. Just as quickly Owens tripped the arming circuits of the defensive torps. In that same move their shoulder harnesses tightened, combat-readiness monitoring equipment flashed on; both men were acting in concert, unthinking, ready without hesitation to make the killer sub live up to her name.

The pilot's laconic speech infuriated Dark.

"Umm, damndest thing I ever saw," came the voice from high above them.

His tone stayed further action on the part of Dark and Owens. The voice suggested surprise but carried with it no sense of danger.

Dark was more than annoyed. His heart was pounding, and he knew that Owens behind him must be experiencing the same physical reactions. You simply don't explode yourself from casual slow cruising into combat conditions without pumping adrenalin into your system as if it were squirting from a fire hose. That and a dozen other things, damn it; slowly he slid down the physical-emotional peak to which he had been hurled by the call, "You got company."

"Spell it out, Foxtrot," Dark barked into his microphone. *"Quick!"*

The Orca crewmen relaxed as the pilot's voice came back to them, still with wonder in it. Obviously the pilot had no idea of what his first description had created within the sealed compartment of the submarine.

"Hard to describe, Bandit," the reply came. "We can see your trail like we said; the swath couldn't be anything else. But on each side of you, there's . . . well, there are three lines that look like streaks of fire. Three on each side of your position. They appear as if they're glowing by themselves—like the things . . . whatever it is at the front of each fire streak, I mean . . . have a glow all around them. The, ah—I know this sounds crazy, Bandit, but from up here it looks like the fire effect is staggered. Staccato would be better like it." Silence for a moment. "And they're keeping up with you. Holding a perfect formation. Over."

Inside the submarine Dark relaxed. Owens watched his

reflection in the wide-angle mirror that showed him the entire area of Dark's control deck and noticed the absence of the hair-trigger wariness evident only moments before.

"Foxtrot, you gave us something of a scare," Dark said, his anger vanished. "Nothing to worry about."

"Yeah? Glad you feel that way about it, Bandit." The voice paused. "Just so we can tell them back home what it was all about, why don't you share your little story with us?"

Dark laughed. "They're porpoises, Foxtrot. Just a couple of friendly critters keeping us company. They'll move off when we start down."

"Porpoises? Maybe you didn't hear me, Bandit. They are keeping perfect formation with you, and—"

"That's the tip-off, you guys. They like their fun and games that way. And those intermittent streaks you talked about—that's the porpoises going in and out of the water. The phosphorescence brightens up when they come above the surface and the air gets at it with all that motion. Like I said," he dismissed the matter, "no sweat. Okay?"

The pilot relaxed. "You're the brainy types down there," he said. "We're far enough from home as it is. Anything else you'd like before we take off?

Dark glanced in his mirror and saw Owens shaking his head.

"That's it, Foxtrot. Keep the beer cold until we get home. Over and out." He killed the transmitter and Owens began to reel in the antenna. The green light went on as the last of the wire snaked into its receptacle and the access doors closed.

"Okay," he announced to Dark, "we're all cleaned up and ready to get out of here."

Dark scanned the instruments before him; the gauge showed the bottom thirteen thousand feet beneath Orca and dropping steadily. The instruments gave him a comfortable feeling, pointing the way to where he was anxious to return.

Some go for the mountains, he thought. They like it where they can crawl back into what the country was once like from one ocean to the other. They're not happy until they're running around like a bunch of goddamned bighorn sheep. He grinned. And then there are other kinds, like that idiot brother of mine who likes to bust open clouds and chase rainbows at a thousand miles an hour or something. Well, each to his own.

Me, he announced to himself, I go the other way. All the way until I'm scraping the belly of old Mother Earth herself.

Two days after departing Base Savage on Isla de Culebra, specified the United States Navy, Conan Dark and Lawrence P. Owens were to deliver the killer submarine Orca to AUTEC—the Atlantic Underwater Test and Evaluation Center in the Bahamas. There, over the shallow curving ledge that extends from the Florida continental shelf to support the islands of the Bahamas, and beyond the ledge to the precipitous flanks of the Blake Escarpment, which falls in a sheer drop to the abyssal plains of the ocean bottom, Orca would participate in her initial ordnance test.

But that was yet two days ahead of them. Orca required not days but hours to rush through the depths from Isla de Culebra to the AUTEC range. Were they to proceed directly, they would arrive on station before AUTEC facilities were prepared for them. Thus they would make the most of the time and the distance—an en-route opportunity—to carry out a running research mission vital to the Navy and not at all displeasing to the two men who had blended their psyches with that of their intricate and mighty machine.

Aboard Orca was mounted a large, cumbersome, and exquisitely complex computer-memory and ocean-current-charting system, linked to the inertial navigation platform developed for undersea guidance. That equipment would dictate their movement to come.

Orca would follow a course outbound to the north, over the Puerto Rico Trench into the waters of the Nares Abyssal Plain. At this point Larry Owens would transfer control of the killer sub from Conan Dark to the Brainbox, their euphemism for the gleaming container within which hummed the electronic memory systems for their en-route experiments. It was the events of the mission—recorded faithfully by Brainbox—that represented the payoff. If it were necessary for Dark to bring Orca to AUTEC at a specific time, he could do so with timing down to the minute. But to accomplish that goal he must exercise full control of the submarine, aided by Larry Owens and his vast navigational-guidance systems. Then they could meet any contingency of their voyage through the performance of the machine at their hands.

This wasn't their purpose where Brainbox was concerned. For they were to attempt an ideal voyage, ideal in terms of their circuitous path and the time factor, *without* exercising full control. Their job was to set out on a preplanned mission and then place Orca at the whims and movements of the forces that surge deep within the world ocean. The Brainbox recorders, keeping an exact detailed record of all that transpired, would then present to submarine scientists a profile of activity within the ocean deeps they had never before had available to them.

Few people are aware that the vast multidimensional arena of the oceans—the cubic space—is anything but quiescent. The depths conceal legions of forces surging, marching, tumbling, carrying within their movement tremendous energies. Vast currents flow with the mass of a thousand giant rivers that course through the lands of earth. Deep tributaries snake their fluid fingers everywhere. And where one finds this miles-wide, deeply submerged river coursing powerfully from south to north, it is also possible—and very often it happens—to discover another vast stream pushing its way from north to south, only a scant few hundred feet beneath the northbound current! They are levels of the hydroworld bent on their mindless paths, impossibly close to one another, moving billions upon billions of tons of sea water by day and night, month after month and year after year. Within that "bowl of quiescence," as so many regard the depths, there are eddies and streams, mountains of water that rise vertically and slide downward with ponderous effect, fast-moving cataracts tumbling down escarpments and miles-high submerged cliff walls with such force they tumble giant boulders as if they were pebbles.

The deeps provide force in manners both powerful and, to those who know only the surface, startling. The density of the hydroworld cannot be comprehended by those who exist under the naked thinness even of an atmosphere a hundred miles high. Water is not water; it is a medium of such cruel, stupendous pressure it seems capable of origin only in some bizarre and alien world. Its density exerts termendous force. The crushing pressure dictates its own rules of movement; under conditions of medium or rapid passage caution is a warning keening in the mind, for one must never forget the nature of the adversary—monster pincers ready to come together with the force of massive battering rams.

Both men knew they were in for an interesting voyage of two days; they were fully aware that their course would bring them through the depths charted by oceanographers as rife with motion. Brainbox could direct, but Conan Dark must control. For any vessel sliding through those depths, when it encounters the turbulent flows, vertical movements, and other forces must necessarily respond to the forces that act upon it. Vertical currents produce pitching movements and side-to-side yaw. Often there is a combination of these forces that can bring on a twisting motion demanding immediate and accurate responses of the submarine pilot.

Far from the sight of man, hundreds and often many thousands of feet beneath the surface waves, there are other waves to be found. Some exert the most gentle of pressures, a great but soft undulation that pulses its course serenely through the depths. And there are the giants—massive waves hundreds of feet high, great hills of cruelly dense water pounding inexorably through the oceans, rising and falling, an aquatic thundering motion. They are of such enormous force that they can buffet and toss about a submarine just as surface maelstroms make of surface ships a plaything of the storm gods.

There were many reasons, all of them compelling, for the Navy to learn as much as possible about these great forces of the inner seas. Immediately obvious, of course, are the effects already described. But there were also riches in those currents and forces—riches represented in knowledge and thus greater control in the murky and complex environment, and, as well, the "free rides" that knowedge of such currents could produce.

A submarine with accurate knowledge of deep currents could utilize them much as high-flying aircraft use jetstreams; if the current moves along the intended course, it is possible to slide into its midst and be carried along at greater speed without the need for increased power—just as it is possible to *avoid* the oncoming mass of a current and be forced not to struggle against its flow. A military submarine with knowledge of such currents could slip into the moving stream and be carried along the midst of the enemy—with all systems shut down and running in absolute silence.

The Gulf Stream—through which Orca would slide on this mission en route to AUTEC—is not the well-defined river so many believe it to be. Instead, it expands and contracts in a strange pulsation much like a living thing, but without the systematic regularity allowing its habits to be charted accurately. It can wander up to twenty miles a day from where it flowed the day before and, on the day following, shift back to its original liquid path. At different times, without reasons known to oceanographers, parts of the stream break away from the main flow and wander off to form rotating eddies as much as eighty or ninety miles in diameter.

And then, just to complicate matters, a thousand feet *beneath* the Gulf Stream there flows a narrow current moving always to the south. Compared to other hydrorivers its speed of less than one knot is slow. But it moves some fifteen million tons of water *every second;* that's about five hundred times greater than the transport of the Mississippi River. At that, it is far down on the list of the truly major rivers within the sea. Along the Pacific equator one current little known outside oceanographic circles has a measured volume of flow of roughly thirty million tons every second.

And sometimes not knowing enough about currents and their effects can kill.

It has killed.

Conan Dark thought of *Thresher*. Like Steve Marchant, Larry Owens, and Hans Riedel, he had lost some close friends aboard the nuclear boat. He had been on the investigating and study team. From the beginning there was an air of helplessness about the whole thing. They knew even before they started what had killed the submarine and smeared its men from existence.

A lack of knowledge of the deeps.

Dark thought of the massive structure and powerful machinery all about him. Orca . . . she could take the worst of whatever the terrible depths had to offer. She was the first boat that could really pick up the gauntlet flung at all intruders—and do with it what her crew willed. Orca, thought Dark, owned a planet.

But it wasn't like that for the other boats. For the thousands of men who cruised in silence, with city-destroying shapes stacked vertically in Sherwood Forest, their amidships launch tubes for Polaris and Poseidon missiles. And the other men in attack boats, utility submarines, and more in the long shapes used for exploration and research and undersea picket lines and a hundred other prime missions.

What happened to *Thresher* could—might—happen to any one of them, any time, and almost anywhere men went beneath the sea in the long shapes.

The greatest enemy: a lack of knowledge.

Conan Dark thought about that; he thought of it many times and always with cognizance of how really vital was that knowledge. And we're one way of finding out, he thought. We're the lucky ones, me and Larry. With this boat under our hands we own the damned oceans.

The Nares Abyssal Plain waited for them, ahead and down. The instruments showed the depth still increasing. Sixteen thousand feet, still lowering.

Dark held up a thumb to Owens and received a nod. They didn't need words for this moment. Not when they were poised on the edge, not now. It was like getting ready to go home.

Dark's hand blended with the grip to his left and began to move forward. Deep within her massive hull Orca stoked her atomic fire; behind them the screws chewed water.

Dark flexed his fingers on the handgrip of the control stick directly before him. He eased forward, carefully, smoothly.

Look out, Neptune. Here we come....

Orca ran for the deeps.

11

"Contact."

"Bearing zero-three-zero, range two miles, four hundred feet low."

Ghostly green fog pulsed at Larry Owens from the sonar-screen display readout. He studied the screen carefully, his brow furrowed in concentration. He searched through his memories for the key of familiarity, knowing he had seen this same sight once before.

"Got something interesting, Larry?"

Owens glanced up at the mirror reflection of Dark. "Yeah," he nodded. "Different, sort of. I'm sure I've had a look at this once before, Con. But it's evading me; can't get it straightened out in my mind yet." He shook his head, openly annoyed with himself at the mental block.

Dark waited; Larry would call the shots in his own good time. They had been under way for some eighteen hours and it was their first opportunity in many long months really to enjoy the performance of the killer submarine.

What they liked most about the brief journey from Isla de Culebra to AUTEC was freedom from the usual demands for experimental and performance data with Orca; prior to this voyage they'd been slaves to technical and engineering requirements. Playing nursemaid to Brainbox was not only a snap, but for the first time since they'd sliced the depths with the submarine they had a chance to search for creatures of the deeps.

Utilizing the wire-controlled ladar—sending it on its flexible cable tether as much as three hundred feet from the submarine—gave them an extended vision double the normal range of the laser beam. In close proximity to rugged terrain or vertical rises, Dark could hold Orca almost to a hover, while Owens directed the ladar probe, electrically powered and sharpened like a small manta, in any direction from the submarine. The data-readout computers of Orca converted the ladar scan to a scope picturization—allowing them to "see" through the ladar almost as if they had been using an optical system.

At various points about the submarine remote television scanners were coupled to powerful floodlights. They had yet to utilize the wire-guided light probes that could send ahead of the submarine, into crevices or *behind* an object of interest, a powerful glow of light.

Above all else Orca was acoustically hypersensitive through her powerful sonar systems, capable of many discrete modes of operation. The combination of powerful probing sonar beams and the "superhearing" of the passive systems, linked to the computer that translated acoustic signals to visual picturization, enabled Conan Dark and Larry Owens to detect the barest whisper or sound originating from distant sources: to detect and then to amplify until the seas became a myriad jungle through which sound roared, hissed, crackled, thundered, croaked, boomed, thrummed, twittered, and snapped; sound that raced along strange thermal ducts comprised of the very sea and that carried more than halfway around the entire planet; sound that became distorted, bent, twisted, doubled back upon itself, and magnified its volume.

Sound originating not only from the marine creatures but great sonic viols as well. The ambient noise of the sea:

waves marching across the surface and through the depths; currents and streams clashing; whirlpools and eddies with strange sucking sounds; liquid slobbering that might emanate from a hundred-foot grouper. Mysterious rumblings and grating noises carry for mile after mile; gas pockets explode just beneath the sea bottom, their thunder reverberating with booming echoes. Quakes and slides along submerged slopes grind their own brand of noise; geysers steam and hiss with boilerlike rasping cries. Volcanic uproars take days to cease their deep thrumming thunder.

Man adds his own touch; screws churning and pounding, explosive blasts deliberate and accidental. Ships, dredges, probes; a million huge pipes discharging the sputum of man-made and industrial sewage, burbling and rumbling from along the shorelines.

Away from all else save the marine creatures, there is still that jungle cacophony, the uproar of liquid every day.

There were all manner of acoustic signatures. . . .

Drumfish slam away at their gas-filled bladders with a vibrating muscle, mad players in a chorus of bassfiddles. Owens knew the sound of the drumfish with a facial grimace inevitable whenever the aggravating, medium-pitched noise slammed through the Orca's passive detection systems.

Shrimp abound in the seas from the surface all the way down to the bottom of the Marianas Trench; from sea level to more than 36,000 feet down! They exist in numbers inconceivable, and they are to be found everywhere, from plankton size to prawns more than a foot in length. Their sounds are as varied as their size and species and equally unbelievable. They babble in their own acoustic language that changes according to the type of shrimp, their number and concentration, the depth, and even what that mass of shrimp might be doing at that particular time. The sonic detectors had brought to Dark and Owens the startling noise deep within the sea of thousands of frying pans in which bacon and eggs sizzled and crackled with a terrible clamor—a sound unmistakably of shrimp. The snapping shrimp also have a distinctive acoustic signature; they snap pincers together with varying speeds and intensities to produce a sonic maelstrom sounding like millions of fingernails snapping against each other. Once they had slipped Orca through a mile-long mass of shrimp; close in the sounds crashed through the sonar pickups like burning twigs. If they produced noise in a sudden community blast of shrimp, the effect was much the same as intense radio static.

Croakers give hard competition to the drumfish for honors in percussive noise; they produce an eerie staccato of sticks being pounded rapidly against a hollow log. Groupers, pompano, toadfish, sea lions, crabs, lobsters . . . they constitute the loudest members of the marine orchestration.

The Orca crewmen had once been startled by the sound of doors opening on rusty, binding hinges. Immediately after this baffling aural cry their earphones filled with high-pitched squeals and shrill whistling sounds. In amazement they studied their screens as a group of whales in loose formation sallied past the submarine. They were high enough in the water to use the television scanners under normal daylight—and in the midst of the giant mammals stared at a whale of absolute white from the huge snout to the flukes.

Drifting near the surface in the midst of cavorting porpoises was to be an acoustic witness to the swift-chattering sonar probes and "conversation" of the highly intelligent mammals. There was much more to be learned from such sounds when they could play back—at greatly reduced speed—the sounds recorded on tape. The bottle-nosed dolphins, they discovered, operated their marine sonar systems with an astounding four hundred high-frequency impulses per second. Bleats, whistling cries, quacks, sonar clicks, and even a sound remarkably like the squawk of sea gulls identified the porpoises.

The night before, shortly after the escort helicopter had swung away over the glowing ocean to return to Isla de Culebra, they had had their first opportunity to secure some extraordinary photographs. Orca was easing along slowly at a depth of fifteen hundred feet, the floor of the Nares Abyssal Plain far below, when Owens picked up a loose swarm of "something" well ahead of their course. The sonar-screen readout began to clarify its pulses' echo. After several minutes more of closing in on their target, Dark and Owens picked up a faint glow on the television screens: something well ahead of them was producing sufficient light to activate their optical systems in otherwise total blackness.

Dark stared at the dim and fuzzy outline. "Larry, you got them on your TV scope?"

"Yeah," Owens replied, "but it's a bum picture. Con, switch off your TV scope for a few moments."

"Roger; TV off."

"Okay, I want to get some light amplification in here," Owens explained. Finally he reported, "Got it. Cameras ready also, Con. You can pick up your TV now."

Dark switched on the set and stared in wonder. "Jesus," he said softly, "did you ever in your life see anything like *that?*" Owens had used light amplification to increase the contrast and clarity of the TV scanning equipment. With Orca now much closer to the marine creatures and the TV equipment adjusted, they had almost a close-up view of the things as they glided toward the submarine.

Owens did not reply immediately. "I've heard of them before," he said after a long pause. He stared hard at the screen and the still-expanding creatures that gripped their interest.

"You remember Nick Massaretti, Con?"

"Think so," Dark replied. "Wait a moment; wasn't he the guy who did all that deep photography with the Italian bathyscaphe?"

"That's the one, all right," Owens confirmed. "I spent some time with Massaretti and he once told me about some creatures he had seen. Called them glowfangs; I think that was his name for them."

"I can understand why," Dark said, shaking his head with disbelief.

"Yeah. He said no one would really believe him outside of a small group who'd also been deep. His cameras went out on him," he went on. "I think he cursed a blue streak for a week afterward when he found out he didn't get any pictures."

Dark laughed. "Let's hope that doesn't happen to us. You all set?"

"Uh huh. Just keep her steady as she goes. I want to use the black-and-white still cameras first; I'll run them on rapid sequence. Then I'll go to motion with the floods," he added. "We'll never get those things on motion color in their own light."

"Steady as she goes," Dark said, staring into the screen.

You could believe *anything* after seeing these; Massaretti used a good name. *Glowfangs . . .*

A milling swarm drifted slowly about them. A swarm of monstrous caricatures of the barracuda; nightmarish dreams come to life. The barracuda was bad enough in itself when it ran in for the kill; compared to these things, it was a playful goldfish.

The marine creatures now all about them, undisturbed by the submarine, each stretched from eight to twenty feet in length, and the larger they were, the more nightmarish were their features.

Each fish drifted slowly with huge jaws extended to their fullest; every animal within view was the same, jaws yawning wide. Within those savage mouths rows of huge razored fangs glowed with a startling light. The teeth differed from those of the barracuda with longer, more curving blade-teeth; many of them bent into the mouth, toward the throat, so that any prey captured within those bayonet-studded gleaming jaws could never escape.

Behind the gleaming mouth bayonets, the nightmare became a surrealistic parody of nature. Directly beneath the lower set of glowing fangs stretched long and slender filaments; on the larger fish they were twice the length of the animal's body—filaments drifting beneath the creature to a length of thirty to forty feet. A second group of filaments extended from the body just before the tails.

Along the ends of the filaments, both from beneath the lower jaw and the tail, glowed blue and red lights. They were so far from the body of each fish that they seemed almost to be other forms of luminescent life moving along with the monsters above them; yet there was no mistake. Both Dark and Owens saw clearly the extensions and the blue and red lights glowing at their extremities. There were also additional blue lights, amazingly symmetrical in form, running along the bodies of the glowfangs like long rows of little windows through which blue light gleamed.

Several of the things turned toward the front of the submarine, presenting to the two men a terrifying view of glowing jaws and deep mouths.

"I don't think I'll ever want to drink again," Owens muttered. "How'd you like to have the DT's and watch *that* coming at you through the walls? Good God!" He shuddered with his own thoughts.

"Never mind," Dark said dryly, "this is bad enough."

"Yeah." Owens paused while he adjusted his controls. "Okay, I'll put on the lights and get some action color. This should make a hell of a movie."

Owens tripped the front floods. Light spread through the depths before them and through the swarming glowfangs. They had only a moment to look with astonishment at dazzling iridescence as the floodlights splashed against and reflected from the bodies of the beasts. Only that moment—

"Jesus!"

Instantly the waters exploded in fury. The sudden intense eyes—the submarine floodlights—triggered an insane paroxysm among the glowfangs. Their reaction came faster than Dark would have believed possible. One moment they drifted along loosely, but the instant the lights flashed among them, they whipped into furious motion—rushing directly at the submarine.

"Look out!" The warning burst instinctively from Dark as blazing fangs rushed at them through the television screen. Reflex caused him to jerk aside from the terrifying view. A dull thud rang through the hull as the nightmarish fish crashed in open-mouthed attack against the prow of the submarine. Another huge body striking metal and glass reverberated through the structure of Orca.

Then—scraping, slashing sounds.

"Christ, Larry! Keep those cameras going!"

Owens' excited voice burst into his headset. "Am I ever, am I *ever!*" he shouted. "Look at those mothers coming in, will you? I never saw anything like—hell, they're attacking *us,* Con! They're attacking Orca!"

Dark had to steel himself against the awesome view; looking at the TV scope was the same as staring right down those monstrous rows of gleaming teeth and the dark throats beyond. It was the most fantastic experience he had ever known in the deeps: being attacked by a swarm of maddened, bayonet-toothed glowing creatures up to twenty feet long. They were perfectly safe; he'd known it all the time, even when instintcively he flung himself aside at that first explosive view of onrushing fangs.

"Listen to 'em," he said with wonder. "They're trying to chew us into little pieces." The sound of knives scraping and clawing at the metal flanks and glass ports of the floodlights had become a bedlam.

Another minute went by with the attack unabated; if anything, it was increasing in fury as distant members of the swarm responded to the sounds of their own kind in their attacking frenzy.

"Got enough film, Larry?"

"Hell, yes," Owens said quickly. "Ran through the reel. Gotta reload, anyway."

"Okay," Dark grunted. "Let's get out of here." He brought in the power to the screws; far behind them the nuclear turbines whined softly as they ran up the temperature scale. Orca surged ahead, acceleration kneading them gently into their seats. They heard tumbling and scraping sounds along the hull as the attacking beasts were brushed aside, then the bayonet teeth were clattering again as the glowfangs continued their blindly furious assault.

"Determined, ain't they?" Dark commented.

Owens laughed, a note of relief in his voice. "Yeah," he agreed. "I think I'll cut the floods and give them a flare to chew on instead of us." He shut down the lights and depressed a switch in a control panel to his left. They barely heard a slim shape leave the upper flanks of the rounded hull. Well above and now behind the speeding submarine a pyrotechnic timer went off; instantly a dazzling star erupted into being as an alloy-flare started to burn. In that intense glare, watching through the stern TV scanners, they saw flashing shapes in a great swarm tearing at the blazing thing that had invaded their domain.

That was last night; an auspicious debut for their two-day journey following the robot-directed circuitous path toward AUTEC and its bristling devices for combat simulation.

Now, eighteen hours after departing Isla de Culebra, rising and falling as the memory tapes of Brainbox demanded, they approached another unknown, the ghostly green fog pulsing on the sonar-screen display readout. The decreasing distance brought greatly improved scope definition; a few minutes later the sonar pulses showed the target no longer as ghostly fog but as individual shapes moving slowly, six thousand feet below the surface.

Owens triggered the cameras and the floodlights in a single motion. The instant the light burst through the inky blackness, the TV scopes came alive to reveal an immense school of sharks.

"There must be hundreds of them!" exclaimed Owens. "I never expected to see something like that six thousand feet down."

"Most people don't," Dark said. He studied the sharp-snouted beasts as they drifted through the artificial light. From time to time one or two sharks would turn to look at the dazzling floodlights and then continue with the rest of the school. The sonar return showed the sharks all about them, an immense gathering of the creatures. Those closest to the submarine drifted easily from its path, riding the pressure waves that pulsed through the depths ahead of Orca.

"Deepest I ever saw a shark," Dark went on slowly, "was about nineteen thousand feet."

"Oh? I thought the record depth was somewhere around thirteen," Owens said.

Dark gestured with disdain. "Forget the records, Larry," he said. "They aren't worth the paper they're written on. Those things we saw last night—the glowfangs. If we didn't get any good pictures, I guarantee that only one scientist in a thousand, maybe even less, is going to believe what we tell them. They'll attribute our story to raptures of the deep or magnification or just a good healthy imagination. Sure as shooting they won't believe us." He looked out at the sharks; hundreds had already glided past them and the end was nowhere in sight as fins and bodies continued the huge procession.

"That thing I saw at nineteen thousand—the shark, I mean," he continued. "It was, oh, maybe twenty feet long or so. That isn't too big when you consider what those things get up to in size. Old fisherman I knew—used to go out by himself for long periods—swore to me he had seen a white, the big killer, that was more than sixty or seventy feet long." Dark looked into his mirror and grinned at Owens. "Y'know something, Larry? I'm the only person ever believed that old man. Everybody else said he was confusing the whale shark—that big mountain of helpless blubber that lives off tiny fish and other small creatures—with the killer. But he wasn't; he described to me every damned detail of both types." Dark nodded slowly. "Hell, yes, I believed him. I'd seen too many things myself that no one would believe *me* about, so why should I doubt *his* word?"

He leaned back, relaxing in his contour seat, watching idly as the great shark procession began to thin. Owens switched off the floodlights and they returned to the darkness ever waiting to swallow everything that slid into the deeps. In the control deck, bathed in the soft red glow of instruments and the greenish cast of their display screens, he waited for his eyes to readapt, to compensate for the lack of illumination the floodlights had sprayed through the depths through which they moved.

The depths hid beneath a thick, pervading blanket of darkness. Only eighty-five feet beneath the surface of the sea, red light disappears from the vision of the human eye. This is the thinnest outer layers of the oceans—the first eighty-five feet out of more than thirty-six thousand feet straight down. Yet the human eye at this shallowest of liquid penetrations cannot discern the red light so common on the surface. Three hundred feet down, yellow-green fades from the resolution of our vision. Four hundred feet and the eye can see only in bluish hues. A thousand feet down, sometimes higher or lower depending upon local conditions, light vanishes for the ocean invader known as man. Some sea creatures apparently can detect the barest glow penetrating from the surface as deep as two or three thousand feet. The most sensitive photographic plates under perfect conditions detect their last dim ghosts of light at a little more than three thousand feet. Beyond that level light must be created; it must be brought down from above by man.

But even without man there is light. Bioluminescence is as much a reality of life within the deeps as are the great currents and rivers that carry millions of tons of water every second of the day and the night. The glowfangs captured on film by Dark and Owens were only one of hundreds, perhaps thousands, of beasts that produce sparkling varieties of light where the sun from time immemorial has been banished.

Iridescent flanks that reflect light appear first on the way down; fish that shine with even the faintest of light reflections make the boundary to a world of self-produced illumination. Here exists a world of colors extraordinary in their variety and richness: a world of living creatures jet black, silver, shades of brown; skins gleaming with strange beauty in green and gold and burnished copper. Crimson worms float gently in the blackness and are pounced upon by shrimp bearing coats of dazzling scarlet. Copepods of red, reddish orange, and a variety of related hues drift through waters which have never known the light of the huge star blazing in the heavens. Fish appear in cloaks of jet black; somehow these *Cyclothone* creatures are made visible to shrimps and prawns more than a foot in length, the color of freshly spilled blood, that lunge unerringly onto their prey of black within black.

The shrimp, however, are not always that tempting a morsel for the larger beasts that hunt them. Many a fish rushing against a huge shrimp finds the chase fruitless as the prey disappears behind an explosive blast of liquid fire—a smoke screen glowing intensely, a cloud of thousands of fireflies discharged by the frightened, fleeing shrimp.

Squids abound in the deeps in numbers to defy the imagination—and remind scientists that their official tomes must constantly have space for revision. A product beyond even the mind of the insane is ten-armed *Vampyro-*

teuthis infernalis, a living, heaving nightmare that should have disappeared millions of years ago but survives to this day—a living fossil-cousin of the squid and the octopus. Certain members of this species—a family extending from a beast only an inch in length to great monsters well over sixty and seventy feet from their bodies to the end of their long tentacles—also are explosively luminescent; from their bulbous bodies they eject forcefully a strange slime that instantly upon contact with the sea becomes a swiftly spreading, startling bright cloud of luminous blue.

This phenomenon is not a rare one in the deeps, where self-produced luminescence was the only kind ever known, until man came upon the scene. There are fish that hang living lights from their tails and extend antennae with brightly glowing extremities of white and red and blue just before their yawning jaws, lights with which to entice prey to come within reach of the ever-waiting fangs and rows of terrible dagger-teeth.

But the squid remains undisputed leader of liquid pyrotechnics. Certain species of the grotesque animal not only produce light within the depths but have developed to a spectacular science their biological luminescence. Prowling the seas thousands of feet from the surface, they produce light of varying intensities and also direct beams of light from their bodies! They do so by activating reflectors along their rubbery hulks to focus their glow, intensifying the beam, and then directing it in the manner of a searchlight. How and why the squid utilizes its body chemical, luciferin, in this manner is a mystery still retained within the depths, just as much as the mystery that enables the squid rapidly to change the color of his biological searchlight.

Soon they would emerge from the wonder of their two days of freedom within the deeps; the grim realism of weapons testing and combat simulation awaited them at AUTEC in the Bahamas. But for this reprieve from their realism Conan Dark was grateful. He was one of a growing but still small band of men in the world who knew and understood the liquid depths of earth, who shared the miracle of which only they truly were aware. It was as if they had been given a whole new planet, a priceless gift too long ignored.

He turned over command of the powerful submarine to Larry Owens. It was time for his sleep period.

But he did not try to sleep. Not yet. One by one he turned down the lights of his instruments and control panels. Slowly he encapsulated himself in a rich womb of no-light. He turned off everything save the TV scope. In the darkness he relaxed and drank in the miracle; he looked into the scope and his eyes took him far beyond.

Above him, lying on his back, he saw drifting off to the side, alone in the all-pervading blackness, a single existence in the liquid night.

A huge luminous spiral, glowing softly, an illuminated breathing as the light pulsed in hues of red and blue . . . his eyes followed it drifting slowly in the liquid space-black.

Beyond the spiral—sudden streaks of light. Vanishing, reappearing; spattering glows in nondimensional blackness.

He slept.

12

"All right," Owens said, "come back to four knots."

Dark eased back on the hydrojet control grip, playing the hydrofoil control surfaces in smooth coordination with the easy thrust of the jets. Fore and aft along Orca the jets whined dully as they carried the boat along under slow forward control. For more than six hours now Dark had maneuvered without the main screws, had drifted and nudged the killer submarine with the stealth of a huge predator preparing lethal confrontation with some wary enemy.

In effect this was exactly what he and Owens were doing, only their stealth—and the weariness of their opponents—was a matter of simulated rather than actual combat. On the surface of and within the vast AUTEC range a hunter-killer team was doing its best to detect, close in upon, and execute a "kill" of their maddeningly elusive prey. For Orca had proved frustrating to a point never before encountered by the men of the HUK force. Armed with ships, helicopters, planes and accompanying nuclear-attack submarines, they had been led astray by the combination of Orca's unprecedented performance and the bristling array of electronic and other devices intended to confuse, distort, and mislead the hunters. Bad enough that the weapons system that constituted Orca and its special devices had given the HUK officers shattering headaches; the submarine itself had driven them almost to despair.

For three days and nights the HUK team, its every move monitored and recorded by the equipment of the Atlantic Underwater Test and Evaluation Center, had pursued Orca with a grim determination approaching the fanatic. Time and again they seemed to have snared the killer submarine; each time they received for their pains confirmation of decoys released by Orca—and the evidence that, had the game been played for real, the submarine that never showed itself along the surface would have chewed its pursuers into mincemeat.

Soon after the tests within the AUTEC range had begun, Dark had taken the killer sub almost to the bottom of the Vema Gap. Miles above them the hunter-killer force swept the waves in patterns of detection and pursuit. The HUK officers and men knew only that they were to "have at it" with a new submarine; they knew nothing of their opponent's tremendous performance in speed and depth. And so they knew nothing of the powerful submarine that pounded through the dense water just above the floor of the Vema Gap, running in a huge circle that encompassed the entire HUK force.

"Damn, just listen to them!" Owens exulted. "They're painting a picture on the scope that's as good as sending us personal messages." He rubbed his hands with glee, watching the sonar-scope presentations while sounds poured into the submarine.

Dark shared his enthusiasm. Far above them the ships of the task force beating the waters for their elusive target poured a deafening racket into the sea. The sonars of the destroyers and the two aircraft carriers were literally boiling the sea about them from the tremendous power generated by their transducers as they hurled acoustic waves downward, hoping for the echoing return that would identify to them a target. But Orca was too far down to present a separate echo. Passive detectors obtained not so much as a liquid whisper from the submarine that now ran with the same forward speed as was maintained by the HUK force.

Suddenly, the pursuers had their target. Miles away, a sudden return of sonar pulses established an arrow pointing to the quarry deep within the sea. Throughout the HUK force the alarm flashed. Attack planes raced toward the exact area radioed to them automatically from the surface ships. Helicopters wheeled about also to close in for the "Kill."

Then, another sonar contact—a second sub! The HUK crewmen grinned at one another; they'd had this sort of trick pulled on them before. Hell, there might even be three or four subs down there! But they had them now, by God, and they would—

Two more contacts came into the Combat Information Center. Helicopters racing to the rough coordinates of the initial contacts—the datum points—hovered above the water to unreel transducer units that dropped down cables to a hundred feet beneath the surface. The moment they had—and held—a contact, a brilliant red light at the tail of the helicopter flashed rapidly to provide a visual signal of target contact to the rest of the HUK team. Aircraft dived from above to mark the datum point with smoke bombs, and then at the lowest altitude possible circled the water in daredevil turns. Now they used their MAD devices to detect the magnetic field of their quarry; the instant that an oscillogaph charting pen in the airplane swung suddenly to confirm the contact, the operator chanted "Madman! Madman!" into his radio to alert all concerned. Swiftly, then, they sought target confirmation—bearing, depth, range, and other target data. As the process went on, duplicating itself with the different target acquisitions, another aircraft flying high overhead played the role of data-transmitter. Every signal from the helicopters and planes near the waves flashed to the data plane in turn was retransmitted instantly to the Combat Information Center of the aircraft carrier that made up the center of direction for the entire HUK force. Planes, helicopters, and destroyers tearing ahead under full power raced in for the "kill."

Conan Dark and Larry Owens grinned as the tumultuous racket of detection and pursuit clattered its way down to them in Orca. Owens glanced at a digital time readout. "Well, that makes four good clean targets they've got by now, Con. Want to spring the big surprise on them?"

Dark laughed; he was enjoying his complicity with Owens. "Uh uh," he said. "Not yet. Let them get a few more contacts to drive them crazy. Then we'll give them the finale."

"Good enough," Owens replied. He thought of the frantic action far above them and sighed. "You know we're going to ruin a lot of people up there, don't you?"

"What do you mean?"

"Just think of all those poor bastards," Owens said with true sympathy, "when they start getting more target returns, and MAD systems all seem to have gone haywire, and—" He broke off to study the consoles. A huge grin split his face. "There they go," he continued. "Right on schedule."

Along the path originally coursed by Orca some oddly shaped objects released during their swift dash had gone into action. Chemical containers came to life; timers released valves to open the way to seawater under tremendous pressure. The water came in contact with the chemical substances and reacted. Huge clouds of bubbles spewed forth from the containers, rising in expanding clouds of gaseous globules that created a thick and opaque screen against which the sonar pulses from the surface ships bounced back to their excited operators. The cry of "Contact, Contact!" rang out in the combat control rooms. More chemical containers bubbled, rumbled, creaked, and grated with their froth, creating additional cries of "Contact!"

The HUK team was good. It didn't take long for them to realize that they'd been had by decoys of thick clouds of bubbles streaming noisily to the surface. Their sudden escape from pursuing the decoys was short-lived. Other targets came in: Orca's robot progeny of steam torpedoes, sound pulsers, timed chains of explosive charges, slim torpedo shapes creating powerful magnetic fields to frustrate and confound the MAD operators. Bedlam racketed through the ocean to bring groans from the sonarmen and black looks on the faces of the operations officers.

Dark listened to the squealing, clattering, thundering clamor crisscrossing the maneuvers area. Just as long as they stayed deep, there wasn't a ghost of a chance for the HUK force to find them. Owens kept a running track of the surface fleet, directing Dark, guiding the submarine through the depths almost directly beneath the center of that HUK team of teeth-grinding pursuers.

"I guess it's time, Larry," Dark said. "Let's slip it to them now."

"Goddamn," Owens chortled. "They are going to be very unhappy with us."

"Yeah. Ain't it terrible?"

They looked at each other and roared with laughter.

A round shape bobbed up and away from the submarine. It rose swiftly toward the ocean surface far above. In the midst of the acoustic uproar it was just one more of dozens of apparently spurious sonar echoes. Long minutes later it bobbed unseen among the choppy waves of the surface. A timer released a small plug and a long whip aerial extended itself above the whitecaps.

Almost at the same moment that the sharp-eyed crew of the helicopter spotted the aerial reflecting the sun another timer went into operation. Within the round shape bobbing in the waves a radio transmitter began flashing its recorded message.

Now hear this! Now hear this!

Astonished officers and men of the task force stared at

one another as the voice broke into their primary radio channels.

Officers and men of the AUTEC HUK Team Five Nine Seven Dash Six, we—

"What the hell is this!"

—greet you one and all. It is—

"Find that blasted transmitter and be quick about it!"

—our sad duty to inform you that we have you surrounded.

In the carrier's Combat Information Center a commander sucked angrily on his cigarette. He turned to his companion.

"Charlie, you know what?"

His friend looked glumly at him.

"Charlie, I think we've been had."

Far in the deeps, Conan Dark and Larry Owens roared with mirth.

In the carrier operations center all eyes turned to the plotting board. The game wasn't over—yet.

A long teardrop shape, its captain taking swift advantage of the uproar still hammering within the sea, swept toward the unsuspecting Orca.

BRAAAAAAAAANNING!

The alarm bell crashed into their ears. At the same instant red lights stabbed from their control panels.

"Bushwhacker!" Dark shouted.

Reflex brought his hands to the power controls, had him ready in the same movement to transform Orca into a living creature of movement. But he stayed his hands, scanning his screens, waiting for Owens to evaluate the clamorous warning. Both men knew even before they saw the readout display what was happening; Dark cursed his own overconfidence. No hunter-killer force worth its salt operated without a one-two punch; the HUK teams had learned their deadliest weapon was not their own detection and attack systems but a coordinated operation that set up the enemy for the *coup de grace* from *within* the seas. And he knew they had an attack sub hard after them right at this very moment; if he'd been too careless, their brand of humor could turn to ashes in his mouth.

But they weren't really sleeping at the switch; not yet. Not with the computerized legerdemain of Orca. As quickly as the alarms stabbed their danger signals to them Larry Owens was evaluating the situation flashed to his data readouts. Then he ordered the main screws shut down; Dark compiled immediately and brought in the hydrojets. There was still enough clamor within the sea to prevent the on-coming attack submarine from getting a clean sonar return that would provide positive identification of the target—Orca—they were seeking. Owens lost no time with their opportunity; electric torpedoes eased away from Orca to rise swiftly and silently. Fifteen hundred feet beneath the surface the decoy torps began to generate precisely the acoustic signature that would emanate from a nuclear submarine.

Then began the contest of wits and stealth. Had it been necessary to flee the area as a matter of survival, Orca could have slipped away without the slightest difficulty. Running under maximum power, Dark could have pulled away even from the homing torpedoes that would have been fired under true combat. But they didn't run; the idea was to find out just how much they could get away with.

Every veteran submariner knows the value of the temperature levels of the seas. With the nuclear-attack submarine thrusting toward Orca, Dark and Owens had sought out—and found—a thick cold river sliding down from the Bermuda rise. Taking advantage of the sonic bedlam still erupting from their decoys, Dark ran Orca on her hydrojets only into the cold current. He came back even more on the power and brought Orca head-on into the current—moving upstream.

The hydrojets ran almost on minimum power, just enough to keep them hovering over the same point of the ocean floor beneath them. The current ran southward with a speed of just under two knots; Dark fed in just enough power to equal the movement of the current. Thus Orca, in terms of passage over the bottom, remained in the same place.

And, quite effectively, "disappeared."

They were far deeper in the sea than the crew of the attack submarine searching for them would believe. That alone would establish a precedent of leading astray their hunters. Then, it wasn't likely that anything at great depth would "hover," especially where the technicians of the attack submarine could determine there was a powerful, wide cold current. Orca gained other advantages from the current. Its cold sponged up the sound of the hydrojets until their murmur became indistinguishable from the other whispers native to the deeps.

Finally, however, the time came to change their role and shift from the hunted to the hunter. They killed all power and Dark controlled Orca on the external control surfaces alone. Her weight carried her down, through the cold running river, deeper and deeper, until the bottom showed clearly on the screens. This far into the seas they were free to come back on power and surge ahead; the attack submarine far above them would be unable to get a clear return on its combat sweep sonar.

Low rounded hills and sweeping valleys rose about Orca; Dark maneuvered the killer sub so as to keep the hills between them and their "enemy." Any sonar pulses that reached this far down and returned to their opponents would show only the jumbled pattern of the hilly bottom.

But theirs was a contest destined to end without a final decision. Several hours later they were coming around in a long ascending path that would bring Orca into attacking position far from where they were sought by the hunter-killer task force, when abruptly an amber light flashed on both their panels.

"What the hell—?" Dark stared at the light blinking on

and off rapidly. He had never expected *this* signal. Not now; not in the midst of the AUTEC combat simulation . . .

"Larry?"

Behind him, Owens stared at the pulsating amber glow on his own panel.

"Yeah, I got it too, Con."

"What do you make of it?"

Owens shrugged. "It's legit," he replied. "I've been checking it out. It's not a spurious signal, Con. The computer ran it through. They're calling us, all right."

Dark swore slowly. He'd wanted to come busting right into the middle of that HUK task force and shake them up like—

"Oh, hell," he said, "we may as well answer the phone, I guess."

Far above them, on the orders of the AUTEC commander, a heavy metal canister had fallen from a low-flying aircraft. At the same time orders flashed to the hunter-killer team to cease immediately all sonar-sweep activity. The canister drifted lower and lower, emitting a thundering acoustic signal as it fell toward the distant bottom.

The acoustic signal was coded, programmed with a series of intermittent signals known only to a few men. And to the computer and memory banks within Orca. The pulsating message, fed into the computer, triggered a receptor and flashed the signal light that now beamed its call to Dark and Owens.

They were to break off the tests and ascend to the surface, where they were to deploy their external antenna. The message they received was brief and to the point.

"Return maximum possible speed home base."

13

Heat waves shimmered in the air above the shell-paved road curving through the thick brush. Above the tangled growth squat and utilitarian structures edged the horizon, wavering in the heat. They loomed like square-blocked igloos, nakedly white and showing salt incrustation under the blistering sun. Far to the right, radar dishes of the tracking station displayed the false colors of Base Savage on Isla de Culebra. It took a careful study of the area to see the double chain-link fences charged with powerful electricity; completely invisible to the eye were the concealed infrared and other detection devices that assured the security of the elaborately disguised submarine base. Even the small harbor lay shrouded in heavy foliage, packed thickly along the slopes of the rounded hill that lifted immediately back of the shoreline. An observer would have to be directly within the harbor, standing on the sand, to notice the high steel arches through their thick camouflage.

Conan Dark and Steve Marchant walked along the sandy beach amid fishing boats and cruisers tied to old wooden pilings. Abandoned "wrecks" lay splashed farther up the sand, bleached white, streaks of rust splaying the lighter wood surfaces. Everywhere the sun struck with oppressive heat, its effect heightened by low cumulus clouds and the stifling humidity of a falling barometer.

Marchant paused to lean against the bleached wooden ribs of an old lifeboat. He eased himself slowly to the sand to take advantage of the shadow from the wreck. Dark joined him, glad of the respite from the heat. Marchant lit a cigarette, handed one to Dark. For several minutes they sat quietly, looking at the cloud shadows that speckled the light-green waters beyond the curving beach.

Dark glanced at the captain; Marchant rested his elbows on his knees. A mood had settled over him and his feelings were reflected in his face. Ever since the previous evening, during a long dinner at the Owens' home, Jerri Stuart with them, Dark had felt that Marchant had told him only part of the reason for their emergency return to Culebra. He hadn't pushed; Steve usually had good reason for speaking in his own good time. But now Dark felt uneasy and impatient; he and Larry Owens were right in the thick of things with the AUTEC tests, and the unexpected letdown was inevitable. He knew the feeling and its cause and yet it did him little good. He wanted to bring things to a head, to extricate from the grim mood suffered by Marchant the real purpose of their return.

No sooner had he and Owens climbed from the submarine when Riedel and his team swarmed over and into Orca. The whole first team was there—Riedel, Ray Matthia, Sam Bronstein, Chuck Harper, Derek Fuller, and a slew of unfamiliar faces who descended on the submarine as if their work were all cut out and waiting for them. And Dark knew it was; intense purpose was in the air, a feeling of time being imperative and needing fulfillment with the utilization of every available minute.

Marchant bided his time to get to the crux of things; but in the biding there was enough information and new reports to create a sense of uneasiness among the others. The man famous for taking any emergency situation in his stride was becoming openly troubled, and when something unsettled Steve Marchant, it wasn't possible to confine it only to that one man.

"We're still running into blank walls," he had explained to Dark and Owens over after-dinner drinks on the Owenses' porch. "Couple of more incidents at sea. After you keep butting your skull against more and more enigmas," he said unhappily, "you can't shake off the feeling that you're being boxed, that it's the other guy who's calling all the shots. It's no good," he said with a slow shaking of his head. "You get jumpy. You get so jumpy that almost anything startles you, and after a while you're at the point where you start looking underneath your bed before you turn out the light."

He looked over his drink at the Orca crewmen. "I don't mind telling you two that it feels like we're dancing to their tune," he said candidly "Only, something has got to break, and soon, because it's building up like a plugged teakettle over a hot fire. . . ."

Steve gave them the running details of another "storm incident" in the Pacific. A major weather disturbance—a rough cyclonic form that was shy of typhoon strength but still capable of causing all sorts of trouble—had built up over a huge area that embraced Eniwetok, Bikini, and other islands in mid-Pacific. Once again there existed a situation perfectly normal in all respects; gale winds up to fifty knots and gusting to sixty or sixty-five.

"And then we started getting reports of unusual wave actions," he explained to them. "Not quite a tidal wave in the true sense of the word—and we couldn't even classify what was going on as tsunamic. For some years we've had a good working system that can pick up seismic activity and give up a quick running extrapolation of what to expect in terms of wave effects. Jerri"—he nodded at the girl—"has tied in with some scientists at the University of Hawaii on their prediction system. But at best all we can predict is the arrival time at any one point of the tsunami. We can't tell the height of the waves."

Jerri Stuart confirmed the basis of Marchant's black mood. "The Hawaii people have good experience with this sort of thing," she said. "They've dealt with tsunamic waves sixty and seventy feet rolling ashore and doing terrible damage. But what Steve is referring to"—she glanced at Marchant, who nodded for her to continue—"is that this time the pattern was—well, call it disrupted, if you want. That's as good a description as any."

"Whoa, there," Owens broke in. "You better run that past me again, honey—and slowly this time."

Jerri laughed. She shook the hair from her eyes in a gesture Conan Dark long remembered; she was getting her teeth into the subject and acting more like a scientist than the girl he—He forced his attention back to the moment.

"Many people confuse tidal with tsunamic waves, Larry," she explained. "The tsunamic wave is really a seismic sea wave; it's the direct result of an earthquake effect, for example. Umm, best examples are those that happen deep within the ocean or along a coastline. The tsunami—you could think of it as an ocean convulsion, Larry, sending out spasms—isn't at all like the popular conception of huge waves. In fact, even the biggest ones ever known can't be detected far out at sea."

He looked at her in surprise. "That's a new one," he admitted.

"Uh huh," she said. "Most people don't have any true conception of the tsunami. Look," she emphasized, "this will make it clearer . . . I mean, why people find it so hard to understand. Most people think of waves as something breaking along the shore. Breakers, huge foaming waves crashing down. Storms do build up tremendous waves, but people are accustomed to putting the two always together—high winds and great waves. The tsunami takes place almost always *without* a storm. The sea is usually calm, in fact, and then these tremendous waves start lifting out of the ocean and come roaring in over the beaches."

Her audience waited for her to continue. "A typical tsunamic wave—caused by an earthquake, let's say —travels through the sea with a speed of four to five hundred miles per hour, sometimes faster, and—"

"*How* fast?"

"I know it sounds impossible," Jerri replied to Owens' startled exclamation, "but it's true. Between four and five hundred miles per hour. Ships at sea can't even detect such waves, though." She laughed at the blank look on Owens' face. "It's a matter of wave motions, Larry. The tsunamic wave has a free wave length of hundreds of miles, but its amplitude is only several feet. This means," she hurried on at the signs of growing distress from Owens, "that it can carry a tremendous amount of momentum—and pass right beneath ships without their being aware of it. It's a pulse, Larry, well within the sea. Then, when it comes to a coastline, where the ocean bottom rises steadily, it's forced more and more to the surface. Finally it gets to the continental shelf and comes up on the beaches, where it becomes evident—it, well, it builds up now in such a way that it's forced to the surface of the water and each pulse becomes a huge wave. A fair-sized tsunamic wave is, oh, say forty feet in height above the waterline, but some of them have reached over a hundred feet."

Marchant rose to his feet and stared out into the night. "Now, the point is," he said, picking up where Jerri left off, "we had some unusual wave action during this storm. Like I said before, we haven't been able to classify it. We checked thoroughly and from the best we can make of things no seismic action has been involved. We didn't get any true tsunamic effect, either," he stressed. "But we got a surface pulse action, a series of high waves, almost like huge swells spaced out in rhythmic fashion."

He turned around to look at them directly. "Never mind those kind of details," he gestured impatiently. "The end result is that we had wave action that was not normal and couldn't be accounted for in any natural manner. And that was so severe, in fact, that we have counted at least three large merchant vessels lost during the storm."

He let the sudden silence fill the room. "So we have questions," he continued after the long pause. "How the devil could a storm like that bring on such wave action? And why should it originate at the direct center of the storm? That certainly seems normal, I grant you. But the measured effects were roughly equidistant; normal surface friction and wind effect should have given us final readings far different from what we actually found."

He returned to his seat, sighing heavily, groping for a cigarette. Jerri struck a match for him. Marchant exhaled a long plume of smoke. "We thought we had a real lock on this thing for a while, but we blew the lead. We still maintain radiological monitoring stations on all islands where we have ever held bomb tests," he explained. "But by the time we got around to taking a look at the instrument readings, it was too late."

"Hold on," Dark broke in. "It sounds like you're doubling back on yourself, Steve. First you hint you got some radiation levels or something and now you're saying it was too late to tell."

"Radioactivity?" Marchant raised his eyebrows in a sign of exasperation. "It was there, all right, Con. But we didn't get word on anything unusual about the storm until the reports of lost ships came in. You just don't lose that much shipping under those conditions. By the time we were able to query some of the survivors and got the word on the wave conditions, several days had gone by. We went after the monitoring sites, all right, and we got readings. But," he shrugged, "it was too late."

"Why?"

"Spotty; too spotty," Marchant replied. "Nothing excessive, no pattern. We tried to run it down closer, but we ended up looking at a blank wall again. The weapons people and some of the big boys from AEC made it very clear that after storms in the past—many times—they'd picked up the same kind of random checkerboard pattern of radioactivity. It could have come from debris brought up from the bottom where we'd held tests before. It could have been"—he shrugged again—"any one of a dozen possible sources."

He smiled at his own frustration. "So we went down swinging," he added. "The radioactive reports were inconclusive and they didn't help us a damned bit. Except, of course, that when you added them to the wave action, and what happened before, along the Alaskan shoreline, for example—and you remember those pictures I showed you?—*then* it made the kind of jigsaw puzzle that pointed to something."

Jerri placed her hand on Marchant's; it was a warm gesture of sympathy and understanding. For several days and nights she had been living and struggling with the problem that bedeviled Steve and his staff. Not only was she beginning to feel the effects, to suffer from the nagging suspicion that they were still being herded about and prodded by the inconclusive nature of these events, but she could now understand what Marchant had been going through for months.

"There's something else Steve hasn't told you yet," she said, turning from Marchant to face Dark and Owens. She smiled. "I think he'd better tell you himself."

They looked at Marchant, waiting.

"It's another piece of the jigsaw," he said at long last. "Like the others, it doesn't mean much by itself. Although," he brooded, "you begin to wonder if you shouldn't really be looking under the bed every night." Unable to stay seated longer than several minutes at a stretch, he heaved himself from his chair and returned to the porch railing, looking into the star-flecked night.

"We had a weather recon plane out," he continued. "We weren't looking for anything in particular; routine data collection. Compare satellite pictures against locally recorded conditions and so on. It was a P3V, and it was going in low to do some pressure trench measurements."

He cracked his knuckles and looked at Dark and Owens. "One of the boys was fast with his camera," he said. "We got a pretty clean shot of a sub."

Dark sipped at his drink. "One will get you ten it wasn't ours," he said.

Marchant stabbed a finger at him and nodded quickly "That's right," he affirmed. "It wasn't one of ours. Now—"

He paused in midsentence as the telephone rang. Betty Owens called from the living room. "It's for you, Steve."

Marchant glanced at his watch and grunted. "Good; I was waiting for this call."

He returned several minutes later. "We've got company coming," he announced. He would say no more until a car pulled into the driveway, when he went out and soon returned to the porch with a young, broad-shouldered sailor. He introduced Lars Svensen to the group and waved the youngster to a chair.

Dark studied the sailor. Even in the dim porch light one couldn't easily have missed his bulk, he was so big. But it was the way he moved that especially drew Dark's attention to the solid frame and musculature of Svensen. Then Steve Marchant brought Dark upright in his seat, listening intently to every word that followed.

"I'll make this brief," Marchant said. "Svensen, here, is a UDT man. One of the best combat swimmers in the business. Con knows what that means; he's gone the route himself. Several nights ago Lars went out with eighteen other men on a special mission into Cuban waters. The long and short of it is that we have known for some time about a secret submarine base along the southwestern coast of Cuba. Air reconnaissance hasn't been any good because it's too well covered. Intelligence has told us only that it's a base for Russian subs. That's all they have on it. We've monitored everything going in and out of there, of course, but outside of sonar pictures we don't have very much else."

He glanced at the young sailor, who listened without a flicker of emotion in his face. "So we brought a UDT team as close to the base as we could, got them to the surface on a cloudy night, and sent them in. Pictures, information; we wanted anything they could get."

Marchant paused, a cheek muscle twitching. His voice faded to just above the level of a whisper. "I told you that nineteen men went in to get that information," he said. His voice was strained.

"Lars Svensen is the only one who came back."

No one spoke. The only emotion Marchant permitted as he fought for his own control was an angry drag on his cigarette. Abruptly he turned to the sailor.

"Tell them what happened," he said.

The soft voice, the matter-of-fact tone, brought a chill through the hot and humid night. It was unreal; Dark wondered if the kid, speaking so calmly, was still somewhat in shock. He seemed to be fully in control of himself, telling the story as if he were repeating the details of an exercise. But it hadn't been anything like training. This one was for keeps.

They never got any pictures, Svensen explained. The area was mined, a superb pattern that crisscrossed the waters with battering-ram shock waves. Svensen counted at least a dozen powerboats cruising the surface, releasing explosive charges at irregular intervals. The men were slowed up by nets, harried by swift currents, and then, with the base defenses alerted, slaughtered like sheep in a pen. Helicopters joined the powerboats and churned the waters with lethal blasts that killed off the UDT men one after the other.

Svenson survived because he was the last man in; he'd just cut through a net when all hell broke loose farther up the channel. His squad leader had given him a frantic sign to get out, to get the hell away from there without wasting any time. Svensen dived to the bottom and hid beneath a large rock outcropping where the men had left one of their electric-powered personnel sleds. He didn't leave at once; he waited for someone else to get out of that charnel house. Staying down, protected and hidden beneath that rock outcropping, not moving, probably saved his life. He had plenty of reserve air tanks from the sled.

Much later, when he knew that none of the men could have any air left, and that no one would come back, he slipped away, staying on the bottom. He made it back to the waiting submarine, exhausted, more dead than alive. The sub commander gambled on a heavy rainstorm during the first signs of daybreak and eased above the wind-whipped waves. As soon as the crew had dragged Svensen into the sub, they ran for it. They had brought nineteen men in and they were taking one out.

There was more to it, Marchant told them as the night wore on. They knew, of course, that the Russians had put together an extraodrinarily alert, deep, and effective defense on that base. Marchant's crack team was still playing chess with the giant Whirlwind computer in the basement of the National Security Agency at Fort Meade, trying to tie together the loose ends of cobwebs that always led to nowhere.

Marchant gave them the details of the spectacular space blast fifty thousand miles beyond the moon. He left Dark and Owens speechless when he added that the AEC had confirmed the yield of that "device," whatever it was, at over a gigaton.

The Air Force hadn't helped them any when they sat down for a high-level meeting with the different services to try to second-guess the blast. The Air Force didn't like the whole thing; they champed at the bit. All they could see—"and I couldn't blame them, either," Marchant admitted—was the power of the booster that could carry such a payload to escape velocity. The Air Force officers at the meeting waved away any connections between that explosion of a billion tons yield and the problems bedeviling Marchant. It was their opinion, and it was hard to contest, that the Russians under their thin disguise of flying a nuclear space drive had actually tested a bomb to be utilized in possible future war. One such bomb, said an Air Force scientist with a worried expression on his face, detonated at an altitude of between 70 and 110 miles, could set several of our eastern states aflame. The thermal effect from such a weapon in just a few seconds, he warned, would burn almost every flammable object exposed to that fireball.

"All of New England could go," he said in a calm voice that sent cold chills down Marchant's back.

Now, sitting in the shade of the abandoned lifeboat, Marchant flipped away his cigarette. He watched the smoke curl lightly where the butt smoldered. Beyond their narrow strip of shadow the sun flailed the sand and the beach.

"There's more to it, you know," Marchant said abruptly.

Dark nodded. Resting on his elbows, he looked out across the water. He didn't turn to look at Marchant. "I figured there was," he said. "Sounds as if it all comes up front now."

"Yeah," Marchant said heavily. "*Now* always catches up to you no matter how fast you run."

He fished for a fresh cigarette, lit up. "I waited to give you the rest of it, Con," he said slowly, "because I wanted everything from last night to settle down inside your mind. I didn't want it coming at you all of a sudden." He turned to Dark, his eyes showing a need for understanding.

"Go on," Dark urged.

"You know Arnold Bowden, don't you?"

"Arnie? Sure," Dark flashed a smile. "One of the best sub men ever lived. Hell of a guy, too. Why?"

"You know his latest assignment, Con?"

"He told me about it couple of months ago, Steve," Dark

said quickly. "He was so tickled pink he was walking on air. Getting the *Charger* was his dream come true. You know what I mean, Steve; having the hottest attack boat in the Navy for your command is—"

He broke off suddenly. The muscle in Marchant's cheek had become a thing alive, twitching and quivering. Marchant's lips were white, pressed tightly together.

"Spill it, goddamn it!" Dark shouted.

"We lost her," Marchant said hoarsely. "We lost her with all hands."

He heard the words, he knew it was true, it had happened. Arnie Bowden . . . he'd known Arnie since they were kids. Christ to hell and back; not Arnie! He knew it, but he just couldn't accept it. It refused to sink in, to make itself stick.

He didn't know he was crying until the tears dripped wetly from his face onto his hands. And it was not until several minutes later that he realized dimly—and was grateful for it—why Steve had waited until now, and here, to tell him.

Steve gave him a few minutes and then he was again Capt. Stephen S. Marchant, United States Navy. With a frustrating, stinking mystery on his hands that swiftly was reaping a staggering toll of lives. Marchant kept it tight and to the point; he didn't embellish what the Navy knew. They didn't know much, either.

Charger was the latest in her line, a swift attack boat of nearly three thousand tons, with a crew of fifty-six. She was a powerhouse of nuclear energy and electronics, packing into her teardrop shape everything science and industry could devise. *Charger* was just about the limit of performance for her class; she could take the pressure of three thousand feet and she could ram her way through that depth with a speed of more than sixty knots. And she bristled with every weapon known to naval science for the destruction of enemy submarines.

For nearly two weeks, Steve told him, *Charger* had shadowed a mystery target in the mid-Atlantic. Throughout that period Arnold Bowden kept the submarine deep, collecting sonar data, sliding through the deeps like a ghost of the unknown vessel. Every day Bowden sent in a report. *Charger* released a buoy that went to the surface. Twelve hours later, far behind the submarine, the buoy extended its radio antenna and waited to be activated by command signal from a military comsat orbiting within line-of-sight range. A rapid-burst transmission of the coded message flashed to the satellite, was confirmed by the robot devices, and the buoy received its remote command to sink itself.

"Ten days ago we failed to get the expected report. We didn't sweat it for a while," Marchant explained. "Anything could have blocked the transmission. The buoy could have failed; Bowden might have thought it best at the moment not to release the thing; the satellite might not have picked up the message—anything. It happens often enough. But when we missed the report three consecutive times, we knew something had gone wrong.

"The next day search planes spotted some debris. You can figure out the rest of it," he said. His voice grated; the strain was showing again. "We confirmed it from the wreckage we picked up. Breakup and destruction; it was all there in the few pieces we managed to get back.

"But how in the name of heaven it could have happened . . ." He beat his fist slowly against his knee, his lips white where he pressed the flesh tightly against his teeth.

"I'm official now, Con." He smiled coldly. "We call it Whip—Project Whip. Full authority and all that crap; right down from the White House. I've been given the job above the board.

"They want the answers. To a lot of things. About *Charger*, and that star the Russians set off beyond the moon, and the tidal wave, and the rest of the goddamned pieces to the puzzle."

Of a sudden his voice hardened. "That's why I called you back, Con," he said, unnecessarily. "Your boat will be ready in about eighteen hours or so. And I have your new orders. Orca will carry full armament. Everything will be aboard; nukes, also.

"You and Larry will take Orca to the last reported position of *Charger*, Con. We've already got boats out there. But no one can get down deep enough. It's right along the Mid-Atlantic Ridge. The currents are hell; we can't use the bathyscaphes or any of the research subs. They can't take it. But we know where to look, and you're going to look."

He stared into Dark's eyes. "I want you to find out what happened down there, Con. I want you to find out how they killed Arnie Bowden and his crew. I want you to do that. For *me*," he said coldly, "as well as the damned Navy."

Riedel and his technicians were working through the night. Orca wouldn't be ready to move out through the tunnel until at least ten o'clock the next morning. Marchant told him they were going to break the long-standing rule of never permitting the killer sub to move in or out of the hidden cavern in daylight; there would be a solid air cover of planes and helicopters to assure a clear path to where they could take her down deep, into the waters of the Nares Abyssal Plain.

But that was tomorrow morning; he had tonight. He had the early evening and the whole damned night and he didn't want to talk about *Charger* or think about Arnie Bowden or the men who'd gone down to the sea for the last time. He'd had the Russians and everything else up to his nose and for these precious hours he didn't want a goddamned thing to do with any of it. He'd be face to face and in the thick of it all soon enough.

He loaded a jeep with scuba gear for himself and Jerri, and packed a small refrigerator with steaks and beer. He picked her up an hour before sunset and they drove to a secluded section of the beach. There was little enough on the island that could be considered private; security had Isla de Culebra locked up tight as a drum. He called the security officer and told him where he and Jerri would be that night and would he please stick his goddamned nose anywhere else but that strip of beach? The man on the other end of the line had heard about *Charger* and he knew that Arnold Bowden and Conan Dark had been kids together; it was his job to know such things and he assured Dark that security would be somewhat more than discreet that night.

He didn't want to eat right away; the hunger had balled into a small knot in the pit of his stomach and the thought of food revolted him. He lay in the sand with Jerri, watching the sun expand into a huge flattened shape of fire and sink into the waves. She sat beside him, her sensitive fingers stroking his body gently. The moon rose early, and finally he sat with her, not speaking. Together they watched the moon sliding higher into the sky. It was clear now, the clouds gone, and the pale silver filled the heavens and rippled a ghostly highway across the ocean toward them. They sat with their fingers together; Jerri had once said to him that fingers spoke for people.

That was it.

Holding hands is braille for the sighted.

She'd said it a long time ago and it wasn't until this moment that he'd really understood what she meant. Through the pain and the grateful silence, the presence she gave to him, he knew that no matter where his thoughts had wandered before, he was in love with Jerri.

Finally he rose and they slipped into their scuba gear. The urge to melt into the sea had become a rising clamor in his mind. He felt compelled to ease his way beneath the surface, not wrapped in a huge metal monster, but of and with his own self; he wanted Jerri with him, sharing his compulsion. Without the words being said, he knew she understood.

The warm sea closed gently about their bodies. With gentle thrusting from their feet they swam away from the shore, going out to meet the moon beneath the waves.

He knew his decision was right. The hardness within him began to diffuse, to leave him like cold gray fog retreating before a warmth beginning deep inside him and then spreading slowly throughout his body and his limbs.

Far out from the shore they drifted close to one another, their bodies touching, looking upward at the miracle of the moment. They couldn't see the moon; the ocean barred the view of the distant orb with a shimmering refraction. But here was no mistaking the silver gleam that spilled a quarter of a million miles down space to spray into the ocean through which they floated. It was a strange, otherworldly scene, looking at a source of light at the far end of a rippled and distorted track, a silver floodlight threading its way through rough-dimpled glass.

Then the water cleared and the rippled distortion calmed; despite the refraction and bending, the gentle silver light, at the end of the tunnel through which they looked, floated and danced, an eyes-closed mental picture of a liquid moon, irregularly formed, moving with inexplicable in-and-out focusing, motions that defied careful scrutiny but that must be gazed upon as a complete shimmering canvas. Time and again the formless shape vanished and impossibly, simultaneously, appeared elsewhere.

They swam in a languorous slow motion toward the beach. Above the water a breeze quickened suddenly, tossed the surface into waves. With undisguised wonder they slowed their limbs, suspended themselves in liquid space to look upward. Moonlight flickered magically in a dancing of silver elves about the roof of their world. Cathedral beams of silver embraced them in ghostly pale gossamer; as quickly as the distant-near quicksilver kissed their bodies it flickered from existence, reappeared again—far away and close, all about them, behind them.

Hand in hand they swam through their cathedral within the sea.

14

Conan Dark held the killer submarine in a wide and slow circling descent into the deeps. They were already passing through three thousand feet and going down steadily in their sweep pattern. On the surface three ships heaved to in support of the grim search mission for the lost submarine. Her deck loaded with helicopters, the attack carrier *Cranshaw* held position almost directly over the sonar-estimated position of *Charger*. Farther out were the oceanographic research vessels *Argonaut* and *Silas Bent*. All three ships had lowered transducers to a hundred feet beneath the surface and were maintaining a careful sonar track and triangulation of the descending Orca. A huge swing-arm crane extended over the side of the carrier, unreeling a thick cable supporting a bulky communications unit and antenna.

Orca was pushing her way to the treacherous spiny backbone of the great Mid-Atlantic Ridge. The currents spilling away from the jagged peaks and slopes of the submerged mountain range were so severe that the Navy had abandoned hopes for using research submersibles in the hunt for *Charger*. The severity of the deep-water turbulence exceeded the control responses of the research craft; Orca's performance and versatility in the deeps and the killer subs' tremendous structural strength were invaluable for the task.

The first shocks came as gentle slaps against the hull.

Dark frowned as the tremors passed through the submarine's structure; he was picking them up in their shock-mounted spherical control room. And that meant it was going to be quite a party down there. They were nearly four thousand feet down in the wide-circling descent when a sledge hammer struck near the stern.

"Damn! Where did that come from?" Owens shouted, gripping his armrests. Orca heeled over, sluing clumsily as Dark fought her back under control. The stern had brushed a sudden downrush of cold water that casually booted the heavy submarine aside. Dark rode her like a fighter plane, treading expertly on the foot controls, both hands sensitive on power and the control grip.

"Larry!"

"Yeah; you got any more surprises?"

Dark laughed. "Get your helmet on before we hit a few more of those things," he said.

He heard Owens grunt as he reached behind him to slide open his equipment locker. The sounds of electrical jacks being snapped together crackled in his headset.

"Right, Con," Owens confirmed. "Helmet and strapped in."

"Okay. Take over for a minute, will you? I want to get squared away up here."

"Right." A pause as Owens switched to dual control. Dark felt the grip shake slightly under his fingers. "Got it," Owens said.

Dark released the controls and hauled his own crash helmet from its storage locker. He placed the protective garb over his head, plugged in the communications jacks, and snapped the chin-guard straps. If this became as rough as it promised to be, well . . . He drew the shoulder straps down over the front of his body and hooked them into the seat belt. He released the inertial reel clutch; he could move forward with ease to control Orca or adjust any of his consoles. But if the submarine went through a violent movement and he was snapped forward, the acceleration of that movement would engage and lock the inertial reel to keep his face from slamming into metal. He checked out the equipment and grasped the controls.

"Okay, Larry, I've got it." He moved the stick slightly from side to side to shake it in Owens' hand behind him.

"Roger. All yours," came the response.

Their headsets crackled. "Larry, you field the calls from upstairs," Dark directed Owens. "It may get a bit hairy down here and I don't want to be bothered with any long conversations."

Owens switched back to his transceiver. "Ascot One, we will be at four thousand in several minutes. We'll level off and hold; we'll give you a call then. Over."

"Very good, Bandit. Please stay open channel at all times. Over."

"Okay; will do. Over and out."

The bottom fell out of the ocean beneath them. A tremendous surge of icy water threw the bow high, mashed the submarine around in a sickening yaw. Dark came in fast with the power, riding the motions, fighting the tremendous downward rush of the current. He brought her out of it by using all his experience and skill.

No sooner were they level when another heavy, thudding blow tried to spin them the other way.

"Son of a bitch!" Dark cried out.

Larry Owens cinched tighter his lap and shoulder harness. "My sentiments exactly," he muttered.

He knew it was going to get worse.

The submerged surface of our world is a grotesque fracturing of planetary scar tissue. For thousands of miles the ocean beds are split and wrinkled, tossed with seamounts, guyots, cliffs, and other upthrusts, a cacophony of terrestrial upheavals speared and slashed with bulging splits and fissures. Between North America, Central America, and South America to the west, Europe and Africa to the east, there runs the massive bulk and length of the Mid-

Atlantic Ridge. This serpentine wall of mountains is a global spinal column flexing and winding its path from Iceland south across nearly half the planet to the mountains of Antarctica. The ridge stands three to nine thousand feet above its adjacent ocean basins and snakes its way generally in the center of the Atlantic, slicing the ocean floor between the curving continental shorelines to east and west. It is a paradox of planetary structure, the longest mountain range anywhere on earth; yet it is almost wholly submerged, giving birth to a scant number of islands that break the surface of the ocean. North of the equator these are best represented by the Azores Plateau and the St. Peter and St. Paul Rocks; the western islands of the Azores rise from the very backbone of the Mid-Atlantic Ridge. For to the south, where the ridge slices northwest-southwest, the St. Peter and St. Paul Rocks break the waves as an actual upthrust of the ridge's upper peaks.

This single mountain chain, fourteen thousand miles along its serpentine length, at places is six hundred miles in width. The entire Mid-Atlantic Ridge appears to be the frozen result of terrible forces that once racked the planet. Running down its crest line, almost directly to the point where the highest peaks thrust upward, is a monstrous fissure. The Mid-Atlantic Rift, canyonlike in its structure, runs from the northern end of the ridge to the far southern area where finally it begins to lose its identity in a tumbled, broken mass. The fissure itself plunges as much as two miles down into the center-backbone of the ridge's curving mass; at various places along the chain of mountains the rift spans to a yawning gap of a width of thirty miles.

The flanks of the ridge running east and west degenerate into the abyssal hills, which are neither mountains, true hills, nor plains. They form a roughly mounded sea bottom of sufficient irregularity and distortion to demand extreme caution from any craft edging into their vicinity. If a comparison might be judged accurate, the abyssal hills would be the oceanic equivalents of the Badlands of the Dakotas.

In the North Atlantic especially they extend to either side of the ridge as flanks of the steeper, rugged central mountain spine. As they extend farther out from the ridge proper, the abyssal hills degenerate into the abyssal plains of organic ooze and silts.

Approximately at latitude 45 degrees west and longitude 25 degrees north, the Mid-Atlantic Ridge suffers an abrupt convolution, as if a spasm had racked the mountainous spinal column and twisted it savagely out of shape. The rift that separates the backbone of the mountain chain is itself torn and ripped. Two separate ranges loom upward from the bottom; the chasm that divides the two is a nightmarish residue of global derangement. Loose rock, jagged spires, swift and dangerous currents create a terror of unpredictable conditions. It was the kind of deep-sea terrain into which not even Orca could plunge with carelessness.

It was here, on some undersea mountain shelf or in a craggy rampart of the shattered mountain spine, that *Charger* lay. Into these waters Conan Dark and Larry Owens probed with their powerful—yet vulnerable—submarine, searching for the torn remains of *Charger* and her fifty-six men.

"Jesus, Con! How much worse can this get?"

Dark was beginning to feel the same misgivings as Owens. At six thousand feet, barely a thousand feet above the jagged spires thrusting upward from below them, the depths had become a churning madhouse. Unseen currents rushed away from distant collisions with the masses of rock below, breaking into twisting tributaries that swirled upward from the Mid-Atlantic Ridge. Orca was pushing her way through such an intertwining series of rivers pounding through the ocean. They were taking heavy forces from different directions, simultaneously, along different parts of the submarine. The temperature changes made matters worse with Orca slipping into the temperatures normal for their depth, only moments later to encounter a channel of icy water that gave them unexpected buoyancy. Charting their path had become impossible in the turbulence that worsened steadily.

Perspiration matted Dark's hair beneath his crash helmet. Owens had gone to near maximum on their air-conditioning system; in a short break of passing the controls to Owens, Dark had pulled on a pair of gloves to keep his hands from slipping on the controls. He wasn't maneuvering the submarine any longer; he was fighting the black elements about them. And he knew a growing concern that it might prove impossible to complete their assignment. Never in all his years of moving through the depths had he encountered a sustained mauling such as they were going through right now.

"Larry."

"Go ahead, Con."

Dark noticed a strain in Owens' voice he had never heard before. His brow creased; he—hell, no time for that now.

"Tell them upstairs I'm reducing speed," Dark said. "I am going to—*damn!*" He fought a violent lurching of the submarine, unable to talk for the moment. "Tell 'em I'm bringing in the jets," he continued. "We've got to have additional control and that's all there is to it."

"R-right, Con."

What the hell's wrong with Larry? His voice almost sounds as if it's . . . oh, Christ, this would shake anyone up.

He heard Owens talking with Ascot One. Their communications were going to hell on them. Whatever were the techniques for hydronic radiations, the turbulence about them was affecting their ability to receive clearly from *Cranshaw* on the surface. Dark didn't want to think about anything except the immediate moment. He peered at the sonar screen, watching the jagged profile of the peaks below them. He was sure—no, almost certain, but not quite, that he could pick out the brighter echo of *Charger's* hull. But in this damned water he just couldn't be *that* sure.

And this was no time to go blundering around in these currents.

"Con, I can hardly read Ascot One," Owens said, his voice unhappy. "They keep breaking up on me. I'm getting only one word out of three from them."

Dark frowned. Damn, they would need some sort of guidance from above the way things were going.

"What do they think is wrong?"

"They don't know," Owens gasped as the bow slammed suddenly to the left. "Think it's got something to do with the antenna system, and—"

Clang!

"What in the name of blue Jesus was th——"

A metal snake scraped and slithered loudly across their stern. The bow pitched down in a harsh jerking motion; again they heard—felt—the metallic blow, a sudden steel whip against the hull.

"There's the goddamned thing," Dark shouted angrily. "It's that antenna of ours . . . it's whipping around like it was alive. For Christ's sake, we can't keep it out like that! We'll lose it for sure."

"It's not going to do the hull any good either," muttered Owens. "Should we reel it in, Con?"

"Tell *Cranshaw* to expect a break in communications from us at any time," Dark ordered. "But until then, ask 'em to keep feeding us coordinates. I'm not too sure of our position any longer. Goddamned scope looks like it's snowing out there."

He heard a harsh laugh from Owens. Then Larry was trying to get his message through to the attack carrier on the surface. Abruptly he heard him repeating the carrier's call sign.

"Come in, Ascot! Bandit calling Ascot One, Bandit calling Ascot One! Do you read us? Over!"

Only a slight hissing in their headsets.

"Come in, Ascot! Do you read us? Do you read us? Ascot One from Bandit! Do you—"

Owens' hand slammed down on the transceiver switch. "It's no use," he shouted angrily. "We've lost them for sure. I got a few words about the cable snapping around badly. Con, it sounds as if the cable couldn't take it any more, and—"

He drew in his breath suddenly.

"Con! They were right over us with that thing!" he cried.

He didn't need to say any more. That communications unit with its antenna weighed several tons, and he didn't have a doubt in his mind but that the wild lashing of the unit had snapped the cable. It could be coming down right on top of them and if it was caught in a current and swept against their hull . . .

"Hang on!" he called to Owens. At the same moment his hand slammed full power to the main screws. The servomotors whined loudly as they retracted the hydrojets; feeling the sudden buildup in pressure from their speed, automatic load sensors cut in to shut down the jets and haul them back within the hull. Dark didn't care if the damn things tore loose; he just wanted the hell out of there, away from whatever might be coming down from—

"Left dive! Left dive!"

Owens' voice burst into his ears. Dark didn't think, didn't take a moment to ponder the shouted, desperate cry. He slammed down Orca's bow, brought her around in a diving turn to the left.

Braaaannng!

The alarm . . . anything close to them kicked in the alarm automatically. That thing from the carrier; that *must* be it, and—

"It—it missed. It's all r-right, now, Con."

Larry's voice sounded hollow, terribly subdued. Con couldn't blame him. He knew now that Owens had gone to upper scan, searching the waters above them just in case that long cable from the carrier had snapped. It had; there might not have been enough time to accelerate away from that thing on the way down if he'd waited until the automatic alarm banged its message at them.

Owens might well have saved Orca from serious damage. Perhaps worse.

Dark studied the scope, searching for the finger needles of rock reaching up. They were almost at seven thousand and he was fast, too damned fast. He brought up the bow, killed their descent and eased into a slow lifting motion. Not until this moment did he notice the ceaseless hammer blows against the hull; there'd been no time to notice anything but getting out from under as the communications unit slid past them toward the bottom.

He came back on the power and brought in the hydrojets once more. Immediately he felt the increased responsiveness of the killer sub. He forced his attention back to their mission.

"Larry, what do you make of it? Can you get a sonar reading on *Charger?*"

For several moments Owens didn't answer. Dark watched his TV scope come to life as Owens switched on the floods. But he couldn't see much. The water was murky, swirling so badly it fouled their optical vision. The sonar didn't do much better; the lines were wavering and every now and then they broke up, merging uselessly before they cleared.

"What about the ladar, Con? Want to give that a try?"

Dark shook his head. "No go, Larry. They'd tear right off their wires before we could do a thing about it."

He chewed his lip, his hands and feet instinctive on the controls. He'd reduced their speed to where Orca came around quickly to his control commands. But this wasn't helping them. They couldn't get close enough to *Charger* this way to find out what had happened. They couldn't even be sure the sonar screen was giving them an accurate picture, that what they saw *was* the lost submarine instead of some rock outcropping.

"I think we'd better go to flares, Con," Owens said

finally. "I'm pretty sure I've got a sonar lock on *Charger*. I've been running through different modes; it's got to be her."

"Okay. How do you want to handle it?"

"Main water flow is from our right and to our left," Owens said. "I think we should try to make it over to the right—about zero four zero degrees, maybe two hundred yards or so. Then start around in a sweep to the right, almost a three-sixty turn and descending. I think the sub's about three hundred yards below us right now. On the way down, in the turn, Con, I can release a string of flares. By the time they're carried along and we come about, we should be just about the level of *Charger*. The flares should light things up pretty good."

Dark didn't consider anything more than he'd received from Owens. Larry could handle the navigation and direction of a sub better than any man he'd ever known. Something had bugged Larry before; there'd been the first wavering signs. But whatever it was he seemed to have grabbed it and held it under control.

"Okay, sailor," Dark replied. "I'll start down now." He brought the bow down and began a timed instrument turn, Owens monitoring his every move.

"When we come around," Owens warned, "be ready to back off with the jets. We're going to be coming in pretty close to what appears to be a hell of a straight drop. It's almost a vertical wall. Best I can make out," he said slowly, "the sub is caught right on the edge of the wall. Probably the hull is jammed or locked in. But you've got to watch it real tight, Con. We can get caught and dragged in with the downcurrents that will be spilling off the cliffs."

"Okay." Dark didn't need to say any more at this point. He watched lights coming on across his auxiliary panel as Owens prepared the cameras, flare releases, and the equipment with which they hoped to get some sort of record of what had happened to *Charger*.

He came through the wide descending turn; he felt the flares releasing from their tubes. They would break up and away from them, eight dazzling globes. If they stayed long enough in position . . . *if*. They could get an eyeball view of *Charger* through the TV screens and Larry would have the cameras moving.

"That's it," Owens said softly. "You're right on the money, Con. Keep her coming around just as you are." He paused. "Thirty seconds to flare ignition."

Dark brought Orca about smartly, playing the controls and the hydrojets with concerted movement. They were close enough now, out of the worst of the turbulence flailing the waters above them, higher up to the edges of the huge cliffs looming alongside Orca.

Light exploded silently. The broken line of flares spilled a savage glare through the turbulence and the inky blackness. Dark held Orca steady, her bow toward the sonar target centered on the scope.

Dead ahead lay *Charger*.

"Holy Jesus. Look at her . . ."

The words spilled unbidden, softly, from Owens' lips. His voice broke, choking him.

Dark froze, his breath stopped. Under the intense flickering light, *Charger* lay mortally wounded, her bow jutting over the edge of the sheer cliff where the rocks had caught and held her. Along that smooth rounded shape—what had been a smooth shape, Dark reminded himself with a sick and helpless anger—the depths had punched in the steel, crumpled the mighty vessel as strong fingers would squeeze and crumple an empty beer can.

They found what they were looking for, what they knew they must find. Forward along the hull; two terrible burns that had holed the steel, punched into her innards, opened the way to the ocean waiting to finish what explosive fire began.

What happened to those men must have been terrifying.

Orca was a creature of the deeps, designed to take everything the lowest levels of the oceans could bear upon her structure, but *Charger*, like every other submarine ever built, was still an intruder. Despite her great strength and her advanced design, her element extended only so far into the oceans and not one foot beyond. There is an absolute that is reached; insofar as hull integrity is concerned, danger is never more than a whisper away.

That's all; it is not even the weight of the last straw that could break her back. Just a whisper of a blow. And when there is a margin for safety, the whisper becomes a thundering roar in the form of two homing torps slicing in for the kill. Coming in, screws pounding through the deeps like the thunder of Judgment Day, happening so fast, so unexpectedly, that in those last sickening moments you know there isn't a blessed, sweet thing you can do about it except know you're going to die.

The omnipresence of the god Pressure. Both Dark and Owens had been deep within the sea many times in the nuclear boats. They had been there enough not simply to know, but to have lived with pressure. It is a living thing; a wild and terrible creature that gives no quarter, that knows nothing of mercy. Mindless, ultimately persistent, always it claws and hammers and slobbers away just beyond the thickness of the hull. Pressure so vast that a minute leak is rammed into the vessel with the cutting force of a huge spinning razor that can decapitate a man. Instantly, with all the precision of a surgeon.

Pressure . . . it weighs as heavily on the senses as it does on the hull. The enemy; oppressive, smothering, choking, squeezing away life.

A vast and mighty implosion; an ocean pouncing, not on—*within*.

But *Charger* didn't just die.

It was murder.

Dark thought of Arnie Bowden and fifty-five other men,

and he didn't want to think of it any more. But he knew he would, for a long time to come. It was burned into his eyes and his mind.

"Holy Mother of God . . ."

Startled, Dark looked up, into his mirror. Larry had his head thrown back against his seat, his eyes squeezed tightly shut. The blood had drained from his face. Chalk white, unaware, he mumbled with the fear that had swept into him on seeing the broken remains of *Charger*. His thoughts came unbidden to his lips, whispered into Dark's ears.

". . . never forget . . . never . . . that diver at . . . over a hundred feet down . . . current slammed him against rock . . . again and again and again and again . . . slammed him . . . water tore into suit . . . oh, God . . . the smoke, the gray smoke in the water . . ."

Dark sat there, helpless, as the whimpers crawled through his earphones.

". . . wasn't smoke . . . blood, his blood . . . water squeezed him, squeezed and squeezed and squeezed . . . the pressure . . . crushed him . . . all jelly . . . a blob . . . we tried; we tried and tried . . . all red . . . looked like jam in the suit . . . buried him that way . . ."

Dark never felt the current until it boomed into Orca. Desperately he threw power to the submarine as it was swept toward the great cliff and the pinnacles of rock. They weren't going to make it. . . .

"Larry! Hang on; hang on!"

The guidance ring around the screws took the blow. Orca shuddered through her length. Dark felt the guidance ring tearing, breaking up. But it took the blow, absorbed the impact. He swung the submarine away, got free of the current trying to slam them again against the great cliffs. Orca pulled around, fighting the current, winning.

It was a Pyrrhic victory.

Thunder grew swiftly all about them. A deep rumbling came from above. Then a groan, a monstrous sawing bass sound. Immediately after the cracking impact of shock waves the cliff collapsed, began to slide.

They were directly beneath the avalanche as the face of the mountain fell away.

15

It was like being caught beneath Niagara Falls. The shock waves hit them in repeated hammer blows, a staccato drumfire crackling along the hull from bow to stern. There was no place to run; in an instant the fury of the disaster swept over and beyond them. The entire face of the cliff was sliding away in a monstrous, rolling rumble that vibrated the depths. Sheets of rock and a rain of boulders and debris erupted out and downward. With each new spasm from the collapsing mountain a huge pressure wave bulled outward, enveloping the submarine and rolling it violently from side to side.

They didn't know what had happened to *Charger*. For all they could tell, the mass of the shattered wreckage might even then be rolling down on top of them.

Despite the fear that assailed Larry Owens, the cry of warning from Dark had jerked him back to reality. Dark didn't know how his friend was faring—he had no time for anything but the controls—but abruptly the forward floods burst into existence and the television scanning screens came alive. It was a terrifying sight; the water fairly boiled with the shocks tearing outward from the great rock masses crumbling and falling away. Rocky debris pulsed through the bizarre scene like shrapnel from bursting fireworks.

Buckshot pounded against the hull. At any moment they might take a blow that would cripple them. Dark's thoughts raced furiously. He couldn't throw the power to Orca and run for it; that could do more harm than good. And if he tried to ascend, it might be compounding what was already a lethal situation. He could take them headlong into a massive boulder where their own ascending speed would crack them open like a brittle eggshell.

"Larry," he gasped out as the boat corkscrewed wildly, "I'm going to try to ride her down, to go with this stuff!"

He twisted savagely at the hydrojet controls to push Orca down in flat attitude. He was desperate to keep the boat horizontal, to maintain control as best he could, while the jets thrust them along in this fashion. The ominous cracking and thudding sounds against the hull continued. If he could kill all forward motion, they would be able to ride out the worst of the sea avalanche thundering about them. He might even be able to speed up, to get ahead of the lethal clouds through which they descended; if he could do that, there would be a chance to bring in the power to the screws and break free. The guidance ring around the screws was gone—the warning lights flashing repeatedly on the screen, an idiot glow repeating its shrill optical message, made that quite clear. But it didn't matter just so long as he could get thrust from the screws when he needed it.

It would help if he could see . . . the jets were at maximum thrust, ramming them downward, building up a strange rolling sense of buoyancy as they descended steadily. The TV screens weren't any help. The water was so turbulent and roiled so violently that nothing that came to view was of the slightest aid.

Another savage blow . . . Worst of all were the overwhelming pressure waves. They rolled Orca wildly, as if the submarine were a log spinning under spiked boots. The fast motions made their heads snap from side to side, pounding painful blows into their skulls, and bruising muscles. If they hadn't secured those lap and shoulder harnesses . . . Even at that the pummeling was brutal. Several times Dark and Owens felt their helmets thud against their seats; once Dark was hurled to the side so violently that in spite of the straps holding him his helmet cracked painfully against a console. Without that crash padding he knew he would have split his skull.

Again and again the pressure waves flipped and rolled them, Dark fighting them every foot of the way.

He was like a man suffering from blindness. They got nothing back from the sonar, and the floodlights showed them only the furious boiling of the deeps. To Conan Dark the entire world had fused into one panel before his eyes, the gyroscopic representations of movement relating to the downward pull of gravity through the seas. He flew, literally, as a pilot must fly when he loses all reference to the horizon, when he is shut off from visual contact with the normal world. He scanned the artificial horizon, a gyroscopic earth sealed within the face of the instrument before him, relating the artificial senses of up and down and rolling from side to side. A small glowing bar against the spherical earth allowed him to "see" the position and attitude of Orca relative to that artificial-real world, allowed him to retain his senses of keeping the submarine parallel to the gravity surface of the planet. He dared not trust the instruments that told him of depth or their rate of descent; the violent motions tearing at Orca were certain to have affected the gauges so that they were unreliable.

"Con! Con, do you hear me! Answer me, for Christ's sake!"

He realized Larry was shouting at him, repeating his name. The sudden burst of Owens' voice into his consciousness startled him.

"Yeah, I read you," Dark called into his microphone.

"I—I've got bottom sonar working," Owens shouted,

fighting for breath control as they continued to be slammed about within their harnesses.

"Christ, that's the first good news that—"

"Listen to me, damn it! I'm getting a strong bottom echo, Con! We can't keep this up much longer." A violent rolling motion made Owens gasp, cutting off his words. Dark heard him gasping for air. "It—it's hard to tell. I think the bottom is only a couple hundred feet below us . . . *We've got to break out of here now!*"

Overload warning lights turned their control panels into strings of flashing Christmas ornaments. Not even Orca could take much more. Larry's right, damn it . . . if we hit bottom like this, we may be caught right underneath the whole blasted mess coming down on top of us.

"Okay, sailor!" Dark shouted back. "Here goes nothing!"

He brought up the power to the main screws and swung the hydrojets around to give them added thrust. If he could break out in a curving line to the left—

The emergency alarm rang shrilly. Something huge bumped and clanged along the hull, gouging metal. You could almost hear Orca screaming in pain and protest. . . .

Ah-oooga! Ah-oooga! Ah-oooga!

General Quarters boomed through every part of the attack carrier *Cranshaw*. The warning came only seconds before the carrier suddenly heaved upward from the ocean surface, rising impossibly, canting the bow over as she lifted. In every direction the surface boiled and thrashed as huge air bubbles ripped away from the depths, splattering through the air-discolored water and the sputum of the catastrophe seven thousand feet below. Men grasped for handholds as they felt the carrier's structure. On the open deck crewmen hurled themselves flat, grabbing at tie-down ropes and fastener rings; anything. *Cranshaw* threw up her bow, sucking water with a terrible sound behind her. Then she came down, hard, fast, smacking brutally into the deep bottom swell left behind her lurching movement. An entire line of helicopters snapped their tie-downs, ground together in a complaining screech of metal and slid over the side. *Cranshaw* pitched like a thing berserk and then began to settle, to diminish the sudden violent movements.

In the operations center, men climbed shakily to their feet, stared at their instruments, at the boiling sea beyond the carrier.

"They'll never get out of this alive," someone said of Orca and her two men.

He was wrong.

Whatever it was that slammed into Orca as Dark brought the nuclear turbines whining shrilly to life was the last of it; the last hurdle before breaking free of the avalanche still thundering toward the foothills of the ridge. His decision to ride down with the outpouring of rocky debris had been the only move that could have saved them; he had just enough separation from the mass of the crumbling mountain wall to evade having Orca pounded by the falling cliffs.

But it had been close; *too* close. Just a few feet either way and . . .

Slowly the terrible shocks diminished. They rode out the blows easily now as Dark brought the submarine upward in a shallow but steady ascent. He could relax now; he smiled thinly as he smelled the sweat that covered every inch of his body. The sweat stinking of fear and the presence of death; he could recognize it. He'd known it before.

He thought of Arnie Bowden and his men. That story was over, now. *Charger* and her crew had gone to their eternal rest miles down, buried forever beneath the remains of the collapsed mountain.

Somehow it seemed a fitting place. Down to the sea; forever . . .

16

They sat in stony silence, the harsh light of the screen flickering across their faces. Three times the small group watched the film from Orca's forward cameras. Each full sequence ran only two minutes. But even that was more than enough. In that distorted liquid nightmare illuminated by the flares drifting high over the cliff, the crumpled remains of *Charger* were unmistakable. There was a sudden swinging blur of film as the current swept Orca around to slam the stern against the cliff wall; at that point the cameras vibrated severely and failed.

Finally Marchant ordered another screening. He asked the Orca crewmen to relate the details of what had happened far beneath the sea. Dark and Owens recounted for their listeners the plunge toward the far bottom as the undersea avalanche hurled its mountainous debris at them. Yet they could convey only the most limited description; personal fear lends itself poorly to narrative.

Despite the reticence of Dark and Owens, Marchant and his staff already knew much of the story. This telling was in the impersonal terms of the data tapes removed from the battered submarine. The tapes in their inhuman origin were extraordinary to the men who studied the mathematical hieroglyphics; there was deep impact to them in the recorded blows and pressures endured while Dark and Owens fought for their survival. At one moment, the tapes showed without the slightest emotion, Orca had been punished beyond her fail limit. Only the fact that her hull integrity had been assured to meet the worst the designers knew of the sea—plus a safety margin over and above that required in the design specifications—brought the submarine and its two men home.

The tapes were analyzed initially without the presence of Dark and Owens; the Orca crewmen were dead to the world. Meeting them in the cavernous chambers beneath the island, Marchant had been shocked at their appearance. Grimy, their haggard faces poorly concealing terrible strain, they emerged from a submarine scarred and pounded the length of her 120 feet. They looked as battered as their vessel.

There were times when you didn't ask questions, and this was one of those time. Marchant knew men; he especially knew Dark and Owens. It might not have been so bad had they been able to rest or relax after their punishing escape; but in a submarine gashed and damaged as was Orca, there could be no rest. They'd both taken drugs to stay awake and alert to bring Orca the long distance home.

Now, Marchant knew, they were at their breaking point. They had come to that moment when they needed relief desperately; they needed escape in their minds from what they had been through. There was that overwhelming pressure of seeing *Charger*, of knowing Arnie Bowden, of all the men crushed into jellied pulp. It was simple enough; their minds demanded rest, quiet, peace. If they didn't get it . . . well, even the strongest can break. Marchant hustled them from the caverns to private quarters, called the base surgeon, and ordered the man to put Dark and Owens out. For a long time. The needles went into their arms without protest, and their eyes were closing even before they had reached their pillows. Marchant and the surgeon personally removed their clothes, slipped cool sheets over their bodies. They were good, the surgeon assured Marchant, for at least ten to twelve hours of unbroken sleep.

Marchant called Jerri and took her with him to the docking caverns, where technicians were swarming over Orca. She stood alongside him, her head shaking in disbelief at the sight of the torn metal and the scars ripped across the tough skin of the submarine. She raised her eyebrows but kept her silence when Marchant called Hans Riedel to the dockside.

"How long?" Marchant gestured toward the battered submarine.

Riedel's eyes narrowed as he ran through the procedures of repair and maintenance. "Three, maybe four weeks," he replied finally.

Marchant glowered. "Too damned long, Hans."

The old veteran of submarine warfare shrugged his shoulders. "It is always too long," he said with a thin smile. "I remember those same words from before, Steve. At Hamburg and—"

Marchant waved his hand. "I know, I know," he said quickly. "I'm not questioning your opinion, Hans, just thinking aloud."

Riedel nodded. "How soon will they be going out again?" he asked suddenly.

Marchant's brow creased in thought. "Sooner than they're going to like it," he said. He glanced across the dry-dock bay at the second Orca. "How long before . . ."

A smile flashed across Riedel's face. "Now," he said. "That boat is ready."

Marchant's eyebrows rose. "What about ordnance, and—"

Riedel cut him short. "She is ready," he said with a note of pride in his voice. "We, ah, anticipated that there would be such a need." He glanced at the glistening surface of the submarine and turned back to Marchant. "Everything is ready," he said in a conclusive tone.

Marchant's hand rested on Riedel's shoulder. "Thank you, Hans," he said warmly. "We don't have any time to waste, I'm afraid. You've saved us a great deal of trouble."

Riedel dismissed the tribute. "You might say, Steve," he

said, a twinkle in his eyes, "that I have had much practice at this sort of thing, eh?"

Marchant laughed with him. "Yes, I suppose you could say that, Hans. Anyway, thank you again."

He took Jerri by the arm and started for the elevator.

"Steve?"

"Umm."

"I was sort of on the outside of that conversation," she began. "You two acted as if you were sharing a private secret of some kind."

He stabbed the elevator button and turned to her. "Not really, Jerri. You mean about his having had a lot of practice in this business?"

She nodded.

He stepped behind her into the elevator and waited for the doors to close. "Well, you could say that he has," he explained. "Hans was the chief engineer for the German Navy's experimental U-boats during World War Two—and in those days you tested your equipment in the big leagues. In combat," he added significantly.

She thought over his words as they walked back to their office complex. "I just thought of something, Steve."

"What, honey?"

The lines on her face were severe. "I was thinking," she said slowly, "about *Charger*, and how Arnie Bowden and Con were such close friends."

He nodded, waiting for her to continue.

"There really isn't much difference . . . I mean, about Arnie and his men, is there? It's just as if there were a war."

He turned to stare at her. "No, Jerri," he said at last. "There really isn't *any* difference at all. They just haven't made any formal declarations about this one."

The steward's grin stretched from ear to ear. He pushed the wheeled cart into their room to display breakfast to them. Dark and Owens sat up sleepily in their beds, eyes wide at the unexpected luxury.

"Gimme that coffee, man," Dark gestured. "I'm hurting."

Owens groaned and stuck out his hand for some of the same. The steward set up trays on the beds, stepped back to survey his handiwork. "Anything more?" he queried.

"Ummph," Dark said after a mouthful of melon. "Just show up in five minutes with a fresh pot of coffee and we'll be friends for life."

The steward threw him a sloppy salute and another grin and slipped from the room.

Later, sipping coffee and smoking, Owens dragged it out. The moment Dark heard the sudden change in tone he knew what was coming.

"Con?"

"Talk low, man, I'm floating on a cloud right now."

"Come down to ground level for a moment, will you?"

Dark propped himself up on one elbow. He kept his face blank as he looked at his friend.

"You sound serious, Larry."

Owens stared straight ahead, his face pinched tightly. He nodded slowly. "Yeah, I'm serious," he said.

"Nothing can be *that* bad, for Christ's sake," Dark muttered.

Owens chewed his lip. Abruptly he blurted it out; Dark was expecting it just like that.

"I crapped out on you, Con."

Dark wanted to reach out and touch him. He saw Larry's face in a binding of pain; he wanted to touch him, to reassure him with that gesture of close friends. But he didn't; he couldn't, not now. He knew what Larry meant. Back in the sub . . . Larry's face chalk white, lips pressed tightly, gripping his seat with all his strength . . .

Dark didn't respond to the admission. He waited.

"Didn't you hear me?"

"I heard you, Larry."

"Is that all you're going to say, damn it!" Owens' face was contorted. "I said I crapped out on you . . . I was yellow down there and—"

"Hold it," Dark broke in, "just hold it, will you?"

He swung his legs onto the floor. He lit two cigarettes and passed one to Owens.

His finger tapped Owens lightly on the shoulder.

"Before you say any more," Dark said, "I want to tell you a story."

"Are you out of your mind, Con? I'm—"

"Back off, Larry," Dark said quickly. "*I'm* serious."

Owens stared at him, not understanding.

"Yeah," Dark went on. A grin spread across his face. "I want to tell you a story about an eagle and a chicken. . . ."

"All right, it's time we got down to some specifics." Steve Marchant sat at the end of the conference table, Intelligence reports in a loose stack before him. Dark, Owens, Jerri Stuart, and Riedel were familiar with the problems that had bedeviled him for so long. And things were getting hotter by the minute; ever since the confirmation of how *Charger* had been lost, Washington was clamoring for answers to a long list of questions. For this meeting Marchant had brought in the Orca specialists. Ray Matthia, Chuck Harper, Sam Bronstein, and Derek Fuller sat in a group; they were the electronics and ordnance specialists for the killer submarine. Marchant wanted them around as a listening audience. Technical specialists they might be, but they had the welcome habit of looking at problems from an entirely different approach. Technical nonentities—items apparently insignificant to the nonspecialists—leaped out like a blazing flare to these people. There was always the chance they might dip into the bubbling kettle of mysteries and come up with another piece to the jigsaw. Marchant had also called in Bob Walters, who was the Navy's leading engineer of bathyscaphe operations.

There was a newcomer to the group; Marchant had pulled strings for weeks to get Georgi Rubinov assigned to his team. Rubinov was the National Security Agency's watchdog on Soviet science and engineering developments; he was as well known to the inner circles of CIA and Defense as he was to his own organization. The man had a startling total recall; he digested factual data of Russian developments with all the aplomb of a computer. And he could put two and two together sometimes and come up with nine or twelve as an answer instead of the expected four. He was the walking equivalent of an analog computer.

Marchant nodded to the girl. "Jerri, give us a capsule on the present status of oceanographic forces."

She separated a sheet of paper from her folder. "As of the latest reports—they are updated every twenty-four hours," Jerri began. "The Soviets have at sea three major oceanographic expeditions. This in itself isn't unusual. But certain aspects of the situation do not dovetail." She glanced at Marchant, who motioned impatiently for her to continue.

"They do not 'fit,' so to speak," she went on, "because of concurrent activities on the part of the Russians. For example"—she glanced at the paper—"aside from these oceanographic teams—which are themselves unusually large in the number of ships—they also have several very large fishing fleets at sea. What makes all this worthy of attention is that there's yet another major ocean force on the high seas."

She glanced around the table; Rubinov sat beside her, his eyes closed, fingers locked together, listening carefully. "There are preparations for a major manned space flight," she continued. She smiled as Rubinov opened one eye and cocked an eyebrow at her.

Marchant broke into her report. "I want you to understand," he said to the group, "that this is a coverup. They have too many ships out for that operation, and Moscow is now making all sorts of noises about how they're using their oceanographic units as emergency rescue teams." His face showed contempt as he glanced at his notes. "Don't you believe a word of it," he added with a sour expression, "even if our own government seems to be buying the whole song and dance."

"What do you mean, Steve?" Georgi Rubinov rumbled the question unexpectedly at Marchant.

"The Intelligence community in Washington," Marchant fired back, "has bought the space agency's evaluation of the Russian moves at sea."

Again the Rubinov eyebrow went into an arch.

"I know, I know," Marchant said with an angry gesture. "*I* can't figure out what the hell NASA has to do with Russian ships on the high seas. But"—he shrugged—"since the Reds are making such a fuss about their upcoming space shot, someone got the bright idea that tracking ships were properly the business of NASA to evaluate. And NASA, which is much more interested in the backside of the moon than it is with the oceans' bottom, says point-blank that the Russian ships are legitimate."

He turned to Jerri. "Please excuse my breaking in like that," he apologized. "Go on."

"The three oceanographic fleets are well distributed," she continued. "All three show a similarity of purpose. Or at least"—she smiled quickly at Rubinov—"the Russians are claiming similar missions for each expedition. They had an international conference recently; it was in Paris, about world oceanography. The Soviet delegates who attended said they were about to make a concerted drive to map the deepest layers of the ocean. They were very sarcastic about the United States' canceling the Mohole program; they made a good many points, I'm afraid, about how they were now carrying the brunt of really deep sea research.

"There's no question but that they are operating in such areas," she confirmed. "They have one expedition now in the area of the Marianas Trench, off Guam, and they have another group operating near Antarctica. That places them in position to study both the Argentine and the Atlantic-Antarctic-Indian depressions."

She paused to take a deep breath. Her next words brought people up straight in their chairs. "They are also concentrating on the Puerto Rico Trench and the Romanche Gap."

They chewed over her words. The Romanche Gap went down to 24,636 feet; it was just off the equator, where the crest of the Mid-Atlantic Ridge broke suddenly and the bottom fell away to nearly five miles straight down. But that was a long distance off, east of the St. Peter and St. Paul Rocks.

The Puerto Rico Trench lay at their doorstep. If the Russians were *really* interested in the true deeps, then their attention to the trench—30,176 feet measured—*was* legitimate.

Georgi Rubinov's voice seemed to start away down in the pit of his stomach; he spoke with an accented heavy growl that provided a startling opposite to Jerri's voice.

"The Russians are being most cooperative," he said without preamble. "In fact, they are almost too cooperative. Um, one would say that their cooperation is dictated along certain lines best suited to their own needs."

He heaved himself to an upright position; beneath heavy lids his eyes traveled slowly around the room as he spoke. "They have made certain to list many of the scientists involved in these expeditions," he noted. "That is not unusual," he added with a shrug of his bearlike shoulders. "But it *is* unusual to provide, through *Novosti Press* in Moscow, printed lists of so many names. "Why"—he smiled—"one could even arrive at the conclusion that they are taking pains to assure that we know so many scientific minds are engaged in their oceanic endeavors. There is no room left for us to doubt their good intentions, no?"

He exchanged glances with Marchant. "But one asks—*why now?* Ordinarily we would look upon such a move as another thaw in the scientific exchange aspects of the cold war. It is to be expected. Harmless, really, on their part. But this is not an ordinary time. There is too much of a suspicious nature, we could say. We might even hold some slight suspicions about a submarine and its entire crew being lost to us through what these gentlemen"—he indicated Dark and Owens—"have established was the direct result of Russian attack. But we cannot *prove* this. We *know* it is so—but we could never prove it before, let us say, an international tribunal. And so they will get away with what they have done."

He smiled at the black and angry looks that had appeared suddenly on the faces glaring at him. "Tut tut," he chided the group, "I am really being impersonal. Perhaps too impersonal for the likes of my associates, no?" Of a sudden his voice grew chilly. "But I have no doubts that the Russians must have felt precisely the same way—umm, yes; it was last year—when one of our destroyers 'accidentally' rammed a Soviet submarine shadowing AUTEC maneuvers. Ummm, most regrettable. Nothing was ever said of the incident, of course."

His hand slapped the table. "But I digress, and you must forgive me. Ah, back to the oceanographic fleets of our friends from Moscow. I have told you about our being told in such unusual detail the honor list of academicians and scientists. Now I will tell you some more.

"We are, of course, shadowing these fleets. We are studying them with surface ships to some extent, but"—he waved his hand to dismiss any importance to the matter—"that is strictly for show. Our submarines have been kept quite busy, as you may imagine. We are also maintaining surveillance through our reconnaissance satellites. Our best results, however, are being achieved through the combination of our submarines and aircraft operating as teams. We have learned, for example, that each Soviet fleet has at least two submarines operating with it. Once again"—he raised his brows in the gesture with which they were fast becoming familiar—"this is not unusual. For an oceanic study fleet to have submarines, I mean. But for *three* fleets to have submarines, all at the same time—ah, this is not usual or normal. Indeed, in the jargon one finds so much better suited to the moment—it stinks."

He returned the sudden smiles. "That is not quite the entire story, however," he went on. "You see, the Russians are also being unusually cooperative. They know we are watching their every move. After all"—he held out his hands palms up—"it is the game we both play, no? In the Pacific, the people aboard their Marianas expedition are almost falling over the sides of their ships to wave at us, they are so friendly. The Antarctic force? Ah, there is less enthusiasm, perhaps, but then it is so much colder there."

Chuck Harper, antisubmarine warfare specialist for Orca, studied Rubinov closely. "I notice you haven't said anything about that third force, Mr. Rubinov."

The NSA specialist brought his fingers together in a bridge; he pursed his lips, delaying his reply.

"No-o-o-o," he said slowly, "that is true. I have saved them for last. Theirs is a different story. Apparently they assembled all their unfriendly Russians and placed them aboard this one particular expedition. They have gone to great pains to exhibit their unfriendliness." Again his hands were extended palms up. "In the most diplomatic manner, of course," he added with his strange smile.

Marchant picked up the conversation. "They're playing things strictly by the rules," he said. "They're on the high seas—international waters and everything it stands for. They have stated the nature of their expedition, the names of the scientists, and—"

"Excuse me, Steve," Jerri broke in. "I think you should mention that we have absolutely no way of knowing if those scientists really are aboard those ships."

Marchant nodded. "Miss Stuart is right, of course," he said to confirm her words. "All we have is their word for it, and I'm inclined to believe that it doesn't really matter what scientists are or aren't aboard that force. As Georgi put it so aptly, the whole thing stinks. They're pushing very hard to keep us as far away as they can."

Sam Bronstein signaled with his hand. "How, Steve?"

"Well, for one thing, they've been posting notice—radio communications on the accepted international channels, for example—that they're carrying out special bottom-sounding and other experiments that require the use of high explosive. The trouble is"—he scowled at the report before him—"they're firing off depth charges at different levels and at irregular intervals. Our subs have had to back off to a distance where they can't really get any information. Any time one of our boys sticks his nose in close, he gets personal attention from their 'scientific experiments.' Since they're legal—they aren't breaking any laws or violating any agreements, and they're on the high seas—we can't say or do much about it."

Georgi Rubinov coughed politely. "There is another point," he said. "Again, it is small by itself. Inconsequential, really. Except that it is one more stick in the growing fagot. They have managed to carry out much of their activities under cover of a low-pressure area. For the last several days their ships have enjoyed the presence of almost steady rain and low cloud ceilings." A look of annoyance clouded his face. "It is making things quite difficult, really."

"Jesus Christ, Steve, it's four o'clock in the morning! Don't you ever sleep?"

Conan Dark glared at the luminous dial of his watch. He had pawed at the telephone like a blind man, struggling out of a deep, drowning sleep. But Marchant ignored his protests.

"Just be thankful I didn't come busting into your room," Steve retorted.

Dark felt Jerri's body snuggled against his own. "Yeah," he agreed sheepishly, "I guess you do have a soul. But what the hell is so important at this—"

"Shut up, throw on some clothes, and come on down to my office," Marchant snapped. "I've got coffee ready for you. Oh, by the way, bring Jerri." Dark could almost feel the malicious joy in Steve's voice.

"You bastard," he growled.

"Sure, that's me all over," Marchant replied. "Hurry it up, will you?" The phone went dead.

Dark looked up from the photographs at Marchant.

"You use the sharks for these?" he asked.

The captain nodded. "Uh huh. We got the idea from Jerri."

She sipped her second cup of coffee and blinked her eyes at Marchant. "From me?" Her face showed surprise. "You never spoke to me about the Bottles for taking pictures of their ships, Steve."

"No, not directly," he said. "But you gave us the clue. Remember your studies on shark behavior?" He turned to Dark. "It's easy to forget things, Con. Sometimes you forget the most commonplace things, too. I was talking with Jerri about sharks and their attacks on shipwreck survivors. Just conversation. Then I remembered something she had said; something about wartime records. Whenever there was a battle at sea, with a lot of racket going on above the surface and underneath it as well, sharks always showed up in droves. Most sea creatures take off for parts unknown when shock waves start tearing up the local scenery. But not sharks; maybe they pass on experience. It doesn't matter, I suppose. But a racket within the sea brings them on; they show up as if they'd all been sent personal messages."

Dark nodded slowly. "I get it," he said. "Sure; you said the Russians were setting off charges all the time."

"That was it," Marchant confirmed. "And there *were* sharks all over the place. We got a sub in there about fifty miles off and sent out six Bottles. They were all shark types; porpoises wouldn't be anywhere near the scene."

He tapped his finger against the photographs. "We lost two sharks; another two didn't get any pictures at all. The fifth got some great scenes of waves and that was all. Pay dirt came with number six, as you can see."

And so it had. Its dorsal fin above the water to expose the camera lens, the sixth "shark" had been able to move in to close range of one particular vessel. In the poor light of shadows and reflections, and water splashed over the lens, they saw a three-quarter rear view of a huge Russian whaling ship.

Dark pointed to the sloping afterdeck that disappeared into the water. He could make out part of what seemed to be a huge metal sphere.

"What is it, Steve?"

Marchant shook his head slowly. "We don't know. Jerri?"

She stared at him blankly. "At first glance," she said carefully, "it would seem to be the spherical personnel chamber for a bathyscaphe. But it's too big for that, Steve! It's several times larger than anything I've ever heard of."

"What does Harper say?" Dark asked. "He's your fair-haired boy on equipment like this, isn't he?"

Marchant nodded. "Chuck went over to Puerto Rico earlier tonight," he said. "I have a chopper bringing him here right now; he'll be in about an hour from now."

He poured coffee all around.

"How would you two like to make a special trip together?"

They showed their surprise. "What kind of trip?" Dark queried.

"Umm, say a pleasant little ride in an airplane."

Dark nudged Jerri. "Beware of Greeks bearing gifts," he warned. "This bastard has that angelic look about him again. And that means he's plotting. *What* airplane flight?" he demanded.

Marchant returned his glare. "We'll leave here by helicopter in twenty minutes; it's a short ride over to our airstrip at Cieba, right off the Puerto Rican coast. A P3V Orion will be waiting for us there."

"An Orion? But what the hell *for!*"

"That front is moving out," Marchant said quietly. "I'm going in for a personal look at that Russian fleet—right on the deck. Want to come along?"

17

"I sure hope this son of a bitch knows what he's doing."

Conan Dark's glum expression spoke with greater eloquence for him than his words. Jerri at his side openly shared his apprehension. They stared through the Plexiglas port of the big Lockheed as the outboard propeller slowed to a silvery blur. Seconds later the four huge blades shuddered to a halt with their edges knife-on to the wind. On the other side of the four-engined Orion the scene was repeated as the pilot shut down both outboard engines.

Steve Marchant leaned back in an observer's cushioned seat, his feet propped comfortably on a worktable. He waved his cigarette at them and laughed. "If I didn't know better," he chuckled. "I'd say you two were worried about something."

Dark jerked his thumb at the window to indicate the dead engine and its frozen propeller blades. "Worried? Damn right I'm worried," he retorted. "I get upset when they lose *one* engine, let alone two of those things." He glanced through the window and withdrew hastily.

"How high are we anyway?" he demanded.

"Five hundred feet," Marchant said with disarming nonchalance. "Why?"

"Why?" Jerri regarded Marchant as if he had lost his mind. "Well, we've lost two engines and we're only five hundred feet up, and—" She broke off at Marchant's renewed laughter and groped in the lurching airplane for her seat.

"We haven't *lost* anything of the sort, honey," Marchant said. "Shutting down two fans on the P3V is standard procedure for search missions."

Dark scowled at him. They were barely free of the clouds that formed a sodden gray blanket immediately above the airplane—it was as if they were flying through some endless building with a low roof instead of rushing through the skies at nearly three hundred miles per hour. And on *two* engines!

"How long do we keep this up?" Dark asked, still unhappy with the sight of two useless propellers.

"Umm, about thirty minutes or so." Marchant glanced at his watch. "We're making a wide swing far to the north," he explained. "The front is breaking in that direction—it's clear to the south."

"But then why not come in—I mean, why not approach their ships *from* the south?" Dark demanded.

"Because that's just what they expect us to do," Marchant replied. "In fact, we'll have a couple of planes in the air to the south to give them some good fat radar targets and take their minds away from us." He smirked at his friends. "*Now* are you satisfied?"

Dark eased his way into his seat. "No," he grumbled, "but these are the best accommodations we could find."

The huge Orion plunged through clouds that filled the airplane with flickering shadows. Jerri gasped and grabbed for Dark's hand.

They watched the propeller starting to turn, the blades twisting to bite the turbulent air. Minutes later the P3V surged through the leaden skies at more than four hundred miles per hour, easing lower and lower to the angry water.

Dark snapped a glance at Marchant. "Damn it, Steve," he rasped, "what's that guy trying to do, anyway?"

Marchant waved his arm to dismiss the matter. "He's going in on the deck," he said easily. "Just like he's supposed to do, Con. Like I said, our friends are pretty well occupied with some radar targets to the south of their position. They won't pick us up until we're right on top of them."

Again he studied his watch. He nodded to the windows. "Okay, we're just about in position. You can see the edge of the front now." He leaned closer to his own port. "You'll be able to pick up the ships in a minute or two. Now, remember," he cautioned them, "our first pass is going to be for the money. Pay close attention because you won't get a second chance like that. Our pilot has been briefed to come up on the whaler from his left and then to rack this thing over good and steep. You'll have a perfect viewing angle—fifty feet up and slightly off to the side. Got it?"

They nodded.

Far ahead of the speeding airplane—beneath them the whitecaps were only a blur—they made out the sharply defined edge of the front. All about them the world was wet and gray; but beyond the heavy cloud blanket, sunshine gleamed like the entrance to another world. The airplane pounded through the low turbulence, smacking its way along with disdain for the swirling winds. Dark had no doubts as to the skill of the pilot in that cockpit, yet . . . Just one slip, one mistake at this altitude, and *blooey!* there would be a big smear of flame and some smoke and a hell of a lot of shredded pieces of metal. . . . He forced the thoughts from his mind, bracing his body to dampen out the rocking motions of the airplane, looking ahead.

They felt the slight vibration as the pilot went to full power, calling for everything the thundering turboprops could deliver. Then—there it was. A shadowy cluster on the horizon, expanding swiftly and breaking up into separate dots across the water. The ships of the mysterious Soviet expedition.

That pilot knew his business. The Orion seemed to explode out of nowhere, leaping from the dismal gray sky. The nose lifted; they felt the sudden body-dragging motion as the pilot went for maneuvering altitude. In their respective positions within the long fuselage, technicians attended cameras and other reconnaissance gear to grasp the greatest possible coverage of the Russian fleet in the brief opportunity provided them.

Expanding magically, the ships appeared to rush toward them. In the few seconds of their final approach they made out a long, modern tanker, still low in the water with its heavy weight of fuel. Then the horizon snapped over and they had a glimpse of a wing whipping through the air just above the waves. Again a steady, body-punishing motion and the stern of a large ship leaped into focus.

"That's it, Con!" Jerri cried. "The whaler! And there, see it? On the ramp; that's where we saw that sphere—" Her voice stopped abruptly. The stern of the whaler was open; in the heady, swift pass over the ship, so low they saw the details of the startled faces raised to them, they saw the ramp to the sea in extended position. But no sphere was visible—a tarpaulin covered the right half of the ramp.

They managed one more low pass at an impossibly steep angle, the pilot handling the big Orion as if it were a fighter plane. Dark and Jerri Stuart forgot the protesting whines of their stomachs, forgot everything with the sight of the fleet spread out before them. Jerri pointed rapidly from one ship to another, identifying the types, noting the conventional oceanographic research vessels.

"Con! Over there; to the right!" she exclaimed suddenly. "See that ship, the one with the long, flat afterdeck?" Dark and Marchant crowded closer to their windows.

"Yeah, I see it," Dark murmured.

"Bathyscaphes—two of them," she said in open surprise. "See the long, rounded shapes—they have a sort of deck atop them—with the spheres underneath? You can barely make them out and—"

"They're bathyscaphes, all right," Dark confirmed, "bigger than anything of its kind I've ever seen and—" He broke off with a sudden exclamation of his own.

"I'll be damned. Steve; *quick!* The right rear of the tanker—you can just make out the shadow. See it?"

The shadow of a submarine; a huge monster just beneath the surface.

"We knew they had a couple of subs with each group," Marchant said, sharing Dark's surprise. "But that thing . . ." He chewed his lip, pressing his face against the Plexiglass to try to see more detail. But the shadow was gone, eclipsed by their own wing as they hurtled low over the ships. Marchant leaned back. "That could be *the* big one, Con," he said slowly. "Remember? That picture we got with the shark?"

Dark's face was grim. "I remember, all right," he said. "I'd give my eyeteeth to get in close to that thing with Orca." He glanced through the window again. "Can you get these guys driving this thing to come around once more, Steve? I'd sure like another look down there if we can."

"Don't know. Stand by one." Marchant yanked a microphone from its hook on the radio table and pulled a headset to his ear.

"Lieutenant Janca, Marchant here. Can you come around for one more pass, behind the tanker?"

Dark leaned close to Marchant to hear the conversation.

"Don't think so, sir," the voice came through the headphones. "Not down here, anyway."

Marchant and Dark glanced quickly at each other.

"What's the scene, Janca?" Marchant snapped.

The pilot's voice remained calm, but his words promised trouble. "They're getting sort of rambunctious, sir," the pilot said with a laugh. "They've put up a couple of choppers. Looks like they're going to try and crowd us a little bit. Get in our way, sort of." The Orion rolled its wings, snapped into a steep bank. "Take a look, sir; you can see them just to the left of the tanker."

Two helicopters rose like angry hornets from the midst of the Soviet ships. One moved slowly to the stern of the tanker while the second machine swung toward the whaler.

The Orion eased into a more shallow bank, coming around in a wide turn. "You give me the word, Captain," the pilot continued, "and I'll take this mother right between their eyeballs."

Marchant frowned. "And he will, too," he said to Dark. "The last thing we want on our hands, however, is something the Reds can fuss about." He nodded to himself, arriving at a decision.

"Lieutenant, I want you to give it a try," Marchant said to the pilot. "But at the first sign of anything going wrong, you haul ass out of here. Get it?"

"Yes, sir. Got it, Captain."

"Okay, just don't cut it too thin," Marchant cautioned.

But they did.

The big Lockheed came barreling in toward the stern of the tanker. Suddenly the helicopter cruising off the vessel pulled up sharply.

"He's trying to ram us!"

"Goddamn it, pull up, *pull up!*"

The voices burst from the headset the same instant the engines howled, the nose jerked up, and a tremendous pressure slammed them down against their seats and the side of the airplane. They had a terrifyingly close glimpse of a bulbous-nosed insect beneath blurred rotors. Then they were free, the Orion straining for altitude, slicing away from the surface in a steep, turning climb.

They stared through the window.

"Jesus . . ."

The Orion never touched the helicopter. But the spinning vortex from the four propellers and the wing tips of the speeding Lockheed left a trail of violent wake turbulence.

It slapped the helicopter from the sky much as a giant hand would smack aside a buzzing mosquito.

The helicopter exploded in a gout of brilliant-orange flame as it struck the water.

18

Steve Marchant dropped the telephone onto its cradle. He rubbed his hand against his shirt in an instinctive gesture, as if he had just released a repulsive maggot. He sighed as he swung his chair around to face Conan Dark.

"Well, that tears it," Marchant scowled. He looked bleakly across the desk at his friend.

Dark lit a cigarette. Casually, giving Marchant extra time, he shook out the match and tossed it into the desk ash tray. He studied Marchant's face through a cloud of smoke.

"They after your ass for what happened?"

Marchant nodded. "Yeah, I guess I'm elected," he said in a strained voice. Dark wasn't sure if the strain was from the physical punishment Steve had been taking, or if it was subdued anger; most likely it was some of both. "The big ass hunt is on in Washington," Marchant continued. "I think they're zeroing in for a chunk of 'prime Marchant butt.' "

Dark laughed at the description. "What's the pitch, Steve?"

Marchant shrugged. "Hell, I should have known it was

coming," he said in resignation. "The handwriting's been on the wall long enough, I suppose." He leaned back in the swivel chair and thumped his shoes onto his desk.

"It's Kuiper," he said suddenly.

Dark's eyes widened "*Doctor* Kuiper?"

"The one and the same."

"But—I don't understand, Steve. I thought Kuiper was one of the fair-haired boys on your Little JCS, and—"

Marchant waved his hand to cut Dark short. "You don't get the picture, Con," he broke in. "Sure, Kuiper's on our ball team. But only when he's wearing that particular hat. He has a couple more. He talks for the National Academy of Sciences and the National Science Foundation. He's on six dozen committees and is an adviser to the President. But he talks loudest"—Marchant made a wry face—"when he stands forth as the paragon of scientific virtue." He gestured unhappily. "Our Dr. Kuiper," he continued, "may well be described as a scared cow of science. With, I should add, an acutely sensitive udder."

"From what you say"—Dark smiled—"there might also be a lot of noise from your sacred cow?"

Marchant couldn't help himself; he grinned at Dark. "Yea, verily, forsooth, and the rest of that jazz. That's a sacred cow loud enough to be heard down every hall and corridor of Washington."

"But how does Kuiper fit in with you, Steve?"

Marchant glared at the telephone. "The Soviet Government has filed a very nasty protest with Washington. Seems like a certain irresponsible group is guilty of violating the traditional freedom of the seas. Said group, through the acts of a few madmen—I quote the descriptive, by the way—has caused the loss of two crewmen of a helicopter. as well as their machine, and threatened directly the security, well-being, lives, and so forth of the other members of the expedition, blah, blah and more blah. And yours truly"—Marchant nudged his own chest with his finger—"is the foremost malicious perpetrator of such inımous deeds. I add the obvious, of course—the Soviet ıovernment is raising every different kind of merry hell. 'hey're playing that scene with the helicopter to the hilt."

Dark nodded. "That was a bum break."

"Yeah, I know, I know," the captain said unhappily. But it played beautifully into their hands. Now it's no ɔnger just shadowing and harassment. Now we're the ullies who are picking on some poor, defenseless scientific ypes. Oh, it's a hell of a flap, all right."

"I still don't get how Kuiper fits into all this," Dark proꞏsted.

Marchant raised his eyebrows. "Oh, nothing to it, eally." His voice was heavy with sarcasm. "He's just backıg the Russians to the hilt, that's all."

"Oh, come off it, Steve!"

"You think I'd make funnies about something like *this,* on?"

Dark shook his head. "No, of course not. Sorry." He tubbed out his cigarette. "How's Kuiper playing the ame?"

His friend shrugged. "He's not sympathetic with the opꞏosition or anything like that," Marchant said. "But uiper has a god that stands above all others. It's . . ."

". . . the sacred cow of science," Dark finished for him.

"With an acutely sensitive udder and a very loud voice," Iarchant said. "Don't forget *that.*"

"So?"

"There's been a private meeting of advisers with the resident," Marchant went on. "At which Kuiper went lear through the roof, from what I've just been told." He lanced again at the telephone. "The good professor made t clear that we—I—are undoing twenty-five years of slow progress toward true-blue international scientific cooperation, that the Russians are liable to take the same attitude toward us, and start pushing around our ivory-tower types. Hell, you can figure out the rest of it, can't you?"

"But what about *Charger!* For Christ's sake, you can't just ignore—"

"Prove it."

Dark stared blankly, caught off balance. "What?"

"I said prove it."

"Don't crap me," Dark said with sudden anger. "You know goddamn well that—"

Marchant held up both hands. "Hold on, Con," he broke in quickly. "Your hearing has gone bad. The words were to 'prove it.' Georgi Rubinov made his point well and it sticks. You simply can't *prove* a damned thing, Con, and in Washington—which is another world, I confess—knowledge of a fact hasn't anything at all to do with your being able to establish, double-dipped in concrete, that the fact really is so."

Dark half rose from his seat, anger flushing his face. "So what does that make me and Larry?" he snapped. "Are we—officially, that is—liars?" He sneered. *"What about the film, goddamn it!"*

Marchant shrugged with the ease of the man who has long wound his path adroitly through many situations similar to the one in which he was now involved. "Oh, we flew a copy of it to Washington. Kuiper screened it this morning, in case you're interested."

"And?"

"He waved it off as next to worthless."

"How the hell could he do that!"

"Easy." Marchant smiled coldly. "He's the biggest of all the sacred cows."

"But, damn it, Steve—"

"According to His Munificence, the films establish certain realities," Marchant continued, ignoring Dark's protests. "First, we have proof that *Charger* is lost." Marchant held up a second finger. "Second, the camera system of Orca is lousy." A third finger went up. "Next, a certain Conan Dark and Lawrence P. Owens are very courageous young men—who suffer from over-active imaginations."

"Goddamn it, I—"

Marchant locked eyes with his friend.

"Admission on our part that the turbulence encountered off the Mid-Atlantic Ridge was entirely unexpected led Kuiper off on another tangent," the captain said. "As far as Kuiper is concerned, *Charger* got caught in the same kind of situation that took *Thresher* down. Like I say, we admitted complete surprise to the conditions you and Larry ran into. So"—Marchant sighed—"Kuiper solves the loss of *Charger* in precisely the same manner."

"But we saw where the hull was pierced! Doesn't that mean anything to—"

Marchant shook his head slowly. "It doesn't mean a thing. It could be spots on the film, it could be your imagination. It could be just one more part of the hull that collapsed. Con, you couldn't *prove* diddly-shit to anyone."

"Steve, have they tied your hands yet?"

Marchant managed a wan smile. "Not yet. That call wasn't official. One of our people has a pipeline into the White House and he didn't waste any time getting a scrambler call in to me." He rubbed his chin, thinking. "At least I've still got some room to breathe, Con. The trick is to use the time we have left before Kuiper's influence gets my ass hung on the nearest cross."

"What else have you found out?" Dark queried.

"Damn it, I knew there was more," Marchant said. "Jerri passed on the news to me. I don't know what it means—not yet, anyway." He searched his desk for a memorandum. "Umm, here it is. Jerri received word a few hours ago that the Russians intend to place instruments on the sea bottom beneath their expeditions. They're not making a secret of it, but they haven't bent over backward to bring attention to it either."

"How did Jerri get it?"

Marchant passed him the memo. "Pay dirt on setting up contacts," he explained. "She has a friend in Reuters, who has stayed close—at Jerri's request—to the international headquarters, the central office, so to speak, where different governments coordinate their oceanographic research programs. Seems like some flunky from the Russian group filed a notice of intent about the—about getting instruments to the deep trenches. Just walked in quietly, left his little piece of paper, and took off. Jerri's friend has been haunting that headquarters, and got the news to Jerri by telephone."

Dark read the memorandum through a second time. He tapped the paper. "What about this last paragraph, Steve?"

Marchant grunted as he leaned forward to glance at the memo. "The volcanic action?"

"Uh huh."

"We've known about that for some time," Marchant explained. "But we don't know much. Volcanic action along the sea bottom isn't that unusual." He smiled. "But why am I telling *you* that? You're the brainy type in this field."

"What I was wondering . . ." He looked up from the memo at Marchant. "Did Jerri say anything—I mean, did she specify anything in particular about this?"

"Not really." Marchant searched his memory. "She did mention that bottom soundings showed unusual heat in this area—one part of the Puerto Rico Trench. I mean—and that she felt the Soviets were probably going to concentrate their instruments there. . . . Con, I want to ask a favor."

"Sure; what is it?"

"Don't be so eager, friend," Marchant advised. "This may not appeal to you."

Dark laughed. "It must be very mysterious. It's not like you to hedge, Steve."

I want you to understand this isn't, well, exactly kosher," Marchant said. "In fact, you're perfectly free to turn me down."

"Jesus, will you get on with it?"

"All right." Marchant studied Dark through narrowed eyes. "I want you to take Orca into that Russian fleet. You might just agitate them enough so they'll tip their hand."

Dark didn't answer for several minutes. "You know it really will be your ass this time if something screws up, don't you?" he said at last.

"Yeah, I know," Marchant admitted. "But I'm asking you, and Larry as well, to risk your necks."

Dark slapped his knee and chuckled. "That's a fair trade any day in the week. When do you want us to move out?"

Marchant didn't smile. He glanced at his watch. "You've got five hours," he said. "I'd like you to be under way before sunup."

19

"Range seven eight zero.

"Depth nine zero zero.

"Five-five knots. Holding beautifully, Con. Steady as she goes."

Dark acknowledged the metronome chant of Owens' voice calling out range, depth, and speed bearings of Orca as they related to the attack submarine dead ahead of their own vessel. Almost eight hundred feet in a direct line forward of Orca, a big American raider surged through the sea at a depth of nine hundred feet, holding a steady fifty-five knots. Mounted within the structural ring of the attack submarine's rudder was a small energized beacon. Every two seconds a laser homing beam flashed out from Orca and reflected back to the killer sub. Electronic scopes before Dark and Owens indicated to each man the shadowy form of the submarine ahead of them to provide range, bearing, relative speeds, and rates of closure or separation between the two vessels. At the moment the bigger submarine throbbed mightily as an acoustic screen behind which Orca moved steadily closer to the Soviet fleet.

Dark glanced at the mission timer. They should be close to their maneuver point.

"Larry, how much longer until we play footsie?"

Owens chuckled. "Just under five minutes," he replied. "I'll give you the count at minus one."

"Right." Dark turned down the gain on his sonar pickup. "They're making one hell of a racket up there," he complained. "Damn sonar sounds as if it's gone ape."

"Yeah," Owens agreed. "Just so long as they keep pulsing like that, we should stay pretty well invisible."

The raider leading them toward the Russian ships kept its sweep sonar turned to maximum possible energy output, its probing signals hammering through the ocean. Despite the bedlam in the area there wasn't any question that the Russians would pick up the American submarine. They couldn't have avoided those powerful pulses even had they wanted to. Their sonar defenses would show the submarine with such intensity that it would blanket out anything else close to the raider.

I hope, Dark said to himself. But the picture changes when those guys take off . . . And if the Russkies have some sharp boys on their scanners, we might end up having fun and games. . . .

"I'll be glad when we get out of this rut," Larry Owens broke into his thoughts.

"I know what you mean," Dark replied. "It does get sort of bumpy like this."

"Christ, I think I'd get seasick if we kept this up much longer," Owens complained. "We're wallowing like a pig in mud."

Dark laughed; the description was true. They remained directly in the swirling wake turbulence of the submarine leading their position. The screws sent back a turbulent, twisting flow that rolled and yawed their own vessel in a stomach-offending motion. It wasn't a rough or seriously disturbing passage, but the effect built up over the hours and gnawed not only at the intestinal area but also at the balance organs within the ears. Seasickness could come faster through their wallowing than from any other motion of Orca. And they had held their position directly astern of the big raider for two hours until, inevitably, their balance organs began to complain. But only for a little while longer . . .

In their chase position the wake turbulence through which they moved funneled a sound-reflecting screen about them. They had the advantage not only of the bulk and sonar-sweeping noise of the big raider but also its trailing wake, an effect enhanced by the booming reverberations of screw cavitation from the lead submarine. In effect they were cocooned within a frothing tunnel of sound. If their hopes were sustained, they would come right up under the noses of the Russians without their presence being detected. *If* . . .

"Two minutes, Con," Owens said.

"Roger." Dark chewed his lip for a moment. "Larry, any indication of that thermocline that's supposed to cut through here?"

"Negative. I've got bottom sweep going, but it's pretty rough to get a clear signal right now."

"Hell, I didn't think of that."

"We should get a clear picture below us," Owens said, "as soon as we're ready to belly-bump."

"Good enough," Dark replied. "Let me know the moment you get something, will you? I'm less than happy about playing Old Pokey close in to those ships. They might be much unfriendly if they pick us up."

"Right. Coming up on one minute. Okay, it is now . . . one minute, *mark*."

Dark leaned forward and punched the digital timer. His left hand gripped the power lever that controlled the nuclear turbines far behind them. The seconds dragged; at the half-minute mark Owens announced the time, received a taut response from Dark.

Exactly as the seconds flashed backward to zero, Dark's left hand moved forward in a smooth and steady motion. Power surged from the turbines into the screws. The response came at once; both men were pushed back firmly into their cushioned seats as the killer sub raced forward. His eyes glued to the gyroscopic flight instruments, Dark took Orca down in a shallow descent, rushing forward as he did so. Owens called out their changing position relative to the raider still ahead but now slightly above their own position.

Several minutes later Dark came back on the power and eased Orca into level attitude, matching precisely the course and speed of the submarine that now loomed only fifty feet above them. This was their "belly-bump" maneuver, holding station with the larger vessel overhead. Once again, only this time much closer to the Soviet oceanographic fleet. Dark and Owens were using their escort as an acoustic shield.

Twenty minutes later they committed themselves: with a swift motion Dark cut the power to the screws. The sudden declaration threw them forward in their restraining harnesses. Skillfully, "flying" the killer sub. Dark used the lifting effect of the hydrofoil surfaces to keep the bow of Orca coming up, trading off speed for depth holding. Above them the attack submarine moved away, the screws at this close range thundering through the structure of their own vessel. For as long as the could, Dark would keep the departing raider between Orca and the Russian ships. He wanted to stretch out to the last possible moment the effective interdiction of their escort. Holding up the bow as the speed fell away, Dark felt naked and exposed. The thunder of the attack submarine's screws faded rapidly, and into Orca seeped the uproar being generated by the four other American submarines holding their pattern about the Russian fleet.

There was no problem with navigation. Whatever the Russians were up to, they had brought their fleet to a halt and were holding position relative to ocean bottom features, simplifying greatly the task of guiding Orca to the ships clustered on the surface.

"Coming down to five knots," Owens announced. "Jets on automatic?"

"Right. Umm—there they go." The whine of the servomotors pulsed through the hull as the hydrojets eased into position from their access ports.

"Two knots, two knots," Owens said quietly.

Dark adjusted the power lever. The hydros thrummed into action, thrusting downward and back, easing Orca along with a slow speed that barely held them at their depth.

With their slow cruise the din racketing through the water seemed to grow in intensity. "Noisy down here, ain't it?" Dark remarked.

"Just like Times Square on New Year's Eve." Owens laughed.

"Well, I hope to hell it's noisy enough," Dark said, reflecting his persistent concern at their slow speed and the possibilities of Russian defensive action too swift for them to counter. "If we could only find that thermocline that one of our boats reported, we could—"

"Hold one!" Owens snapped out the words, excitement clear in his voice.

Dark waited.

"Con, I'm getting a bounce . . . hard to tell." Owens was muttering, thinking aloud as he studied his instruments. "I'm on minimum gain with bottom sweep, and—by God, it *is*! About two or three hundred feet below us, Con! A nice, fat cold one!"

Dark didn't waste a moment. The control grip went forward immediately, dropping the bow to take Orca down in a slanting dive. Two hundred and eighty feet farther into the sea, Orca seemed to nudge a soft, yielding obstruction. Both men felt the slight lurch, almost a bump, as the killer sub eased into the layer of icy water coursing through the depths.

"Whoo-eee, but that *do* feel good!" Owens cried.

"Yeah," Dark agreed happily. "Nice to have a blanket over our heads again. Say, did you get a reading on—"

Owens anticipated the question. "Not really, Con," he broke in. "But it looks shallow. It's not moving very fast, either. Um, I'd guess about a hundred and fifty feet thick."

Dark pondered the information; they might have come upon too much of a good thing. He studied the instruments showing the gradual increase in depth. Finally, beneath the layer of cold water, he brought the submarine back to level. The thermocline through which they had passed and that now lay above them as a sound-bending shield was a hundred and thirty feet thick. The instruments showed him a depth of nearly fourteen hundred feet.

"We might be too low," he said. "I don't know if we can hack it with the laser cameras, Larry."

"I know, I know," came the response. "But at least we can keep moving in with this thing over us. What the hell," he said with hope in his voice, "it might just lift higher and we'll be able to ride it all the way, Con."

"I don't know," Dark muttered. "We'll play it by ear; that's all we can do for now. How much longer until we're in position?"

Owens checked his instruments, punched the computer controls for a re-evaluation. "Looks like about ten minutes or so," he answered finally. "No question but that our friends are holding their same position."

Dark thought about blundering upward in an area far from their targets—but not far enough so that any sonar scanning they did couldn't be picked up and zeroed in by the Russians. At least that problem was out of the way.

"We should get our fanfare in a minute or two," Owens said. "If our people make enough noise and that thermocline holds, we could end up being real fat."

Dark nodded slowly. "Hope so."

"You sure as hell don't sound enthusiastic, Con."

"I sure as hell am *not,*" Dark retorted.

"Thanks for keeping up my morale," Owens shot back. "Us lowly members of the crew deserve better than that. Don't you think you—"

Whummmpf!

"There they are!" Owens said, breaking into his banter. "Right on the dot, too."

Bedlam erupted from all quadrants about the Russian ships. Sonar operators within the oceanographic fleet grimaced and cursed the Americans soundly. For two days now they had kept up their infernal noise. They would raise the very devil for anywhere from thirty minutes to an hour, and then suddenly and strangely fall silent. No one knew when it would begin again, but it always did, and the worst of all was trying to understand *why.* If the acoustic blasts were to serve as a ruse—but why would they keep it up for so long? And what were they hoping to accomplish when all they did was to . . . *bah!* The sonarmen remained at their equipment, alert, ready, and waiting for anything that the Americans might try. But they were much more annoyed than they were apprehensive. They worked with the most advanced military detection systems produced anywhere in the world; nothing, they swore, would escape them in the depths. Their sweep sonar pulsed steadily, unremitting, downward and away from their fleet. . . .

"Goddamn it to hell and back," Dark cursed. "It won't work. Christ, we're so close and—" He ground his teeth in vexation.

They had slipped undetected to a position directly beneath the Russian vessels. He knew the sonarmen would be sweeping every area about their task force. At the same time Dark realized that those sonarmen, in sweeping vertically, would seek—or be expecting—the kind of sonar echo that would be produced by a deep-diving submarine easing its way toward the surface. And that would be the sound of compressed air being blown into the ballast tanks, lightening ship, ascending slowly through increasing buoyancy.

I'd bet a year's pay that Arnie Bowden was convinced they knew nothing of his playing shadow with *Charger,* Dark thought grimly. And they nailed Arnie right to the cross. I thought we had this thing hacked, but now . . .

"We're too deep," he said, anger sharpening his words.

Owens reflected his mood. "I know Con. We won't be able to stay down here much longer." He didn't like the idea of sliding above the thermocline any more than did his companion. But they had extended the laser robots to their maximum reach and they still couldn't get a clear picture. Steve Marchant wanted detailed photography; he needed ammunition he could take back to Washington to ram down some throats. He needed proof that this wasn't any simple scientific expedition. For that matter, what the hell were the Russians in a scientific fleet doing with complete military sonar systems! That one fact alone should have convinced Washington that this whole thing stank; Owens shrugged in resignation. He couldn't figure it; Con had explained the reason for the pictures, and that was good enough for him. But now things worsened swiftly. They would have to come above the thermocline, get closer to the Soviet ships, expose themselves to the sonar sweeps they were picking up on their passive radar. Like Dark, he didn't know if they could get away with the acoustic shotgunning the American subs were sustaining.

Because you just don't maintain this kind of sonar surveillance without something to back up your effort. . . . The thought made him think of *Charger* and he felt his blood run cold.

Knock it off, he reprimanded himself. You're already collecting flowers for yourself, Owens. Pay attention to what you're doing. . . .

"It's time for fun and games," Dark said with a grim tone. "We're starting up now."

He brought her up with the hydrojets alone, easing through the ascent with minimum energy and the least possible disturbance of the seas about them. The cold current, beneath which they had sought protection against the probing sonar of the Russian ships, dropped sharply as if following an invisible riverbed that plunged away and beneath them. Suddenly the seas came alive: stripped of the sound-bending cold blanket, they felt within their chamber the racketing orchestration produced by the American submarines. Muffled thuds and booms resounded over a constantly fluctuating patter of sonic rain.

The depth gauge read nine hundred feet.

"This is as far as we go," he said quickly to Owens. "We're starting to drift . . . don't know where the hell this current came from . . ." He twisted the hydrojet control, cursing the need for additional power not merely to hold their depth but also to maintain their position along a vertical line, to keep them within effective range of their wire-guided laser robots.

"Larry, get 'em out quick!" he snapped. "I'm going to have to bring in more power. . . ." Owens heard the murmur of the hydrojets increase to a higher-pitched whine. He moved his own controls with deftness and speed. At the end of their flexible cables the manta-shaped probes hurried higher through the seas, running silently on electrically-powered screws. *Almost silently,* Owens reminded himself. *Almost, but not quite.*

The sense of urgency communicated from Dark to himself, kept his nerves taut. Within moments the laser scouts reached out their full distance, hovering five hundred feet above and ahead of Orca. Both men studied their green-pulsing screens, watching intently as dim shadows far above them resolved into definite forms and shapes.

"By God, there they are," Dark exclaimed. "We're right on the money. How about the cameras, Larry? We can't hang around here for—"

"They're rolling," Owens shot back. "I won't need long. I'm trying to get one of 'em close to that whaler."

They looked through the pulsing vision of the laser scouts; on their screens they studied the distinct hull lines of the tanker, of several smaller ships. In the distance—

"Christ! Subs—two of them! See 'm, Con?"

"Yeah, and I don't like it one bit," Dark murmured.

"Look!" The intensity of the moment lowered Owens' voice to a hiss. He drew in his breath sharply, a reaction instinctive to the sight that swam into view on their screens.

The huge sphere Dark had seen in the reconnaissance photographs . . . look at the size of that damned thing! It must be thirty-forty feet in diameter. What could they be doing with something like that? It doesn't fit; it just doesn't fit! It's too damned big for instruments. . . . Beyond the sphere he studied the lower assemblies of two bathyscaphes, personnel spheres linked along the bottom of huge truncated tanks that rose and fell along the surface swells.

"See the cables?"

"Yeah, I see 'em, Larry. They're hooked around the float tanks of the 'scaphes; you can see the cross linking."

"Right; I'm getting a good picture. Con, what the hell is that thing all about? I've never seen anything like it before."

"I can't figure it. I don't know. But it smells to high heaven." Dark scanned his instruments. "Larry, we just can't hang around here any more, we've got—"

"You can bug out right now. I'm through. Got all the pictures we'll need."

"Thank the Lord for that, fella." Swiftly he reversed the hydrojets, rotated them on their extension arms to turn their thrust upward. Orca began to slide back toward the depths, to the safety that awaited them far below.

Dark kept his left hand on the main power lever, his

fingers itching to ram the control forward, to send raw energy surging through the shafts into the silent screws. The feeling of naked exposure made his skin crawl.

Eyes watching his instrument panel, his thoughts returned to the sphere, its cable rigging to the huge bathyscaphes. They're going to take that thing down, all right. No question of that. But what for? The question nagged at him. Maybe Jerri or Rubinov will come up with something. I thought I knew every gadget and piece of machinery that could be used for the real deep stuff. But I've never seen anything like that!

Wait a moment; just wait one stinking moment! What did Jerri say in that memo to Steve? Damn it, I'm right on the edge of it, the pieces are all starting to . . .

His blood ran cold. *Good God Almighty . . . it couldn't be that. It's . . . hell, that's possi*ble! It's—

BRAAAAANNG!

"DIVE! DIVE!" Owens' voice burst in his headset at the same instant the alarm erupted with its shattering clang.

"Dive! Torps! Torps! They're coming in fast . . . . Get us the hell out of here!"

20

Orca shuddered through her length as Dark threw the full strength of his arm behind the power lever. Until this moment the screws had been silent. Now raw energy slammed through the shafts to whip the screws around at full speed. Drag threw a tremendous overload into the system; immediately the inertial load sensors cut in to regulate the power flow. Dark raged at the delay, but there was nothing he or Owens could do except sweat out the brief interval Orca needed to absorb the energy howling through the drive system.

Dark's left hand gripped the power lever with savage strength, his knuckles white under the pressure. Owens' fist beat slowly against his control panel. The men cursed silently as spasms wracked their vessel, shook the shock-mounted instruments and control consoles. At full emergency power the hydrojets cut in to maximum thrust automatically. Then, finally, after heart-squeezing seconds that seemed like hours, the killer sub answered the call of energy. Water boiled explosively as the screws grabbed, churning, driving Orca ahead. The howl of the turbines, free now to drive the screws with raw atomic fire, swept through the control sphere; just as quickly the cry of energy subsided, fed through the thrashing screws to the depths.

Acceleration started slowly, built rapidly until both men felt the welcome pressure shoving them back into their seats. But would it be fast enough? Owens' face turned chalk white as the sounds of the oncoming torps increased in their buzz-saw intensity.

"Con . . . we're not going to make it! They're coming in fast; too fast . . . sixty knots. . . ." Owens snapped out the words in staccato bursts. "We're not accelerating quickly enough. . . ." A brief pause, then Owens' voice cold and machinelike.

"Full red, full red," he intoned.

Panel lights flashed on. Owens had sealed off their chamber from the remainder of the submarine, closing off all pressure and air lines, creating within their limited space an environment removed from Orca. Massive case-hardened steel, alloyed with Carboloy-cemented carbide, the hardest steel known to man; this was their sealed wall that would endure between them and the smashing over-pressures that at any moment could tear through the depths.

Dark glued his eyes to his instruments, the power control beneath his left hand all the way forward. Red lights screamed silently from the panels with their warnings of power overload. It didn't matter; nothing mattered except speed and more speed. He cursed the situation into which he had taken Orca; you just don't throw away the insurance guaranteed you by your vessel. And they had violated every goddamned rule in the book. . . .

"Decoys away," Owens snapped.

They could barely feel the slight vibration through the hull. As quickly as Owens punched his combat controls, a swarm of needle-nosed missiles tore away from the submarine. Then they felt the sudden hard cracks as solid propellant rocket charges came to life in the sea in a ripple of flaming crashes.

"Decoys hot, decoys hot," Owens chanted, monitoring his boards, working desperately to save Orca—and themselves. He didn't think of himself or Dark as separate entities; they were one and the same, that *gestalt* of man and machine that made up their powerful system and at this moment was in mortal danger.

Rocket flame ripped darkness, cracked its sharp bullwhip of shock waves against ths swiftly receding hull of the submarine. Seconds later chemicals reacted within the slim torpedo shapes rushing away from Orca. Superheated steam raged against turbine wheels and whipped propellers into gleaming blurs. The decoys burst away from the fleeing submarine with programmed interference, deliberate sonic cries intended for the oncoming missiles.

The acoustic uproar ran the scale of sounds precisely as those emanating from the submarine; other cries—thrashing screws, a howl rising and falling in a liquid banshee wail, deep brooming thumps, explosive clouds of bubbles expanding swiftly, the sputtering hiss of chemicals flaring nakedly against seawater, pulsing sonar—erupted through the depths. Several decoys rushed toward the oncoming torps, homing in to the sounds of the attack missiles; the others fanned out along a hemispherical pattern behind which Orca might reach safety.

Owens locked his eyes onto the digital timer, his finger

brushing but not yet applying pressure against a brilliant-red firing stud. Then—it was time.

Explosions came thinly through the water, fed through their detectors to their headsets. Almost at that same moment the digital counter swept to zero.

Owens' finger jammed against the firing stud. "Missiles away, missiles away," he chanted. He was amazed at the coldness and steely sound of his own voice. He had the wild thought that he was listening to someone else, that he observed and heard a stranger with icy nerves and control of his every action. It didn't seem possible; somewhere in the back of his mind he knew he was that other person. But it seemed too incredible to believe.

You've made it, a voice whispered in his mind. Con was right about the eagle and the chicken. A smile rustled through his thoughts. It's nice to see that eagle fly. . . .

Con . . . all this time he hadn't said a word, hadn't made a single comment. Owens grinned. But he damned well would have sounded off if there'd been reason, he thought.

"We should hear the secondary explosions any moment," he said to Dark.

A hell of a time for the man to close up like that! All he received in return from Dark was a quiet reply. "Yeah; right about now."

They waited. Muffled explosions rushed through the sea. Far behind them, Owens' second defense ran through its period of waiting. The initial decoys had led several of the oncoming torps astray, fired their warheads. Those were the first blasts they had picked up. But some of the Russian torps could have gotten through, might be running for a time interval on their gyros alone while their sensors remained blanked out. Then, after waiting long enough to get through whatever defenses the Americans would have sent out, the Russian torps would "come alive" and actively seek out through their sonar homing systems the shadow of Orca.

They still needed time. The killer sub raced now with a speed greater than forty knots; the indicator crawled around, building steadily. Soon they would be plunging down and away from the pursuing robots with a speed greater than that of the Russian missiles. Soon, but not yet. Owens waited, timing every move with exquisite precision.

The second bank of torps went out from Orca, each with a homing system and a powerful warhead.

Those were the final blasts cracking through the sea. Their own defensive torps seeking out the oncoming missiles, getting within range for overpressure to be effective, setting off the warheads.

Immediately Owens went to maximum gain on their active sonar, sweeping the waters behind them. The sonar screen blurred with the snowstorm effect of water boiling and heaving from the explosions. But that was all.

"Got anything?" Dark shot at him.

"Negative," Owens replied, his voice triumphant. "Just a lot of snow back there. There's nothing moving any more under its own power."

"Great. We've got eighty knots," Dark advised. "What's your pitch now, Larry?"

Eighty knots . . . clear behind us. . . . Owens made a snap decision.

"Come around in a right diving turn," he said quickly. He glanced at their gyro indicators. "Bring her around, steady descent, and roll out on two-six-five degrees. Maintain descent all the way."

"Right. Two-six-five it is." Orca began to swing; the side pressure of the turn nudged them against their harnesses.

Silent, they studied the instruments. Owens snapped off his search sonar and went to passive, listening for the telltale pulses of Russian sonar seeking them out.

"They're still beating their gums upstairs," Owens said, referring to the sonar transducers tearing at the sea just beneath the Soviet expedition.

Dark laughed harshly. "I'll just bet they are," he said. "Those sons of bitches . . ." He glanced at Owens in his mirror. "That's some scientific expedition those jokers have going for them, isn't it?"

Owens nodded, grimacing. "Well, one thing we know," he replied. "At least one of their damned submarines isn't a research job." He thought of the suddenness of the attack hurled against them and shuddered. "Those guys are on their toes, Con."

"Sure they are," Dark said. He was bitter and he didn't try to hide it. "Those bastards just sat there, waiting for us to come in," he said, almost with a snarl. "They must have done the same thing to Arnie Bowden, just kept chugging along and setting the spring on their goddamned trap. They got away with it once and they almost got away with it again just now."

His eye flicked up again to the mirror. "They were sure they had us cold-cocked, Larry. And I'll tell you something else. Short and sweet, no frills." He paused, glancing at his instruments, waiting while the killer sub rolled through a current. At their speed the bumpy passage was brief.

"You saved our ass just now, sailor," Dark continued.

Owens looked blankly at Dark's mirrored reflection. "That's ridiculous, Con. I—"

Dark gestured impatiently. "Never mind the protests, Larry," he said. "You were right on the money all the way. It's not a matter of badgering compliments. They cold-cocked *Charger* and they figured they had us neatly sewed up the same way." He shook his head with admiration. "Mister, I am very glad you weren't sleeping at the switch."

Owens chuckled. "It's easy, Con. All you gotta do is stay scared into the middle of next week, like I was."

Dark grinned at him.

"Okay, start rolling out now," Owens said, all business again. "Coming up on two-six-five." He took the moment to stretch, luxuriating in releasing his cramped muscles. He hadn't realized how stiff and cramped he'd become in those few minutes.

"They'll never be expecting us down here," he said with growing confidence to Dark. "They'll pick up our speed and they won't believe it. And—"

"Hold it."

The words came with urgency vibrant in Dark's voice. Owens kept his silence, waiting. He glanced in the mirror and saw Dark's brow furrowed with a sudden intense concentration.

A sixth sense was clamoring a shrill, insistent alarm. He felt a prickling cold sensation scraping along the back of his neck. . . . *Something's wrong . . . think, damn you! You're in danger, danger, danger. . . .*

The mental alarm tore at him. What the hell was it? Something in his memory; he had been through it only a short time ago. He groped for the answer and abruptly a shout of realization, of heart-stopping danger stabbed through his mind.

His left hand jerked back on the power level to disengage the screws from the whirling shafts. The fleeing energy hummed low through the ship as he snapped to Owens, "Silent running! Silent running!"

He raced his eyes across the gauges, checking everything. "Passive sonar only," he barked to his crewman. Moments later Owens confirmed sonar status.

"I want status red on all systems," Dark said quickly.

Owens' hands flashed among his controls. "Roger," he said quietly, not questioning Dark. "Passive sonar, status red."

With diminishing speed Orca sailed along a shallow line of descent, a huge ghost arrow in the black liquid depths. Not a sound, not a whisper, reached out from the gliding shape.

Dark stared at his control panels, muscles taut, his

nerves razor-edged. He caught himself trying to *hear* something through the seas, a gesture human but futile. He focused his attention on the panels before him, waiting.

Fear trickled from his armpits along his ribs. . . .

21

Memory trickled through his awareness of the moment; he knew their survival could well depend upon how swiftly and thoroughly he put together the thoughts so elusive in his mind.

"Maintain silent running." His voice was distant; listless. Even as he spoke he knew the words were unnecessary, that he was simply vocalizing a part of his mind. Larry would maintain silent running without a single question until hell froze over, if that was what they needed. Yet the words had come unbidden, emphasizing to himself the critical need for silence while their passive sonar strained to ferret every whisper, near and distant, from the depths within which they ghosted.

The painful memories of their recent terrible need for speed and the mind-scrabbling slowness of response remained in the forefront of his thoughts. As Orca slid through the inky waters, Dark eased forward on the control grip to drop the bow; he wanted the killer sub sliding downward, maintaining movement so that when necessary he could come to power—effective power—with the screws without any of that wild churning they'd experienced just a short time before.

If only they could pick up something . . . !

They didn't dare use their search sonar; it would be a dead giveaway to anything else within the oceans within a range close enough to be of concern to them. *There—that's it!* With a grim sense of satisfaction it came back to him: that meeting with Marchant and the Bottle photograph of that—

"Contact! Contact!"

Dark snapped his sonar input to audio and went to full amplification on his sonar screen. Larry's voice overrode the whispered sound ghosting into his headset.

"Screws. We have screws contact," Owens intoned.

"Where the hell are they?" Dark snarled the question, intent on a need for defense, knowing the Soviets were well into the maneuvers with which they'd hoped—skillfully, damn them—to snare the prey that had escaped. "We're not that easy," Dark muttered to himself.

Owens' voice came back, confusion open in his words. "Can't tell. Christ, this set must have gone ape," he complained.

"What's the scoop? Quick, man!"

"I don't know, Con," Owens confessed. His fist thumped the sonar screen. "According to this gadget, we've got two targets *beneath* us—and that's impossible!"

"What do you mean?"

Owens' vexation was apparent. "Hell, they're *below* us—and I'm getting screws, for Christ's sake. That—"

"Rig for combat." Dark's voice cut through Owens' words and thoughts. Despite his surprise he swept his hand across the arming board, setting up Orca for immediate attack.

Screws . . . ! Goddamn it, they're really pulling out the plug to nail us, Dark swore to himself. Two targets on the screen . . . they've got to be figuring we won't be expecting anything like this. Orca has them baffled; they can't hack the way we've been cutting up down here. They're sure anxious to keep us away from whatever it is they're doing with that fleet of theirs. Scientific instruments, my ass! They're—

Owens' voice broke through his thoughts. "What the blazes is going on, Con? We're at three thousand and the bounce shows the targets—I've still got two of them and I still don't believe it—a hell of a way beneath us. I can't get anything really accurate on the passive, but if this thing is working at all, I show them at nine thousand!"

"They're real, all right," Dark said grimly. He stared at his scope, anxious for better range data. "Let me know the instant there's any change."

"Right."

"I think I know the name of the game, Larry."

"Jesus, this is a hell of a time to play—"

"Steve showed me some pictures a while ago," Dark said, ignoring Owens' vexation. "A real whopper of a sub; Russian. Bigger than *Triton*. A lot bigger."

Owens took that in silence.

"The picture showed two belly hull compartments," Dark went on. "I'd lay fifty to one they were for handling two deep submersibles and—" He broke into his explanation. "Remember that report, Larry, the one I told you about from one of our oceanographic teams? They picked up one, maybe two targets? Well, our people swore they were getting a clear sonar picture—they also got triangulation, by the way—of those targets at twelve thousand feet."

"Twelve thou——!"

"Yeah," Dark said slowly. "It looks like they were right, after all. I think those are our little playmates."

Owens thought about two unknowns—unknowns hell!—and what that meant to Orca. Could the Russians have developed a killer sub like Orca? With their performance? Owens didn't believe it. He shook his head in dismay.

"From the best we could learn," Dark went on, "they're

a sort of bastardization between a deep-diving research hull and a jury-rigged combat system."

Owens' didn't care any longer what the devil they were; the words "combat system" struck through his bewildered thoughts. To hell with the explanations. They could come later. First you had to be sure there would be a "later"; jawing about it now was a sure invitation to disaster. He started running through his mind the battery of defensive and strike weapons in Orca's arsenal. *This time, you bastards, we're playing for keeps. . . .*

"Larry, I don't think we're going to have to sweat anything close in from our friends out there," Dark said. "From the looks of things, it's going to be some long-range shooting on their part." He paused. "Now, listen. We've got to get some accurate bearing and range—especially how cozy they're playing it by trying to box us."

"Keep talkin'."

"Those boats are solid; no question of that. They can take at least two thousand fathoms, maybe a lot more. But from the way it shapes up, they're rugged but probably clumsy as pigs, sort of like a floating barge . . . and loaded for bear. That means the moment they're sure of target data on us, they're going to cut loose with everything they have."

He paused to study his scopes. "They're probably confused about us; can't figure out how we're managing to get around the way we have been. They're scared of us, and when you're scared in this kind of party you don't play for second best. So they're going to salvo us; let everything loose at the same time."

"Got it."

"All right," Dark went on. "From the way they're lying low, they're going to stay off their sweep sonar until they get a really good return from us. And we're not helping them any the way we're going. Now, here's how we'll play it. You go to max gain on the sweep; get a real good target-data picture. I'll give you a count. The moment we zero it,

I'm going full on the screws; everything this baby can put out." Dark licked his lips; the taste of battle was in his mouth.

"I'm going to run directly at them, Larry. They won't be expecting it. Anything but," he added for emphasis. "I don't want to forget their friends upstairs. They'll be looking for us as well. My idea is to cut at them and just tear up the scenery hard as we can. Then we're going down; fast. With all the mess we're going to leave around, it'll screen us." He paused. "Got it?"

Owens nodded. "Got it. You can sound off any time you're ready, Con." Owens' fingers poised over the firing studs; this was the kind of music he knew better than any other.

"Right. You going to salvo the nukes?"

"Uh uh."

The reply puzzled Dark. "How come, Larry?"

"I figure they'll be expecting us to do just that," Owens replied. "They've got us sandwiched in neatly between the two of them down here and the surface ships. We've got to be on the edge of panic; no way out. That's the way *they're* going to think. That means they'll expect us to bust loose with all the fireworks we can throw at them. I'm going to give them a surprise, just what they're not expecting."

Sometimes Con could say everything with just a few words. "Hope you're right. You're betting our asses on it, you know."

Owens laughed harshly. "Don't I ever!"

Dark didn't answer for several moments. "Okay, sailor," he said. "Let's show 'em how to play the game."

"By *our* rules, if you please."

"Amen."

A final study of the scopes, then. "Fire control is yours at zero." Dark snapped.

"Right."

They were again the efficient, smooth team.

"At my mark minus five and counting . . . *Mark!*"

"Two . . . one . . . *Go!*"

They moved in concert. Dark rammed forward on power; the hydrojets grabbed at water. With their descent giving them speed, the screws chewed wildly, spun; only for a moment. Orca dug in hard and threw her power into acceleration. Even as they were going back into their seats, the killer sub starting to run, Owens went to max gain to sweep sonar. Long seconds later the pulsing sonics bounced back from their targets. The fire-control board began to light up like a Christmas tree as it displayed target information.

Orca shuddered.

"Decoys away!" Owens' fingers rippled across the firing studs, releasing a salvo of decoys, sending forth the bedlam to lead astray the enemy sonar.

"*Jesus Christ!* We just— *Torps! Torps! I have four targets*—"

He cut off his own words, fingers stabbing fiercely against the studs to release interceptor torps. Eight shapes ripped away from Orca's hull, spat flame from their rocket charges, rushed off through blackness, seeking with the optics of sound, homing in on the increasing sharp thunder of the Russian torpedos racing at them.

"Don't know how close . . ." Owens' face whitened as he saw the numbers on the fire-control board. "*Hang on!*" Instinctively they braced themselves for the blasts that seemed inevitable.

Seconds before the first crackling blow tore the depths, Owens hit the firing stud again. Two shapes vanished away from Orca; two Mark IX Needle Homers, long and deadly. For the first part of their journey they ran blindly on their gyros, obeying the programmed command taking them in the general direction of the two distant submarines. When they got past the hell that would be grinding up the ocean and their instruments could probe ahead without the false messages of hammering shock waves . . . like faithful bird dogs they'd hunt for their targets—targets with men. Nothing less than a direct hit by a defensive homer would stop them. And they didn't need to hit dead-on; not with a compact nuclear charge that went off with a blast effect equal to three hundred tons of TNT.

WHAAAAANG!

"We got their torps! *We got 'em!*" Owens shouted with jubilation at the reprieve. Orca rocked sharply, a physical blow from afar smacking against the speeding hull. She rode out the blast of their defensive torps homing in against and detonating the enemy warheads. Another blast slammed into them.

Lips pulled back in a death mask, Owens hands flashed across the firing studs. Six log cylinders left Orca, two Mark IX's mixed in with four decoys, hammering bedlam all about them.

They were eleven miles from the scene when the Mark IX's demanded their pound of flesh. Even at that distance they took a mauling worse than the blasts of the incoming Russian torps.

A deep-diving submersible can take a tremendous amount of damage; it can suffer leaks and distorted metal and still ride out the blows. It's designed to take everything the oceans can inflict and that's a hell of a lot when you're talking about *normal* pressures of six and seven tons to the square *inch*. The Russian submersibles could take that and more. That was their purpose; they were clumsy but tremendously strong deep-sea dread-noughts.

But they couldn't take the punch of a Mark IX nuke at what is even a complete miss for a conventional warhead. The effect of three hundred tons of high explosives going off in the depths . . . it's like being at ground zero for an air burst where the shock wave is so insane that the air becomes steel hard and burns with a savage, awesome light.

The first Mark IX exploded directly over and only two hundred feet from the closest Russian sub. Instantly a mailed fist a hundred feet wide opened about the vessel, then closed with a force inexorable and beyond human conception.

The titanic fist squeezed; tighter and tighter. The spine and flanks of the Russian submarine became pulpy fruit beneath a hammer striking its blow from all sides. With that savage, everywhere simultaneous breaching of the hull there came final implosion.

The sub and its crew, in that instant, were smeared from existence. What had been a powerful machine with a living crew in that instant became jellied garbage.

Thirty-seven seconds later Orca took the head-punching blast of their second Mark IX. But the sonar screens had gone crazy. There was no way to tell if the nuke had claimed the second Soviet vessel or if it had mauled a decoy.

It didn't matter. Orca was free and running.

Dark took her down; deep. The depths swallowed the long shape plunging forward at nearly a hundred knots, racing for Isla de Culebra.

22

"It's a bomb.

"There's no question about it. A bomb. Thermonuclear; the biggest goddamn thing the world has ever seen.

"It fits. Now. For Christ's sake, it all fits. Everything drops right in the slot. Everything they've done since the beginning. That tidal wave in Alaska; the explosion in space, beyond the moon; the subs; hell, even the deliberate cover of the oceanographic fleets. All of it leads neatly, very neatly, right up to this moment.

"And you know what's happening? Now? I mean *right now?*

"They're getting ready to blow that son of a bitch while we sit here arguing about it!"

Conan Dark shook his head in dismay. He sprawled in his chair, oblivious to the discomfiture of the others who were captive audience to the unexpected bitter exchange between two close friends. With little side comment permitted in their verbal contest, Dark and Steve Marchant had been having at one another.

"Steve, I swear I don't figure you. For months you've been on a wild-goose chase. You've made enemies from one end of Washington to the other. You've turned half the country upside down. You've been playing blindman's buff while putting together the wildest jigsaw puzzle that's come along in years." He glared at his friend. "And now, goddamn you, when all the pieces finally come together," he said, his voice taut, "you start back-pedaling like you're in a bicycle race. What the hell do you *want,* man? Arnie Bowden and his whole crew are dead, you're on top of tidal waves and ships lost at sea and God knows how much else. And—"

"Let me explain something to you, Con," Marchant said carefully. "In this room it all fits. It's neat; the pieces all slide together and they interlock and we can see the whole picture." He leaned forward, intent, trying desperately to hake his friend understand. "In Washington," he continued, "they don't see things the way we do. They—"

"That's a lot of shit and you know it," Dark snarled.

"Will you shut up and let me finish, damn it! I want you to understand something, Con," Marchant went on. "I said that in Washington they don't see things the way we do and I mean it. This is one crisis. No matter how big or rough it is or may seem to us," he emphasized, "it's just one more flap in one day and night after other flaps. And don't wave Arnie Bowden at me, Con; I knew him as well as you did and he was just as close a friend of mine as he was of yours."

He watched the fire smoldering in Dark's eyes. If he could just keep him quiet a while longer. . . .

"I want you to see Washington's point of view. You can knock the idea of the 'big picture' all you want to, Con, but it's there and it's real and it's also realistic. Cuba, Vietnam, the U-2, espionage . . . hell, we've been weaned and sustained with one crisis after the other."

"But this is different! They're getting ready right now—"

"They're *always* different."

Dark stared at him.

Marchant gestured tiredly. "See that telephone? It's a direct line to Washington, straight to the Chief of Naval Operations. A call from me will also alert the Joint Chiefs of Staff. It will get people out of bed in the White House. Oh, it will make the flap scene, all right."

"Then why don't you pick up the goddamned thing and use it!"

"Because," Marchant replied with a note of impatience in his voice, "it won't do you or me or this country one damned little bit of good if I get shot down. Or," he added caustically, "if the story I tell is so diluted or has so many weak points or questions I can't answer that I tie everything up in knots. *That's* why, Mr. Dark. I must, I absolutely *must,* have every answer to every question before I make that call. Otherwise I will defeat everything we have worked for. I—we—will be playing right into the hands of the Russians. Do you understand me now?"

Dark swung around to lean his elbows on the table. He kneaded the bridge of his nose with his thumb and forefinger, trying to ease away some of the pain that bound a wire around his skull. He looked up at Marchant.

"Sure, I understand you, Steve," he said quietly. "But I don't think *you* understand what I've been trying to tell you. That thing is in the water. They've linked it by cable to those two bathyscaphes. For all we know it's on the way down now. We are running out of time," he added, deliberately spacing his words for emphasis.

Then he stabbed a finger at Marchant. "Remember Jerri's little note about volcanic action at the bottom of the trough? Do you know what that would—"

"No, I *don't* know what the bomb effect would be," Marchant said, anticipating Dark's words. He turned to the people with them. "Maybe we'll have the specifics now." Ignoring Dark and addressing the group at large, he asked if they were ready to come up with answers to the questions he'd given them immediately after his first briefing with Dark and Owens.

Sam Bronstein gestured idly with his slide rule. "I think it's good that you're sitting down, Steve," he said slowly. A chill covered his words.

"What is it, Sam?"

Bronstein gestured to a thick stack of papers and reference manuals. "Umm, it imposes a heavy load on the imagination. But then"—he shrugged, his whole attitude one of resignation to the inevitable—"I have been living for many years now beyond the looking glass." A smile passed quickly across his face as he made his Alice-in-Wonderland simile.

"Based upon what Con and Larry have reported," he went on, "which seems verified by the films, even if they leave much to be desired . . . umm, well; based upon a sphere approximately thirty-five feet in diameter . . . we have considered the size of the machinery necessary for protection against pressures at the bottom, and so forth"—he waved his hand to dismiss the side details—"and considering the known results of what they have accomplished in weapons technology, we are talking about—"

He paused and let his eyes meet those of every person with him.

"We are talking about," he repeated, "a single thermonuclear device that will yield an effect equal to"—he faltered for a moment—"thirty gigatons."

No one spoke.

Bronstein again scanned the room. Still there was only silence.

"You do not believe me?"

Ray Matthia's face was masklike. He and Bronstein had worked for nearly ten years on nuclear ordnance programs. Of all the people in the room none knew better than Matthia that Sam Bronstein never—*never*—spoke in his professional role without being absolutely certain of his words. When Matthia heard the conclusion voiced by Bronstein, he was, more so than anyone else present, devastated by his statement.

Matthia forced himself to stir in his chair. He raised one hand, let it drop weakly back into his lap.

"What's there to believe, Sam?" Matthia said in almost a whisper. "You've just announced the end of the world. What the hell do you want, a critique?" His eyes looked hollow in a setting of chalk-white skin. Anger flared dimly in his glance.

His friend smiled sadly. "You act as if I were responsible for the facts, Ray."

Matthia shook his head. "No, it's not that," he said in a wavering voice. "It's just that I'm so sick and goddamned tired of kilotons and megatons and gigatons." He closed his eyes for a long moment. "Now that you come up with thirty gigatons in one banana bunch. . . ." He shrugged and lapsed into silence.

"Does everyone understand what Bronstein has told us?" Marchant looked about the room. Dark swore in a low monotone; that was the only visible reaction. The others were in either a state of shock, disbelief, or, Marchant knew, incomprehension.

"Sam is telling us that that bomb—*if* it is a bomb, and I for one am convinced that it is—will yield an explosive force of—of," the words stuck in his throat, "thirty billion tons." He shook his head. "I know," he said to all of them and to no one in particular, "it just doesn't seem possible."

Bronstein slipped a sheet of figures across the table to Marchant; the nuclear ordnance scientist addressed the conferees. "So that you will understand how I came to the figure I have given you," he said, "understand that much of it is extrapolation. A single bomb equal to thirty billion tons of high explosives must seem impossible." His brow furrowed as he thought carefully of his words. "Thirty gigatons seems impossible also to me. But no matter how impossible it appears, you must understand that there is nothing technically difficult involved in building a thermonuclear weapon *just as big as you want it to be.*

"And based strictly on that device they released beyond the moon, the Soviets could pack into a sphere such as Dark and Owens have described a device of approximately thirty gigatons yield. I may be somewhat off in my figures," he warned. Then, to assure his listeners his error was insignificant, he went on: "But I daresay the error would be no more than ten percent, and—"

"What would be the heat generated at the core of such a device?"

Bronstein looked up in surprise at the sound of the woman's voice. He held his gaze level with Jerri Stuart, who with several technicians sat behind a table spread with charts.

"In excess of one hundred million degrees centigrade."

"Good Lord, are you *sure?*"

Bronstein shrugged with the unhappy gesture of the man who has been in bed for years with a living nightmare. "I am sure," he nodded. "Even the smaller devices produce this temperature. It is, of course, many times greater than the heat that exists at the center of the sun itself."

Jerri lit a cigarette, her fingers shaking visibly. "Sam, wouldn't such a bomb produce . . . I mean, what about the radioactivity? Wouldn't it be overwhelming?" She shuddered. "Thirty *billion* tons—! What would that do to the entire world? The cloud—"

"No, no," Bronstein interjected quickly. "With a device such as this, my dear, the gross radiological product is a matter of intent. The user obtains in the way of long-lived contaminants what he desires."

"You mean you can keep radiological effects to their minimum?"

Bronstein smiled gravely and nodded at Jerri Stuart. "If

hat is the intention; yes," he confirmed.

"Thank you," she said, turning away quickly to the harts that had occupied her attention. Bob Walters, speialist on deep-ocean research systems, hurried to her side vith a thick filing folder. They conferred briefly, then Jerri urned again to Bronstein.

"One thing more, Sam."

"Yes, Jerri?"

"What would be the maximum depth for a bomb such as his one if, say, if the agency using the bomb wanted to reate a maximum radiological effect."

He scratched his cheek. "There are so many factors, you inderstand?" She nodded. "Well, then," he continued, "all hings being equal, considering, umm, blowout effect, the avity effect, and blowout upward from the surface, and, imph, let me see. . . ." For perhaps thirty seconds he numbled to himself, made a hasty reference to his slide ule, and looked again at Jerri. "The nominal depth would e somewhere around fourteen thousand feet," he said.

Jerri Stuart, Bob Walters, and two oceanographic echnicians assigned to their office, Jay Young and Chris Bonoventi, swept the note pads, ash trays, and other clutter from the end of the large conference table. Working quickly, they spread across the table sea-floor charts, geologic structure profiles, temperature readings, and other studies which altogether painted a picture in depth of the Puerto Rico Trench—nearly six miles beneath the surface of the ocean. The group assembled in the room watched them closely. Bob Walters' face was pinched, his hair shockingly stark against the whiteness of his face. Jerri Stuart was a startling contrast with her agitated, nervous movements. That alone brought Conan Dark and Steve Marchant, who knew her better than any of the others, who knew her for her self-control and coolness, straight up in their seats.

She spread across the other papers charts of the sea flo
of the Puerto Rico Trench, and placed alongside the
charts a structural profile of the terrestrial crust of t
same region. She spoke with halting phrases, gesturing ne
vously.

"Here." She tapped the top chart with her pencil. "Th
is where we have been keeping a seismic profile. It's a
recorded with the oceanographic and hydrographic offic
in Washington; most of the work is carried out from Puert
Rico, of course. Along the northern flank of th
trench"—her pencil traced the outline of the area to whic
she referred—"is where there has been unusual he
generation. We don't know too much about what is going o
down there," she said, brushing the hair from her eye
"That makes things difficult, of course.

"From everything we have learned," she adde
carefully, measuring her words, "there is a section of th
ocean bottom, within the Puerto Rico Trench prope
where there may be only a thin crust covering an exposur
to a—a—" She turned to Bob Walters. "It would be bes
described," she went on after a moment's talk with th
bathyscaphe expert, "as a flue, or a thin finger of volcani
activity. It's not a case of a great volcanic mass separate
from the ocean by a thin crust," she hastened to add. "Ac
tually, the crust is quite solid. There is this single flaw
however, poking upward through the crust.

"Far beneath this flaw there is, apparently, major volcanic activity." Her voice took on a sense of grayness. A
she continued her explanation, her eyes seemed to witnes
some cataclysm still to take place.

"Seismic studies of a localized area are at best questionable," she said. "But I do not believe we are in erro
here. There is a most substantial, well, a giant pocket o
volcanic activity well beneath the crust, the crust that form
the ocean bottom.

"And if this is so," she said, her voice shaking, "and the sphere that Con has been talking about—the one I myself saw with Captain Marchant—then everything that Con says is, *must be* true."

She stared white-faced at Marchant.

"The bomb itself is only the trigger to set off a chain reaction far worse than anything the bomb may do."

Steve Marchant listened to Sam Bronstein as if the voice reaching him traveled for miles down some huge corridor. Even as he digested the technical descriptions of the ordnance specialists, a part of his mind marveled that a group of sane, adult human beings could be seated together on a sun-swept island, discussing with relative calm what might well be the fate of an entire planet. Marchant felt in a mild state of shock; unreality crowded him, pressing in from all sides.

Sam Bronstein was providing to the assembled group an exquisite review of what happened when thirty billion tons of energy tore loose in the bowels of the earth. The man is fantastic, thought Marchant. He's perfected the technique of separating himself from reality. It must be some sort of miracle to crawl into the world of mathematics and hide within the lofty pillars of matter and energy. God pity him when he has to come out. . . . He and his kind talk about the toppling of cities and the destruction of millions of human beings as if they were moving pawns on a board. But he knew the injustice of his own words even as they slipped through his mind. Who am I to judge? Am I, or the rest of us who have ordered men to their deaths, any more blameless because we wore uniforms and we could hide within our own labyrinths of organization and uniform and our own sacred cows of honor and duty? What does it feel like to dump a load of incendiaries on a city and know that someone, that night, is responsible for burning a couple of hundred kids to death? And how many scientists were in the ranks of the camp guards at Belsen and Aus— With growing anger at his self-preoccupation, he forced the thoughts from his mind.

History was bad enough; the future that lay heavily in the room, at that moment, could be worse. So he listened to the nonhuman description of a hundred million degrees centigrade and the shock wave that would claw and rend and rip outward.

A long silence followed Sam Bronstein's analysis of thirty billion tons of unmitigated hell.

Finally Marchant knew he had to ask the question. He didn't want to. But . . . he shrugged mentally and took a deep breath.

"Jerri?"

She turned to face him.

"Yes, Steve."

"To the best of your knowledge—based on whatever information you have been able to collect so far, what would be the effects if such a device were to expose the volcanic area, on the scale we have been discussing, to the ocean?"

She didn't answer immediately. She had the answer, she knew what those effects were. But she didn't have the words. Finally, she took a deep breath. Her voice was rock-steady.

"We are talking about the rape of a planet."

There it was, dragged out stark naked and exposed in all its hideous charred, bubbling flesh for them to see; *all* the Caribbean torn to shreds; Cuba, Hispaniola, Puerto Rico, Jamaica, the Bahamas to the north . . . all of them, gone; savage, deep quakes would rip Central America, Mexico, the underbelly of the United States, the entire northeastern flank of South America; the triggering of faults could in turn trigger more, send quakes raging and tearing for thousands of miles beyond.

But that would be nothing compared to the tsunamic forces that would be unleashed. Tidal waves would account for the deaths of tens of millions of people. But the tsunamic effect? Beyond comprehension . . . it would inundate not only entire islands, but would maul and shatter continental coastlines, even devastate faraway Africa.

What was it Sam Bronstein had said?

". . . calculated years ago the effects generated by sea-bottom explosions of entire merchant vessels transformed into thermonuclear devices. A fifty-megaton bomb burst at a depth of twenty-seven hundred feet in deep water would generate wave heights of fifty feet at a distance of one hundred miles. But that is a minor yield. . . ."

I must be going mad. He sits there and describes fifty million tons of thermonuclear hell and waves fifty feet high as a minor yield. But he means it. . . .

". . . and a spherical chamber with a thousand tons of bomb material, the raw fuel for the thermonuclear reaction, would generate effects quite predictable. We did some computer runs in our nuclear-war games. If you placed such a bomb at a depth of two miles, on the sea bottom, say, two hundred miles off the western coast of the United States, the average wave height as it struck the western coastline would be approximately two hundred and twenty feet. That is only average, of course . . . What? Oh, certainly. Much, much bigger than that . . ."

But that thing cable-slung to the Russian bathyscaphes didn't have to be that big. Not at all. It would slit open the belly of the earth and expose water under terrifying pressure to raw volcanic fire. The secondary explosion would make the bomb seem puny in comparison. I wonder what they would all do in this room if I suddenly got the giggles?

". . . pulverize all of Florida and destroy the coastal regions northward along Georgia and the Carolinas . . . wipe out Miami and many of the Gulf cities . . . could totally inundate the entire state and far beyond . . . destroy the Kennedy Space Center and throw us years behind the

Russians in the fight for the moon and Mars . . . destroy the Panama Canal . . . devastate much of Mexico and Latin America . . . depending upon what was happening in terms of crustal-block shifts or movement, of course. What was that? If that happened? There might be a massive shift of the planetary crust in this region. Certainly . . . would topple undersea mountain ranges, trigger seismic action through much of South America . . . the tidal wave would be felt around the world . . . no, no; they could rig it either to produce radioactivity or to virtually eliminate it . . . the techniques are really quite well defined. . . . How many?

"Several hundred million, perhaps more."

"Say that again. . . ."

"It could kill several hundred million people, perhaps more. To a considerable exent it would affect virtually the entire planet. As bad, possibly much worse than a fullscale nuclear war . . . hell, that's a moot point . . . you're nitpicking, man! Listen to you, for Christ's sake . . . what's a lousy few million one way or the other . . . I think I'm going to be sick. . . ."

"The nation least affected would be the Soviet Union. . . ."

23

Conan Dark glanced at Larry Owens, then turned to Steve Marchant.

"What are you going to do, Steve?"

Marchant's face was bleak. "I know what I would *like* to do, Con," he replied, gesturing helplessly. "I'd like to go in and take over that whole damned Russian fleet. But there's another side to that coin. If they resist and we cut loose, it could be the spark that would open Pandora's Box. With," he grimaced, "all those nuclear goodies inside just waiting to bust out."

His eyes looked coolly into those of Dark. "I like to walk easy when what *I* recommend may start a third world war. And no one," he said grimly, "neither you nor anyone else, is going to make me rush into something like that."

Georgi Rubinov stepped into the breach. He rapped the table sharply with a heavy pipe, scattering ashes across a notebook opened before him. "Gentlemen." The intrusion caught them by surprise. Rubinov coughed apologetically. "Gentelmen, I would be grateful," he said, smiling, "for your attention. I have some thoughts I would like to share with you, eh?"

Rubinov half turned to take in Dark and Owens with his steel gaze. "It would help matters, I am sure," he said, "if you two were to understand, truly, why our good captain seems to be hedging his decision, as it were. Let me speak for him, although I fear he does not appreciate my intrusion into matters he feels are intimate and, well delicate."

Rubinovs' voice and his unsettling eyes had an effect that was almost hypnotic. No one made a sound as he wove his spell. "Let me tell you why he hesitates," he went on without so much as a further glance at Marchant. "I do not believe you people were aware that Captain Marchant and I were together in the late summer of 1945. Steve was still on active duty then—submarines you will recall. I myself was attached to military Intelligence, and immediately after the Japanese capitulated, I flew into the airfield near the city of Nagasaki. The Navy had sent our friend Marchant into the port area, and as fortune would have it, we were thrown together. We entered a city which only six days before had been struck with the second atomic bomb."

Rubinov's face was like that of a heavily lined granite statue; only his lips moved. "I will not burden you with the details of what the aftermath of a nuclear holocaust is like, with the stench of so many burned human beings. I will tell you only one thing."

Silence hung in the room like a thick cloud of dust as they waited for the man to continue. Rubinov's ice-blue eyes were clouded, unseeing, as for a moment in his mind he turned back the years. "Yes, only one thing," he went on. "Even that is too much." The mist left his eyes; once again the others encountered his penetrating gaze. "We went to an emergency hospital. It was not really a hospital, however. It was a concrete building, swept clean by the blast, into which the burned victims had crawled and dragged themselves. We stopped by a Japanese woman holding a baby, both of them burned, horribly burned.

"And just at that moment the woman swooned. Faint

and weak, she fell. A man reacts at such a time; there is no other way. I supported the woman; Captain Marchant instinctively reached out to catch the child—a little girl, maybe four or five years old. Steve took the child from the mother.

"As I said, she was burned.

"The little girl's body fell away. Her skin . . . it sloughed off. He was left holding the skin from the little girl's torso. The rest of her fell to the concrete floor."

George Rubinov turned his head slowly to look into the eyes of every person in the room in turn. "So now you may better understand, my friends, when I tell you that one does not approach lightly, or with undue haste, what could make such things again come true."

He scratched his nose, silent for the moment. Then his body half turned in his chair to face Marchant again. "Time presses us, Steve," he said with urgency in his voice. "You have made your decision and now you must give it voice. Really, there is no other way."

Something broke free within Marchant. He sighed and leaned closer to the table.

"I know, I know," he said in a voice so low they could barely make out the words. A shudder passed through him. Whatever it was that had clawed through his mind was put aside. He jerked the telephone from its cradle and put through a call directly to the Chief of Naval Operations; they listened as he ordered the call through a military communications satellite to prevent jamming or tapping. "And as soon as you reach Admiral Masterson," he said into the telephone, "alert the President's military aide at the White House. Got it? Right. I'll hang up but I want you to keep this line open. No other calls through here, understand? Right." He replaced the telephone.

Four minutes later it rang.

"Admiral. Captain Marchant here. Yes, sir. I'm afraid so, sir. . . .

"That's right, Admiral. It is my urgent recommendatio that immediate preventive action must be taken. I mus stress immediate and unrestricted action on our part, sir. I we delay too long . . . the consequences, Admiral . . . yes sir . . ."

More than ten minutes went by as Marchant related in detail the latest findings of his group. Every word he spoke was being recorded simultaneously in the Admiral's office, in the conference room where the Joint Chiefs of Staff would meet, in the White House, at the National Security Agency, and in the office of Combined Intelligence, Department of Defense.

"That's correct, Admiral. Yes, sir, the line will remain open. What was that, sir?"

Marchant's eyes widened. He turned in his seat to look at Rubinov. "W-why, yes, he's here, Admiral. Of course; I'll put him right on."

Marchant cupped his hand over the mouthpiece, surprise evident in his face. "It's Admiral Masterson. He wants to speak with you, Georgi."

Rubinov extended his hand for the telephone. Marchant studied his face carefully. "You don't seem surprised," he said.

An enigmatic smile was his only answer as the NSA agent took the phone.

"Ah, yes, Admiral. Rubinov here."

Rubinov listened for several minutes, not a word from him during that time. Eyes widened as he finally spoke. "Yes, yes. That is correct, Admiral. Now, you must do this at once. It must come directly from you, Admiral Masterson. It is how we have prepared the continuity. Good! Can you reach Williams right away? *Very* good. Tell him, Admiral, that the reference is nine-three-seven. It is to accompany Marchant's report. Aha; yes, I am grateful to you. Yes, I will. Good-bye."

He replaced the telephone.

Dark slouched in his chair, his eyes locked on Rubinov's face.

"What was that all about, Georgi?"

Rubinov smiled thinly. "You will know soon enough," he said at last. "But I will tell you something. You—all of you"—his hand gestured to take in the entire room—"have done your country, and the world, as well, a great service." He filled his pipe slowly, concentrating on the effort.

"One thing more I will tell you," he said, again with his enigmatic smile.

"You have done the Soviet Union an even greater service."

He refused to say more.

Twenty-three minutes later every alarm bell in Base Savage went off. The strident clamor rang through corridors and offices, echoed throughout the cavernous chambers where the two Orca submarines were berthed, sent hundreds of birds whirring in alarm from the surface of Isla de Culebra.

In the conference room men leaped to their feet with shocked surprise. The alarms kept up their shrill warning as shouts filled the room.

"Christ, it's the combat alert!"

"Outta' my way, goddamn it; I've got to get down to the sub!"

The first man had started through the conference-room door when he glanced at Steve Marchant. The captain stood before his chair, staring at Georgi Rubinov, who had remained seated, a picture of relaxation. The NSA agent blew a cloud of smoke from his pipe and smiled at Marchant.

At the door the men came to a shoving, pushing halt, their eyes turning to the strange tableau before them.

Rubinov gestured to the clamoring alarm. Marchant crossed the room in several quick steps, unlocked the access panel, and tripped the "off" switch. The silence was almost deafening; then, distantly, they heard the other alarms still racketing through the base, mixed in with the pounding of feet running through corridors and the shouts of men. Marchant walked slowly back to his chair, never taking his eyes from Rubinov.

"You don't seem surprised, Georgi," Marchant said.

Rubinov shook his head, spilling ashes from his pipe. Moving with exaggerated care, he brushed off his jacket. "You are right, Steve," he said finally. "I am not surprised. In fact, I was expecting it."

Marchant raised his eyebrows. "I see." He thought for several moments. "Umm, that call to . . . ?"

Rubinov nodded. He withdrew the pipe from his mouth and gestured at the alarm.

"The alert, by the way, is global."

"What?"

"Umph." Rubinov blew out a match. "The United States at this moment is on a war footing."

"You can't be serious, Georgi!"

The thick brows arched. "But of course I am serious," he replied. "There is much that you do not yet—"

The instant the telephone rang, he jerked the instrument from its cradle. "Rubinov here," he snapped.

A moment later he cupped his hand across the mouthpiece, looking at Marchant. "Williams."

Marchant turned to Dark and the others. "It's the director of the NSA," he said. He shook his head, as bewildered as the others in the room. They took their seats as Rubinov's words into the telephone continued the mystery.

"Steve! The extension phone . . . yes, yes; pick it up!"

Marchant brought the earpiece to his head. Dark and Owens watched the captain's eyes widen as he heard both ends of the conversation. But what Rubinov said was enough to let them know the crisis in which they were involved extended far beyond their own knowledge of the matter.

"No, no; there is no question," Rubinov repeated. "I have both of them here in the room with me. What? Yes; that is them. Dark and Owens; I have seen the films and I have talked with them at great length. There is absolutely no question."

Rubinov glanced briefly at Dark and Owens as they sat listening. He turned back to his notes and went on with his conversation with the director of the National Security Agency.

". . . make it absolutely clear. There must not be any misunderstanding; you must make certain of that. The sphere; it is thermonuclear. Even now, *now,* I tell you, they are moving ahead with their plans.

"Wait. I must ask you certain questions. Then the last of it all will be clear. All right? Good! Now, first of all . . ."

Dark, Owens and Marchant listened with growing amazement. Most of the men in the conference room had left for their posts; the technicians were already in the cavern with the two submarines. Jerri Stuart and Bob Walters quietly moved closer to the three men who waited while Rubinov continued his enigmatic conversation.

The manner in which he fired his questions at the NSA director startled them; Rubinov spoke with authority unmistakable in his voice. As he went on, they began to skirt the edges of what Marchant previously had said: Washington is another world where crisis is a daily byword and national emergencies are found waiting behind every dawn.

". . . any signs of alert through their military command structure? Uh huh; it is as we expected, then. Tell me; is there anything, anything at all in regard to code security with the Kr—— No? No other signs, either, eh? Then we are receiving confirmation, are we not? It is exactly as we had suspected."

A long pause followed. Rubinov's next words went off like a bomb.

"So! It has happened, finally. Their fail-safe system has broken down completely, eh? It looks like old Doroshinskaya is making his bid, after all. He is clever, that one."

Rubinov listened. Then: "Yes, yes, there is not a moment to lose. We should place this on the tie-line directly to the JCS—they are together, no? . . . and to the White House. Yes, of course! To the President directly. It will be in his hands; it is he who must give the orders. . . ."

Abruptly Rubinov turned to face the group, his finger stabbing at Conan Dark. "You must stay here; there may be questions only you can answer." He nodded to Larry Owens. "There is no time for questions right now. Do as I say; it is most urgent. Get that machine of yours ready for immediate departure. Be certain you are fully armed. Do it, please—*now*."

Owens came to his feet, glancing at Marchant. The captain nodded. "Anything he says," Marchant said, motioning to Rubinov.

Owens took off at a run.

Dark and Marchant sat in silence as Georgi Rubinov answered the questions fired to him through the telephone; several times Rubinov responded directly to the President.

There was yet one final hurdle. The Army member of the Joint Chiefs came into the conversation; Dark placed his ear near the receiver held by Marchant to hear the exchange.

"Mr. Rubinov, there is a serious flaw in all you say. I am well aware that we have lost *Charger* and also that the Russians are up to something. But what you say is more than fantastic; you are referring to a doomsday weapon, Mr. Rubinov."

If the General expected an argumentative protest, he was disappointed.

"Precisely," snapped the NSA agent.

"There is that flaw I mentioned. There is a total lack—and I do mean total, Mr. Rubinov—of any form of military or other preparations on the part of the Soviet military forces. To go ahead with the plan you have outlined seems not only foolish, but insane, without steps taken on their part to follow up what their bomb would produce."

This was the crucial moment. . . .

"I can hear you quite well, Mr. Rubinov. Please go ahead."

"Thank you, Mr. President.

"I must take a moment, sir, to note the concept with which we have lived for years and with which you are closer than any other man. I am talking, of course, about fail-safe. It is not always remembered, Mr. President, that this is a two-way street, that it is possible to move in either direction. Everything we have been doing for the past several months, and especially what has taken place more recently, convinces me that we have just run into the traffic going in the opposite direction.

"Mr. President, there is no question but that the Russian fleet—this so-called oceanographic task force—intends without delay to emplace this monster bomb deep within the Puerto Rico Trench. The consequences of its detonation have been given to you, so I need not belabor that issue further. There is another matter, however, that must be considered.

"It has been brought up, Mr. President, that our Intelligence shows absolutely no signs of military or other preparations on the part of the Soviets that would preclude their risking a war. *That is exactly the point, Mr. President. No such preparations have been made.*"

"Would you explain that further, Mr. Rubinov?"

"Of course, sir. Please be reminded that we have been following a lead for many months, Mr. President. We have stayed close to reports, many of which have been verified, of a major power play going on within the hierarchy of the USSR. Now, after all this time, everything is taking its proper place.

"The Soviet Premier does not know a thing about the true intent of this fleet. That is the key, Mr. President. Under the aegis of this oceanographic expedition, which the Russian leaders believe to be what it represents—a scientific task force—it is apparent that this secret group within the USSR is making its bid for power.

"Once again, Mr. President, all this is taking place without the knowledge of the Soviet leaders. This clique which seeks to overthrow the government leaders now in power is carrying out this entire venture, which is absurdly easy to disguise, entirely on their own.

"Mr. President, this is a complete breakdown of the fail-safe principle within the Russian government.

"We suspect, but we are not certain, that Adm. Vadim Doroshinskaya is behind this secret group. Mr. Williams has full details of our work ready for you at any time, sir.

"Mr. President, everything they have done—the deep explosion south of the Alaskan coastline, the destruction of the submarine *Charger*, their almost fanatical attempts to prevent any close study of their oceanographic force, the manner in which they tried to destroy the Orca submarine, their bomb test beyond the moon . . . all this leads to this very moment, to the attempt to wreak unimaginable destruction.

"When this holocaust is a reality, with all that it implies, it is then, Mr. President, that the Doroshinskaya clique will make its move. We can predict with accuracy what will take place. There will be a closed session when Admiral Doroshinskaya strikes; he will reveal himself as the leader of the group.

"You are aware, sir, that the military has been fighting an uphill battle within the hierarchy of Soviet government ever since the days of Nikita Khrushchev. In such a showdown the military, to further their own interests, will support Vadim Doroshinskaya. It is their dream to sustain their dominant role in Soviet affairs, to stand militantly against the world, to deal with us from a position of power.

"With this weapon, Mr. President, they can accomplish everything they seek."

Rubinov paused and took a deep breath. "Sir, I would stake my life on the fact that the Soviet Premier, and the people close to him, are unaware of what is happening. They are entirely in the dark about this terrible threat."

Rubinov waited for a response. Finally, terse, it came.

"Is there anything further, Mr. Rubinov?" They could tell nothing from the tone of the voice.

"Mr. President, this is most unusual, and I would like your permission before I proceed further. I would like your permission, sir, to make a recommendation."

"Go on, please."

"Yes, sir. I am recommending to you, based on everything that we have discussed and that has been determined with actual contact by Mr. Dark and Mr. Owens with the Soviet fleet, Mr. President, that the Soviet Premier be contacted and presented with the facts. But even more important, and I cannot overemphasize the urgency of the moment, I recommend, sir, that the Navy be directed at once to take every step necessary to prevent that bomb from emplacement.

"We are losing time, sir. Once that sphere is at the bottom of the Puerto Rico Trench, no power on earth can save the hundreds of millions of people who will be lost.

"That is all, Mr. President."

"Thank you, Mr. Rubinov. I am grateful for your candor."

A click indicated the closed line to the White House. Then: "Captain Marchant?" It was Admiral Masterson.

"Yes, sir."

“Please stand by, Captain. This line will remain ope
with my aide at this end. We will get back to you directly.”

“Yes, sir.”

They waited.

24

"Captain Marchant, you will take every step necessary to sieze control of the Soviet fleet in your area. Do you understand—?"

"Loud and clear, Admiral."

"You will effect this move without military action, if possible. But at the slightest opposition or any sign of duplicity on the part of the Soviet authorities who are involved, you will not hesitate to bring to bear all the power you command."

Admiral Masterson hesitated a moment. When he spoke again, his voice had changed slightly.

"Steve?"

"Yes, Admiral."

"Don't waste any time. Stop that damned thing before it's too late. Let me kn——"

The telephone went dead. Steve Marchant and Conan Dark were already through the door and running toward the elevators that led down to the submarine pen.

The servicing crew took the verbal lashing of Hans Riedel and Steve Marchant without complaint. They slipped Orca from her berth into the flooding locks, shuffled their feet and swore with impatience as the water level rose, and then watched in grim silence as the killer sub vanished into her domain. Conan Dark took her through the tunnel shaft into the waters to the north of Isla de Culebra, running with reckless speed through the shallows, eager to break free of the mud and sand flats and plunge down the continental slope that led to the cruel gash in the earth's surface formed by the Puerto Rico Trench.

Simultaneously with the movement of the killer submarine from Base Savage, military units of the Navy and Air Force rushed to the scene of the oceanographic fleet of the Soviets. The encirclement of the expedition took place swiftly and with overwhelming force. Strategic bombers thundered from the runways of Ramey Air Force Base in Puerto Rico to take up high-altitude stations over the fleet, a long curving train of B-52's always in position to unleash hydrogen bombs were that final move necessary. Tactical aircraft, fighter-bombers and electronic ferrets, took up circling attack stations at lower heights. Several warships on maneuvers—two cruisers escorted by six destroyers—were close enough to cut the Atlantic at flank speed to come up on the Russian ships.

Boarding parties would soon be on the scene: large helicopters to descend directly to the landing platforms of several vessels. Reluctance on the part of the Soviets to accept the armed helicopters would be tempered by an escort of missile-armed fighters and attack aircraft.

Time was running away swiftly for the Russian force.

Time . . .

Was there still time? One question, unanswered, invaded the minds of all concerned with the strike units moving against the Soviet fleet: *Where was that bomb?*

No one knew; they did not know to what depth the bomb had already been taken by its bathyscaphe escorts. Was it still within reach of the attack submarines that for so many days had circled the Russian ships? Could the American submarines prevent the massive sphere from reaching its destination?

No one could tell.

Only time.

25

Two thousand feet beneath the ocean surface Orca ripped a swirling path through the Atlantic. Holding a course to the northeast, Dark kept power to emergency maximum, slamming the killer sub through the sea at almost 110 knots. He scanned his instruments and cursed their depth. Deeper, they could run with greater speed. The more pressure around their killer sub, the better her reactions to that pressure. But they would soon have to break close to the surface; it was necessary to contact Marchant exactly one hour after their departure from Isla de Culebra.

"Con, it's time to go upstairs," Owens reminded him. "Uncle Steve will be champing at the bit for his telephone call."

Dark came back gently on the control grip, lifting Orca's bow and driving toward the surface. "I hate to do this," he complained to his crewman. "This is a hell of a time to come back on the power and poke along. I'm getting all sorts of unhappy thoughts about that goddamned sphere."

"I know," Owens agreed. "But who can tell? Maybe the party's over already."

"Not on your life," Dark said grimly. "I'd make book on that."

Owens didn't answer. "Take her up to about fifty feet," he said finally. "You can start easing off on your speed now, Con. It will give me a chance to get the antenna out."

"Roger."

Orca eased her rush through the seas. As the power and speed fell away and the pressure about them lessened, they could feel the turbulent flow scrubbing along the rounded flanks of the killer sub.

"Fifty feet it is."

"Right. Got a dime for the phone?"

They laughed. It was their first comic relief in many hours.

". . . coming in garbled, but we can read you. How . . . you?"

"Pretty much the same, Steve. What's the latest?"

"Plenty, Con. It looks as if Georgi Rubinov was dead on target from beginning to end. The President's been on a hot-line contact ever since you two left; Masterson's office is feeding the reports to me down here. The long and short of it is that the Soviet Premier is adamant about knowing nothing about a plan to set off a bomb within the seas. At the same time he was forced to admit that unless we had good suspicions, we were spending a lot of energy on just an oceanographic expedition.

"The Russians were told that every plane and every missile this country has is on combat-strike readiness and that if the bomb ever does go off, the USSR, to put it bluntly, will get creamed."

"Isn't that what Rubinov and you were trying to avoid?"

"Absolutely. But Rubinov drove home in this area as well. The very fact that we *are* ready to cut loose with everything we have has made it clear that we're not playing games. Masterson said you could hear that hot line between Washington and Moscow just sizzling."

"I'll bet!"

"But that's not the clincher, Con. The Premier bought what the President had to say to him. Now, listen to *this*." Marchant couldn't hide the jubilation in his voice. "The Russian Premier has given orders—he's broadcast *in the open,* by the way—as a sign of good faith that the oceanographic fleet is to cooperate fully with our forces. He told his people our boarding parties are to be allowed on their ships and that nothing is to hinder our movement." A chuckle came into their headsets. "To say the least, the people aboard the ships act like they're confused." Abruptly Marchant's voice sobered. "From the first reports we got, Con, most of the Russians on those ships knew nothing about any bomb plot. Just a few kingpins and a minimum number of people they needed for the job."

"Did we have any trouble with them?"

"Some, I'm afraid."

"What happened?"

"The characters who've been running the show were pretty well concentrated on a large oceanographic ship. When things started coming unglued, they tried to make the scene by transferring to that big sub we've run into a few times. The boat came alongside and people started getting off the ship. We brought a destroyer into the act, but it was on the side of the ship opposite that of the sub. Then all hell broke loose."

"You mean a fight?"

"That's what we ran into, Con. Remember the old Q-ships, the merchantmen with false sides concealing guns? It's a cute trick and it worked for them. For a little while, anyway. As soon as our destroyer got up close, the sides of that oceanographic ship dropped away and our people got it point-blank. Our planes couldn't do anything because they were so close. In all the confusion that big sub got away."

"Jesus! What about our attack boats?"

"No sweat. We've got two boats after that sub right now."

"What happened to the destroyer?"

"We lost her, Con. Went down, heavy loss of life, I'm afraid. Our planes tore up the Q-ship, but it's a lousy exchange no matter how you look at it."

"Christ, yes."

"There's a . . . stand by, Orca."

"Roger."

They waited, chafing at their slow speed. Several minutes went by. When Marchant came back they could detect a change in his tone.

"Orca, Marchant here."

"Go ahead, Steve."

"Are you familiar with *Rapier*, Con?"

"Damn right I am. *Charger*'s sister boat, right?"

"Right as rain. I thought you two guys would like to know that a few minutes ago *Rapier evened the score.*"

"You mean that big one?"

"Uh huh. *Rapier* took her neat, Con. No question of the kill. Their top crowd was aboard, too."

"It's a bum trade, but it helps, Steve."

"Yeah, and"—Marchant's voice cut off suddenly. Several moments later he came back into the radio line, his voice reflecting agitation.

"Orca, come in, come in."

Dark answered immediately. "Orca here."

"Con, we show your position, uh . . . damn! You're about an hour or so away from the Russian force. How do you look?"

Con fielded it to Owens.

"Steve, Larry here. What's wrong?"

The answer sent cold chills through them.

"The two bathyscaphes and the sphere are gone! They're beyond our reach. Sonar contact shows the bomb just pass-fifteen hundred fathoms."

"Hell, that's too deep for our boats!"

"I know. And the Russians were talking to say they have no direct contact with the 'scaphes. They insist the crews have orders to follow and that they're completely on their own. There's no way we can contact them. Con, you and Larry are our only chance now!"

"Wait one, Steve. . . ." Dark thought quickly. They had to have more information. Owens broke into their conversation.

"Steve, can you reach our people in the area?"

"We're in open contact."

"Good. Tell them to drop a sonar beacon in the water. Get it as deep as they can and let it beam on full power."

"Okay."

"No, wait a moment. Tell them that as soon as the beacon is in place and transmitting, to shut down all sweep sonar. I want to get as clean a signal as I can at max range."

"No sweat. We'll take care of it."

"Steve, this is Con. I'm going to want some fast answers to a couple of things."

"Shoot."

"What do you have on the descent so far; I mean with the sphere and the two 'scaphes?"

"Little enough, Con. The scientists our people are speaking to said the bathyscaphes are extremely limited in their maneuverability. Apparently that rig, the cables between the 'scaphes and the sphere, is sensitive as—"

"Skip the rest of that," Dark broke in. "From what we saw of it, the bathyscaphe operators are going to have their hands full, all right."

"Well, that's what we got from our side. Their people said it will have to be a matter of their drifting with the side currents, playing it by ear as they go. When they get near the bottom they'll . . . well, apparently they feel their best bet is to get as close to the bottom as they can to avoid the thermal effects, and then drift in from the side, the bathyscaphes dragging the sphere slowly behind—between—them."

"Sounds reasonable, Steve. Do we have anything on how they plan to arm the thing?"

"Can't tell," Marchant said unhappily. "All their people didn't get away in that sub. We have their ordnance man, but he won't talk, and—"

"Stick a rifle up his ass. He'll talk," Dark snapped.

"We did. No dice. He just tells us to go ahead and shoot him. Claims that we're all as good as dead, anyway."

"Nice."

"Yeah. Steve, what about Sam Bronstein? Does he have any ideas? This could be important."

"Stand by, Con. I've got Sam on tap in the next room."

"Okay."

Twenty seconds later: "This is Bronstein. I've been monitoring your conversation."

"All right, then. You know what the score is, Sam. What can you come up with? And keep it tight, fella. We've got to crank this thing up as fast as we can."

"Con, the only sensible thing for them to do—in fact, it's the only way I can figure out they *would* do—is to get the bomb into the trench before it's armed. It's simply got to be a pressure-sensing arming system; once it reaches a depth where the pressure actuates the mechanism . . . that's when it comes alive. It probably has a time-delay built into it so that the Russians can get away after it is in place. It would have to have that unless they were all willing to commit suicide."

"I think we can forget that possibility, Sam."

"I agree. The important thing is we can count on the bomb remaining dormant, unarmed, until it reaches a preset depth. Con, if you can keep that thing from getting into the trench proper, there's every chance it will remain harmless."

"Sounds reasonable."

"I just don't see any other way to do it. It's too dangerous to rely entirely upon a timer mechanism, and at that depth you couldn't count on the reliability of a direc arming device, I mean, something between the bathyscaph and the bomb itself. It's too risky for them that way."

"Anything else, Sam?"

"Well, it's hard to say, Con. What I'm keeping in mind i that their whole plan is to get maximum effect from tha thing. There isn't much use in their detonating it unles they have a chance of rupturing the crust and starting natural chain reaction between the ocean and the volcani heat."

A harsh laugh escaped from Dark. A hell of a chanc they had *now!* If only they had moved in faster, committe themselves sooner, they could have stopped that god-damned thing before it ever started down. Now, even witl five big attack subs right on the scene, we couldn't do blasted thing about it! Even once they cut communication and he drove Orca down, into the depths where the kille sub could run with all the efficiency built into her powe and her lines, they would need still nearly an hour to ge there. And *then* they still had to locate those sons o bitches in the bathyscaphes. . . .

"Con, we still have a chance." Larry had broken hi silence. "We've got a good chance if we can just kill all thi and get going."

Dark racked his brain; this would be a hell of a time tc forget anything. He had to be certain they had every las scrap of information before they cut communications and ran for the deeps. . . .

"Con, Bronstein here."

"Go ahead, Sam."

"I'm convinced that if you can disrupt their plans to lower their device to the preplanned depth, to the bottom of the trench, you can stop this whole operation. You can still block them, Con, and—"

Dark thought of their homing torps. If they got in anywhere close, Larry could salvo the Mark IX torps with their nuclear warheads. There'd be no radiation effect, just the steel-hammer blow that would tear into the 'scaphes and finish the job *fast*. It would be—

It was almost as if Sam Bronstein anticipated his thinking.

". . . whatever you do, for God's sake, Con, don't—*do not*—use any kind of explosive."

"How's that, Sam? Say again, please."

"You can't use any warheads, Con. The—"

"Why the hell not?" Dark shouted.

"The overpressures; it would be suicide," Bronstein shot back. "If you set off any explosives close to the sphere, the over-pressures could easily exceed the levels at the bottom of the trench. *You'd trigger the bomb, Con. You would be setting it off yourself!*"

"One-one-five, Larry," Dark said. "That's all we can get out of her right now."

Owens worked the circular dials of his computer. He nodded grimly. "It's gonna be close, Con. They'll be down to about twenty thousand feet by the time we get there."

"I know," Dark grated. "But I've got those turbines about ready to scream now. I don't dare go over the redline for any more power. This is hardly the time to get an automatic shutdown."

"Yeah." There wasn't anything more Owens could say.

Maybe . . . just maybe I've got the key. If I'm wrong that thing will go off and . . . hell, it won't matter one way or the other if that happens. Christ, it's going to be a bloody mess. We'll be in darkness; maybe the floods will work okay if we're real close in. And we're going to have to cut it very thin, Dark thought, so thin we're liable to bust right into them. . . .

For a fleeting moment he thought of the American vessels in the area; a ghostly vision of Puerto Rico and

Jerri and Betty and the Owens children, then an upwelling of millions and millions of faces, a sweep of a monster tidal wave smashing from five hundred feet above the ocean level . . . mountains shaking, cities coming apart at the seams. . . .

Knock it off! he shouted in his mind to himself. That isn't going to do anybody any damned good. . . . A chill rippled along his skin. . . . There's got to be a way out of this. He ground his teeth with rage and frustration.

Goddamn it, there's got to be a way . . . !

Think! think!

26

Orca rushed through the depths like a thing alive. Twin nuclear turbines at maximum-emergency sustained power surged energy to the screws. Along the body of the great machine sensors felt the pulse of pressure, responded with bands of heat, slipped the killer sub through the oppressive weight of more than four tons along every square inch of the hull. Eighteen thousand feet beneath the other world far above, Conan Dark and Larry Owens raced against an enemy impassive, uncaring, totally indifferent. . . .

Time.

"How much longer?"

Larry Owens compared the computer-screened sonar pulses against his predicted time to the Soviet fleet.

"Five minutes or so, Con," he said, scowling at the screens, "ten at the most. It's hard to tell with this beacon mix we're getting."

"Damn!"

"I'll let you know the moment I get any break in signal," Owens assured Dark.

The sonar beacon they had requested through Marchant pounded its sonic cry through the depths, an unmistakable acoustic lighthouse directing them to the specific area they sought above the Puerto Rico Trench. But another signal drifted through the seas, weaker than the one Owens recognized as a standard U.S. Navy sonar homer. The second pulsation he picked up through Orca's systems confused him until he recognized the definite code pattern of repetitive sonics.

"I think I've got something," Owens said with suspicion still in his voice. Dark recognized the "thinking aloud" tone of his friend and did not answer.

Owens stared at the green lines rippling across his scope. "It's got to be," he breathed. "It couldn't be anything else! If that's—Con? I think I'm picking up a Russian homer . . . *and it's on the bottom.*"

"Are you sure?" Dark snapped out the question. If Larry was right, they could save a—

"Hard to be positive," Owens mumbled as he struggled to obtain a clear identification of the sonic pulsation. "It's mixing in with our own beacon," he explained. "I'm trying to get a computer separation so that I can—hell, yes! No question about it, Con. Bearing zero-five-two degrees. That's it, all right! They must have placed it down there a couple of days ago to guide the 'scaphes. . . ."

"It would be . . . sure, clumsy as they are," Dark said, "it would have been the only smart thing for them to do. They could descend up-current and then drift down carefully. One will get you fifty, Larry, they're maintaining some sort of directional control. Crude but effective. Can you get anything on sonar?"

"Negative on the sweep," Owens said. "Nothing like screws down here coming in."

"They could be using jets."

"We couldn't pick 'em up yet. No cavitation this far down, and they'd be operating at low thrust anyway."

"How about a bounce?"

"Negative so far. I'm getting a lot of clutter, what with

the thermoclines and both beacons going. Lot of turbulence near the trench as well. As soon as we get a bit closer, I want to go to computer separation and—stand by one."

"Roger." Dark waited, his eyes scanning the "flight" instruments. Sooner or later they'd get something on their sweep sonar; they had to. Something as big as that triple target of the two bathyscaphes and the sphere; Christ, they'd stand out like a transponder yelling its sonic head off before too much longer.

Dark didn't envy the crews aboard the 'scaphes. The Russian bathyscaphes at best—and best was a short step only—were awkward research vessels designed only for solo maneuvering with great caution and the slowest possible movement within the crushing pressures of the deeps. Except for sonar sorely limited by size and power supply, and their limited-range searchlights, the Soviet crewmen groped their way haltingly and with severe myopia masking their vision. They had entered a world of sonic optics, of discontinuities, where cruel and terrible pressure ruled a region in which stars and vacuum and the universe itself were concepts of heretical madness.

The sonar beacon was little more than a candle flickering dimly in a storm where snowflakes were as hard as diamonds and heavier than lead; and yet, balancing themselves on feel and the fluttering signals of whirling gyroscopes, they struggled their way ever downward, drifting along their steeply slanted line of descent, two huge, clumsy, and wingless moths with a painful and weary fluttering to reach their goal. With every foot deeper into the liquid abyss, the pressure increased. Dark had gone down himself in a bathyscaphe. It was a horrible thing to do, with metal creaking like old hawsers on a three-master, feeling constantly and always more fiercely the sense of that building, overwhelming pressure. Clumsiness was a reality in this eternal darkness, and it seemed a pitiful thing indeed to stab through the black wetness with great floodlights powerful enough in the darkness of a surface world's night, but which down here were swallowed almost at once in the insatiable maw where light existed only from living things.

Creaking metal and straining glass and the pieces groaning inward, squeezing tighter and tighter and tighter; rocking awkwardly from side to side, then undulating like a great swollen balloon at the mercy of temperature and pressure and a plaything of currents and turbulence. It was bad enough in a single bathyscaphe, but in that contraption he and Larry had seen just beneath the surface, it could have been nothing less than three steps through the doorway to some gibbering liquid nightmare.

I'm going to try to kill them, Dark thought, because I have to and there's no other way out. But whoever they are, they've sure as hell got three brass balls to each man.

"Contact! Contact! Target bearing zero four six, repeat bearing zero four six."

"What's the range and depth? Quick, Larry!"

But you didn't budge Owens when he merged himself with his instruments and control panels. "Hold one," came the maddening reply. Dark waited, on edge, wanting to shout for the data he needed.

"Come to data remote display," Owens said calmly.

Dark stabbed at the switches. A row of panels came to glowing life before him. As quickly as Owens confirmed the target information he obtained from the sweep systems and computers of Orca, he punched the data into his display panel. Dark received a duplicate of the final readout rather than the confusing multiple data imputs that fed to Owens. He stared hard at the lighted strips; the range flashed on: *3,000 yards*. The bearing was still zero four six. Owens went to search-and-look through the inputs to the computer. A guidance ring blipped into life; within the concentric circles appeared a single blob of light. That was their target: the Russian bathyscaphes and the bomb. Just so long as Dark kept the light blob centered within the glowing circles he would approach that target along the shortest route possible. Right now the light appeared in direct center, low. The Russians were below their own depth of eighteen thousand feet; how far below, they couldn't yet determine.

Orca slashed her way through the sea, prow coming down as Dark went deeper to center the target light within the glowing rings. He had driven the killer sub with punishment, the great nuclear turbines howling just beneath their danger limit to ram the long shape through the steel-hard water. Now he eased off power, decelerating slowly but steadily. There wasn't much use in plunging beyond their targets and wasting time to come around again. . . .

He brought Orca to a slow drift with the hydrojets. Like a great lethal shark of the ocean deeps, the killer sub moved with deceptive slowness, her prow held in the direction of the descending Russian lash-up of bathyscaphes and their terrible weapon. For several minutes they studied the crude, greenish forms outlined in glowing fog on the sonar screens.

"The sonar's lousy," Dark complained. "We've got to get in closer."

"Roger. Range one thousand yards," Owens intoned, now more an integral element of Orca's electronics than an individual human being. "Close to two zero zero yards."

"Right." Dark brought power into the hydrojets, nudging the submarine along carefully. He kept one eye glued to the range panel, playing his power with the steadily decreasing distance.

"Lasers coming out," Owens said.

Dark felt the slight shudder as the access panels slid back and the wire-guided mantas, searching the blackness with their green-ruby monochromatic light, slid away from the submarine.

"Sonar to standby," Owens directed.

Dark hit the switches. "Okay; standby," he confirmed.

"Roger. Go to laser scope, please."

"On laser."

"Mode is dim," Owens warned. "Max amplification coming on."

"On dim," Dark said. He waited until the lasers moved in closer to their targets and the shadowy forms on his display scope hardened, gaining clarity and distinctiness.

"Increase to point six laser scope."

Dark turned the dial to its reading of .6, watching the scope display increase in brightness and clarity.

For a long moment he stared, silent. Owens did not say a word. They shared a view into another world, through the depths of a planet not their own.

And of a creature alien, ultimately lethal.

A monstrous swollen ovum of death swung slowly from side to side beneath a bathyscaphe, the cables supporting the great sphere appearing in the laser light like tentacles from some huge bloated jellyfish. Immediately below the great truncated shape of the bathyscaphe they saw the smaller personnel sphere, ports showing as unlidded multiple eyes, the gaze of a creature suffering the terrible pressure of twenty-six thousand feet depth. Every square inch of surface creaked and groaned with nearly twelve thousand pounds pressure; the alien, tentacle-connected creature on their screens seemed almost to be sending forth a silent shout of agony.

For the grotesque form staggered in its movement. This far down, close to the heat-soaked portion of the Puerto Rico Trench, the depths had lost their quiescence. Thermal layers shimmered and rent the black waters; the upwelling, heat-roiled seas mixed with deep currents. The Russians had taken pains to avoid the obstacles of turbulence they knew awaited them anywhere close to the fault within the trench. There was not yet violence, but of turbulence and unpredictable currents there was no lack.

The Russians had their hands full; they were on the edge of trouble. Either bathyscaphe alone could have surmounted the difficulties of their descent and the waters about them. But the 'scaphes were restricted from what feeble movement they would otherwise have possessed. They were like two men running each with a leg tied together while someone kept thrusting a stick between their clumsily stomping feet.

And they were on the edge of compounding their difficulties. High above the lip of the trench flowed a wide and deep river of cold. Where the icy current met the heat twisting upward from the area of the trench, the depths swirled with eddies, reverse currents, and vertical flows. Everywhere there took place an unpredictable rippling and cross-flowing that every passing minute increased the danger to the lashed-up assembly of bathyscaphes and the giant bomb.

The main assembly of the bathyscaphe with the cable-slung bomb swayed and rocked dangerously. With a determination and skill apparent to the watching Dark and Owens, the Russian crew struggled to sustain equilibrium. Hydrojets attached at critical control points about both the truncated tank and the personnel compartment kept shifting, thrusting in different directions, fighting the unpredictability of the dangerous motions from side to side, up and down, a multiplicity of rolling and twisting as the Russians fought to ease their devastating cargo to its destination. The men within the primary sphere, to which was linked the thermonuclear bomb, strained for balance and control in the blackness-shrouded world where only gyroscopic senses were real and men obeyed implicitly the readings of their instruments.

Nearby hovered the second bathyscaphe, its crew working frantically to maintain a kaleidoscope of balance, tautness, position, and matching movement. It was not so close that it endangered immediately its companion; it remained slightly above the first 'scaphe and to its side. A single brilliant floodlight sprayed its flickering illumination across the sphere and its bathyscaphe. The water absorbed the light with all the soaking qualities of a sponge, but the floodlights fulfilled their role well enough. From the second bathyscaphe the men within monitored the behavior of the heaving and swaying companion vessel with its ill-behaved sphere. Through their laser screens Dark and Owens made out thin strands reaching like gossamer webs between the bomb sphere and the second bathyscaphe. The purpose of the arrangement was clear; the second vessel provided a necessary counterbalance to the undulations of the ponderous sphere, the side cables generating tautness and some limited control to ease the task of the men directly guiding the descent of the bomb.

"Close to two-five yards."

"Roger. Two-five it is." Dark brought in the power gingerly, rotating the hydrojets to thrust Orca closer to the bathyscaphes.

Owens waited until they reached their position only seventy-five feet from the swaying tangle before them. "Hold two-five and you can come to optics now."

"Right." Dark held the control grip in his right hand. With his left he twisted power to hold its setting, then he leaned forward to punch off the laser input to his display console. He flipped another switch to change the scope to direct optics.

"Hang on," Owens said sharply. "I'm going to hit the floods."

"Okay."

Two brilliant beams of light splashed across the bathyscaphes and the bomb sphere, throwing the entire assembly into stark relief, reflecting brilliantly from glass ports and knobbed equipment. Now they had an excellent view of the machinery before them. The cables showed up clearly, and in the same moment they saw the writhing motions of the clumsy suspension system; not until now could they tell how truly difficult a time of it the Russians were having.

"Christ, look at those cables!" Dark exclaimed. "They're twisting like snakes."

"I'll be damned. . . ." Owens studied his screen carefully. "See what happens when the thing gets away? They can't hold a proper separation, Con. Look how it jerks against the rigging of the 'scaphe."

"Right. You can see where it's torn a few of the mounts loose already."

Owens nodded. "Doesn't seem to have bothered them too much yet," he observed.

"They figured it pretty good," Dark said. "Probably rigged that mess with three times the cables the scientists said they needed."

"Yeah, and—hold one, Con. I think I'm getting a track on their drift."

"Go ahead."

Several moments later Owens reported. "Look, we're down to nearly twenty-seven thousand; dropped nearly a thousand feet since we got here. But the bottom sounder is giving a strong trace, Con. We've got some pretty strong lateral drift."

"Right," Dark affirmed. "You getting a Doppler change on your sonar?"

"Affirmative. It looks like a two-to-one ratio; two down for every foot of lateral drift. They're playing that thing tight. They've got to kill their descent before too long and start edging along the bottom. We're only a thousand feet above the bottom right now, but it slopes down sharply pretty soon toward the lower region of the trench." He paused, checking his instruments and studying the assembly as it edged deeper into the ocean.

"They've got to make their play before too long, Con," he warned.

"I know," Dark replied. "I'm just chewing this thing over before we commit ourselves. This is no time to trip over our own feet."

"I see what you mean," Owens said. "You want to keep this same distance? We can—hey, *look!*"

Garish in the floods, they saw faces within the ports of the second bathyscaphe. Even at their distance they couldn't fail to recognize the astonishment of the Russians staring through thick glass ports at the dazzling twin lights hovering with them five miles under the sea.

"They must be going out of their minds trying to figure us," Owens commented, not without some sympathy for the men behind those ports.

"Yeah. It's too bad. Those guys have what it takes, Larry."

"Do you think we could get them to start up with that thing, Con?"

Dark shook his head. "Never in a thousand years, fella. They must have picked that team damned carefully. I bet they'd swim over here and start hacking away at us with knives if they thought they could get away with it." He paused for a moment. "Nope," he went on. "Soon as I get the lay of the land, they're going to have to give their all for Mother Russia."

Owens chewed over what they had to do. He forced the concept of human beings from his mind. Out there, less than a hundred feet away, hung the thing that could tear apart his country and twenty more. That's the way it goes, he thought, shrugging to himself. There's no contest; it's them or maybe a few hundred million people.

"How are you going to handle it, Con?"

"Hold one, Larry, I'm trying to hack this thing now."
"Roger."

The Russians in their crude vessels slid down the wet darkness along a steep, swaying line of descent, like a balloon falling out of the sky before the wind. They had attempted to calculate their side drift from the moment they left the surface, hoping to sail the currents so they might reach the ocean bed only a few hundred feet from the final sheer drop to the bottom of the Puerto Rico Trench. Passive sonar picked up the sounds of their struggle, carrying the thrumming vibrations of the hydrojet thrusters mounted on the bathyscaphes. But what lent even greater unreality to the scene were the sounds emanating from the jury-rigged systems. They could hear cables twanging against each other, stretching taut and then undulating in serpentine writhings as the distance between the sphere and the bathyscaphes shortened unpredictably to slacken the rigging. It was the sound one might expect of some grotesque creature inhabiting these depths, not of man-made equipment bumping clumsily toward the bottom now less than a thousand feet below them.

The turbulence that increased steadily as they drifted closer to the trench came as a surprise to Dark. There were no currents here, only the sluggish heaving of the ocean itself and finger tributaries that nudged gently rather than pushed what came within their reach. But currents weren't the problem; down there, still beneath a thinning crust, was a hellish magma of naked fire under awesome pressures and temperature.

Still some distance away, within the final bottom cleft of the trench proper, volcanic gases seeped through the crust, emitting great bubbles that weaved drunkenly as they thrust upward. Over the sounds of the Russian 'scaphes and their whispering cables they could, now for the first time clearly. detect the distant licks of fire seeping upward through the fractured crustal rock where they encountered water squeezing down; the trench bottom was a series of intermittent and endless explosions as superheated steam boomed and cracked through the seas. The closer they drifted to the crustal fault, the worse became the turbulence about them; shock waves punched with increasing severity, and great gusts and sighs of liquid wind rumbled through the blackness to roll and yaw even the solid mass of Orca.

With every passing moment the going became tougher for the Russians. Too bad. "Too bad, hell," Dark snarled to himself. "Those guys don't seem to be objecting to what they're doing. . . ."

His fingers caressed the firing studs for the Mark IX torps. He jerked his hand away as if he'd burned his skin.

Goddamn it! I didn't even think . . . like my hand was acting on its own, wanting to salvo the nukes . . . but I can't! How the hell do I handle this? If Sam is right—and damn him, he's always right—I don't dare fire even an explosive warhead. This far down it would be suicide . . . the overpressures. . . . If that thing is armed by a pressure reading, I've got to come up with some answers damned quick. Let's see; the trench goes to exactly 30,176 feet . . . they couldn't be certain of getting to the precise bottom point; couldn't even be sure of just what it was . . . sonar isn't that damned accurate . . . they must be going for a generalization, say, thirty thousand . . . that would be low enough to do the job for them. . . .

He brought Orca to five knots, thinking furiously as the killer sub moved in a wide circle about their quarry. Orca was a killer from bow to stern, but the nature of the bomb arming mechanism had pulled their teeth.

Christ, what do I do now? We can't use any torps. How do I stop them? They must know we're backed against the fence. They're ignoring us; going on as if we weren't even here. What the hell, they couldn't do anything else anyway. And if—

"I've got sonar contact with the edge of the trench, Con."

Owens' words cut through him like a knife.

They were running out of time! They were too close, too close to the trench. He had to do something—*and fast.*

And then it came to him, so simple it had remained deceptive, beyond his reach. In this fantastic world of steel-hard water and the nightmare before them, reasoning and deduction rolled into a single destructive weapon.

He had the answer.

The weapon; he'd found it.

It was Orca itself. . . .

27

"Con?"

"Yeah, Larry."

"I want to ask you something."

"Go ahead."

"I was thinking of Betty and the kids."

"I know what you mean."

"Maybe."

"Say again, Larry?"

"We haven't got much time left, Con. We're getting close to the trench."

"I know. . . ."

"No, you don't; hear me out."

He glanced in his mirror, saw Owens' face, white, a mask.

"Shoot."

"Like I say, I was thinking of Betty and the kids."

Dark waited.

"Jerri, too. And—and . . . a lot of things, Con. People and things . . . we can't use the nukes. . . ."

"Hell, man, I know that!"

"And we can't leave here. Con, we can't go back up again unless we cream that thing."

"I know that too."

"We can't go back up until we finish what we came down here to do. And we're running out of time."

Dark said nothing.

"What are you going to do, Con?"

Angry; his voice hard. "I've got it figured."

"What if it doesn't work?"

"What do you mean!"

"Just what I said. What if it doesn't work?"

"Then I'll come around again, and again, goddamn it, until it does!"

"Time, time, time."

"Don't you think I know that?"

"I've got a different perspective, Con. I'm looking at it through the eyes of a couple of kids."

"This is a hell of a time to—"

"No; you're wrong." Owens' voice was soft, almost wistful. "This is the right time."

"What the blazes do you want, Larry? Do you think I won't do everything to—"

"We might have to ram, Con."

"Do you know what you're saying?"

"The good Lord help me, yes. I know. We might have to ram."

Dark didn't answer for a few moments. Then: "You're talking suicide, you know."

"No. You're wrong."

"Then what would you call it?"

"I haven't got the words, Con. Call it . . . call it a—a—well, a payment on tomorrow. Call it love. I don't know and I don't care. I just know we have to finish what we came here to do."

"Don't you think I intend to do just that?"

"Sure, I know you do. But this is bigger than you or me

and a lot more. So if you can't make that thing harmless—and I still don't know how you're going to do it—we're going to ram."

"You seem sure of yourself, Larry."

"I am."

The tone in Owens' voice brought Dark to glance in his mirror. His blood ran cold.

Larry held a .45 in his right hand. Dark could see the hammer in position, cocked to fire.

"I'll be goddamned."

"I'm sorry, Con. But I've got to be sure; absolutely sure."

Dark didn't answer.

Owens waited. Finally: "Time, Con. There's not much left."

"I'm thinking, goddamn it."

"I love you more than I do my own brother, Con."

"That's a hell of a thing to s——" Dark glanced into the mirror again. *"I know, Larry,"* he said softly. *"I know."*

He didn't have to destroy the sphere. Their need was to prevent its emplacement within the trench, keep it from reaching the pressure level that would trigger the arming mechanism.

He studied the screen carefully, judging, estimating in his mind, watching the swaying, dangerous motions of the huge bomb beneath the clumsy bathyscaphe. He caught a glimpse of a face at a port, looking out, a mask peering through liquid hell.

"Lasers in!" Dark snapped.

"Roger," Owens confirmed. "Lasers coming in."

The servomotors whined as they reeled in the long cable tethers and the laser robots. A panel light chanted from amber to green.

"Confirm lasers in."

Owens hit the arming switches. "Flares on standby."

"I want them two hundred feet over our present depth."

Owens punched in the data to the computer which set the depth controls of the flares.

"Two hundred up. Okay."

"How many can you dump at one time?"

Owens scanned the board. "Six," he replied.

"I'm going to come around upcurrent," Dark explained. "Start about a hundred yards before we reach them. I want those flares strung along the area a hundred yards before and a hundred yards behind the 'scaphes. Ripple 'em out when I give you the word."

"Okay."

Dark made his move.

He poured the power to the screws, notching the lever for fifty knots. Orca surged ahead, starting around in a wide circle that along its flank would take them past the two bathyscaphes and the bomb. A hundred yards before he reached the Russian vessels he called for the flares.

"Owens punched the ripple-fire control. "Flares starting out," he said, his voice flat.

Dark didn't respond. He took the killer sub several hundred yards away and brought her around in a tight turning sweep that pushed them against the sides of their harnesses. The optical screen flashed and rippled as the flares overhead blazed through wet blackness, scattering light so dazzling that the bathyscaphes and sphere appeared almost in stark relief.

"Hang on . . . here we go!"

The turbines howled as the screws took the punishing surge of full power. Orca burst forward, adding to her already great speed. Faster and faster the killer sub plunged toward its quarry, closing the distance. The scaphes and the great gleaming sphere expanded swiftly in the screens. Front searchlights blazing, Orca ripped after her prey like a giant monster of the deeps.

The speed built swiftly as the killer sub literally was

hurled toward the Russians.

My God . . . Con's going to do it! He's going to ram! Betty . . . The faces of his children passed before Larry's eyes.

Our Father . . .

28

He chopped power, slammed his controls with wild abandon. The guidance ring around the screws groaned audibly beneath the terrible punishment of the sluing, skidding turn that Dark demanded from the killer sub. He played the hydrofoil controls and the guidance ring and power in a blending motion that slammed them against the sides of their seats. Orca was still groaning her way through the banked, rolling turn when Dark again pounded the power lever forward.

He studied the screen, searching for results of his thundering run just beneath the great sphere. It came abruptly. As he and Owens watched, the bathyscaphe and sphere descended directly into the boiling, vicious turbulence of Orca's power-screaming run.

"Jesus . . ."

Something in the depths reached upward and crashed against the Russian vessel and its thermonuclear cargo. As if it had cracked into a solid wall, the sphere was hurled aside, a gnat brushed away by a giant, inexorable hand. It rocked wildly, snapping its cables back and forth in a violent whip-cracking motion. The cables rippled along

their length, snatched at the bathyscaphe, imparted to th
huge and clumsy ark the writhing energy absorbed by th
sphere.

"It looks like a forest of snakes . . . goddamn, look a
the 'scaphe! There go some cables see 'em? They jus
broke away . . . they can't take much more of that."

The Russians struggled frantically to regain control, t
slow their descent, to overcome the savage punching motions started by the turbulent wake of Orca and now
transmitting to the carrying bathyscaphe. The secon
vessel suddenly was jerked wildly by its cables. Stee
strands snapped like string, hurling the bathyscaphe ove
to its side, swirling it around like a cork in a whirlpool.

The huge sphere drifted down, the cable slack giving i
freedom. The Russians reacted too late; they were alread
slowing their descent. When the cables extended after th
dropping sphere and again drew taut, the impact strain wa
visibly tremendous. Another cable snapped . . . the bathyscaphe yawed almost out of control. Dark swore
through clenched teeth. "Damned mothering son of a
bitch! I thought we had them. . . ."

"Bring her around, bring her around!" Owens shouted.

"Hang on, sailor. . . ."

Again Orca rammed through the depths, again the turbines screamed as the screws chewed steel-hard water.

He came in closer this time, nearly scraping the cables,
hurling the killer sub between the sphere and the bathyscaphe. Screws pounding, the great shape of Orca twisted the
water into steely knots and whips. . . .

They turned just in time to see the turbulent wake take
its effect.

The cables were alive, writhing and twisting like huge
snakes in agony, striking blindly. They whipped tight, then
rebounded, throwing tremendous pulling strain on both the
sphere and the bathyscaphe.

Unable to speak, holding their breath, they watched the

macabre scene beneath the sputtering flares. The sphere rocked violently from side to side, spinning, twisting the cables. Directly above, the bathyscaphe, pitching its bow up and down helplessly, drew closer and closer to the sphere.

The behemoths met, crashed into one another.

The massive sphere crunched, irresistible, into the great truncated tank of the bathyscaphe. Metal crumpled like tissue paper; the thin aluminum wrinkled, split, gave way before the inexorable punch of the sphere.

Dark came off power, the movement unbidden by his mind, a reflex. Together they watched the men in the bathyscaphe condemned to die. It would take hours yet, until their air gave out. Or they might wish to meet the inevitable sooner. It didn't matter; the end could no longer be changed.

The truncated tank came apart at the seams; without that tank, there was no way possible for the personnel sphere ever to return to the other world nearly six miles above. There was only one way to go.

Down.

The cables parted, shredding along their lengths. For long seconds the monster bomb and the doomed personnel sphere, the latter still attached to its ruptured and torn flotation tank, fell together, drifting in a helpless, slow-motion fluttering toward the ooze waiting below.

Then they began to ease apart, shredding bits and pieces of broken and twisted metal. In the final light of the flares they looked like mindless, fluttering moths of the deeps.

They followed the bomb sphere down, circling slowly as the terrible weapon rolled and wobbled the remaining distance to the ocean bottom.

A cloud of silt and mud lifted in a great fog. When the water began to clear and their floodlights pierced the disturbed seabed, they could see a curving metallic flank gripped by the mud.

"Con."

Exhaustion in the answering voice. "Christ . . . I'm shaking like a leaf."

"Me too. Con?"

"Yeah."

"Look at the depth . . ."

The needle pointed to 29,377 feet.

"Jesus, I think I'm going to be sick. . . ."

They released a communications buoy that rose swiftly and would broadcast immediately its antenna broke the surface. The message Owens taped was short and to the point:

Mission accomplished. Bomb on ocean bottom depth two nine three seven seven. Sonar homer alongside. One bathyscaphe lost with crew. Second 'scaphe ascending, harmless. Returning surface. End message.

It was short but it said everything.

The nightmare was ended.

They began the long climb to the surface.

"Con?"

"Yeah."

"Take her up, Con. All the way."

"That's the way I feel."

"You too?"

"Christ, yes.

"I want to see the sun.

"For a little while there it almost went out."